Promise Me Always

NEW YORK TIMES BESTSELLING AUTHOR

A.L. JACKSON

A.L. Jackson
www.aljacksonauthor.com
Cover Design by RBA Designs
Image by Wander Aguiar

Content editing by SS Stylistic Editing
Line editing by The Ryter's Proof
Proofreading by Julia Griffis, The Romance Bibliophile
Formatting by Champagne Book Design

ISBN: 978-1-946420-96-1

More from

A.L. Jackson

Redemption Hills
Give Me a Reason
Say It's Forever
Never Look Back
Promise Me Always

The Falling Stars Series
Kiss the Stars
Catch Me When I Fall
Falling into You
Beneath the Stars

Confessions of the Heart
More of You
All of Me
Pieces of Us

Fight for Me
Show Me the Way
Follow Me Back
Lead Me Home
Hold on to Hope

Promise Me Always

Chapter One

Milo

IT WAS JUST BEFORE TEN P.M. AS I EDGED THROUGH THE CROWD.

Every muscle in my body was coiled and ready to strike.

Absolution was packed wall-to-wall, filled to capacity with a line at the door, same way it was most nights.

Though, as I moved beneath the lights that flashed in time with the chaotic rhythm of the band that played onstage, the throng broke apart, instinct warning them they'd do best to keep out of my way.

My job was to keep tabs on those who came to the club for a taste of the excess offered within its walls.

Kult cut through the roiling mass, heading in my direction. He was the second head bouncer here at Absolution, and the two of us were running circuits on the main floor tonight.

Dude had buzzed his once long-blond hair. The effect of it only doubled the threat that oozed from him in waves. He slowed to a stop in front of me, and he lifted his voice over the din. "All quiet?"

"If you mean I haven't had to haul any unruly assholes out back, then yeah."

He cracked a shit-eating grin. "Tell me why you seem so glum about that."

So, I might come with a reputation. I chalked it up to it being a part of the job, but my crew knew better. Still, I played it off. "Glum? Not even close. Hell, I'd pay for one dull night."

Cracking up, Kult pointed a finger in my face. "You, my friend, are a liar. But don't worry, the night's still young. No need to sulk. Your face is way too pretty for that," he razzed.

I grunted at him.

He laughed again, though he was holding his hands up in surrender. "Just messin' with you, brother. No need to go beast on my ass. I know you only give a beat down if someone deserves it."

God knew there were plenty who did.

I'd been a bouncer here at Absolution for the last three years. There weren't a whole lot of nights that shit didn't go down.

It was on me to draw the invisible line. On me to decide what forms of corruption were acceptable and when those boundaries had been breached.

No, the irony wasn't lost on me, considering I had never been so good at delineating them for myself.

"Besides, we'd be out of a job if people decided to behave themselves. You're not going to find me complainin'," Kult said. "I'm going to make the rounds. Let me know if anyone gets rowdy."

"Will do," I told him.

Truth was, I took protecting those who came to this club seriously. It was always the innocent that got in the line of fire. The ones I could tell with a glance didn't belong in a place like this and had stumbled into a viper's den, without a clue how to navigate the seedy, sordid waters.

Deviants could scent that shit from a mile away. Sniffing out the vulnerable, getting off on the thrill of tainting something pure.

So this? I used it as an offering.

Penance.

Reparation.

A guardian of the innocent and a reaper of the corrupt.

Fools didn't know how desperately they didn't want to be the latter.

I let my gaze wander the cavernous space.

Housed in an old warehouse, Absolution was two stories of luxury cut with a slice of biker bar. Plush booths lined the walls, and leather couches and high-top tables were set back from the dance floor to fill the open middle area. Blue neon lights glowed from the main bar that ran the length of the entire far end of the building and illuminated the wall of bottles that ran up its height.

Upstairs quartered another bar and a bunch of pool tables, done balcony style so there was still a view of the stage.

People flocked here night-after-night, searching for escape.

For a good time.

A fuck.

Freedom.

Whatever they couldn't find outside these walls.

As long as they weren't hurting anyone else? Then for me, it was a go.

My attention roved over the disorder. It snagged on Trent who stood at the end of the bar. He lifted his chin, gesturing for me to approach.

I headed that way, weaving through the groups of people who were huddled around the high-top tables.

"Trent," I said when I got within earshot of my boss.

Trent was one of the club owners, along with his two brothers, Jud and Logan, plus Sage, a guy who used to be the general manager but who had bought in recently.

Trent was intimidating as fuck, tatted from head to toe, an ex-biker who'd known the dark life but had come to our small city of Redemption Hills, California and started over.

I'd met him when he'd first come into town. Two of us had taken one look at each other and had known we were one and the same. We'd become instant friends, and I'd been working for him ever since.

"Hey, man, need a favor," he said.

"Whatever you need."

"Eden and Tessa are coming in tonight."

I ignored the spark that popped in my chest at the mention of Tessa's name. I locked it down tight, where it belonged.

"School wrapped this last Friday, and they want to celebrate," he continued. "Should be here in five, and I need to meet with Sage in the office for a few. Need you to keep an extra eye. Make sure none of these pricks decide to get *friendly*."

His voice turned dark when he issued the last.

No one messed with his wife.

Eden was his world. She was the only woman on the planet who could take this broody motherfucker and turn him into a cheesy sap who melted whenever she came into the room.

"Not a problem. I'll see to it they make it to your private booth."

That didn't mean every drop of my blood wouldn't be boiling with the thought of Tessa coming through the door.

Tessa McDaniels was Eden's best friend. She was this wild, untamed thing with a big, bleeding heart.

Kind to the core.

Someone I counted as a friend, and I sure as hell didn't have many of those.

Problem was, somewhere along the line, she'd become the tormenter of my dreams.

"Thanks, man. Trust you to keep a close eye. I appreciate what you do."

"Just doing my job." I shrugged like it was simple.

Cut and dry.

Ignoring the truth that I used this job as an outlet. Better to pour my wrath out here than take it elsewhere.

Turning, I weaved back through the crush of bodies that roiled and thrashed. I broke out the other side and ducked into the employee hall that ran the far side of the club. At its end was the door to the employee lot where Eden would park.

Oz took up that post. He was a new bouncer who'd been hired on earlier this year. He was older than the rest of us by probably fifteen years. Rough around the edges, and he had this massive scar running the length of his face.

"Hey, man, boss's wife is on her way. Going to step out to meet them," I told him as I approached.

"Of course, sir."

He opened the door for me to duck out.

That was the precise time Eden came bobbing through the other side.

She was dressed up for the night. Her blonde hair was curled in fat waves, and she had on a black cocktail dress that was modest compared to what most wore here.

Eden sent me a warm smile. "Hey, Milo. How are you tonight?"

"So far, so good."

I did my best to keep my focus on Eden and not the girl who came ambling up the steps behind her.

Impossible.

Because Tessa was wrapped in that same shiny red dress that never failed to send my thoughts spiraling in a direction I couldn't let them.

It was strapless and hugged every sharp curve of her body, landing just at the top of her thighs to show off her long, long legs.

She teetered on these sexy-as-fuck, strappy heels that made my stomach clutch.

Sight of her always twisted through me like a knife.

But she had a douche-dick boyfriend that I hated with every fiber of my being, not that I'd ever touch her if she were free, anyway. Still, the thought of her with him made my insides quake with the thirst for violence.

Dude was a grade-A prick.

"Milo!" Tessa nearly squealed when she saw me.

Eyes the color of the ocean lit.

Complex layers of teals and deep blues and speckles of green. Made me feel like if I went to any beach, I could find her there.

Her face was this angelic thing, her cheeks high and her nose tiny, her mouth nothing but a plump rosebud ripe for devouring.

Every inch of her face was dappled in freckles, promising the lush, red locks rolling down her back didn't come from a bottle.

But it was the goodness that ran from her like a current that kicked me in the gut, evoking all the shit I couldn't feel, but when I was in her space, I couldn't stop the sense that I was standing in the light.

Then she went and threw herself around me. Her arms tightened around my neck, and she pressed her cheek to my heart that threatened to hemorrhage out, rocking us back and forth as she hugged me like she was relishing the moment, too.

Knew better than to let my thoughts go sliding in that direction. This urge to dip my dirty into the purity she embodied. Drink of the light that glowed from her.

My chest fisted as I leaned down so I could wrap my arms around her waist, careful as all fuck, doing my best to quell the urge to crush her against me and push my nose into that wild mass of hair and inhale.

"I missed you! How long has it been?" she rushed.

I quirked a brow at her when I managed to untangle myself from her hold. Only thing it did was shift her hands to my sides.

Heat curled up my spine.

"It's been a week." You know, because the girl liked to come in here and torture me.

She grinned, so damned sweet. "Way too long. I've totally missed you. And seriously, have you grown since the last time I saw you? I always thought of you as a mountain man, but I changed my mind…I think you're an actual freaking mountain."

Stepping back, she held on to my arms while she looked my giant frame up and down.

A tease played across those red lips, warmth dripping from her being.

Girl pure fucking sun.

"Hardly." The word was rough.

"I dunno," she drew out, "you're looking extra big to me."

Eden giggled at her side. "Tessa, leave the poor guy alone."

She glanced at Eden. "What are you even talking about? Milo loves me."

Her attention swung back to me, red hair swishing all over her bare shoulders. "Don't you?"

Without answering, I took a step back to put some space between us. "I hear we're celebrating tonight?"

"That's right, baby! School's out." Tessa gave a sloppy slug to my shoulder.

Eden shook her head. "She's acting excited right now, but she went and took the director position at the foundation, and now she's going to have to work all summer break."

Aghast, those blue eyes widened, and Tessa pressed a hand to her heart. "Do I look like the kind of girl who wants to miss out on all the fun?"

"Working overtime at the foundation?" Eden's brows lifted on the tease.

"Says the girl who will be teaching ballet classes there all summer," Tessa tossed back.

The two of them taught at a private school, and they could razz each other all they wanted, but there was no question they loved it.

"So, where is this one's husband, anyway? I'm surprised Trent wasn't at the door, ready to go caveman on her adorable ass." Tessa knocked her hip into Eden's.

Eden giggled as she peered down the hall. "Is it weird if I agree with Tessa?"

Tessa feigned offense. "Why would you not agree with me? I know all the things. I told you Trent was your Ace, didn't I? You should be forever grateful for my stellar intuition. Your mouth would still be watering for a taste of that bad boy if I hadn't intervened. You're welcome for your kids, too."

Tessa waggled her brows.

Light laughter rippled from Eden. "Is it sad you're probably right?"

Fucking cute, the two of them, tied at the hip the way they were.

"Nothing sad about it." Tessa took her hand. "You're my ride or die. I complete you. Well, me and your smoking hot hubby, and I may not give you all those yummy O's, but I was here first, so you're stuck with me."

"I'll be forever in your debt."

"You know it." Tessa was all grins.

I angled my head down the hall. "Trent is tied up in a meeting."

I stepped around them to start walking. I needed to get the hell out of that confined space. "He asked me to meet you two and make sure you got to your private booth. He should be finished in a few minutes."

"*Oooo*, we get an escort. I feel like a celebrity right now. The perks of being this one's bestie." Tessa fumbled along behind me, trying to book it up to my side while wearing those heels.

Felt her like chaos at my side. Like one of those summer storms that were really fucking gorgeous to look at but could cause outright annihilation.

The second we dipped out into the main room, I was on edge.

I began to wind them through the crush, ready to pounce on any fucker who got the wrong idea.

People parted like they felt the intensity that gushed from my being, that intuition to step aside. I cut a path to the booth tucked at the far back corner of the club that was reserved for the Lawsons and their guests.

"Here we are," I said, standing off to the side so they could slip in. Tessa touched my arm as she passed, slanting me a sweet look that made me itchy. "Thanks, Milo. You are the best."

Reining my wayward eyes was hopeless as she slipped into one side of the booth. There was no goddamn way to stop my gaze from tracing the length of her silky thighs, the way her knees parted just enough to give me a veiled glimpse of what had become nothing but a fantasy.

Like I said, the torturer of my dreams.

Tiny Tease.

Except she didn't have a clue what she did to me.

"I'll be nearby if you need me."

Tessa winked. "As if we'd expect anything less of you."

I set up post about five feet away, hidden in the corner, and leaned against the wall with my arms crossed over my chest.

Far enough away to give them some privacy, close enough I could get to them in a blink if the situation arose.

Tessa and Eden kept tossing back dirty martinis.

They were laughing and giggling and likely conspiring.

Everything about them became more animated as the minutes passed.

The fuckwads out on the prowl must have felt the ferocity vibrating from my bones because they gave them a wide berth even when they had to be the two most gorgeous women in the club.

An hour passed.

Then two.

Trent checked in every so often, but there was a problem in the kitchen, so he kept slipping out.

The longer Tessa sat there, the more the giggles coming out of her grew in volume, her voice getting louder, her spirit free.

Had to wonder if she came here to find the things she couldn't outside these walls, too.

If she found respite here.

Relief.

If she was always this fuckin' happy or if once she was out the door, life's burdens got heavy.

I guessed I'd always sensed an undercurrent of something beneath that joy.

The thing that really pissed me off was it became most apparent when her boyfriend came around.

Asshole dimming her light.

The same way as he did right then.

A cloud gathered around her, shuttering her warmth, when the pompous fucker broke through the crowd and came striding her way.

A tacky hatred slicked across my flesh, violence threatening to rise to the surface. I did my best to swallow it down before I did something I couldn't take back. Still, my mouth watered with the thirst to just let go. To release the chains that kept me in control.

Karl Haller was one of those pretentious pricks who thought he owned the world, with too-straight teeth and over-styled blond hair.

Wearing an expensive suit and arrogance on his face.

He'd caused trouble here last year, and I'd personally wanted to give him the official stamp of unwelcome and make sure he never waltzed through Absolution's doors again, but over time, he'd somehow swindled his way back in.

I never could see what she saw in him. Wanted better for her.

Hell, what I really wanted was to knock him flat when I saw the way she shrank when he came to stand at the edge of her table.

Tessa was the farthest from weak. Not close to being a doormat. She was this fierce, fiery spirit that chased after the good things in this life.

Whole of it left me confused, whatever this clutch was that he had on her.

I was close enough that I could make out the false pleasantry he tossed at Eden, a cool, "Hello," before he straightened his suit jacket and turned toward Tessa.

He stretched out his hand, but the gesture didn't come close to appearing kind. "It's time to go."

"I didn't text you yet to come get me." Her voice had gone raspy, cut with revulsion.

"And you didn't return my text an hour ago. Now, it's time to go."

"Karl—"

I surged forward. I figured there was no reason to stop myself. Even if some other asshat was trying to pull this in the club, I'd be all too happy to intervene.

But there was something about this that sent venom coating my tongue. "It seems the girl isn't interested in leaving with you."

Worry filled Tessa's face when she looked up in my direction. "It's—"

"I'm pretty sure you don't have a say in it," he sneered, disgust in the curl of his nose, like the asshole thought he was better than me. The second I hauled him out back, he was gonna find out that was not the case.

A soft hand landed on my wrist. "It's okay, Milo."

And shit, I nearly stumbled.

Nearly turned and gathered her up so I could stand between her and this fucker she clearly didn't belong with.

"It's not okay if you don't want to go with him." The words were a snarl as I stared the bastard down.

Karl scoffed and turned away from me, though there was no missing the tremor in his hands. "I don't have time for this tonight, Tessa."

"Tessa." It was a plea from Eden.

Tessa slipped out of the booth, turned to her best friend, and whispered, "It's fine."

Karl spun on his heel and started to walk, and the girl glanced at me in some kind of apology before she followed the asshole out.

"Damn it," I rumbled, scrubbing a palm over my face to break up the haze of red as I watched her disappear into the fray, hating that I couldn't do one goddamn thing about it.

It was hard as fuck continuing with work like nothing had gone down. To act like my insides weren't a web of anger and frustration. I'd barely had the willpower not to rip the face off every asshole who dared to even look at me sideways.

It'd made it even worse that Eden had been super upset after Tessa had left. It was clear she didn't get it, either.

Why Tessa would give the way she did.

I was more than ready to call it a night when Kult and I dipped out the side door and into the employee lot at just after three a.m.

The air was cool, brushing against my heated flesh like a balm that might soothe the fire that burned within.

I locked the heavy metal door behind us before I ambled down the three steps to the pitted pavement below. The deep darkness was cut by the hazy glow of lights that streamed down from the sides of the brick building.

I took a furtive glance around, making sure we were in the clear and ready to roll.

Head bouncers were always the last to leave, ensuring the rest of the staff made it safely to their cars after closing up and doing one last sweep of the interior to verify it was empty.

"Looks good, yeah?" Kult asked.

"Yup."

"See you tomorrow night, then, brother," he said as we crossed the lot.

"Night."

He climbed onto his Harley that was parked next to my old truck. Cranking open my door, I hopped into the driver's seat.

"Ride safe," I told him.

"Never." He winked.

Chuckling, I shut my door, turned the ignition, and the loud engine rumbled to life. I'd restored the ancient blue Ford about two years before, and I took it out every now and again to keep the old girl alive.

Kult's bike grumbled as he kicked it over, and he gave me a little salute as he pulled out and took to the road.

I backed out, and the spray of headlights illuminated the dense forest that enclosed the area.

My heart nearly jumped out of my chest when I made out a grainy figure leaning against a big boulder just off to the right, hidden in the shadows of the towering trees. The wash of headlights flooded over her, sending that red dress glittering like a dizzying mess of stars.

What the fuck was she doing out here alone?

Throat closing off, I rammed on the brake right where I was, and I shoved the truck back into park.

Her expression nearly made me lose it.

She looked lost.

Broken.

Beaten down.

Rage coiled down my spine.

I couldn't handle the idea of the girl out here by herself.

Of someone hurting her.

The other part of me was fuckin' relieved that she was here. At least for the moment, she wasn't subjected to that dick.

I breathed deep to rein the chaos that caught me up in her cyclone before I tossed open the door and slipped out.

Didn't feign to know the details about her and Karl's relationship, but I'd bet my goddamn life he was responsible. It'd been close to three hours since she'd walked out, and I had no clue what'd transpired between now and then, but I was certain it wasn't good.

I rounded to the front of my truck, the words coming out rough. "What are you doing out here, Tessa?"

Eyes the color of a thousand seas roiled.

Tumultuous and uncontained.

Every cell in my body clutched.

Tears streaked down her stunning face, and those thick locks of red hair were a disaster. She swallowed hard, her delicate throat bobbing as she did. "I…"

She blinked as her gaze drifted to the side before she brought her focus back to me and whispered, "I don't even know. I came back to wait for Eden, but I just sat here and watched her leave."

Torment rippled through her expression, and her smile cracked at the side.

Lost.

Definitely lost.

"It's okay, Little Dove. You're not alone." Carefully, I approached. Every step I took sent swells of protectiveness rising from the depths. It made it hard to keep my head on straight. To remember my boundaries. The places I couldn't go.

That was the problem with Tessa.

She got me off-kilter. Made me itchy. Made me want to forget.

Fucking heresy.

"Are you hurt?" The question was shards.

"No. I'm fine. Completely fine. Totally fine." She swiped at the lines of tears that tracked over the freckles dappled on her cheeks.

She gave me the biggest, fakest smile. That was when I noticed the tiny cut on the edge of her mouth.

Rage blew through me so hot and hard it nearly bowled me in two. Acid burned in my stomach, and fury curled my hands into fists.

Had spent years working to control that shit.

The kind of violence that spiraled fast and cracked me in half.

"Don't look so fine to me." It came out the rumble of a warning.

She laughed a shaky sound and gestured at herself, the girl still wearing that red dress that hugged her slim curves so tight it was hard not to get stuck there.

"I'm not *fine*? Pssh. Have you seen me?" she attempted to joke and shimmy her shoulders, but it was soaked in misery.

"What the fuck did he do to you, Tessa?" I tried to keep my voice even when I was pretty sure it came out a growl, and I knew from experience I was a hot second from going on a rampage.

"It was nothing." Another faked smile.

Bullshit.

This wasn't the girl I knew. Not even close.

"Little Dove." I said it soft and urging because shit, I knew she needed someone right then.

A supporter.

A friend.

"Let me take you home."

She cracked at that, and she turned her head away and looked into the distance like it could cover her distress, though I could tell she was tripping toward a breakdown.

Her shoulders hitched and shook as she tried to keep the sobs silent that wracked through her being.

Possession wound me tight, this sense that I needed to gather her up and hold her. Promise her it would be okay.

Such a goddamn fool, but still, I slowly erased the rest of the space, trying to discount the way the air sizzled as I got closer.

Reaching out, I took her by the chin and prodded her to look at me.

Bad move.

Fire flamed and lapped, and those eyes were staring at me, where I towered over her like I might be someone I was not.

"Tell me, Tessa. He did this?"

He had.

Of course, he had.

Karl was a piece of shit. I just needed her to confirm it, and I'd be glad to take care of the rest.

She sucked in a shattered breath. "I've put up with so much crap from him, Milo, but tonight, he actually hit me, and that was it. It's over. It's over, and I have no idea what I'm going to do."

Thank fuck.

Somehow, I managed not to shout it toward the heavens.

The moon lit the angles of her face. Her nose and jaw were sharp, but her lips were soft and trembling. "I was so tired, Milo. So tired of him treating me the way he did. So tired of his demands. So tired of his control. I couldn't take it any longer. I couldn't."

"That's good, Little Dove."

"No, it's not." A sob hitched in her throat, and her gaze seemed disoriented, as if whatever had gone down tonight had just caught up to her. "I have no idea what I'm going to do."

"You're going to be free, that's what."

Pain echoed through her features.

"How could I just let him down like that? How could I be so selfish?"

The words were slurred, and she swayed a bit to the side. Clearly, the effects of the martinis she'd been sucking back earlier tonight still glided through her bloodstream.

My hands went to her waist so I could hoist her from the rock and onto her feet.

It brought her too close.

Energy sparked through the connection. I ground my teeth to tame it and angled my head down closer to hers, trying to break through the disorder that had her trapped in a storm.

"Let him down? You don't owe Karl anything, Tessa."

Tears streamed fast down her cheeks, and guilt contorted her face. "Not Karl. I hate him. I hate him," she stammered. "He hit me. I can't believe he hit me. That was it, Milo. I cracked. I couldn't do it anymore."

It was like she was apologizing to the world, and there was nothing I could do but sweep her into my arms, holding her tiny body against my chest.

I was slammed with her presence. With her scent. Strawberries and cream and something far too sweet.

"It's okay." It was a gruff promise.

"It's not," she whimpered. "How could I be so selfish, Milo? How could I do this to him? How could I do it? After everything?"

I had no idea who *he* was, though it was clear she wasn't talking about Karl. Clear whatever she was going through held a profound pain.

I understood that kind of pain far too well.

This went so much deeper than being about the asshole I wanted to pound into the ground until he no longer existed. A thousand questions burned through my mind, but the girl was in no shape to be answering them then.

"Going to take you home," I rumbled at the side of her head.

It was a horrible idea, but I couldn't force myself to come to an alternate one.

She buried her face up under my beard. "I don't have a home."

I tightened my hold. "My home, Tessa."

Trying to keep my cool, I carried her in the direction of my truck.

"Don't worry about me, Milo. You don't have to take me to your place. I've got this." I felt her resolute nod against the panging in my chest.

I held her so tight in my giant arms I was afraid I might crush her. "You do have this, Little Dove. Know you do. But let me help you tonight, okay?"

Curling in deeper, she whispered, "Are you sure?"

"Yeah, I'm sure."

"That's what friends are for, right?" she hiccupped, her heart beating so hard I could feel it thrumming against mine.

"That's right. That's what friends are for."

I carried her to the passenger side and settled her onto the seat, holding my breath because I kept getting assaulted by her scent as I leaned in to help her get buckled.

I eased back, trying to keep my cool at her sitting there, the way she had her head angled toward me and her cheek pressed to the seat.

That fiery hair blazed around her precious face, and those ocean eyes swam with a million things. "Mad love, Milo. Mad, mad love."

Her smile was soft.

My heart flailed in my chest. I stared at her for a beat too long before I murmured, "Yeah, Tessa, mad love."

Chapter Two

Tessa

FAINT RAYS OF SUNLIGHT BLED THROUGH THE EDGES OF THE drapes that covered the window, nudging me from sleep. My senses spun, touching on my foreign surroundings.

The cozy bed I was in and the quiet energy that hummed through the space.

Peace and safety.

It was so quiet, I could hear my pulse in my ears, could count each one, as if my heart were reminding me I still had a chance at a life I'd never believed I'd have.

I floated in it, trying to get my bearings, to rein my thoughts that immediately wanted to spiral out of control.

That was the thing about waking up to a new reality. You hadn't quite taken hold of your direction.

Your new purpose remained hazy, and fears of pushing forward through the unknown to find a better destination tended to run rampant.

Knowing I'd made a decision that was going to change everything hadn't been so easy to sleep on.

My sleep had come in fitful spurts.

Rife with a worry so intense that Bobby's face had chased me into my dreams.

Still, there'd been a part of me that'd felt...light. A burden that had been eating me alive lifted.

How could my soul be so heavy but still feel as if pieces of my heart had been unchained?

Guilt at the choice I'd made threatened to consume, but I had to accept I'd come to a breaking point.

For years, my meaning in life had been my brother's comfort, but last night, it'd become clear I couldn't remain with Karl.

He'd always landed somewhere in the middle of being a petulant brat and a manipulative tyrant.

That I could handle. Bobby was worth it.

But when he'd struck me?

I'd seen something I hadn't seen in Karl before, and I could feel that things were getting ready to splinter.

Then who would be there for Bobby?

There had to be another way. There had to be.

Blowing out a sigh, I pushed up to sitting.

The room spun, and a dagger pierced through my brain.

I rammed the heels of my hands into my eyes.

Freaking martinis.

They were dirty, all right.

But my nights out with Eden were my escape. My reprieve. My joy.

Karl didn't get to ruin that anymore.

Tossing off what looked like a handmade, patchwork quilt, I sat up, fighting a blush when I realized I was wearing a giant T-shirt that swallowed me whole.

It smelled of him. Like the deep, dark woods.

Pine and cedar.

My palm slipped over the black cotton fabric.

I hadn't been wearing a bra last night, and the only thing I had on underneath the shirt was a slip of satin that could barely be considered underwear.

Heat bloomed across my flesh as memories bounded.

Milo had insisted on taking me home with him when he'd found me in the Absolution parking lot after I'd been unsure of where to go. I had been drawn back there because within its walls had been the only people I could trust, though it'd turned out I'd been too upset to face them.

I remembered him placing me in his truck, and I'd barely stirred when he had carried me in after I'd fallen asleep—okay, passed out—in his truck, barely coherent when he'd pulled me back into his arms and rumbled all those reassuring words to the top of my head.

"It's okay."

"I have you."

"You're not alone."

I bit down on my bottom lip as I remembered him changing me into his shirt.

The care he'd used.

The caution.

He'd slipped it over my head and fully covered me before he'd slid off my dress.

I was pretty sure I'd also mumbled something about him being beautiful.

Awesome, Tessa.

But he was. I was pretty sure in every way. Even though I'd done my best to ignore the fact since I'd met him. But there'd been something about him that'd been there in an instant. It was the type of attraction I'd never felt before, which had only made me feel guilty. I mean, it wasn't like my heart had held any sort of devotion to Karl, but still…

Faint rustling echoed outside the room, and my thudding heart pounded harder. I slipped off the edge of the bed. My bare feet hit the hardwood floor, and I eased over to the door and pressed my ear to it, listening to the subdued shuffling and the quieted clanking of pans.

My senses were impaled with too many sensations.

Coffee and bacon and the man.

My stomach rumbled, and I took a steeling breath before I carefully turned the knob and cracked open the door.

It opened to a hallway that ran farther down to the left of me, and straight ahead was the opening to the main area of the house.

I tiptoed to the edge of it and peered out into Milo's home.

Well, cabin.

Rugged and rough and gorgeous.

Rustic floors and wood-paneled walls. The living space had an over-sized maroon leather sofa and two matching chairs. Light infiltrated the space, blazing in from the huge bank of windows that seemed to take up the entire back wall of the cabin.

But it was the hulking shape of the man who stood at the stove that stole my breath.

He was on the other side of the long, butcher-block island, the top half of him exposed where he faced away. His hair was a thick shock of black, and he'd cut it so it was cropped on the sides and a little longer on top. I'd always had a really hard time not thinking about what it would be like to scratch my fingers through it.

His shoulders were massive and wide, and even from this distance, I could see the brute strength of him rippling from beneath the black shirt that stretched over his body.

As if he felt me there, he glanced at me from over his shoulder.

Intense eyes stared back.

Amber dipped in warm honey.

My stomach took a swooping dive.

A freefall.

He slowly shifted around.

Did the ground tremble?

No, that was only my stupid, wayward heart clattering in my chest.

Because he was looking at me with this harsh softness that made my belly tumble, his eyes dragging over me in a slow sweep, grazing over his shirt, down my legs to my toes before it leisurely dragged back up.

Energy crackled.

The man breathed contradiction.

His voice was always held low, his actions measured, though he glowed with a severity unlike anything I'd experienced before.

A volatility that writhed within him that he kept tapped.

Then he went and smiled this concerned smile that melted my insides, the weight of it twitching beneath his trimmed black beard.

"How'd you sleep?" His voice was a low rumble that skated my skin.

Flustered, I took a couple steps into the room. "Great."

His gaze narrowed, those honey-dipped eyes taking me in from across the space like he could see straight through me.

Gah, why did he have to be so…everything?

Big and intimidating and rough.

Soft and kind and real.

He crossed the small area between the stove and the island, and he planted his palms on top. The position only emphasized his hulking muscles. The mass of them flexed beneath the intricate ink that rolled down his arms and onto the back of his hands.

I swore he was like looking at bottled mayhem.

His attention dipped to my lip.

Nerves had the tip of my tongue poking out at the spot.

His expression darkened. "How are you feeling?"

"Like I drank a gallon of vodka, then got smacked in the face by an asshole." I attempted a joke.

Milo clearly didn't think it was funny.

A dark sound rolled through his chest.

"I'm really okay," I amended, coming forward. "It didn't hurt that much, and it's not going to happen again, so I feel…"

Terrified.

Exhilarated.

Freed.

Trapped.

"Better."

He seemed to war, like he wanted to say something else, then changed his mind.

"Coffee?" he asked instead.

"Milo Hendricks, you are speaking my love language." I couldn't help but grin.

A soft quirk lifted at the edge of his mouth. "Happy to oblige. Have a seat."

He gestured to a stool at the island.

I padded over and slipped onto it, trying to play it like this was all completely normal.

Like he didn't make me shake.

Like I hadn't sported a very scandalous crush on him since the moment I'd met him.

I wondered what he'd think if he knew I'd fantasized about waking up in his house before, although the previous night's activities had looked quite a bit *different* from the way they'd actually gone down.

And on all things holy, was it a stunning house.

It was somehow everything I expected, but more.

Rustic and raw, but also warm and cozy with a touch of luxury.

My eyes wandered, taking it in.

It was one giant room, and the ceiling was pitched and had to be at least two stories tall.

Sunlight gleamed in from the windows that ran the backside of the kitchen, expanding out to run from floor to ceiling on the far-right side. The glass segments were framed in the same color of wood as the walls.

They gave way to an elevated porch and the forest beyond.

Tucked about a hundred yards back was a small lake hugged by the expanse of soaring trees.

Blue water rippled and glittered beneath the rays of morning sun.

My chest squeezed at the beauty of it.

"This is gorgeous, Milo," I whispered in awe. "And I'm not just being polite. It's…a dream. I can't believe you live here."

A soft grunt left his mouth as he moved to a cabinet, pulled out a mug, and poured me a cup from the carafe. "My grandparents left me the land when they passed. Spent a couple years building this place."

Surprise unhinged my jaw. "You built this place? Like, with your bare hands?"

He slid the mug across the island in my direction, and I did my best not to gawk at those tattoo-covered mitts as he pushed them out in front of me.

But they were so big and nice, and he was so damned intriguing it was hard not to get lost at the sight.

"Yup."

"Magician."

He shook his head in gentle disbelief. "Hardly, but I do like to work with my hands."

Redness flamed.

I wondered what else he could do with those hands.

"Creamer?" he asked.

I blinked myself out of the lust-induced stupor. "Is that even a question?"

He let go of a low chuckle and turned, moved to the refrigerator, and opened the door. "I think I should have known based on the drinks you typically choose at the club."

Pleasure glowed in my stomach.

He paid attention?

"What can I say? I like sweet things. Which is why Eden is in so much trouble this morning since she swindled me into martinis last night rather than my go-to. If I have to pay for it, Eden does, too."

Clearly, we were skirting the subject that sat in the room like a hot-pink, inflatable elephant.

"Oh, I'm sure she's paying for it just fine," he rumbled as he dug for the creamer while I sat, trying not to ogle him.

Talk about a miserable failure.

But who could blame me when he wore a pair of gray sweatpants that were really dangerous to my sanity? Holy crap, his thighs were thick, and his ass was this muscular, sublime thing.

Not to mention all those yummy muscles were bulging out from the tight black tee, his shoulders wide before his frame tapered down to a narrow waist.

He was so freaking tall that he filled the entire opening of the door.

A fortress.

The colossal kind.

Then he turned around.

Do not look, do not look. Do. Not. Look.

Yeah, I looked.

I gulped around the knot that formed in my throat.

Every inch of this man was magnificent.

"There you go." He passed me the creamer like just looking at him hadn't rocked my world.

My attention snapped up to his face. "Thank you."

"You hungry?" he asked as he moved back to the stove where he removed the bacon, then proceeded to break eggs into the sizzling grease.

All mountain-man style.

"You don't have to feed me."

He peeked back. "What if I want to?"

My chest tightened.

"Then I'd say thank you...for everything." I added that on really quick because this was obviously about more than him making me breakfast. It was time to broach the topic that simmered around us like a secret I didn't want to share.

He slowed, his voice lowering in emphasis. "Was glad I found you, if I'm bein' honest."

Discomfort clattered around in my spirit, and I fumbled to pour a big dose of creamer into my mug.

I met his eye because he deserved the truth. "I'm glad you did, too."

A grunt vibrated from his being. "What were you doing out there?"

Disquieted laughter rolled up my throat. "I don't even know, Milo. I came back because I didn't really have anywhere else to go. I waited for Eden and Trent to leave, but I just...couldn't get up the nerve to come out of my hiding place and tell them what happened."

Or really, I hadn't been ready.

"You were in shock." Milo said it like he'd plucked it right out of my brain.

My head dipped. "I think so. I guess that happens when you lose direction."

"Or maybe you were just stumbling into it...the right path."

Right into you.

I kept that to myself.

Tension bound the air as he plated the eggs and bacon.

Every movement he made was filled with caution, as if he knew he was treading into territory I was uncomfortable to visit. Or maybe he was just building up to something.

Easing over, he placed the food in front of me.

Then he planted his hands on the island as he stared me down.

Severity gushed from him on an unanticipated wave. "I want to destroy that bastard, Tessa. Have wanted to since the second I had the displeasure of meetin' him. But after last night?"

Fury crawled across his ink-covered flesh, the muscles writhing and rippling, his jaw clenched in restraint.

He looked like he might actually commit murder.

"It's not your problem to deal with, Milo."

The last thing I wanted was for him to get himself in trouble because of me.

"No?" The word cracked in the air. A direct threat.

Shivers raced.

God, he was a lot to take in.

He might have been soft-spoken, but there'd always been a current that ran beneath it.

Explosive.

"I would never want to drag you into my mess."

Air puffed from his nose. "Think I'm already there. Besides, life is made of messes. I'd be more than glad to clean this one up for you."

"Believe me, I'm more trouble than I'm worth. You know what they say about redheads." I tossed back a lock of my hair, going for light when everything felt like it weighed a hundred pounds.

"Guess it's your lucky day because red just so happens to be my favorite color."

Heat rushed up from the volcano that suddenly erupted in my stomach.

Note to self: Milo Hendricks was a stone-cold charmer. Who knew?

"He's honestly not worth either of our time, Milo," I told him, licking my lips and trying not to make too much of his statement. "I just want to be done with him."

"Then why stay with him?" His question punched through the atmosphere.

Distress clawed its way through me, and my tongue stroked out to wet my dried lips. "Because sometimes, we have to sacrifice our own well-being for the sake of the ones we love most."

Confusion pulled across his brow. "Who—" he started to ask before a phone started buzzing on the counter where it was plugged into the wall.

I frowned when I realized it was mine.

Milo shrugged. "Last night, it was beeping that it was about to die, and I figured you might need it this morning. Hope you don't mind."

"That's really kind of you, Milo."

"The least I can do," he said. He ambled to the opposite counter to unplug it.

A disbelieving giggle got free. "I would say you're doing plenty. Overboard, baby. A girl could totally get used to this...waking up to coffee and breakfast and the most breathtaking view I've ever seen."

He grunted like it was no big deal.

"Here you go." He passed me my phone, and I entered the code. Instantly, I cringed.

There was a slew of waiting messages that had come in throughout the night.

Really, I shouldn't have been surprised, but still, it sent a bout of anger rebounding.

Bouncing through my spirit because seriously, the freaking nerve.

Karl: I don't appreciate the stunt you pulled tonight.

The stunt I pulled? My teeth ground. Was this douchenugget kidding me?

Karl: Where are you?

Karl: I don't have time for your games, Tessa. If you aren't home by 8:00 a.m., I'm calling the police.

It was 8:09, not that I cared. But it was the last text that had just come through that sent blood sloshing through my veins. A disorienting thunder. The very thing that had kept me tied to him for far too long.

Karl: You know what happens if you don't come home.

For years, I'd nod and smile when Karl made his demands. I'd bent to his will that had grown uglier and uglier as time had passed because I hadn't seen how there was any other choice.

And no, I still didn't have a solution. An answer. But there had to be one, right?

I struggled to breathe through the sickness that clawed at my insides, a tacky qualm spoiling in a pit of dread.

"What is it?" Milo's voice held a wicked cut of violence.

My hand shook as I set my phone on the island. "It's nothing."

"Don't do that, Tessa. You don't have to pretend with me. Have no clue why that asshole has you in a clutch, but I can see you're scared. That you feel trapped."

"I just don't know how to move on from here. What I'm going to do." The confession came rushing out.

"You want to stay with him?" Malice shook through the quieted question.

"No."

Absolutely not.

"Then there's your answer."

"It's not as simple as that."

"It never is, but it's on us to figure out how to work around our circumstances."

I peeked up at this man who'd become a friend.

Someone I trusted.

But I'd never come to the place where I'd trusted anyone else with this.

"These circumstances might be too great to overcome," I whispered.

"So, we deal with today and figure the rest out later." His voice was gruff.

"Just like that?" I asked.

"Just like that."

Affection gathered at the base of my throat. "Well, then, I guess the first step is finding an apartment."

That obstacle?

Easy.

It was Bobby who haunted my mind. Bobby who made me wonder if I was committing the greatest act of selfishness.

But this had gone too far, and I would find a way. I had to.

Milo raked his teeth over his plump bottom lip. Crap, that was distracting. "Was thinkin' maybe you should stick around here for a bit."

"Don't tease a girl, Milo. That's just rude."

"Not teasing, Tessa. This place is huge and empty except for me."

Hold the phone. Was he serious?

"Milo." The tone woven in his name held the thousand reasons this would be a very bad idea.

Mostly, the sound of him in the shower. Well, the thought of him in his bed. Hell, just standing in his kitchen he was dangerous.

Clearly, I was starving for a taste of the man.

But really, I'd meant it when I'd said I didn't want to drag him into my mess.

"Would make me feel better, knowing you're here, under my roof, where I can keep an extra eye out for you."

Turmoil wound its way deep into my psyche, the ache that wanted to give in and let Milo hold a little of my burden.

That's what friends were for, and all.

But I knew better than asking so much of someone else.

My smile came soft. "You're so kind, Milo, but I can't—"

He suddenly shoved off the island and stalked around the side of it.

The words stalled on my tongue as he came to tower over me.

All that burly intimidation on display.

Beautiful Beast.

He grabbed the arms of the stool and swiveled it so I was facing him.

The man clutched them as if they were a life raft and he was in danger of going under.

Still, he angled down to get close to my face.

God, he was really freaking hot, and my mouth went dry as that dark intensity pulsed from him in shattering waves.

Stealing my breath and pounding my heart so frantically I thought it would bust through my ribs.

"You think I'm doing this for you out of obligation, Tessa? Because I'm a *nice* guy?" A growl filled the words, and I was getting sucked deeper into his mystery, into the deepest woods where the light couldn't make it beneath the shroud of heavy, dense leaves.

A safe haven that whispered of destruction.

This man, who clearly wore a beautifully broken halo.

I struggled to draw oxygen into my thinned airways.

He dragged the stool even closer, so close I might as well have been in his arms. "I won't sleep knowing you're out there by yourself, and I'm already a flat second from rollin' out that door, finding that prick, and showing him just what I think of him. Believe me, Tessa, that shit wouldn't be pretty."

He lifted one hand and ran the pad of his thumb over the tiny cut on my lip.

Gently, though it nipped with a current of rage.

His attention dipped to that spot for one second before his eyes cut to mine.

"So, no, Tessa, I'm not asking you to stay here because I think it's the right thing to do. I'm asking you because I need you here. Just for a little while, until I know you're safe and you've found your way."

My tongue swept over my lips, every part of me shaking, my hands and my words and my unsteady heart. "I mean, because we're friends, right?"

He peeled himself away, staring me down as he grumbled, "Yeah, Tessa, because we're friends."

Then he pointed at my plate. "Now eat, before your food gets cold."

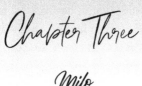

Chapter Three

Milo

WHAT THE FUCK WAS *I* THINKING?

I stormed into my bedroom, slammed the door shut behind me, and drove my fingers into my hair. I started to pace, nothing but a madman tearing up the floor.

Of all the goddamn ideas I could have, I had to go and invite her to stay here? Hell, I'd all but demanded it.

And I'd done it already knowing having her here last night had nearly pushed me to a boiling point.

The entire night, I'd been torn between sitting in the corner of the guest room and watching her sleep to make sure she was fine and whole and hopping into my truck and taking a quick jog back into town so I could hunt a motherfucker down.

Ruin him for daring to touch on that beauty.

For tainting it.

Marring it.

I paced the other direction, doing my best to get my shit together. I needed to actually be there for her instead of inciting the type of *mess* there was no chance she would be prepared for.

I'd made the snap decision to ask her to stay here when I'd caught a glimpse of what that asshole had texted her, sure there would be no letting her out of my sight.

There was no taking it back now.

I had to suck it up.

Pretend like the woman didn't needle into places I couldn't let her go.

Support her like the *friend* I was supposed to be.

Inhaling a steadying breath, I forced myself to focus. I strode through the ensuite bathroom and into the closet on the opposite side so I could at least find something for her to change into. Suffice it to say her parading around in my shirt was not gonna do.

There was a drawer in the built-in chest that I tended to stuff odds and ends into. My mom loved hanging out on the dock, and she was constantly leaving crap behind.

I opened it and started to rummage around to find her something that might work, tossing old pieces of random clothing out of the way. I stalled out when my fingers brushed on the worn fabric tucked at the very back.

Recognition hit me so fast it punched the air from my lungs.

Agony raced in to take its place, filling my chest cavity to the point of bursting.

Warily, I pulled out the small pair of yoga pants.

Hidden away.

Forgotten.

Except there was no fucking chance I could ever forget.

I turned around and slumped back against the drawers, bringing the fabric to my nose and inhaling deep.

A tiny giggle rippled from her lips, her smile pure adoration. "I know you better than you think I do, Milo Hendricks."

He could only smile back, propped on an elbow as he gazed down at her where she lay on their bed. "Is that so?" he teased.

"It's very so and so very plain to see how much you love me."

His heart soared, and he touched her face. "More than you'll ever know. Forever and always."

"I'm sorry, baby," I whispered as I balled the fabric tighter and pressed it deeper against my face.

Like it could stand as a bridge back to her.

"I'm so fucking sorry."

Sorrow whispered and howled from the darkness.

From that void that would forever live on.

From the place where I'd destroyed the one beautiful thing that had ever been offered to me.

Forcing the torment down, I stuffed the yoga pants back into the very back of the drawer and rifled through until I found an old shirt and some shorts of my mom's that would have to do until we could get Tessa something better.

Then I slammed the drawer shut and moved back out into the main living space, slowing my footsteps as I eased toward the hall on the opposite end. My heart that was already feeling flayed got chopped to shit when I saw Tessa wasn't at the door to the room where I'd placed her last night, but rather was standing in the doorway to the one at the far end of the hall.

Her hand was still on the knob, the girl frozen in confusion as she stared inside.

Or maybe she'd just gotten snagged on every mistake I'd ever made.

Every misstep.

Every failure.

Every sin.

A slow, dense intensity pulsed along the narrow hall, and I struggled to breathe around it. Struggled to process this connection that throbbed between the two of us.

A live wire.

Echoing and curling and rebounding.

My skin crawled, and the vacancy in my spirit ached.

There was something about Tessa that made it seem like she got people without them having to say a thing. Like she knew things. Saw things. Felt things.

And shit, I was feeling all of them right then, too.

For an eternity, we stood in it together. Silent as we floated on this gutting confusion that rippled with understanding.

Finally, she looked at me from over her shoulder. Caution filled her expression. This girl who knocked me senseless every time I caught sight of her gorgeous face.

The guilt of that truth nearly knocked me to my knees.

A smile pulled to her mouth, soft and awed and perplexed. "I didn't know you're a dad, Milo. That's amazing."

There was a question behind it, and regret coiled with the adoration, my throat feeling like it might lock up as I scrubbed a palm over my face.

"Yeah," I finally managed. "A girl and a boy. Remington and Scout."

"How often are they here? I mean, I can leave." Her words became hurried, like she suddenly felt uncomfortable or out of place when I was the monster who didn't want her anywhere else. "Get my own place. It's no problem. I don't want to get in the way. I didn't know you had children here, and seriously, the last thing they need is my crazy ass running around—"

"No." The single word cut her off.

She slowed, caught in my storm, blue eyes adrift. Lapping and swirling and drawing me to a beautiful place.

To the place where the sun touched the sky.

Too bright for those who'd been condemned to the darkness. I forced myself to speak around the shards of glass lodged at the base of my throat. "They don't come here."

A frown pulled to her brow, that blaze of red hair a burning halo piled on top of her head.

Her gaze was soft. Penetrating. Digging deep into the recesses where my demons lay.

Swore to God, she took up every molecule in the space.

"Do they live with their mother?" Caution stole all the lightness from her voice, and I was pretty sure the woman could sense the pain that was leaching from me in a torrent.

My head barely shook through the misery. "No."

She blinked, troubled, the question a rough scrape. "Where?"

"With their grandparents." It grated out, the admission nothing but razors of affliction.

"Oh." It was a slight curl of her mouth, and her teeth raked her bottom lip like she was trying to hold back every question that wanted to come rushing out.

While I stood there feeling like I was coming unhinged.

"I didn't mean to pry," she finally whispered, pulling the door shut. "I was looking for a linen closet so I could grab a towel and take a shower, and I opened this and…"

She trailed off, the smattering of freckles on her pale skin glowing in the sunlight.

"It's fine," I told her, when it was the farthest from the truth. None of it was fine. But that wasn't on her. It was on me.

Her tongue stroked over those rosebud lips, both nervous and bold. "I'm sorry."

"What do you have to be sorry for?"

"I'm sorry that my friend is in pain."

Understanding passed between us, the two of us there, hovering in this weird awkwardness that somehow didn't feel all that uncomfortable.

Finally, I cleared my throat and shoved the clothes out in front of me. "Found these…they're my mom's. She probably left them on the dock or something. I hope they fit okay."

Tessa eased forward, her eyes still on me when she reached out and took them. She smiled at me like it was okay I'd just revealed a jagged piece of my heart.

"Why does it feel weird for me to wear your mom's clothes?"

"It shouldn't. My mom's the best. She lives on the property to the west. I'm sure she'll be by to check in."

She hugged the clothes to her chest. "Well, if she's half as awesome as you, I can't wait to meet her."

Air huffed from my nose. "I'm sure she'll be excited to meet you, too."

That was sure to be a whole fucking fiasco in itself.

Tessa rocked back on her heels, staring at me, but somehow giving me privacy.

"Thank you for everything, Milo," she finally whispered.

My stomach fisted just from the breathy sound of her voice.

I blew out a sigh because I didn't think I had the first clue what I'd gotten myself into. "Get yourself a shower, Tessa. I'll be out back if you need anything."

Chapter Four

Tessa

"THANK GOD YOU ANSWERED. I AM IN DESPERATE NEED of my BFF right now, and I'm not even kidding." I whispered it all dramatic-like into the phone as I ducked around the gorgeous main room of the cabin. Why I found it fit to go stealth, I wasn't sure, but somehow, having this conversation felt like a covert mission.

Especially when I kept peeking out the edge of the bank of windows that overlooked the sprawling backyard.

Milo was outside on his hands and knees as he sanded a piece of wood, working on what looked to be an elaborate fort.

He'd ridded himself of the atrocity that was his shirt, because holy crapballs, it was a sin to cover up all the deliciousness that was the man.

From this distance, I really couldn't make out any of the designs, but I could tell his back was almost completely covered in ink, and the muscles in his arms and shoulders flexed and bowed as he manually roughed the sandpaper block over the planks of wood.

Power tools would have been an unnecessary invention if all men were made like him.

But what sent my spirit sinking was the knowledge he was out there working on a treehouse after he'd just confessed that his children didn't come to visit. My heart was already in tattered shreds at the adorable room that had been set up, waiting for two kids to fill it.

There had been no missing the way the room ached, and in turn, I could only ache for my friend. But it'd also triggered a million questions.

Eden giggled from the other end of the line. "Uh-oh, tell me what kind of trouble you got yourself into this time. Do I need to bring bail money?"

If Milo would have been left to his own devices, I was pretty sure it was him who would have needed the bailout.

"Well, some things did go down last night," I hedged, my nerves spiking.

I could feel the mood shift, Eden coming to the quick conclusion that my night hadn't ended the way it usually did—with me giving into Karl's demands. For years, she'd begged me to leave him, unable to understand why I'd stay. Maybe I'd been a fool not to give her the truth. I'd never been sure myself if I'd kept her in the dark to protect the arrangement or because of shame.

"What happened?" Her voice lowered in concern.

I inhaled a shaky breath. "I ended it with Karl."

Shocked silence compressed the air, then she whispered, "You left him?"

Emotion gathered in my throat, anger and hurt and resolution. "He struck me last night, Eden."

Pain infiltrated the small sound she released before she cautiously asked, "Has...has this been happening?"

I paced in a small circle, running my free hand through my hair as I tried to figure out a way to explain this to my best friend.

She was going to be hurt.

She had the right to be.

We were supposed to share everything with each other.

"It was the first time, and it was my breaking point. A person can only take so much."

Confusion curled through the connection. "I don't understand why you let yourself get pushed to that place, Tessa. You are the most amazing person I know."

Affection pounded in my chest. "I know I'm pretty great," I tried to tease, to lighten this moment, because crap, it was hard letting go of a secret I'd kept in my clutches, like hiding it would make it less painful.

Less real.

An alternate reality.

She waited. She knew me well enough to know when I was joking to cloud the seriousness. I blew out a sigh. "I have something I need to tell you."

"You can tell me anything. You know that."

"Karl has been paying for Bobby's care."

Silence stretched long, and I could tell she was processing. She warred, then pressed, "What do you mean? I thought the state paid for it?"

The laugh I let go was ashamed, and my voice quieted as I rushed through the confession. "It was Karl paying for it the entire time."

We'd only been dating for a short time when the accident happened, and I'd moved in with him pretty quickly after.

"I don't understand. Why didn't you tell me? Why didn't you come to us for help? The church would have helped. We would have—"

"I know you would have, and that's exactly why I didn't tell you. Your dad already gave so much to me and Bobby. There was no chance I was going to ask for more."

When our parents had died when I was fifteen, Bobby had stepped in as my guardian. He raised me when he'd barely been more than a kid himself.

Eden's father, Gary, ran a nonprofit called Hope to Hands out of the church where he was the pastor, helping those in the community who were in need.

At the beginning?

That organization had made it possible for me to remain with Bobby. Providing groceries and covering our rent for a full year until Bobby had gotten a promotion at work.

After Bobby's accident, there was no chance I could ask more of them. I couldn't take away from the other families who needed that money when I had another option.

Unfortunately, it was an option that had begun to destroy me.

Eden was silent for a long time before she carefully asked, "Is that why you took over Hope to Hands? Because you felt like you've already taken too much?"

God, sometimes she knew me too well.

When Gary had been ready to retire from the position, I'd felt called. I needed to give back after everything that had been given to me.

"Of course not. I was bored and needed a reason to stay away from Karl's house for longer. I did it for purely selfish reasons." I let it go as a tease.

"You really are the most amazing person I know," she murmured instead of laughing.

My voice softened. "You guys took care of us, Eden. I don't know where I would be right now if your father hadn't stepped in."

Over the years, he'd become like a father to me, especially after Bobby's accident. I'd had no one left but these incredible people who'd welcomed me into their family.

"And that's the hold Karl has always had on you. I should have known."

"You didn't know because I kept it from you, and I'm sorry for that."

"Still, I should have dug deeper," she argued, like any of this was her fault. "I always knew there was something. It wasn't like you lit up anytime that jerk came around. I never could understand what you saw in him."

I'd actually liked him at the beginning, though, until he'd shown who he really was. Once he'd started giving me money? His offering had been nothing but chains.

"I definitely didn't see a whole lot in him…he was like…sour cake with mold on it." My nose curled at the vision.

Eden giggled. "Gross."

"Totally gross."

We both laughed before the lightness drained. "I can't believe it. What are you going to do now? Trent and I can—"

"Don't you dare say you guys can give me money. That is not happening. I will figure this out."

"Why not, when you would be the first one to give me the shirt off your back?"

"Well, I'm actually going to need yours." I looked down at the outfit Milo had given me to wear. It was an old, ratty tee with holes in it and a pair of gym shorts.

It was going to go awesome with my heels.

Dawning blazed from my bestie. "Wait a minute, where are you?"

I inhaled a deep breath, taking another quick peep out into the backyard. Milo was now on a ladder hammering a piece of wood.

Tingles raced.

Good God, the man was delicious.

"Milo's."

A beat of silence passed before she laughed. "Oh my God, did you call him? I knew you had a thing for him. You were always in denial, claiming you had a boyfriend, while you were salivating over him, weren't you?"

All true.

"No, of course not. Who do you think I am? And it so didn't go down like that. He found me loitering outside Absolution."

"You went back to Absolution?" she gasped. "Why didn't you call me to come get you?"

"Because last night was the first night in forever that you and Trent didn't have the kids, and I knew you were over there eating all that yummy, delicious cake." No mold to be found. "What kind of BFF would I be if I interrupted that?"

"I would have come."

"Well, I certainly hope you did. I mean, come on, tasty O's with your uber hot man or rushing out to save me in the middle of the night? This is not a toss-up, Eden."

They'd been so cute when they'd come out the door. So in love. Trent couldn't keep his hands or his mouth off my bestie as he'd led her to her car. I wasn't about to interrupt it, even though I'd never felt so alone than when I'd watched them drive away.

"I would have been there for you in a heartbeat. Ride or die, remember?"

"Well, you were riding that big D, soooo…"

She choked. "Tessa."

"I am the teller of the truth. Tell me I'm wrong."

She giggled.

"Uh-huh, that's what I thought."

I wasn't jealous or anything.

But I wanted it. Ached for it. A connection that was real. It was hard going at life alone.

I peeked at Milo again. There he was, intense as he worked, sunlight burning down and blazing against all his toned, chiseled flesh.

Snap. Crackle. Boom.

There went my lady bits.

"Tessa?"

I jolted out of it, realizing she'd called my name three times.

"Oh, sorry, what?" I asked, completely flustered.

"I was just saying I'll come pick you up. Kate will be up from her nap in about a half an hour, and we'll head over there."

Of course, she would invite me to crash at their place.

I loved her so much for it, too.

But she had a family now.

Nerves raced, streaking through my veins, because was I really doing this? I hesitated, then rushed, "I'm actually going to stay here at Milo's for a while."

"Excuse me?" Her response was loaded.

"Yeah, so it turns out he needs a roommate."

It was only a tiny lie, because the man did seem like he needed someone.

I understood lonely.

Recognized it.

But his was even more severe.

There was a deep, penetrating sorrow that lined his bones. His aura this convoluted, distorted thing.

I'd never seen it so clearly than when I'd been the idiot who went hunting through his house like it was my own and stumbled into that room.

It was painted to be a replica of the view outside, the walls the lake and the forest surrounding it, the ceiling a whisper of the summer sky. Two beds were fashioned like treehouses, close to what he was building outside, like just lying in them would be an adventure. They were covered in handmade quilts that matched perfectly.

Two toy boxes were in the middle of the far wall, and a bookshelf bracketed each side. They were stocked with toys and books and stuffed animals.

But it'd been too perfect.

Too clean.

Too empty.

"Hey, did you know Milo has kids?" I was back to whispering.

Eden hesitated before she blew out a knowing sigh. "Yeah, Trent has mentioned it a few times. I guess their grandparents have custody of them."

My heart squeezed in a fist.

"Where is their mother?"

"I'm honestly not sure."

Unable to stop myself, I glanced out the window again, my pulse chugging in dread. "Do you think he...hurt them?"

I couldn't imagine. Couldn't believe it.

He might have oozed ferocity, but I also felt his goodness. His loyalty.

Tenderness filled her voice. "My gut says no. Every time I'm around him, I feel like there's something really big and difficult going on in his life, but you know I don't really know him that well. He rarely speaks, and when he does, it's never about his personal life. For the most part, he keeps to himself, but Trent trusts him around our kids, and you know that would never fly if that weren't the case."

"Yeah." My agreement was quiet as I gazed out.

A painting of peace and heartbreak.

A picture of grief and solitude.

"So, you said you needed the shirt off my back…" Eden hedged.

I laughed. "Um, yes, I'm wearing an old shirt and shorts that belong to Milo's mom. Save me. I'm going to have to go get my stuff from Karl's soon, but I'm not up for it yet."

I'd say screw it all if it weren't for the fact my car was there.

"Don't worry, Eden to the rescue."

"And bring me shoes…but not the ugly old lady ones you like to wear sometimes because they're *comfortable*. Bring me those cute slides with the heel."

"Wow. The love, Tessa." Her tone was droll.

I grinned. "Like I said, I'm the teller of the truth."

"Okay, then, truth teller, are you okay?" Care filled her voice.

I inhaled a shaky breath. "I think I am. I'll figure this out, whatever I have to do. All except lying beside Karl for one more night."

"I know you have this, but please, if you need help, ask us. We are here for you. You may not be blood, but you are my sister, Tessa. I hope you know that."

Affection clogged my throat. "I know. You're my sister, too."

"No more secrets."

"No more secrets," I promised.

She paused for a second before she continued, "You are the most selfless person I know, Tessa, and I know you'd give anything for your brother, but it's time for you to live for yourself, too. You deserve to be happy."

"I am happy."

"I'm not talking about that kind of happy. Not the surface kind or the merely content kind. You deserve the fullness of it. I know you're lonely, as much as you try to hide it. You deserve *cake*."

A soggy laugh jutted from my mouth as moisture filled my eyes. "I think I'm taking my first step toward it. I finally realized last night that I wasn't helping anyone by staying with Karl. Not when there was going to be nothing left of me in the end. And yeah, I want *cake*."

I wanted a life that was sweet.

Fulfilling.

And sure, I could do it on my own, which would be just fine. But a partner, finding my *person*? That sounded really nice.

"You know Salem and Aster are going to be banging down your door, wanting to know the details," she warned.

Aster and Salem were Eden's sisters-in-law, each married to one of Trent's brothers.

Aka: The Fantastic Foursome.

They'd been pushing me to ditch Karl since they'd met him.

"Ugh, I'll send out a text."

"You deserve every question you have coming your way," she teased.

So maybe I badgered them for details about their relationships, finding joy in what they had found when I'd succumbed to what I would never have.

"Hey, my only choice has been living vicariously through the three of you. Don't blame a girl for her needs. I needed deets. Visuals."

"That's called porn."

"Your hubbies are all way better to look at. I'll take the blessings I'm given."

"You are so messed up," she giggled.

"And you're my hero. Now get your cute butt in your car once Miss Baby Kate wakes up and bring me some clothes. Do you know where Milo lives?"

"I can get the address from Trent. As soon as she's up, I'll be on my way."

"You are the best, Eden. Mad, mad love."

"Mad love."

The line went dead, and I was fighting a smile as I tapped out a message in our group thread. They were going to love this shit.

Me: The douche-canoe has been set at sea. Buh-bye, tiny-dick, prick-face.

It only took a second for the responses to come rolling in.

Salem: Shut your face.

Aster: Are you serious? Tell me you're saying what I think you're saying.

Salem: If this is a joke, I'm going to kick your scrawny ass.

Me: No joke. I ended it last night.

Salem: OMG, WHAT HAPPENED?

Me: Get together soon and talk about it?

Salem: Margaritas, Friday.

Me: As long as they're bottomless.

Because I was definitely going to need them.

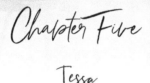

Chapter Five

Tessa

THE NEXT MORNING, I SLIPPED DOWN THE BRIGHTLY LIT halls of St. John's Meadows.

The summer sun stood proud where it shined through the windows and cast its cheery warmth on the tenants of the long-term care facility.

St. John's Meadows boasted thirty private rooms. There was a big, shared living space and a few smaller alcoved dens, a dining room, not to mention a theater, game room, and a craft and art room.

It'd been designed to give off the vibe as close to a house as possible in hopes of offering its residents a form of comfort and tranquility. Its grounds lush and brimming with giant trees, the lawn perfectly trimmed, and the shrubs and plants overabundant with colorful flowers.

But it still had *that* smell.

The smell of medicine and antiseptic and forever crushed dreams.

I guarded myself against it. Against the sorrow that gripped my chest every time I stepped through the doors.

Bobby's room was one-eleven, midway down the right hall and situated on the left.

My heart squeezed so hard it might as well have been one of those stress balls that could be flattened to nothing as I stood in the open doorway and peered inside.

Every prayer and promise I had ever made rose to the surface and threatened to clot out the resolution I had made to myself.

Because he was the reason. The catalyst to every choice that I made.

He was strapped to his wheelchair to keep him safe, staring out the window at the gardens.

I never knew if it was unseeing or not.

If he recognized its beauty. If he wished he were out there walking its paths. If he felt the loss of every memory and experience he would never get to have.

If he understood.

I carefully eased into his room. Loud noises startled him, so I kept my footsteps quiet as I crossed the floor.

I thought I could feel his spirit lighten when I approached him. My big brother who'd been hidden away and forgotten by everyone but me.

Well, me and Karl, who had used him like a bargaining chip.

No more.

"Hey, Bobby, it's me, Tessa," I whispered.

His arm and shoulder tremored just a bit, the only response I ever got.

I moved around his chair and knelt in front of him, my spirit flailing at the sight.

In love.

In agony.

His hair was a dark russet, a deeper red than mine, though I'd always liked to believe that we'd matched.

That we favored each other.

That we were a pair.

Inseparable.

Family.

Bobby had always been the one I looked up to. Idolized. My protector.

The obnoxious big brother who gave me crap and ordered me

around and told me who I could and couldn't date, which was basically everyone, but he'd done it with big vats of love and a gentle smile.

My chest ached as I thought of how he smiled no more.

He'd sacrificed everything for me, his freedom, the nights in his early 20s when he should have been off at a bar picking up girls, in favor of working two jobs to take care of me.

When he'd had his accident, there'd been no other choice than sacrificing everything for him.

Guilt threatened to suffocate as I carefully reached out and touched the hand he kept clasped tight against his chest, his right hand the only one that had any function at all.

"How are you today?" I asked, keeping my voice low.

My eyes made a quick path over him to ensure he had everything he needed, checking that he was secure, even though I trusted his caregivers took excellent care of him, which was the exact reason I was desperate for him to remain here.

He was always freshly bathed, his clothes and bedding clean. He had daily physical therapy, and they fed him his meals regularly.

He had at least improved to the point that he could swallow when prompted, improved to the place where he could breathe on his own so his trach could be removed.

It'd made me hopeful that he would recover.

That he would walk.

Talk.

But he'd never progressed beyond that.

He was nonverbal and fairly nonresponsive, only making a few grunting sounds that I never knew if they were communication or just locked-up energy that his body expelled.

His eyes that were the same color as mine were always distant, gone to a faraway place.

A place I had no idea where he existed.

I felt desperate to meet him there. So he'd know I'd never leave him alone, that I'd never turn my back, that I loved him with every fiber of my being.

"You look good, big brother," I murmured.

I took the fist he held against his chest, and I carefully pulled it onto his lap and opened his hand.

In it was a small, round charm, an intricate locket that made a ball, but when it was opened, it contained four small pictures.

One was of our parents, two were of him and me, and the other was of the four of us when we'd been young and our family had been complete.

This...this was how I knew he remembered.

Because he kept me close when I was away.

I set the charm aside and wound my fingers through his.

He breathed a heavy breath, and I knew.

I knew he felt me.

So I would never stop talking to him. Would never stop communicating in the only way we could.

"Are they taking good care of you?"

I ran my thumb over the back of his hand.

"It's beautiful out today, isn't it? Windy last night, though. I hope it didn't keep you awake."

I knelt there for a minute, unsure of what to say, how to admit what I'd done.

Feeling the pressure of it, I pushed to standing and started to move around his room. I fiddled with the remote on the wheeled table that sat off to the side of his bed, touched the bouquet I'd brought him on Saturday when I'd visited him last, and glanced at his chart where the nurses and caregivers scribbled their notes.

Mostly, it was a distraction. Something to do with my hands to ward off the panic.

What if I couldn't provide for him?

What if I couldn't find a way?

There were a couple of new drawings on the pinboard that hung on the wall. One was from Hank, who was nineteen and a hopeless flirt. He never failed to ask me out every time he saw me in the hall.

The other was from Lynette, a young girl who had learned to paint with her mouth and spent her days out in the gardens, painting pictures for those who rarely made it outside.

I unpinned them and moved back to Bobby's side. I pulled up a chair, angling it so I was almost facing him.

I lifted the first, the almost nondescript scribbles made by Hank.

"Get better, Bobby!" A tweak of a smile edged my mouth as I read it aloud. "Hank is always rooting for you, Bobby. He thinks one day you're going to roam these halls with him, causing all sorts of trouble. What do you think?"

I held it up and traced my finger over Hank's crude words.

Bobby only gave me a slow blink.

Sorrow crested.

A swelling wave.

It always felt like it was right there, ready to consume.

I held up the other picture that was incredibly good. "And here, this one is from Lynette. That's the fountain that is right outside your window. Look...there were birds in it that day. Five of them."

I counted them out for him.

I had to wonder if he was in his head thinking, *No shit, Sherlock.*

I so badly wished I knew.

I set them aside.

Normally, I could ramble at him all day, talking about everything and nothing. It wasn't like words didn't come easily for me.

But today, it felt like a lie. Like dishonesty.

I eased to the edge of the chair, and I sat forward and gathered both his hands between mine. I squeezed tight as I let the confession ride into the air. "I left Karl, Bobby. I left him because he wasn't good to me or good *for* me. Because my heart aches to find its freedom. To find love and joy."

Was it selfish? Wanting those things for myself when Bobby would never have them?

"I'm living with a friend now. It's kind of weird and awkward, mostly because he's stupid hot, and I don't know what to do with myself when I'm around him."

I got so sweaty every time Milo was around, I worried I was having hot flashes.

"Don't worry. I'm safe there. Milo is kind. A total good guy. You'd definitely like him." My tongue stroked out to wet my dried lips. "I'm going to be honest and tell you that I'm scared. I'm scared that I won't be able to figure this out on my own. That I'll let you down. But I want you to know I'll never let that happen. I'll do whatever it takes. I'll take care of you. Always. I promise I will find a way."

Pushing to my feet, I leaned over him so I could press my lips to his temple. "I love you so much, big brother. Mad, mad love."

Tears stinging at the backs of my eyes, I pressed the charm back into his hand. I curled his fingers around it and held it tight as I whispered, "I hope you at least know that."

Blinking away the moisture, I stood and walked from his room.

I followed the couple halls into the administration area. I knocked on Nancy's door that rested halfway open.

She looked up from her desk. "Tessa, hey, come in."

"Hi."

Her brow dented in worry. "Is everything okay?"

I gulped around the torment and eased down onto one of the chairs across from her. "Can you let me know how far Bobby is paid up to?"

Concern played through her eyes, but without saying anything, she shifted so she could type on her keyboard and look at the screen that was angled off to the side.

"He's paid until the end of the month."

That was like…three weeks.

I tried to swallow around the grapefruit-sized ball of dread lodged in my throat.

"Has something happened?"

"No, no, everything's fine, I just wanted to make sure the last payment came through," I lied.

Clearly, she picked up on my agitation because she studied me for a beat before she turned and dug into a drawer and pulled out some pamphlets. "We love having Bobby as a resident, but there are other options if you need them."

She passed the pamphlets toward me.

The top one was for a state funded facility in San Francisco.

I felt sick.

"Thank you," I whispered as I gathered them and stood.

I made a silent promise that I wouldn't need them.

I ducked out of her office and hurried down the hall with my head lowered, not wanting to face any of the caretakers who would definitely pick up on the fact that something was off.

I usually came through here trying to brighten everyone's day.

This place often radiated sadness.

I knew it wore and whittled and cut. It was hard. Both for residents, the caretakers, and the family members who came to visit.

I pushed out the front doors and into the bright morning light, inhaling deeply as the fear of what I'd done rushed up from the depths where I'd tried to keep it contained.

Guilt and worry filled my chest to overflowing. I struggled to breathe. To fight off the panic that sank into my skin like sharp talons.

I started in the direction of Milo's SUV he'd let me borrow, almost at a run because I had to get out of there before I had a breakdown.

I screamed when a hand wrapped around my arm from behind.

Hatred.

Disgust.

Revulsion.

They roiled through my body.

I whirled around so fast it tore my arm out of Karl's hold. "What the hell are you doing here?" I demanded, trying to keep the shaking out of my voice.

I doubted he'd pull anything in public. He had his reputation to uphold, after all. But I couldn't handle him *here*.

Near Bobby.

By the one person who meant the most to me, who Karl had wielded like manipulation.

Karl kept his rage checked, though I could see it writhing behind his eyes. "I've been trying to get in touch with you, and you haven't returned my calls."

"That's because I don't want to talk to you."

His teeth ground in restraint, his expression pompous and hard. "I told you I didn't have time for your games, Tessa."

"That's good, because there is no *time* left for us. I told you I was finished, and I meant it."

"You're being ridiculous. Overreacting, the way you do about everything. You can do me a favor and stop acting like a spoiled brat."

My brow pinched tight as the hatred roared. "I was a fool for ever staying with you. This went on for way too long, and it ends now."

A scoff ripped from his mouth. "Are you fucking kidding me? After everything I've done for you?"

"You didn't do any of those things because you care about me."

His hand scraped through his too-perfect hair. "I did it because I love you."

What bullshit.

"I don't think you ever loved me. You just needed a pet project to show off to your friends and colleagues. Look at what a good guy Karl Haller is taking care of the poor girl, while you treat me like garbage behind closed doors. I'm finished with you degrading me. Of you making me feel stupid and small. I'm tired of you trying to control my every move."

It was plenty without him becoming physical.

But when he had?

"It's done, Karl."

He flew into my face. The venom spewing from his mouth held me just as tight as if he held me by the arms. "Well, I'm not done with you."

Fear slithered down my spine, but I lifted my chin, refusing to give into him.

"Screw you, Karl. You don't get me anymore." I started to back away as I spoke. "I'll be by your house to get my things tomorrow. I'd appreciate it if you weren't there when I come."

I turned on my heel, digging into my purse to get the keys to Milo's Tahoe.

I slowed when the snarl of words hooked me from behind. Quiet but delivered with the deathly strike that Karl intended. "You know what happens if you walk, Tessa. Don't try my patience."

I barely turned, my voice a thin sheet of sadness. "And there it is,

Karl. Proof that you don't love me. You'd gladly let my brother suffer if I don't do what you say. That's not love."

His mouth slashed in a downward sneer. "Do you actually think I'm going to continue to spend $15,000 a month for your brother to stay here after you've made me look like a fool?"

Regret wrapped around my ribs. "You are a fool, Karl, because if you did love me? If you had treated me with respect? I wouldn't be walking away."

I honestly didn't even know how I'd ended up in this position. When I'd first started dating him, I was young. He'd been charming and charismatic, and it wasn't like he was bad to look at. I'd thought there might actually be something there.

And after losing my parents?

I'd wanted it.

Love. A family. Security.

My *person* who cared about me the way I cared for them.

Maybe I'd been a fool for thinking that might be Karl.

Somewhere after Bobby'd had his accident and Karl had offered to put him in this facility, things had changed.

Maybe he'd resented me for the promise he'd made to provide for Bobby. Maybe it'd become too much for him. Maybe he knew just how much Bobby had disliked him when Karl and I had first started dating.

Most likely, the asshole just got off on having me under his thumb.

Whatever the case, our relationship had twisted itself into this ugly thing of bitterness and hostility and shame.

Before I'd recognized what was happening, I'd been stuck. Basically contracted to a man I'd come to despise.

Gathering myself, I turned back around and headed for the SUV I'd parked in the lot.

Karl's voice echoed behind me. "You don't get to just walk away from me, Tessa," he warned.

I clicked the lock and opened the door, glaring at him when I said, "Watch me."

Chapter Six

Milo

"PAULA, PLEASE..." MY VOICE WAS RAGGED, MY HEART squeezing so fuckin' tight I thought it would implode as I pressed the phone to my ear.

I wasn't sure I would physically make it any farther.

Not when she dug deeper at the guilt. "How could you be so selfish, after all you've done? After everything you've already taken from us?" she spat.

Anger coiled with the shame. "You know there's no chance I'm just going to turn my back on them."

"Like you didn't before."

Grief clutched my spirit, right along with a giant slab of guilt. "I was mourning, Paula."

Her voice was bitter. "They're better off with us. You can't actually think they'd have a better life with you."

"I'm their father." Agony spiked through the air.

"You don't deserve to be." It was spite.

Hurt.

Part of me wanted to agree with her. Take on every single thing she threw my way.

God knew it was my fault.

The other half knew my kids needed me. I knew it to my soul.

"I'll fight for them." Those words came out hard, laced with that truth.

"If you had any heart at all, you'd let us live. They're safe. Well cared for. And you see them every week. Isn't that enough?"

An afternoon at the park. She thought that was enough to make up for every memory that was lost? For every holiday and birthday and chaotic morning trying to rush them out the door to make it to school on time?

Misery crawled through my bloodstream. Clotting off life and love and hope, but it was the last vestiges of that hope that had me whispering, "I love them, Paula. I love them. They're my children. They need me."

"Are you sure it's not the other way around, Milo? Are you sure it's not you who needs them, and you are too blind to see what is best for them?"

Torment flayed and cleaved.

"I'm not backing down. They are my children."

"And you stole *mine*." The heaving of her grief slashed through the too-dense air, impaling me in the chest, this torture that would never end.

"I would have died for her." The words croaked from my trembling throat.

"But you didn't."

The line went dead before I could say anything else. I threw my phone to the mattress beside me, slumped over, and buried my face in my hands.

I did my best to lock down the riot of emotions.

A war that raged and fought to take hold.

The truth of Paula's accusations at odds with the truth of my soul.

I couldn't sit still.

I pushed to my feet, my boots slogging slowly over the planks of my cabin floor, the call of my heart drawing me to the destination.

I crossed the great room and turned down the hall. Outside the closed door, my forehead dropped to the wood. Inhaling a shuddering breath, I pushed into my children's room.

Sunlight filtered through the window. It pitched a glittering glow over the room my mother and I had painstakingly poured our love into. Her fingers had woven the patchwork designs of their bedspreads and painted the images on the walls, while I'd carved and nailed and drowned myself in the making of the treehouse beds, praying one day they would be filled.

Agony I would never be free of lifted from the pit of hell where my soul was condemned.

Suffocating.

Crushing.

Excruciating.

Every fuckin' horrible memory, every mistake, impaling me as I stood there in the middle of it.

A prisoner to the vacancy within the walls.

I was so lost to the turmoil, I guessed I hadn't heard my SUV roll up to the front of the house.

It didn't matter.

I felt her.

I felt the shift in the air and the tremble of the ground and the warm energy that infiltrated the space.

I needed to guard myself against it. Ignore the pull that tugged and whispered and coaxed.

A gravity I'd do best to resist. I never should have asked her to stay here because there wasn't a single piece of me that could handle her presence.

Her smiles and her goofiness and her laughter.

Her quiet insight and soft spirit.

The way she filled the walls of the cabin like she was supposed to be there when it was supposed to be Autumn who roamed the halls.

Guilt nearly choked me out.

How could I even think it? Want something good after what I'd done?

Motherfucking heresy.

Knowing it didn't stop it.

Heat crawled up my spine as Tessa slowly approached from behind, each step quieted and cautious as she crept up to the door.

I could feel her peering in. "Hey. Am I intruding?"

I shifted to look over my shoulder. "It's okay."

When it came to Tessa, I couldn't seem to refuse her anything.

She took another cautious step forward.

Shit, I could actually sense her inhaling my grief, experiencing it, her attention carefully moving around the room like she was newly categorizing everything.

Ocean eyes swam.

Calm on the surface and a riptide underneath.

"Tell me about them?" she whispered.

Telling her no would be the correct answer. Instead, like a fool, I scrubbed a palm over my face before I fully turned around to face her.

Tessa stood just inside the doorway.

The sight of her tugged at every forbidden place inside me.

A blaze of red hair framed her gorgeous face, all those freckles bright beneath the shimmery rays of light.

She wore jeans and a cropped white tee. Casual and sexy at the same time.

Her lips parted on a breath, like she was hinged on my next words, waiting on me to invite her into a place I shouldn't let her go.

"Remington is my daughter. We call her Remy. She's eight. She's shy but super intuitive. One of those quiet spirits that get things on a deeper level, especially for her age."

Emotion clogged the description.

Love and grief.

I might only get to see her once a week, but she and I shared a special connection. A bond that would never break.

A soft smile touched the edge of Tessa's mouth. "Remington's a beautiful name."

"Yeah. Her mother named her."

The admission cracked at the end, and before I lost the nerve,

I forced myself to continue. "Scout, he's five. A handful like nothin' you've ever seen."

My own smile was fighting for dominance, plucking at the edges of where everything had gone dim, my tongue locked on all the painful parts.

"Well, I'm a teacher, so I've seen some wild ones." Her voice was a soft tease as she watched me, like she was searching for clues in my expression. Or hell, maybe she could already read every single thing inside me, and she knew she was traipsing into a minefield.

A place riddled with darkness and ghosts and destruction. The place I would be forever chained.

Maybe Paula was right. Maybe I should give up.

At the thought, a spike of agony speared me so deeply I nearly buckled, a gasp coming up my throat before I could stop it. My hands curled into fists as I tried to force all the shit back down where it belonged.

Tessa caught it, anyway. "I'm so sorry, Milo. I realize I don't know the circumstances, but I can feel what's here…"

Her gaze moved around the room, taking in every emotion and intonation.

"Yeah, and what's that?" Didn't mean to sound like a jerk, but anger came ripping out.

Anger at what I'd done.

Anger at what I couldn't stop or change.

It was too late.

Too fuckin' late.

She watched me without judgment, without disgust, and when she spoke, her voice was both a plea and understanding. "It's your life. Your hopes and your dreams and where your love lives. And it's locked behind a closed door in your house."

Felt like I'd been kicked in the gut.

My teeth ground, pain splitting through my head.

Turmoil spun, everything dense, too tight, too narrow.

"What happened to their mother?" Tessa pushed beyond the boundaries.

I was moving before I even knew it.

Her eyes went wide as I backed her against the wall.

I towered over her where I caged her in, and the woman stared up at me in quiet ferocity.

In fierce care.

While I glared down at her stunning form that made me feel like I was going to lose it.

"I didn't invite you here for you to try to crawl into my head, Tessa." The words were shards.

"I know," she said, unwilling to look away from the agony that had me crushing my teeth. "But sometimes, friends need to go there, anyway."

My head angled down, my nose so close to the cut of her jaw.

Her scent invaded logic.

Strawberries and cream.

The sweetest temptation.

Tiny Tease.

I inhaled deep, and the words I exhaled scruffed against her cheek. "Not a safe place to be, Tessa. I'd suggest you stay away."

I started to pull back, but she fisted her hand in my shirt, keeping us nose-to-nose.

"What if I don't want to?" she whispered, those eyes rushing all over my face.

Penetrating.

Tempting.

Destroying.

Everything clutched.

Urges slammed me from all sides, this need to stand in the light.

To feel her tight little body against mine.

To kiss and fuck and take.

Before I did something stupid, I uncurled her fingers from my shirt and pushed away.

I could feel myself slipping.

Getting sucked into a trap.

The foot of space separating us came alive.

Boiling with that energy.

"Milo," she almost begged.

"Just don't, Tessa."

Without saying anything else, I had my feet pounding out the door because I couldn't spend a second longer with her in that room.

Not with her grace, and sure as fuck not with her understanding.

Because I already ruined my chance. Destroyed. And I'd never fucking spoil beauty again.

Chapter Seven

Milo

ROCKS FLEW UP FROM HIS BACK TIRES AS HE BARRELED DOWN the dirt road. Sweat streamed from his temple and blood pooled on his shirt at his side.

His hands gripped the steering wheel like it might keep him chained to sanity as he struggled to see through the blur of fear.

Rushing ahead to meet it.

To cut it off.

To stop it.

"You failed." The memory of the venomous voice played in his ear like the tolling of the dead. **"Your betrayal won't go unnoticed."**

It was said one second before the shearing pain had impaled him.

Darkness had sucked him under.

How many hours had passed, he didn't know. Night had possessed the earth, crawling through the trees and sinking into the crevices.

He shoved the gas pedal to the floorboards, the tail of the truck fishtailing as he whipped around the curves.

It was little relief when the building finally came into view, his headlights illuminating the trailer. The tires skidded as he rammed on the brakes and threw the truck into park.

He didn't shut it off.

He jumped out and ran.

Searched.

Shouted.

"Autumn? Autumn?"

Only the vacancy echoed back.

A sickly awareness that sank into his flesh.

Dread.

Desperation.

He burst out the back door and into the night.

His footsteps pounded.

The water glittered like black ice.

Milo plunged into the freezing cold.

It swallowed him whole.

An abyss.

A chasm.

Darkness. Darkness.

He sank to the bottom where it reigned for eternity.

Where his life was left without light.

A roar erupted from my soul, so loud it battered the walls and shook the panes of the windows.

A reverberation that curled through the darkened cabin like the call of the forsaken.

The lost.

The abandoned.

The desolate.

Air heaved on tormented shockwaves from my lungs, and my shoulders jutted in spastic quakes as the room spun.

Agony crawled across my flesh like tiny demons searching for a home, infiltrating the fissures that were torn open wide, pain squeezing my ribs in a fist so tight I was sure I was being crushed.

Night after night.

It gathered like dust and dirt.

A heaped grave at my feet.

I sat upright in my bed, half disoriented and half seeing too clearly.

Each time the nightmare came to collect, I felt like I'd been dragged in front of a mirror that replayed every hope I'd dared to dream on a distorted loop.

Round and round and round.

All while forcing me to stare at the one responsible for destroying it.

I inhaled through the pain, fuckin' desperate to reel it back in, but it was only getting deformed and contorted when I felt the shift in the dense, dark air.

That was one second before I heard the creak of the floorboards.

My chest squeezed in a fist when there was a light tapping against the door.

The sound crawled through the atmosphere and wrapped me like solace.

A blanket of comfort that I didn't deserve.

"Milo?" Her voice was a timid call, a whisper that panged against my heart.

Despair gusted from the depths.

"I'm fine, Tessa." The lie lashed from my tongue.

Seconds raced, and I swore that I could hear her heartbeat thundering from the other side of the door.

"I don't think you are," she finally whispered through the wood. Her voice a crutch.

A lure.

Peace.

"Can I…come in?"

I needed to tell her to go. Hell, I needed to tell her that this whole thing had been a bad idea from the start. After the way I'd reacted this afternoon when she'd asked me about Autumn? I needed to end this before it was too late.

But it was my fool mouth that was muttering, "Yeah, Tessa, you can come in."

Chapter Eight

Tessa

MY HAND TREMBLED AS HARD AS MY HEART AS I SLOWLY twisted the knob to his bedroom door. The latch clicked and gave, and I drew in a steeling breath before I barely opened it an inch so I could peer through the crack.

My pulse still sprinted and clanged from the shout that had hammered through the cabin like the heavy carnage of a bomb.

Guttural.

Anguished.

My eyes narrowed as my sight tried to adjust.

Milo's room was shrouded in shadows, dark and grim. Within it, I could almost make out the shape of the ghosts that howled and whipped and haunted the space.

His huge silhouette vibrated in the middle of it where he sat upright on his massive bed.

Somehow, he still managed to overpower it with his sheer size.

Every muscle in his body was rigid.

Coiled.

Ready to strike.

My spirit clutched.

All afternoon and night while he'd been at work, I'd reeled from the severity of the interaction we'd shared earlier in the day.

He'd been filled with a rage that hadn't been directed at me.

A torrent of grief so great it'd erupted from his mouth and fired from his tongue.

Now, his aura danced in a glow of flames. Red and orange hues that lapped and simmered and seethed, as if the man were being burned alive where he sat struggling for control in the middle of his bed.

Carefully, I eased the door open farther and took a tentative step inside. In an instant, I was pummeled by the energy that ricocheted chaotically throughout the room.

"Hey." The word was held in caution.

It would be rude to ask him if he was okay when he clearly was not.

His bed sat horizontally across the room, the headboard against the wall to my right.

Warily, he turned his focus toward me. "What are you doing in here, Tessa?"

There was no anger behind it. It was just another of those warnings that I shouldn't try to get inside his head.

A warning that I couldn't handle it or maybe that I couldn't understand. Maybe I was ignorant to disagree. But his pain had jolted me from my own agonized, fitful sleep, and I couldn't help but wonder if maybe we could be there for each other.

"I heard you," was all that I said.

Energy swelled.

Whispered and blew and compelled.

The attraction I'd always felt for him was different this time.

Bolder and darker.

It was the kind that made you fearful to step into it because you knew your infatuation had turned dangerous.

It wasn't light or frivolous.

It wasn't a tease.

It was deep and desperate and terrifying.

And I was sure, right in that second, I felt it down to my soul.

Milo roughed out a cynical sound as he stared blankly at the window opposite him. "Never should have asked you to stay here."

"Because you don't want me here?" I figured I should lay it out. Tiptoeing wasn't exactly my thing.

He looked at me then, with that strikingly gorgeous fury that he kept locked down tight. His jaw was clenched beneath his beard, and he leveled me with a stare that made me both want to run and drop to my knees.

"No, Tessa, because of how much I *do* want you here."

Severity crashed.

An intense awareness that swirled through the room.

It compelled me forward.

"You're lonely," I murmured.

The air shivered, and the racing of my heart turned erratic.

His attention dipped to his legs that were covered by a dark comforter, his big body this fortress that I could so clearly see had been damaged.

Battered and barraged.

The foundation cracked.

Pieces missing.

He rubbed the heel of his hand against the center of his chest. "It wasn't supposed to go down this way."

"What way?" I pressed, pushing for details as I floated toward him, so slow it might take me an eternity to get there but compelled all the same.

"That I would lose every single thing that I loved."

"Your wife?" The question was a ball of sympathy I lobbed at him.

"Gone." He bunted it right back.

I didn't need him to clarify. It was written in the single word.

She was gone.

Forever.

He had no chance of getting her back.

Heartache pulled tight, and my feet kept shuffling across the floor until I found myself standing at the edge of his bed.

He looked up at me in a way that clutched so tightly that it yanked me down onto the edge of his mattress.

No longer able to stand.

He'd told me to make myself at home, but I doubted that had included me creeping into his room at night.

But I didn't think there was a bone in my body that could have resisted the lure of his spirit.

The need to come here.

"I'm sorry," I mumbled, refusing to look away from the harsh planes of his face.

I had the urge to sweep the pad of my thumb over the stark slash of his eyebrows, like it might be able to erase some of the strain.

A low, rough chuckle rumbled the air, a sound that came completely at his expense. "I'm sorry, too."

Part of me wanted to ask what happened to her, but I wasn't sure we were there yet. Pushing my way into a place he'd asked me not to go. But there was something about what had transpired earlier today that had the words escaping without permission.

"What's going on with your kids, Milo?"

Driving his fingers through his hair, he inhaled a sharp breath. Tension rippled over his flesh before the gruff confession left his mouth. "I just want them back."

"How did your in-laws get custody?"

Self-hatred filled his laugh, and his honeyed eyes dimmed, a thousand shades of black that raged in the shadows.

"After Autumn died…" His teeth ground with the pain that rocked through him.

An earthquake.

"Let's just say I wasn't in the best frame of mind."

"Anyone could understand that."

His laughter was hollow. "No, Tessa, not everyone could understand that. I…" He hesitated for a moment before he admitted, "I pretty much disappeared for a year. Fell off the face of the earth because I wasn't sure how to walk it any longer."

I gulped and forced myself to remain sitting, quietly waiting for him to continue.

"When I returned, I told them I'd gotten myself back together. That I was ready to care for the kids. But they fought me on it. Took me to court. The judge saw me unfit, citing the kids would be better off with them."

"How could anyone judge in their favor?"

"Look at me, Tessa." He gestured at himself.

Slowly, I shifted, climbing onto my hands and knees so I could crawl up to face him. Crisscrossing my legs, I reached out and curled my hand around the top of his.

Sparks streaked up my arm.

Attraction.

Want.

I guarded myself against it, tried to ignore it.

What kind of selfish jerk would think about him in that way when he was finally opening up to me?

He needed a friend.

Someone who supported him.

"I'm so sorry, Milo. I can see how much you love them."

"I got one day of visitation a week," he continued on a heavy rasp, like now that he'd started, he didn't know how to stop. "One fuckin' day, Tessa."

His sorrow spun around me, tendrils that pulled me in his direction.

"And what do you want?" Somehow, it came out a plea.

His thick throat bobbed when he swallowed, his confession low and hard. "I want to be there for them. I want to be the one who tucks them in at night and the one who wakes them up in the morning to get ready for school. I want to be the annoying dad who makes fuckin' horrible jokes and the same one who patches up their skinned knees when they fall down. I want to raise them, Tessa. I want them to know every day of their lives that they are my reason. The purpose I have to go on." Desperation ground through his words. "I want them to know they are the meaning of my life."

Emotion pressed down. A thousand pounds on my chest.

The man was conflict.

Sweet and good.

Rough and fierce.

A beautiful beast with that broken halo tipped to the side.

I wanted to reach out and straighten it.

Promise he was decent and right.

True, I hardly knew him. It didn't matter. I could still see.

Could feel.

It was something Bobby had always said I possessed—the ability to barely brush into someone's atmosphere and know the state of their heart.

Whether it was ugly or honest.

Corrupt or kind.

"What are you going to do?" Caution filled my quieted words.

Hope shimmered around his big body. "I've hired a new lawyer, and I'm petitioning the court for full custody. Didn't want it to come to that, had hoped that we could come to some sort of resolution, but…"

He inhaled heavily before he slowly blew out, the gentleness that was this man at odds with the ferocity that radiated from his flesh. "My in-laws won't budge. They keep claiming I'm unfit. A threat to my children's well-being. It doesn't help they are loaded. They basically pay for things to go down the way they want. But if they want to fight me, then I'm going to fight back hard."

"What can I do to help? I could be a witness. Tell them what a really awesome roommate you are. I mean, who wouldn't want someone like me vouching for them?" I joked.

But I meant it.

"I'll do anything you need, Milo."

"How is it you're so good, Little Dove?"

"I am pretty great, right?" My smile was soggy, hoping he understood. That I truly wanted the best for him.

"I mean it. Anything you need," I reiterated as my hand tightened around his.

He shifted it to thread his fingers through mine. We both just kind of…stared at where we were joined.

Contemplating what it meant.

Friendship, Tessa. It meant friendship.

But I couldn't deny the way my guts were tangled in a coil of excitement, sitting there with him like this.

I had to blame it on my own loneliness.

Sure, I had friends. Eden was my world. The best friend I could ask for.

But there was always something missing. With each loss I'd suffered, the void inside me had been carved deeper.

Karl had done nothing to fill it.

He'd only amplified it.

Filled it with chains and shame and this gross feeling that had seeded itself so deep in my being I'd thought I'd never be able to uproot it.

With Milo?

My throat thickened, and I tried to swallow around the rising of something fascinating.

Enchanting.

Lovely and formidable.

And I was suddenly struck with an idea. A freaking crazy, wild, reckless idea.

Milo frowned, catching up to the shift in my mood. "What is it?"

Anticipation had me stroking my tongue across my lips. "I have an idea."

"What's that?"

"We pretend to be engaged."

Shocked, he started to yank his hand away, but I held on tighter. "You said it yourself that your in-laws have painted you in a bad light. Let's repaint it. Show them that you've moved on with your life. That you're healthy and happy and in love. Building something new. Let's show them that you deserve to have your kids back."

"Tessa." My name fell from his lips like a reprimand. Like I'd jumped off the deep end.

I wasn't swayed. "Think about it, Milo. Why do you think they haven't given you custody? Because you're some dude who lives by himself, right?"

He flinched like I'd hit him, and I gathered up his hand tighter. "I'm not being flippant about this, Milo. Think about it. What would your attorney say if they were told you were engaged? Be honest."

He shifted his gaze away, looking to the wall. He might have wanted to reject my idea, but I could tell the way his chest heaved that there was some validity to it.

"What would your attorney say?" I pressed again.

"She'd probably be thrilled to hear it."

"See," I drew out, holding too tightly to his hand, excited by the prospect.

"This is a terrible idea, Tessa." His voice was a deep rumble.

"All the good ones are." I grinned.

A soft chuckle tumbled off his lips, and he raked a hand through his hair, eyeing me carefully. "Are you serious about this?"

"I meant it when I said I'd do anything to help you, and I'm pretty sure this is the best thing I could do. We're friends. We're supposed to help each other."

"I don't think I can ask that of you."

"You aren't asking anything of me, Milo. I'm offering it."

Disbelieving amusement flitted through his strong features. "You're insane, you know that?"

"Completely. That's why you love me." I said it light, but emotion wobbled through the air.

"Do you think we could pull it off?" I rushed, trying to ignore the way my insides quaked with how close he was.

The smile that kicked at the edge of his mouth was sad. "It couldn't be all that hard imagining getting to love you."

My knees knocked with the impact of it. "But don't you worry. It's all just fake. Completely fake. Right?" I didn't mean to let the last word hitch with hope.

My stomach flipped as the foolish girl inside me hoped this might include the two of us getting naked.

His eyes took a quick jaunt over my body. "Wouldn't dream of touching you, Tessa."

"Well, now you're just offending me." My lips curled a fraction. Like all of this was no big deal when I was pretty sure what I'd just offered wasn't going to come without consequences.

Being in his space like this. Wanting him when he would never want me. Already half in love with a man who would never love me back.

"You know you're stunning, Tessa. Every fuckin' inch of you. Inside and out. I just won't be the fool to dream of it for myself."

That lump in my throat throbbed, and nervously, I wrung my fingers together.

"I want to help you," I whispered, so quietly. "I want to help you get your kids back. This is where they belong. Let's do this, Milo. Together."

His big palm glided up my neck and settled on the side of my face. "Are you sure?"

"I am," I promised.

No matter the cost.

The affection in his gaze threatened to burn me to bits. "Thank you. I won't ever be able to repay you."

"I'm not asking you to repay me, Milo. This is what friends do."

"Never thought I'd have a friend quite like you."

"Well, I am pretty amazing." I winked.

His thumb slipped across the apple of my cheek, no lightness in his tone when he murmured, "You are completely amazing."

I gulped, caught in the intensity, in his warmth that was nothing but a trap.

I hopped off his bed before I did something stupid like crawl into his lap. "I'd better get back to bed."

He nodded slowly, his gaze tracing me in the lapping shadows. "Okay."

Turning, I headed for the door because I had to get out of there before it became too much.

I had my hand on his doorknob when his voice caressed me from behind. "Thank you, Tessa. I mean it in a way you don't understand.

Even if it doesn't turn out in my favor, my gratitude toward you will be unending."

From over my shoulder, I peered back at him. "This is going to be risky, isn't it?"

"Yeah. But the risk is all on me, and there's nothing I won't do for my kids."

I nodded around the disorder that blew through my spirit. "Then I'm happy to do it with you."

Before either of us could say anything else, I opened his door and made a beeline for the guest room, thinking it might sever the attraction that had left me a needy mess.

My body aching for him was one thing.

That, I could handle.

But I knew, deep down, it was my heart that was at risk.

Chapter Nine

Milo

IT WAS A BIT AFTER EIGHT THE NEXT MORNING WHEN SHE shuffled out of her room the same way as I'd come to expect her to do.

All cute and rumpled and looking like she needed a straight shot of coffee injected into her veins.

Red hair a flaming mess, eyes sleepy, a slight grin on her rosebud lips that always grew when she saw me standing in the kitchen.

"Hey, Little Dove," I murmured, trying to keep my cool as she crossed the room.

Hard to do when she wore a tight tank that matched these tiny sleep shorts that barely covered her ass and showed off those long-ass legs.

The woman had really set her sights on doing me in.

That in itself was enough to do stupid things to my dick. Pair it with what she'd offered me last night?

Tessa had me totally off-kilter. Pitched in a place where I didn't know whether to be ashamed or dropping to my knees in gratitude.

"Morning, Milo." Her voice was cautious, something almost shy about it, her gaze unsure, like she was trying to decipher if what'd gone down last night was real or if it'd been a bad dream.

I poured her a cup of coffee before she even made it to the island, and I slid it her direction as she propped herself onto a stool. I passed her the creamer, too.

She hummed. "My hero."

I grunted. "Hardly. I think you're mine."

She stared at me from behind her coffee cup. "You're kind of amazing, too, you know that?"

"Not always, Tessa." Half of me wanted her to understand the truth of it, the other wanted to hide it. Keep her in the dark, where she'd keep looking at me like I was something good and right.

Like I hadn't chased down sin and started a fallout that had cost everything.

Silence hovered in the air between us, two of us contemplating what we'd gotten ourselves into. She took a sip of her coffee, studying me carefully before she set her mug on the counter, going all business. "So, how are we going to handle this thing?"

From where I stood across from her, I planted my palms on the counter. "The fiancé thing?"

Redness kissed her cheeks. Was she actually blushing?

"Yeah, that thing." The words were wispy, tugging at that dead spot that once had been my heart.

I inhaled deep before I set the fantasy free.

"We met each other through Trent and Eden. I've secretly wanted you since I met you, and when you finally broke up with your boyfriend, I took the chance that you might feel the same. It all happened fast, our love. You came here one night, and you never left because you found the place where you belong."

Didn't mean to choke over the last, this lump of something gathering at the base of my throat, making it difficult to breathe.

Tessa made a tiny noise. "That sounds about right."

My gaze ate her up, the girl sitting at the island like an artifact that had been here all along. Waiting to be discovered.

Her delicate throat tremored. "When are we getting married?"

I continued on with the delusion. "In the spring, out on the dock by the lake because you fell in love with this place, too."

"Right, yes. I definitely did. And I'll wear this gorgeous white dress and flowers in my hair and these crystal Manolos that I've wanted forever but could never afford."

She actually squealed at that.

My stupid mind went to conjuring the vision before guilt stabbed into the picture with a violence so fierce I didn't know how I wasn't bleeding out on the floor.

"Oh, you're a lucky man, Milo Hendricks. I'm going to be gorgeous." There she was with her sweet, sassy tease, shimmying her shoulders.

"No question about that," I told her. There was a small, twisted part of me that wished this was real.

Her expression softened, the same as her words. "Remy will be our flower girl, and Scout will be the ring bearer."

My chest tightened, and I forced myself to smile. "The only thing I want is to be fully back in their lives."

Reaching over the island, she squeezed my hand. "They will be, Milo."

I slipped my fingers between hers, shifting to twine them together. "Because of you."

A soft grin slid to her face, and those freckles lit. "I am pretty great."

Zero arrogance.

Pure Tessa.

"That you are," I told her.

Hesitating, she dipped her gaze to the far side of the kitchen.

"What is it?" I urged.

She slowly returned her attention to me, her eyes raging with a tumult I hated to see there. "I need to get my things at Karl's today. Would you be able to go with me? I really don't want to go alone."

Possession pulsed through my blood. "That's good, because I don't want you going there alone, either."

That blush was back, and she squeezed my hand again, her head tipped to the side when she whispered, "I think you and I are going to make a pretty good team."

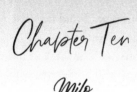

Chapter Ten

Milo

"KNOCK, KNOCK," THE VOICE CALLED FROM OUT OF nowhere.

Ah, shit.

I knew that voice, and I knew it well.

I jerked around from where I was loading the dishwasher, needing something to do with my hands, all around trying to get my head on straight while Tessa went to shower and get ready to go get her things.

That right there fucked with my brain.

I couldn't stop from picturing her under the spray.

Bare body beneath it.

Girl perfect and wet and, motherfuck, there I went, losing direction all over again.

I tamped the visions down because I had a brand-new situation to attend to.

I forced a smile just in time to catch my mother poking her head through the front door.

She gave me a giant grin when she saw me and slipped in without invitation like it was just another day.

Funny, considering there wasn't a single thing about this day that felt normal.

"Hey, Mom, how are you?" I roughed a flustered hand through my hair as I fumbled out from around the island.

"I'm great. It's gorgeous out, so I decided to take the long route and swing by to see how my favorite son is, you know, since he hasn't bothered to call his poor, lonely mother in the last week."

"Your only son," I gruffed, though there wasn't an ounce of annoyance to it since my mother was the best woman in the world.

She'd been there for me when no one else was.

Dragging me out from the pit where I'd fallen and into the land of the living when living was the last thing I'd wanted to do.

Reeled me back from the edge of destruction where I'd hunted like a beast.

Bloodthirst on my tongue and vengeance on my hands.

Going after it hadn't done anything but steal the rest of my joy, and she'd been the one who'd gotten through to me, forced me to see I was only spoiling what I had left.

I had to stand for my kids.

Little did we know what a battle that was going to be.

"Pretty sure Matthew is keeping you plenty busy, anyway." I arched a brow.

My mom had gone and fallen in love, and the guy was over there constantly.

My mother was a knockout.

Her hair was thick and black, and she wore it in a long bob around her defined face. She had this vibrancy about her that glowed. But make no mistake—she wasn't up for taking anyone's shit, either.

She'd been through hell and back when I was young, and she wasn't going to make that mistake again.

With a giggle, she waved me off. "Pssh. He's no replacement for you, and for the record, just because you're my only son doesn't mean you're not still *my favorite*. Accept it."

Casually, she stomped off her boots on the rug. It sent her hair swishing around her shoulders, and her eyes that were the same color as mine danced with love as she peered over at me.

"Fine. I'm your favorite." A tweak of a grin hit the edge of my mouth.

"Busy week?" she asked, seriously that time, staring at me in question.

No doubt she'd taken note of the anxiety that had to be zapping from my skin in strikes of chaotic colors.

I rubbed a hand over my beard. "Somethin' like that."

It was just then that the shower turned off in the guest bathroom, and with the stark change in noise level, my mom realized we weren't alone.

"Oh." There was a slight furrow to her brow, then the dent got compounded by a bolt of glee that lit in her eyes.

Shit.

Of course, she was going to jump to conclusions.

Hanging onto a hope that was never going to come to fruition.

I hated she was going to have to believe this arrangement with Tessa was something it was not, but there was no other way. That didn't mean I had a clue how to deal with it, and panic sped through my veins when the bathroom door creaked open.

"I'll be ready in ten, Milo!" Tessa called before she appeared at the opening of the hall.

Wrapped in a black terrycloth robe, her red hair as wet as could be.

Tessa was this natural, stunning beauty.

The sight of her did just that.

Stunned me.

My tongue locked in my mouth, and my stomach fisted in want.

Shit.

I had to get this attraction under control.

Her blue eyes rounded when she saw we had company, and she shifted on her feet like she was standing in hot coals, stammering, "O-o-oh, hi."

Taking a step forward, Tessa pinned a bright smile on her face that was only partially faked. Her freckles sparked in the sunlight that slanted in through the windows, and I could feel her discomfort coming off her in waves.

She swallowed, forcing back the agitation. "You must be Milo's mom."

My mom's attention swung to me in pure speculation.

I didn't have women at my place.

Not ever.

And certainly not ones soaking wet and wearing only a robe.

When I didn't say anything, she returned her gaze to Tessa. "I am."

Tessa's smile grew sincere. "I am not shocked. Seriously, he looks just like you, and believe me, that is about the highest compliment I could pay you. Have you seen your son?"

She sent me a gentle yet ribbing grin.

Warmth radiated from her spirit.

This girl so kind.

She had a way of making the people around her feel welcome.

Important.

I'd seen her do it a hundred times at the club, not to mention the times I'd hung out with the Lawsons.

The woman shining her light.

Making the world better just by being in it.

Friendly laughter rippled from my mom. "He's about as handsome as they come, isn't he?"

Two of them.

Now I was in trouble.

"Oh, yeah," Tessa agreed. "Good DNA."

My mom's eyes were wide when she looked over at me. "I like this girl."

In an instant, Tessa came rushing from the hall. "I'm Tessa, and it's so great to meet you."

The warmth Tessa exuded also made her a smidge erratic.

She was nothing but a streak of joy and excitement as she rushed my mom, like my mother's statement had given her the go.

She opened her arms and wrapped my mom in them, swaying her back and forth and making a bunch of squealing noises. "I knew you were going to be amazing."

My mom laughed before she pulled back a fraction so she could look at Tessa. "Is that so?"

Mom's voice was soft curiosity and a slow thrill.

Something I could feel climbing from her spirit.

It made me itchy.

"Well, your son is crazy amazing, so I figured you had to be, too."

"That he is."

They both looked at me.

I fidgeted, antsy as fuck.

Tessa shifted to take my mom by both hands, and she looked her up and down. "How are you so gorgeous?"

"Okay, I *really* like this girl," Mom said, voice a sweet tease, gaze speaking in silent code that shouted, *Oh, you snagged yourself a good one.*

She had to know it was an impossibility.

But if we were going to pull this thing off?

We had to convince people it was real, and shit, my heart sank at what I had to do, but my mom would never fucking approve if she knew the plan we'd concocted.

I forced myself to move, boots thudding the floor as I warily approached where they stood together like they were the best of friends.

My heart climbed up to take residence in my throat as I stretched a shaking hand toward Tessa.

Confusion filled her expression before she slowly reached out and accepted it. Warmth streaked up my arm.

Exactly the way I wished it wouldn't.

I tugged her to stand at my side, shifting her around so we both were facing my mom.

I sucked for a steadying breath, holding on to Tessa like it would give me strength.

"Oh, good, he's going to say something," Mom teased.

I sent her a soft glare, then struggled to keep my voice light when I said, "Figured official introductions are in order. Tessa, this is my mom, Cheryl." Hesitation held the confession for a second before I pushed it out. "Mom, I want you to meet Tessa, my fiancée."

A tremor rocked through Tessa's body at my proclamation, though she managed to keep it together.

My mother didn't fare so well.

She went pale and came close to buckling, and her hand shot out to the wall to keep herself steady as she was rocked with the impact of my lie that she believed only as the truth.

"What? How? When?"

The questions tumbled fast.

Guilt locked up my tongue.

Tessa gave me another squeeze, her voice this low, compassionate thing when she quickly spoke, "I met Milo through our friends, Trent and Eden. I always had this secret thing for him, like instant, from the second I saw him."

A husky, nervous giggle rolled up her throat as she peeked at me before she returned her attention to my mom.

"But I had a boyfriend at the time, who was a total jerk. Things were never going to work out for us. So, when Milo found out I'd ended it, he asked me to dinner. We clicked. And I know it's fast, but this… what we have? It's beautiful."

Her hand twitched against mine. That message for me.

It was beautiful.

What we were doing.

Fighting for my kids.

Swallowing hard, I lifted her hand and brought the back of it to my lips.

"She's the best thing that's ever happened to me," I muttered.

I should have known this wasn't gonna end well when I didn't have to dig all that deep for the deception.

Still, shame flared.

Clawed.

Gutted me from the inside.

Tears started streaming down my mom's face.

Fuck.

This was brutal.

She breathed a couple haggard breaths before she rushed back for Tessa. For the longest time, she hugged her hard, the two caught up in some sacred place.

Murmurings rumbled from their mouths.

"Thank you. Thank you for loving my son."

"I'm the one who's thankful."

I was wrong. This wasn't just brutal. It was devastating.

Finally, Mom peeled herself away. Her cheeks were red and soaked, and she smacked my chest with the back of her hand. "I am so mad at you for keeping this from me."

There was no anger.

Just joy.

Sheer, fucking joy.

"I'm sorry. It's brand new, and we needed to figure a few things out before we announced it," I forced out.

Mom curled her arms around my waist and set her head on my chest since she was an entire foot and a half shorter than me. "I'm so happy for you, Milo. I knew the time would come. I knew you'd find love. Joy and peace. Everything you deserve."

Agony twisted me in two.

Easing back, she turned her affection on Tessa. "And I'm so thankful he gets to share it with you."

Tessa looked at me. Ocean eyes a calm, vast sea. "So am I."

Chapter Eleven

Tessa

NERVES BATTERED MY RIBS, AND MY PALMS WERE SLICK with sweat as Milo pulled to a stop at the curb in front of Karl's house. Years of bad memories flooded my brain. Every one of them was a reminder of why I had to take a leap in this direction.

A leap I was taking for myself.

Fear had stopped me.

The worry that I had no other options.

But I had people who cared about me, and I knew they'd help me figure this out.

I glanced over at Milo who vibrated in the driver's seat.

He was all burly monster then, aggression so clear in the way his hulking muscles twitched and flexed as he held on to the steering wheel like it was the only thing keeping him from flying out the door and seeking retribution.

Beautiful Beast.

"Don't like the idea of you going in there by yourself," came as a low rumble from his mouth.

Was it wrong that I liked it so much?

"If he's here, it's only going to make things worse if you go storming in there with me. He's going to take it as a threat, and we don't need that trouble. I'm going to grab a few things and my car, lickety-split, then we'll get the heck out of here. He won't even know I was here."

Ferocity blazed through Milo's expression. "You have any issues, you call me. I'll be right here waiting."

"I know you will, and I hope you know how much I appreciate that."

I ducked out of his idling truck and rushed up the walkway toward the ritzy, modern house. I'd think it really super gorgeous if the douchenugget hadn't ruined it with all his ugliness. Painted it in his overinflated ego.

Now, the monstrosity oozed with Karl's pretension and snobbery.

I could feel myself getting tripped up in it where it leaked from the cracks and leached out in a thick, slimy bog.

Fighting the force of it, I climbed to the columned front porch, my pulse racing so wild I thought I might pass out.

I might have put on a brave face for Milo, but I'd rather spend an entire day locked in a classroom full of six-year-olds who'd popped a dozen cases of Red Bull than deal with Karl's petulant ass.

I stole a quick glance behind me.

Milo watched me through the windshield, his expression coiled in pained restraint.

My chest panged.

It looked like he physically ached letting me do this alone.

And crap, this was all getting extraordinarily complicated.

These feelings.

These wonderful, horrible, terrifying feelings.

His kids.

His mother.

But most of all, it was the man.

I gave him a thumbs-up before I turned and moved for the door.

I eased the key into the lock so slowly, I could hear each of the bullets sliding into the groove. My breaths were shallow, and I pushed open the door to the spray of afternoon light that speared through the row of windows that sat high up on the two-story wall.

The alarm started to beep, and I rushed over to the pad and entered the code to shut it off.

It was a miracle.

Karl had actually respected my wishes for once and wasn't there.

Maybe he didn't want to deal with me, either.

My attention swept over the main room. Everything was white and sleek and posh and probably the most uncomfortable thing I'd ever seen.

Disgust pooled in my stomach.

This place was nothing more than a prison to me.

No more.

I took a quick breath and jogged up the stairs to the second floor. I went into the master bedroom and directly into the enormous closet.

I snagged a suitcase from the top shelf, tossed it open on the floor, and began to stuff as many things into it as I could.

Shirts and jeans and my favorite dresses.

Shoes.

I stuffed in as many of those as I could.

Obviously.

I dumped in an entire drawer of underwear and bras.

There.

Snagging a big tote from a shelf, I hustled from the bedroom, across the landing, and into the office.

Second to my car, what I needed most were the important documents I kept in a bin. I knelt next to the bookcase that had a row of drawers on the bottom, and I opened the one where I stored my things and began to frantically pull out what I needed.

Bobby's medical records.

My birth certificate and social security card.

Pictures of our parents and a few of me and Bobby from when we were children.

The information for the storage locker where I kept Bobby's possessions because I'd never had the heart to get rid of them.

I stalled out when the shadow fell across me from behind.

My racing heart chugged, and my blood thickened to sludge.

I'd never been afraid of Karl before.

Honestly, I'd felt little of it the night he'd hit me. Most of that adrenaline had been fueled by my anger.

I hadn't ever felt an innuendo of it until yesterday.

And I felt the full force of it right then.

I thought maybe a veil had been lifted.

The one that had cloaked him in chivalry and hidden away a vileness I could feel curling through the air.

"What do you think you're doing?" Venom cut through the room.

I hid my alarm behind a scowl, glancing at my phone, unsure how to play this. I could easily call Milo, but him barging in would only escalate whatever bullshit Karl wanted to throw my way.

I intended on throwing it back.

"Getting my things, like I said. Don't worry, I won't be long. Give me one second, and I'll be out of your hair." I said it like it was no big deal.

I went back to grabbing the few files I needed, doing my best to keep my hands from shaking as I stuffed them into the bag.

"You don't get to do this."

"And what's that?" I kept it all so casual as I zipped the bag and stood.

Karl was at the doorway, dressed in his typical suit, not a blond hair out of place. But his blue eyes were cold as he stretched his arms out across the doorway. "Leave."

I huffed. "We already went over this yesterday, Karl. Like I said, I'm finished with you. It's over." I moved around the desk and started his way with my head held high. "Now get out of my way."

When I got to within a foot of him, he grabbed me by the throat, his hand cruel and unforgiving.

My mouth gaped open with the surprise, and a slosh of terror slithered down my spine.

This was different.

So different than I'd ever seen him before.

"Let me go, Karl, I'm not joking." I hated that the pressure slurred my voice. "You're not going to back me into a corner, and I'm not going to change my mind or conform to your will. In case you didn't notice, I don't give a shit what you say anymore."

"Do you have any idea how much money I've spent on your worthless brother? He'd be dead if it weren't for me."

"And I'm grateful for that." It was true. That money had mattered, even though it'd come from this jerk. "But you tainted it, and that's on you."

He squeezed tighter, and I did my best not to panic, but there was a fury in his eyes that I'd never seen before.

And my breaths, they were wheezing, my throat constricting to the point of pain.

My mind spun with a swirl of dizziness, and my fingers itched with the regret that I hadn't tapped out an SOS to Milo.

I had little choice then.

Fight or flight.

I decided on the first.

I dropped the bag to the floor, and the sudden movement caught Karl off guard. Before he recognized my intention, I reached up, grabbed him by the shoulders, and shoved my knee between his legs.

Hard.

I found a sick satisfaction in the crunch.

Roaring, his hand slipped from my throat, and he stumbled back as he bent in two.

There was no time to relish in it because he straightened before I had the chance to grab my things and run.

He took a menacing step forward, and I took one back. Another, then another. The backs of my thighs hit the edge of the desk. "Leave me alone, Karl, I'm warning you."

Condescending laughter rolled from him. "You're warning me? I think you have this situation completely twisted around. I own you, Tessa. Bought and paid for."

"You bastard," I seethed. "It wasn't like that, and you know it."

"Wasn't it?"

He kept coming, and he reached out to grab me by the arm.

I wasn't about to let it happen.

I'd go psycho on his ass before he ever touched me again.

I slapped his hand away. "Don't touch me."

"You don't get to make that choice."

When he moved for me, I went feral.

Clawing and hitting and kicking.

Nails scraping as shouts ripped up my throat.

I was only half-shocked when I got in a good hit. My fist connected with his mouth, and his lip split open.

Blood dribbled from the wound.

It only made him angrier.

"You bitch," he hissed.

He shoved me hard, setting me off balance, and I gasped when he had me by a wrist, then the other. He bent my arms back and pinned me to the top of his desk.

I flailed and tore and struggled to break free.

"It appears you need a reminder of your position. I spent fifteen-thousand-fucking-dollars a month to pay for your pathetic brother. This is the least you can do."

He shifted both my wrists to one hand, the asshole trying to work his other hand between us like he was going to shove off my pants.

It created a gap between us when he did.

I took the chance.

This time, my knee hit him in the stomach when I drew it up fast. The impact knocked him off to the side, and I shot up to run, but then froze with the storm of violence that suddenly descended on the room.

Held in the dark malice that rained.

"What the fuck are you doing in my house?" Karl snarled.

"This."

I couldn't decipher if it was in fast or slow motion, the way Milo moved before he had Karl by the shirt, dragging him up and toward him. He cocked his giant arm back at the same time.

He delivered a punch to Karl's nose.

One hit.

One blow.

Karl was facedown on the floor when Milo let his shirt go.

Shock hurtled from my lungs in rasping juts, and Milo glared down at him, too freaking calm for how Karl was bleeding out on the white carpet.

"Is he dead?" I whispered in abject horror.

"Unfortunately, no," was all he said, his jaw clenched so tight I thought his teeth would shatter.

"Are you injured?" he finally grated.

"No."

"Are you sure?"

My nod was shaky. "Yeah."

"Then let's get the hell out of here."

I nodded again, still trying to process what had happened, my attention on Karl, who wasn't moving, as I slipped off the desk. I stared at him for a second before I rushed to grab the bag from the floor.

A frenzy lit, and I tossed the strap over my shoulder before I ran back into the master bedroom and into the closet.

I dropped to my knees, frantic, barely able to get my hands to cooperate as I tried to get the suitcase zipped shut. Milo was suddenly there, kneeling in front of me, taking my hands and setting them in my lap.

"Let me." His voice was low. Back to that reserved quietness he wore at the club.

He zipped it closed, his gaze cautious as he stood with the suitcase and stretched out his free hand. "Let's go."

I nodded again.

Numb.

Shocked.

I didn't know.

I rushed to keep up with him as he hauled butt out of the room and across the landing to the stairs. I warily glanced through the double doors of the office to where Karl had begun to moan as we went by.

Holy crap.

Did that just happen?

Milo gave my hand a tug, and he bounded down the stairs. I almost followed him out the door before I realized what I'd forgotten.

"I need to get my car."

"Shit." He almost looked like he was going to tell me to leave it.

"This way." I turned directions, and Milo followed me into the garage. Three luxury cars were parked in the first bays, and my Corolla was in the fourth. I jammed at the button to open the garage door, and I moved for the car, Milo right behind me.

I got into the driver's seat, my shaking hands going to the steering wheel, my breaths labored.

"You sure you can drive, Little Dove?"

"Yep, I'm fine. Great. Perfect, actually. You kicked Karl's ass." I grinned. All manic-like. But could anyone blame me?

Milo grunted. "Pull out and onto the road. I'll follow you home."

Home.

Right.

With my fake fiancé.

I laughed.

Laughed and laughed because this shit was hysterical.

Huh.

It looked like the insanity of it all had just caught up to me.

Chapter Twelve

Milo

M Y CHEST PULLED IN ALL THE WRONG PLACES AS I LOOKED out the bank of windows to the view out back.

She was there, sitting on the edge of the dock with her legs dangling over the side, her feet bare, her arms propping her up as she tilted her face back to the last fragments of sunlight that hung to the pink-hewn sky.

A breeze gently blew, and those fiery locks of red billowed with the soft gusts, in time with the ripples that shimmered across the placid lake.

She looked like a fucking painting right then, framed by the trees that towered on each side, the mountains a gorgeous backdrop behind her.

But the girl was the focus.

The center.

The light.

Like the painter had gotten the shading just right.

Throat thick, I eased open the door and stepped onto the porch. The air was cool as it brushed my overheated flesh.

Pushing away the reservations, I eased down the three porch steps and took the path that cut through the middle of the lawn. My footsteps slowed as I trekked across the yard to the beach, slower still as I took the first step onto the dock.

The wood groaned, and I could feel Tessa's spirit race out to meet with mine.

That strange connection thrummed on a thread of peace.

Crazy, since I'd never had such a disorder toiling from within.

She sat up a bit and ran a hand through her hair to tame it, tucking it to one side and exposing the delicate slope of her neck as she shifted to look at me.

A slow smile moved across her stunning face, the sharp angles somehow so fucking soft while every part of me remained rigid and hard, my blood still boiling from the showdown with Karl earlier today.

"Hey, you," she whispered into the quiet rustling of the forest.

Blue eyes swam.

A welcome.

Calling me to their depths.

"Hey."

"Want to join me?" Tessa lifted her wine glass, her voice shifting into a tease. "I'm about to polish this baby off. Clearly, I need someone to save me from myself."

She had a bottle of pink, bubbly wine chilling on ice in a wooden bucket, and a Bluetooth speaker hummed some indie band I didn't recognize.

"Have to work." I was having a hard time responding in anything more than grunts.

Amusement played all over that tempting mouth. "At a bar."

Air puffed from my nose. "What, you think we sit around doing shots all night?"

"Isn't that what people who work at bars do?"

"It's my job to haul the drunk assholes out, not *to be* the drunk asshole."

Her smile spread too wide. "Are you implying I'm an asshole, Milo Hendricks?"

Rough laughter scraped out. This girl just had a way of soothing the soul.

"Think you're the farthest thing from it, Little Dove. Think you deserve that entire bottle after what went down today."

Cautiously, I eased the rest of the way over and sat down beside her. That energy went to whispering around us the way it liked to do, calming, almost disarming, while my insides stormed with her claim.

Her smile softened, filled with this gratefulness that spun around her like silk. "Thank you for what you did earlier. I really hate dragging you into my mess."

I huffed. "Dragging me into your mess? Pretty sure it's the other way around."

Her head barely shook. "You were there when I needed you."

I warred, unsure of what to reveal, unable to stop the confession from bubbling out. "I wanted to be there for you. Needed to be. Walking in on that?"

My throat locked on the violence that still screamed for release. The truth that I'd wanted to end him. It'd taken everything in me to remain standing over the piece of shit and not let go.

Give in.

"I heard what he said, Tessa. About your brother?"

I hadn't even known that she had a brother.

"That he's been paying for his care?" I continued. "That's why you stayed with him for all that time? That's why you've been walking around looking like you're gonna fall apart?"

Her nod was soft. "Yeah."

"I never fully got it, but I guess I still knew he had a hold on you."

Her head drooped between her shoulders, and I couldn't help but reach out and tip her chin toward me, forcing her to look at me. "You don't have to be ashamed, Tessa. You didn't do anything wrong. You were just fighting for someone you love."

"And now I have no idea what I'm going to do."

"It's covered, Tessa."

I had more money than I could ever spend. Autumn had had a life insurance policy when we'd met. She named me the beneficiary when we'd gotten married. It was money that made me sick where it festered in an unused bank account. I'd thought a million times to donate it, but

I'd needed to use a portion of it to finish the house to give the kids the home Autumn and I had hoped for. Plus, I needed it to use for attorney fees, and the rest would go to the kids when they got old enough.

It would go for this, too. To the one who was fighting for my kids. To bring this family back together.

A sharp gasp raked from her lungs. "I can't take money from you."

"You can. It's just been sitting there in my bank account. I want you to have it."

She scoffed and tried to jerk her chin away. "I won't be indebted to someone else, Milo."

I slipped my hand down to her neck, my thumb tracing her jaw, coaxing her back. "There's no debt, Tessa. No trade. This is a friend taking care of a friend, same way as you're taking care of me."

Tears blurred in those blue eyes. "Milo, I can't—"

"Please, let me do this for you. Because I can. Because I care for you. Just like I know you care for me."

Her throat tremored. "Milo."

"Please. We're a team, remember?"

A soggy giggle slipped from between her red lips. "Twisting my words on me, huh?"

I grinned. "Whatever it takes."

She blew out a sigh. "Okay, but just until I figure something else out. I won't be mooching off you forever."

"It's yours for as long as you want it."

"I promise I'll pay you back as soon as I can." She exhaled a choppy breath. "Ugh, this is a total mess, isn't it? I can't even believe what he tried to do."

Remnants of the fear she'd worn earlier traipsed through her features. "I had no idea Karl could be such a monster. A jerk? Sure. But something has changed."

"Men like him don't like bein' told no. They think whatever they want is owed to them."

"He can't have me anymore."

"And he doesn't like that."

"No, he doesn't," she whispered. Her gaze drifted out over the water, contemplation and worry, before she slowly shifted her attention back to me. "I'm not sure he's going to give up. I think I might have pissed him off even more."

"He gets near you again, it's not gonna turn out so good for him, Tessa." The words rang with a warning of truth.

Flames sparked where she touched my arm. "You can't do anything reckless, Milo. You're fighting to get your kids back, and the last thing you need is to get into trouble on my account. Karl…"

Tessa swallowed, her throat bobbing hard. "He has connections. He's friends with the mayor. He'll twist everything in his favor, and I'm already worried that he'll find some way to retaliate after what happened today."

"He doesn't get a free pass for touching you, Tessa. I don't care about the consequences."

And fuck, I did care. Of course, I cared.

My kids.

The thing I wanted most in this world was to prove to my kids that they were worth it.

My love and my devotion and my everything.

But I couldn't stand aside and let the bastard mess with Tessa. Not on my watch.

"I don't want to be a burden to you, Milo."

Taking her hand, I threaded our fingers together. It was becoming a nasty habit.

"Don't think you could ever be that, Tessa. You're giving me a gift."

Uncertainty billowed from her spirit, and she peeked over at me. "I'm sorry you had to lie to your mom this morning."

There was almost a question behind it, but more so, understanding.

I raked my free hand over my face to break up the discomfort. "She would never approve of this sham. She'd try to talk me out of it. Tell me I'm only going to make things worse. I think it's best if she believes this is real. Otherwise, she's going to worry more."

"She's going to be heartbroken when she finds out it's not."

"No doubt about that."

"She's amazing." Tessa's voice was wonder. "She loves you so much."

"She is amazing. She's always been my rock. The one who was there, no matter what."

"Unconditional," she whispered.

"Yeah."

"My mom was like that, too, before she passed."

My chest squeezed, and I rubbed my thumb over the back of her hand, feeling the slow swell of sadness ripple across her flesh. "How long has it been?"

"I was fifteen. My brother is four years older than me. He stepped up and took care of me when he was barely more than a kid himself."

"And now you're taking care of him."

Her smile was frail. "I'm not doing a very good job of it."

"Not true, Tessa. Most people would never go the lengths you have."

"I just wish I could do it myself, but I seriously doubt my teacher's salary or the small amount I'm making as the foundation director is ever going to cut it." She choked out a little self-deprecating laugh.

"We'll figure it out," I promised.

The two of us sat there with our fingers threaded like it was the most natural thing in the world while the sun continued to sink behind the mountains.

Rays sparked behind the skyline, striking the wisps of clouds in oranges and purples and fiery reds. Twilight cast the air in that grayed vapor you could almost reach out and touch.

"It's so beautiful here," Tessa whispered into the duskiness. "A girl could get used to this."

Playfulness kissed her mouth as she smiled over at me.

My chest fisted at the sight, lust curling in my gut.

"It's yours as long as you want it. But if it becomes too much? If it gets to be too much pressure or gets in the way of you finding your joy, you tell me, Tessa. I won't be the bastard to hold you back."

My hand that was twined with hers was suddenly tight against her chest, and Tessa shifted, pulling up a leg so she could face me. "I'm here for you, Milo. It's what friends do, remember?"

"I doubt many friends ask something like this."

"Oh, you should see the things Eden comes up with. She's really pushing it, if you ask me." The razzing played all over her face, her gaze knowing, kind and genuine.

A chuckle got free before my nerves were making a rebound.

Every cell in my body locked up tight as I shifted so I was facing her, too. It brought us knee-to-knee and breath-to-breath.

Just a fool who was letting my palm slip to the sharp curve of her jaw, my thumb running along her cheek.

Heat burned at the connection.

"Thank you." My words were rough.

"It's my honor, Milo."

"Are you sure you want to do this?" I pressed. I had to offer her one last out. I was quickly realizing this was going to be more difficult than I'd imagined.

"Positive."

Pulling my hand from her face, I gave her a tight nod. "Have somethin' for you, then."

Rosebud lips parted, and interest flared in her eyes. "Oh, what is it?"

I shouldn't have been making it such a thing, but I was having a hard time keeping myself from feeling like this marked something.

An oath.

A pact.

Or maybe it was this affection that grew and grew. This emotion I needed to kill before it became a threat.

Still, I dug into my pocket and pulled out the antique ring, and shit, Tessa gasped a giddy, shocked squeal before she bit down on her bottom lip like she wished she could annul the sound.

She giggled nervously then, peeking between my face and the ring that I held up like a promise.

"Is this necessary?" she rushed like a secret.

"Think it is if we're going to convince anyone we're actually getting married."

"Oh…um…right…of course."

I took her left hand that was shaking like mad.

"Will you be my fake fiancée, Tessa McDaniels?" I fought for a tease, but the words were thick and choppy.

"Only if you buy me the Manolos, Milo Hendricks."

I would have laughed, but her smile was wistful, and I was getting hooked on the expression on her face, the way those blue eyes got a little too misty, and her mouth tweaked at the side.

She lifted the ring. "This is like…crazy gorgeous, Milo."

"I saw it in the window of Reid & Co. Instantly thought of you."

Surprise pinched her brow when she realized where it came from. "Oh, God, are you serious?"

I gave a slight shrug, like it wasn't a big deal.

I'd learned the hard way that money didn't matter.

"I will protect this baby with my life, Milo. We'll sell it when this is through. I mean, I'm kind of notorious for losing things, and I pretty much only buy really inexpensive jewelry because hello…Tessa. But this?" Each word left her with escalating intensity. "No way. It's on this finger until the end."

She waved her hand in my face.

"It's yours, Tessa. Keep it. Sell it. Give it away. Whatever you want."

"Milo—"

"Mean it. I want you to have it, as a thank you."

"You are really stacking this generosity against me. How am I supposed to compete?" She tried to play it off as fun.

"There's no competing in friendship, Tessa. We just take care of each other where we can."

Something shifted in her features. "Okay."

Our gazes locked there, tangled with the twilight that seeped away, darkness pulling at the edges of the earth and preparing to take the day in its grasp.

Had the urge to loop my arm around her waist and pull her close, rest her head back against my chest so we could watch the rest of the sun melt away and the stars blink to life in the sky.

The music soft. A love song that'd just begun.

Nothing but a fool's game.

Clearing my throat, I hopped to my feet. "I should probably get going."

Tessa seemed shocked out of the trance, too, momentarily disoriented, blinking and searching for lost breath, before she pinned on one of those smiles that I wondered if anyone else could tell was fake.

"Okay, great. Have a good night. I'll just be over here nursing this."

She dug out the wine bottle and emptied it out into her glass.

"Are you gonna be okay here by yourself, Little Dove?"

Her smile changed, real this time, edged in sadness. "Don't worry about me, Milo. I've been alone for a long, long time."

Chapter Thirteen

Tessa

"**Y**OU SIT THAT CUTE LITTLE BUTT DOWN RIGHT THERE and spill."

Salem pointed at the chair across from her as I sashayed my way into our favorite Mexican restaurant.

The vibe was casual, the margaritas were epic, and the owners were awesome.

I made no apologies for frequenting the place.

But this evening, I wasn't sure if it was excitement or dread that would be the winning emotion that crawled over me in a slick sheen of sweat as I stepped through the door.

All I knew was my nerves had gone haywire.

A breaker tripped.

Circuits crossed.

I gave my friends a giant grin as I approached our table. "Um, I know how much you missed me and all, and my presence is required, but can't a girl get a drink before you tear into her?"

"Hello, and no." Aster rolled her dark brown eyes, though the action was riddled with affection. Her hair was in a high ponytail, and she sat back in her chair because her baby belly took up her lap. "I don't think you've ever done anyone else that favor in your life, and I've basically been waiting for this for all of mine, so let's hear it."

Pride filled her voice.

"Hugs first. Have you no manners?" I let the feigned atrocity wind into my response.

Salem, Eden, and Aster all jumped up, and I came clomping over on my five-inch heels because hello, mama got her shoes back, and I threw my arms out and pulled my besties into an awkward hug. We were all swaying and squealing and clinging to each other and probably garnering the attention of every person in the restaurant.

I had this thing about hugs.

They weren't frivolous to me. They were a connection. A direct link of spirits.

Whenever I hugged someone, I got a sense.

A wash of warmth. A roll of rightness.

Or a slow slide of cold callousness.

Some people masked it better than others, but it was always there.

Bobby had called me a weirdo, but I swore I could tell. I tried not to use it like a tool, but it'd gotten to the point where it was like radar.

Intuition.

I guess I should have listened to it the first time I'd hugged Karl.

Hugging my girls?

It was pure joy.

Murmurings of their love filled my ears. "So proud of you. This is a brand-new start. Good things are waiting for you."

Crap.

Were my eyes stinging?

The truth was, I'd been dealing with so many conflicting emotions, I was having a hard time processing up from down.

Being at Milo's had twisted me inside out. Made me want things I wasn't supposed to want. Question my direction. My intentions. What the heck Milo and I actually thought we were doing and how it was going to affect our friendship in the end.

Salem was the first to pull away, and she straightened herself out, tossing her hair over her shoulder as she pointed at a chair. "Sit."

"Bossy," I said around the anarchy wreaking havoc on my spirit.

She scoffed. "Have you even met me?"

Salem was one of those black-haired, blue-eyed beauties who could slay you with a look. A total badass but a softie. She was married to Trent's brother, Jud, and damn, they were freaking scorching together. They had a new baby boy who was only two months old, plus Salem's daughter, Juniper, who was the sweetest little girl I'd ever met.

"Excuse me, then. I can see I don't want to get on your bad side." I mumbled beneath my breath.

I pulled out the chair across from her, and we all took our seats.

Aster sat next to Salem, and Eden sat next to me.

Salem slid a giant margarita glass my direction.

I groaned. "You do love me."

"Barely." A smile tugged at her lips.

"Keep lying to yourself."

The second everyone got settled, the four of us leaned over the small table, drawn to each other.

Creating a bubble like we were getting ready to share the dirtiest of secrets.

No doubt, there would be plenty of that going on.

Eden reached out and took my hand. "How are you doing? I've been worried about you all week."

We'd interacted over texts a couple of times, but I'd been so wrapped up with everything going on that we hadn't gone deeper. I hadn't even told her about what'd happened with Karl the two unfortunate times I'd run into him.

"I've been busy." I kind of shrugged.

"You'd better have been *busy* gallivanting all over town and making up for lost time," Salem tossed out.

"I second that," Aster said before she took a sip of her club soda because...*preggers*. It seemed to be a sickness with this bunch, not that I minded getting to be auntie to all their cuties. "I'm praying this means you're going to stop digging for details on the rest of us because you finally found a real man to put you out of your misery."

"Now, why would I ever do that? That sounds boring."

"Oh, dear, poor Tessa, finding yourself a man who does it right is not boring." Salem grinned.

Pure Cheshire.

My stomach tilted when I thought of the raw power Milo had unleashed on Karl yesterday. I was pretty sure he would do it right.

"You did already, didn't you, you dirty dog?" Aster slapped the top of the table.

Redness flushed.

Crap.

I fared way better when I was the one plying them for details.

"No."

"Then why are you so red?" Aster pushed.

Both my hands flew up to cover my face. A round of gasps went up.

"What is that?" Eden whispered in horror. "Please tell me you didn't let that monster talk you into going back to him?"

Oh, shit.

The ring.

Flustered, I ripped my hands away, flailing around the one sporting the most gorgeous ring ever created, like I wasn't wearing the evidence of the cluster I'd gotten myself into. All dainty, twining bands and filigree, capped off with a huge, pear-cut, pink diamond.

"No, absolutely not."

"Then what is that?" Confusion bound Eden's expression.

"Milo gave it to me." It flew out way too fast.

These girls were good at the coercion.

More shocked gasps rang out, and Salem grabbed my hand and jerked it across the table so she could inspect it. "Holy fuck, Tessa, this is like a $20,000 ring. And it's on your freaking ring finger. What is going on?"

"Are you engaged?" Eden pressed.

Almost hurt.

Eden and I shared everything, but everything about this had *bad choices* written all over it, and I hadn't had the guts to call her up and confess what Milo and I were up to.

The same week I'd promised her no more secrets.

I was not going to win the best bestie award this year.

Eden and Salem gaped at me, a thousand questions spinning through the air.

"If she's engaged to anyone, Milo would certainly be my pick," Aster rushed to fill the tension. "Have you seen him? And he's super sweet."

Maybe I'd gotten lost in the fantasy. Or maybe I'd just wanted to help a hurting man so badly that I'd convinced myself this engagement façade was a great plan. Convinced myself we could actually pull it off.

Right then, it wasn't seeming like such a terrific idea.

Because explaining this out loud?

It sounded like I'd signed myself up for a load of trouble.

"It's fake, you guys." It came out thin. Wisps of disappointment.

That tension stretched tighter between us.

Slowly, Eden shifted, taking my hand again. Her brow twisted in emphasis. "What are you talking about, Tessa? What is going on?"

"It's fake. I'm fake engaged to Milo." I choked an incredulous laugh because yeah, saying it out loud? I sounded like an idiot.

A smirk lit on Salem's face. "That sounds like a fine way to piss off Karl."

"I don't give a crap about Karl." There was some honesty.

Aster blinked, working her way up to worry. "Then why?"

I pulled my hand away from Eden's, and I took a long swig of my margarita, buying time before I was whispering toward the glass. "His in-laws got custody of his kids when his wife died. He's trying to get them back."

"Oh shit, Tessa," Salem breathed.

A vat of distress dumped itself onto the already heavy atmosphere. I could feel the weight of Eden's stare from the side.

I nodded. "He needs to show the court that he's settling down and building a stable home. And he's been so kind to me, so I offered to help him."

"That's..." Aster drew out.

"Complicated," I supplied.

"Crazy and amazing and selfless." Eden's words were a breath, and she reached out and took my hand again. I shifted to look her way to find the concern written in her features. "But it's a lot, Tessa. How long are you supposed to pretend like you're marrying him? I can't imagine anything related to a custody suit is going to be quick. It could be months…or years. Are you willing to sacrifice your freedom for that long?"

She didn't have to say the rest of what she was thinking. I saw the implication of it in the tilt of her head.

After you've already sacrificed for years for Bobby.

She wouldn't say it aloud, anyway. I knew she'd protect the secret I'd shared with her on Monday.

"I care about him." It was the best way to explain it.

"I know you do…but you need to take care of yourself, too. And what happens when he gets his kids back? Do you just…break up? Isn't that going to mess with their heads?"

Dread slithered beneath my skin.

I knew those were things Milo and I needed to discuss. We'd been so focused on the hope of getting them back that we hadn't taken the time to address what would happen after.

It'd seemed logical in the shadows of his room.

But the daylight ushered in a thousand complications.

A groan grumbled from my throat. "I don't even know. We haven't planned it out yet. I just know that I want to help him, any way that I can."

Aster leaned closer. "And you're just living with him like this whole thing is real until God knows when? Aren't you going to get tired of pretending? It seems like it's too much to ask of you."

My head shook. "I think the problem is how much I like being there."

She tried to hide the glee lighting at the edge of her mouth. "You do like him, don't you?"

"What's not to like?"

All of it.

Everything.

All except for the undercurrent of darkness that curled around him like a building storm.

The ghosts that haunted him in the night.

But the truth was, I'd gladly take those on, too.

Crap.

I was screwed.

"You cannot be blamed, Tessa. The man is stupid hot." Salem casually popped a chip into her mouth. "And you know the quiet ones are wild in bed."

"Don't tease me," I whined.

"Someone needs to get laid, and she needs it hard." She spoke no greater truth. "Maybe you can convince Milo to do you the favor since you're giving up so much for him." Salem sent me a salacious grin. "You know you want it."

"Or maybe you go after what you really want, Tessa," Eden cut into the joking, her voice serious.

I glanced at her. "And what do I really want?"

"You're the only one who can answer that, but I remember not too long ago this really incredible friend telling me to take a chance. That the man I thought was all wrong for me, but who I couldn't get off my mind, might be meant for me. That he might be my Ace."

She'd been terrified of loving Trent. I mean, the guy was actually terrifying, so there was that. But together? There was something special about their connection. I'd pushed her. Told her she would never find what she was missing if she didn't open herself to the possibility.

And I wanted that...someday, I wanted that.

My Ace.

Sadness stretched across my chest. Pain for Milo. For that hollowness I could feel echoing inside of him. "I doubt he could be my Ace, because I think he already lost his."

And I didn't want second best. I wanted someone who loved me with every fiber, the way I would love them.

I wanted passion.

Friendship.

An unending connection.

I wanted my *person*.

"I don't know, Tessa. I've seen the way he watches you when we're at the club, and believe me, it's spicy," Aster said.

I gave a small shrug. "I think he might be attracted to me, but his heart is all kinds of battered, and I'm pretty sure he's boarded it up."

"And if it wasn't?" Eden asked.

"Then I'd hike that man like he was a mountain." I waggled my brows, then cracked up.

"You are such a goober, Tessa McDaniels." Salem laughed.

"Okay, hold up." Aster lifted a hand. "We haven't even talked about Karl, which is the whole reason I've been dying to talk to you. What happened? I honestly thought the three of us were going to have to take matters into our own hands. Tie him up and float him to the bottom of the sea where he'd never be found."

My brows reached for the sky. "You really are a mafia princess. I'm scared for my life right now."

She giggled. "I didn't mean literally."

"Sure," I sang before I let the lightness bleed away. "There's not much to tell. I finally couldn't take his assholery any longer, and I told him it was over. He actually hit me. Can you believe that?"

I ignored the shiver of fear at what had happened when I'd gone to get my things.

"What I can believe is he's dead." Fury slipped over Salem's face. "Aster's plan is sounding incredibly reasonable right now."

I gulped down the rest of my margarita before I grinned and poured myself another from the pitcher. "You don't have to worry about it. I went over there to get my things, and Milo kicked his ass."

It was out before I could stop it.

Eden's eyes bugged out. "Um, what?"

"Yep. Karl decided to be an asshole." I left out the gory details because the three of them would lose it, and Karl might, in fact, find himself floating at the bottom of the sea.

We definitely didn't need a murder on our hands.

"One punch to the face and Karl was out cold. It was kind of embarrassing for the poor guy. I think he might have pissed himself, too."

"Oh my God." Aster laughed. "I love Milo. Such a beast."

I giggled, and my chest stretched a little too wide with the affection I had for the man.

"I kinda love him, too," I admitted.

"Crap, she has it bad." Salem looked between Eden and Aster.

"I can hear you, you know," I pouted.

"Honestly, we're just proud of you." Salem's tone filled with sincerity. "I hated that you were with Karl. Hated the way he treated you. Hated that I saw you were unhappy. I never understood why."

I searched for a valid explanation. "Once I make a commitment to someone, I have a hard time walking away."

"I'm glad you came to the point where you realized Karl doesn't deserve your commitment."

No.

Only Bobby did.

But now…now I could care for my brother and be a better me while doing it.

My voice lowered with the significance. "You guys can't tell anyone about this. Not your husbands. No one. I mean, it's serious. I know you talk to them about everything, but this has to stay between us. We can't risk any kind of rumors going around that we aren't real."

"Of course," they all promised.

"Not even if they catch a whiff of a secret and try to withhold those delicious O's they are so fond of giving you. Do you understand me?"

I pointed around the table at each of them.

Salem whined. "I'm not sure I'm that strong."

"Suck it up. I've had to for years."

"Fine, fine. I promise."

"Promise," Eden and Aster agreed.

Our hands were all back in the middle of the table again, clutching each other.

"Fantastic Foursome Oath," I proclaimed. "It cannot be broken or unsealed."

"That's not a thing." Salem laughed a throaty laugh.

"It is now. You break it, and bad, bad things will befall you." I made sure the words came out all kinds of ominous.

She laughed. "Goober."

"This might be rough, Tessa," Eden whispered when the lightness wore off.

Determination took over the discomfort of her warning. "I know. But he's my friend, and friends do whatever they can to support each other."

"Your friend, who I bet has a giant dick." Salem just had to add that.

"I hate you. I'm getting more margaritas." Standing, I grabbed the pitcher and strutted toward the bar like I hadn't wondered that very thing a thousand times.

"You know you love me."

I swiveled to face her, walking backward when I gave her the same response she'd given me earlier. "Barely."

I turned back around, and she called from behind, "Mad love, Tessa. Mad, mad love."

My heart fisted, and I fought a grin.

The brat had learned all my tricks.

I set the pitcher on the bar and dug out my phone when it buzzed in my pocket, and I couldn't stop the smile that spread across my face when I read the text.

> Milo: How are you, Little Dove? Are you having fun with your friends?

So maybe the two margaritas I'd gulped down had already hit my bloodstream because I tapped out a response without giving it thought.

> Me: Are you thinking about me, fiancé?

It took an entire minute for him to respond.

> Milo: I shouldn't be, but I am.

Wings fluttered in my stomach, and I jerked when a voice hit me from the side. "How about I get that pitcher for you?"

I turned to find this crazy-sexy guy who was watching me with a sly smirk from where he leaned against the bar.

Like, *hello, Hottie McTottie.*

I should so take him up on his offer and then have him take me to his place later. It wasn't like there was any mistaking what his intentions were.

Unfortunately, there wasn't a speck of me that wanted to do it.

I flaunted the fingers of my left hand in his face. "Oh, sorry, I'm engaged."

"Well, that's too bad."

My phone buzzed again.

   Milo: Be safe, Little Dove. I'll see you later tonight.

No.

It wasn't too bad at all.

Chapter Fourteen

Tessa

"OKAY, GARY, SEE YOU TOMORROW," I CALLED TO EDEN'S father as he pushed open the door to the office that housed Hope to Hands.

Standing in the doorway, he grinned back at me where I sat at my desk. "Don't stay too late. You work yourself too hard, you know?"

"Um, I didn't show up one time last week. I would hardly call that working hard. You're going to have to change my official title to slacker."

So maybe I'd been distracted by a man beast who made my belly quiver.

A light chuckle left Gary. "We all deserve a break once in a while. It is summer, after all."

"You know I like staying busy."

"That you do, but I expect you to take care of yourself, too."

He sent me one of those fatherly glares that made my chest stretch tight. Gary was in his mid-sixties, his hair grayed and the burdens he'd carried on his shoulders written in the deep lines set in his face.

But his eyes—they were kind.

And his heart was genuine.

Affection wobbled in my spirit.

"I am. I promise."

Better than I'd been in years.

"Okay, then. Lock up."

"Will do. And I expect *you* to go home and put your feet up and relax."

He laughed a slow sound. "I just might do that. Drive safe, sweetheart."

"Goodnight."

The door swung shut behind him, and I returned my attention to the paperwork I'd been working on.

Hope to Hands was the nonprofit foundation affiliated with the private school and church that Gary had founded years ago.

I'd become a teacher here the same year Eden had.

She and I had gone to college together, and at that time, I'd had no clue what I wanted to do with my life.

Shocker.

But Bobby had sacrificed for me, worked like crazy to have the funds to put me through college, insistent that he wanted me to have the full experience without the worry of debt, so I wasn't about to screw that up.

So, I figured, why not?

I'd tag along with Eden and go into education.

Sure, I enjoyed being in a classroom, but not the way Eden did. She was incredibly invested in each child.

It wasn't like I didn't love them, but there'd always been something missing.

No true passion.

But I'd found it here.

Helping the families who came to the church who were in need.

I'd taken over as executive director when it'd become clear Gary needed to let some of his responsibilities go.

I wasn't quite sure why he was so worried about me overextending myself when the man would work his fingers to the bone, which he'd basically done.

We'd had a big scare about a year ago when Eden had found him dizzy and confused in his office. We'd worried it was a stroke, but it'd turned out to be exhaustion.

Eden had demanded he give up at least one of his positions.

I'd been volunteering at the foundation for years, so it'd made sense that I'd stand in for him since it was the source of a lot of his stress.

It turned out that I loved it.

Thrived in it.

My heart had found the place where it flourished.

Giving back in the same way as Bobby and I had received years before.

It just felt right.

I scanned over the submissions for rent assistance.

Why I felt the need to print them out, I didn't know. But I guessed it made it tangible.

Something palpable to hold on to.

Something real because there were real people behind these forms.

I needed something that didn't blur into another number on the screen.

The hard part was there was always more need than resources.

I separated the applications by urgency, prioritizing those who were in the process of being evicted.

A light thud that sounded from outside had me freezing.

Unease prickled through my senses, and the fine hairs lifted on the back of my neck.

I sat completely still.

Listening.

Barely breathing.

For a long time, the only sound was the manic pounding of my heart. Until there was the unmistakable crunch of a footstep just outside the door.

Fear spiraled down my spine.

A cold, icy dread.

Crap.

I should have immediately hopped up and turned the lock when Gary left.

It was a little after six, but camp had ended at four. The rest of the staff would have already left for the night. The maintenance crew worked overnight, so they shouldn't be here for another six hours.

I tried to swallow around the terror that thickened my throat, and I reached for my phone and stood at the same second the doorknob slowly turned.

I rushed to punch 9-1-1 into my phone. My hand shook as I hovered my finger over send, and my stomach was panging with a gnawing fear.

The door swung open, and Karl appeared in the doorway, venom in his stance and a snarl on his face.

Fear throbbed, heavy and dark.

But I stood up straighter and held my ground.

I had to cover my shock when I saw his face marred in the black and blue bruises that covered the entirety of the right side.

There was a scab on his lip, compliments of me.

Clearly, his perfected arrogance had been knocked down by a notch or two.

And oh, man, he did not look happy about it.

"You need to leave right now." There was no use trying to keep the tremoring from my voice.

Karl already knew what he'd done.

The line he'd crossed.

I would never look at him the same.

"I'll call the cops if you come any closer. You are trespassing."

I held the phone out between us like I was wielding a weapon.

A sneer curled his expression in hate. "Have at it, Tessa, and I'll gladly press charges against the thug you brought into my house."

I almost scoffed.

Milo was the thug?

"Good. Then we get to tell them all about how you attacked me, nearly choked me, then tried to force yourself on me."

My chin quivered, half in fear and half in defiance.

After everything, I couldn't believe he would come here.

Or maybe I should have expected it.

I'd already warned Milo that I was worried we'd only pissed him off more.

Karl was not the type of man who liked to have his ego stripped.

Feigned confusion twisted through his features. "Are you sure about that, Tessa? How could I force you when we've been together for years, devoted to each other? And after I've been taking care of your brother, providing for him? Poor guy."

Artificial sympathy cut into his expression.

Sickness clawed at my being, and I swallowed around the bile that coated my tongue. "I ended it with you, Karl. There is no devotion. It was all a sham."

One so different from the one I was parading with Milo.

"And even if we were still together? It doesn't give you the right to touch me when I tell you no."

"You owe me, Tessa."

"I don't owe you anything."

I lifted the phone higher, ready to push send.

He froze for a second before rage flash-fired through his eyes. "What the fuck is that?"

The ring.

Crap.

I inhaled a sharp breath. "It's none of your business."

Disbelieving laughter tumbled from his tongue, the sound coated in disgust. "Were you fucking him? The whole time that you kept running off to that club, you were fucking him, weren't you?"

"No." I didn't need to defend myself to Karl, but I didn't want to incite his wrath, either.

Retribution flashed through his glare and flitted through the malign of his grin. "I don't like being played for a fool, Tessa."

"I didn't—"

He stepped forward, and the words locked on my tongue.

Every cell in my body was cut in a razor-sharp edge.

Ready to dial but also knowing it would cause a bigger mess for Milo if I did.

A blight to the picture we were trying to paint.

Karl cocked his head. A severe, ugly warning. "You owe me, Tessa. Make no mistake, I will collect."

Then he turned and pushed back out the door.

I bent in half, and my hand shot to my desk for support. Ragged gasps of relief and fear rushed from my lungs.

I swallowed it down, grinding my teeth, searching for fortitude.

Because I couldn't back down, even when Karl had me backed against a wall.

Night had taken hold of the sky as I eased my car down the winding dirt road that led to Milo's cabin tucked deep in the forest. Stars blinked from the heavens, and the spiked tops of the soaring pines danced beneath the darkened expanse.

My tires crunched on the gravel, and my heart continued to batter at my ribs.

Pained affection stretched tight when my headlights illuminated the front of the cabin.

So quaint and quiet within the storm that raged in the periphery.

Both his truck and his Tahoe were parked in the front.

Milo was home.

I came to a stop and shut off the engine, then I took a steeling breath before I got out and climbed the steps to the front porch.

I put my key into the lock, my chest squeezing at the memory of Milo offering that to me, too, telling me this was my home for as long as I wanted it.

And our lines seemed so very blurred right then.

Boundaries set that I didn't know how to live within.

I pushed open the door.

Silence echoed back.

Shutting and locking the door behind me, I tossed my bag and keys onto the entryway table, then slowly moved through the space.

Instinctively, I knew he wasn't inside.

Drawn, I edged to the glass-paned door and peered outside.

It was still out back, no sign of movement.

It didn't matter.

I carefully eased open the door to the lapping night.

Rays of moonlight shimmered over the placid lake, and I gulped for a lungful of the crisp, clean air before my feet took to the planks of the porch. I eased down the steps and traipsed across the lawn to the nearly completed treehouse.

Somehow, I knew he would be there.

The treehouse was just shy of being extravagant, a little like Milo's home.

Large and lavish yet exuding a rugged charm that made it comfortable.

The children's fortress took up the middle section of the grand maple tree that stood towering and proud to the right side of Milo's rambling yard.

Energy whirled and whipped on a gust of wind.

I swallowed any reservations down and started up the stairs, holding on to the railing as I wound my way up the trunk to the platform that surrounded the entire treehouse.

Energy crashed through the tepid air, his presence profound.

Inhaling a slow breath, I nudged open the door that was about half the size of a standard one and poked my head through.

I found him sitting with his back propped against the wall, the warm glow of the light fixtures he'd installed in the ceiling illuminating his shape.

His face in stark profile.

His big, burly body appearing even larger in the confined space.

My stomach tilted.

The man was so gorgeous I was lucky I didn't trip at the sight.

But what squeezed my chest was the subdued sorrow he continued to emanate. Since returning from his visit with Remy and Scout yesterday afternoon, it had hovered over him like a dark cloud.

His aura dampened.

As if every time he had to walk away from his children, another tattered piece of his heart had been whittled away.

"Hey," I managed around the thickness in my throat. I tamped down the fear that still held fast after the confrontation with Karl.

He didn't need me rushing in and dumping my problems on him.

The man would likely go on a rampage, and I was pretty sure that was exactly what Karl was banking on.

That Milo would seek retribution.

Karl wanted to shift the focus from himself and make Milo look like the bad guy, and Karl would come out looking all shiny and squeaky clean.

If people only knew.

Gold-hewn eyes drifted my way. Soft tenderness filled his expression. "Hey, Little Dove."

His welcome wound around me like a caress, and the attraction I couldn't shake flared from the depths.

"What are you doing up here?" I whispered, worried my voice might break into the solitude, but not so worried that I didn't duck my head so I could enter.

There were some tools strewn around him, though it looked like he'd been sitting for a while.

"Figured I'd finish the shelves before I need to go into work," he muttered, gesturing to where he was building them into a corner.

His attention to detail was insane.

"It's almost finished," I mused as I looked around to take it in.

He'd been working on it nonstop since we'd made our pact.

Constructing.

Preparing.

Hoping.

The floor area was large enough to be a bedroom, though the ceilings were only about five feet tall.

He'd put in two real windows that overlooked the lake, and they opened to let in the breeze.

There was a section of the roof that still remained unfinished, and everything would need to be sanded and stained.

I eased down onto the wood floor and sat beside him.

For a moment, we rested in the silence before I murmured, "They're going to love it, Milo."

He let go of a small grunt, and his attention swung to me. "Yeah. They will. Because of you."

After I'd hung out with my besties on Friday, it'd become clear that we needed to talk. We'd spent too much time skirting the difficult parts.

Nerves rattled, and my tongue swept my dried lips as I looked at him.

"If we're going to do this, I need to meet them, Milo. Become a real part of your life."

Worry gushed from his spirit. "I know."

"What is it you're afraid of?" The question rushed from my lips.

Milo hesitated, roughing one of those big hands through his hair.

Attraction blazed. I couldn't stop it. There was no chance of keeping it contained.

Finally, he let his head roll to the side where he was leaned against the wall, that gaze so intense as he stared at me. "I'm afraid of taking another person from them. The way I did their mother. That it's goin' to hurt them in the end."

Pain pierced me, a blade shoved right into my heart.

God, he lived with so much unfound guilt. Didn't he see he was good? That he deserved to have his children in his life?

I forced a faked smile, the playful words thin. "They won't even like me. Heck, they'll probably be glad to get rid of me."

Milo grunted. "Hardly, Little Dove. Nothin' not to love about you."

I twisted a piece of my hair and tried to keep it together.

Especially when crawling onto his lap seemed like a mighty fine plan right about then.

"Redhead, remember? I'm trouble. You'll all be better off without me."

"Is that what you think? That people are better off without you?"

"I think they can take me in measured doses." My laugh was hollow.

"That's not really what you believe, though, is it?"

His fingers threaded through mine.

Fire flashed.

"Can feel you aching for a home." He gruffed it like a claim.

My soul fluttered. "But this is *your* home, Milo. I'm just pretending like it's mine. But I'm here for you…as your friend…as long as you need me to be."

Friend.

I was an idiot.

It wasn't close to what I felt.

And I was never so certain than right then that I was going to get my heart slaughtered.

"We just need to be careful with their hearts…and I think…" I glanced away, then back to him, shifting a fraction to face him. "I think maybe we should plan that I remain in their lives in some way. I can be their crazy Aunt Tessa, just like I am for Gage and Juni. Once you've gotten custody and they're settled, we tell them we decided you and I are better off as friends."

He lifted his back from the wall. The man overpowered the space. I could barely breathe.

"You'd do that for me?" The words were low and grumbly.

I liked them far too much, and I had to keep myself from shouting I'd probably give him anything.

"For us? Stay in their lives permanently?" he added.

"Just try to get rid of me." I forced a wobbly tease. "Once I claim you, you're pretty much stuck with me."

"You claimin' me, Little Dove?" His voice was gruff, and it was making me all kinds of tingly.

"I just might, Milo. I mean, because you're my friend."

Tell me I'm wrong. Tell me you feel something different, too.

His eyes caressed over my face. I got the sense he might be counting every freckle.

A needy sound crawled out from my spirit.

"A friend?" He scoffed, like it was an insult. "You're the light, Tessa. The goodness I'd never expected. You have any idea what I see when I look at you?"

Could he ever see me the way I saw him? Because every day I spent in his house, the harder it got to pretend like I didn't want more.

Harder to pretend there wasn't something that burned between us.

Harder to pin on faked smiles and easy laughter when what I felt wasn't close to being light.

Not when the man made me want to fly.

We'd both somehow come to sitting fully upright, our legs drawn up so we were facing each other.

Hope lit in the space between us.

A warm, flickering glow.

"I think we kick this plan into gear on Sunday. You come with me to my visitation. Then I'll talk to my attorney this week to schedule an appointment so we can set things in motion. Are you ready for that?"

"Absolutely," I promised, because right then, all the concerns and questions I'd had with the girls didn't seem so important.

We'd figured this out.

Together.

I squeezed his hand tight. "We've got this, Milo. We're a great team."

A smile tweaked the edge of his distractingly sexy mouth. "Nobody else I'd want to do it with."

My stomach took a swooping dive.

"I know I'm great and all." I pinned on a bright smile, and crap, his big palm came up to cup the side of my face. He ran his thumb along my jaw.

My belly twisted with want, and a needy throb pounded between my thighs.

Oh, this man made me feel things I'd never felt before.

"That you are, Little Dove."

Intensity blazed in the space, a pull tugging between us.

I swallowed down the arousal and pushed myself to broach the topic I really didn't want to broach. "I think we might have another problem," I rushed like maybe we could skip right over it.

His entire demeanor darkened. A black storm gathering on the horizon.

Nope.

No skipping for Milo.

"What's that?"

I attempted to hide it, but fear made a rebound, and a shiver raced down my spine. The confession shook when I set it free. "Karl came to my work tonight."

Fury flashed through Milo's face, and every muscle in his body flexed.

The hand on my cheek curled in protection.

Beautiful Beast.

"Did he hurt you?" It was nothing less than a growl.

Frantically, I shook my head. "No. But he threatened us. He saw the ring, and he thinks there was something going on with us when he and I were still together. His ego took a hit, and I don't think he's going to let it slide. He warned about pressing charges against you for assault, but I told him if he did, I'd press charges, too. I'm not sure it's enough to keep him from taking action, though."

Any upstanding judge would never rule in his favor.

But Karl had connections.

He would twist and manipulate.

Make himself look like the victim in the situation.

Worry fluttered through my being.

He gripped me by both sides of the face.

Powerful.

Fierce.

Pure, bottled mayhem.

I sucked in a shallow breath as every cell in my body came alive and leaned in his direction.

"Told you if he came around you again, things weren't going to go so well for him."

"And you absolutely cannot do anything reckless, Milo. We are in this to get your kids back, not so you can end up in jail because of my asshole ex. Promise me."

My hand found his shirt, and my fingers curled into the fabric that stretched tight across his chest.

His heart ravaged at his ribs, and I could feel his ghosts in the tremor of his hands.

Violence.

It writhed and thrashed where he kept it chained.

He leaned in and grated the words so close to my mouth I could taste them. "Make no mistake, Tessa. I'd burn the fucking world down before I let him get to you."

Then he stood and was gone.

Chapter Fifteen

Milo

I PROWLED THROUGH THE CROWD THAT HAD GATHERED AT Absolution.

It was no different from any other night. Except for the unhinged rage that streaked through my veins.

Eating me raw as it clawed and gnashed and searched for a way out.

Lights strobed in a dizzying whorl, and the band onstage thrashed to the chaotic rhythm.

A slew of bodies slammed in time.

My hands were in fists, and my teeth were clenched as I shouldered through the crush that vied to push deeper into the fray.

It had taken every part of my haggard soul not to veer off course on my way to work and drive straight to Karl Haller's house and show him exactly what I'd wanted to do that day last week.

Somehow, I'd managed to drive my ass directly to the club without taking a disastrous detour.

Had worked on this shit for years.

Controlling the rage.

The pit of ugliness that seethed.

Now, it boiled and blistered and seared my flesh.

A tattoo of destruction.

I stormed through the crowd, eyes peeled for anyone stepping out of line.

I wondered if I was the inciter of it. If my fury had spilled out from my pores and into the crowd to feed the mayhem.

Because I felt when the disorder had shifted into a riot.

A bunch of people came stumbling back while a small group went ballistic in the middle.

Half of the crowd hurried to get out of the way, but a ton of others pressed in to get a better look at the fight that had broken out at the base of the stage.

I shouted to get out of my way as I pushed through the ring of madness.

About half a dozen assholes were in an all-out brawl.

Arms swinging wide.

Punching and kicking.

Three tumbled to the floor.

Heavy metal played on like an anthem to the frenzy.

I nabbed one of the assholes by the collar and jerked him to his feet.

A woman came rushing for us, shouting the guy's name.

Out of the corner of my eye, I saw it, but not before it was too late.

The motherfucker to the side of her threw an errant fist as she ran past him, no fuckin' care of where it landed.

It cracked the woman in the temple.

She stumbled to the side in shock, grabbing hold of her head and bending in two as a shout of pain wailed out of her. Someone grabbed the woman and pulled her back to safety.

But there was no safety for the scum who'd hit her.

The violence inside me broke its chains.

The sleaze hadn't even slowed after he'd assaulted her but had gone for another man.

I tossed off the guy I'd had in my hold and stalked toward him.

In a flash, I had him by the throat. "You piece of shit."

His eyes went wide as I squeezed.

A second later, Sage, Kult, plus two other bouncers broke through the frenzy.

Trent barreled in behind them.

"Get these assholes out of here," Trent shouted.

Took all of a second for my crew to round them up. I shifted the fucker who was raging against my hold so I could drag him out, and in a flash, we were shoving back through the gawkers and hauling their asses to the side door.

Violence clouded and compelled, a vicious scream that howled in my ear.

I fought it.

Pounded it back down into the depths where it belonged.

Where I couldn't let it free.

One of the bouncers held open the door while Kult, Trent, and two others dragged the guys out.

"Cops or the door, sir?" Kult asked Trent.

Trent shoved the guy he had a hold on out the door, sending him sailing.

"Fuckers can take their bullshit outside." Trent pointed at the guy he'd tossed to the curb. "Don't want to see your face in my club again. Got it?"

"Whatever, asshole," the guy swore, backing away and swiping the blood from his mouth.

I slipped out, angling to the side so I could wrangle the bastard out who was kicking and flailing.

"You're lucky I didn't end you," I growled at his ear before I shoved him toward the road.

I turned around to head inside.

I heard the rush of footsteps before he jumped on my back. He slammed me so hard I lost my balance and got knocked to my knees.

He landed a punch to the back of my head.

Pain splintered, but it had nothing on the red that blurred my sight.

Rage full.

I had him flipped around and pinned to the pavement before the asshole could make sense of the motion.

I let one punch free.

It cracked against his face.

Blood gushed.

In an instant, my sight bleared over.

You worthless little shit. You'll never amount to nothin'. **Blow after blow.** *Come on, fight back, you pussy.*

End him.

Your betrayal won't go unnoticed.

Autumn, baby. I'm so sorry. I'm so sorry.

Karl hit me. Can you believe it?

You bitch. It appears you need a reminder of your position.

Voices spun through my mind.

So many. Too loud. Too much.

Sanity slipped.

Blinking in and out.

Tessa.

Autumn.

Fists flew.

I no longer realized they belonged to me. Not until I was being hauled up and pushed against the wall.

Trent flung his arm across my chest to hold me back. His voice broke through the chaos. "Cool it, man. You've gotta snap out of it. Someone called the cops, and they're on their way. You hear me?" he hissed, his face close to mine, breaking through the disorder.

Pants rushed my throat, and my entire body writhed with the thirst to destroy.

"Listen to me," he urged low. "You're fine. Take a deep breath."

Worry rushed through his pitch-black eyes.

I squeezed mine shut and tried to gather the rage that still burned in my fists.

I slammed my head back against the roughened bricks.

"Fuck," I groaned as the reality of what I'd done bled through.

"It's okay, man. Get out of here and go into my office. I'm going to take care of this shit, and I'll be in."

⊂୦

Trent handed me a tumbler of amber liquid before he leaned back on the edge of his desk and crossed his feet at the ankles. He blew out a heavy sigh before he looked down at me, where I sat trembling in a chair.

"Is he hurt?" I could barely force out the question.

Trent cracked a grin. "More than likely since you went beast on his ass, but he and the rest of them took off as soon as they heard the sirens." Trent smirked. "Saves paperwork."

I grunted. "You should fire my ass for pulling that shit."

Trent actually laughed. "Fire you? I hired you because of that shit."

I took a shaky sip of the whiskey. Hot liquid burned as it rolled down my throat. "Not supposed to lose it like that."

"Would have lost it, too. Kult told me he hit that girl."

My throat threatened to close off. "Yeah."

"Asshole deserved it."

I inhaled deep. "I can't do it, Trent. Can't lose control like that. Can't become *him* again."

Trent rubbed his fingers over his mouth, contemplating, before he stared me down. "You fought to survive, Milo. Don't ever fucking apologize for that."

"Did it for the wrong reasons for a long, long time."

"Did you have a choice?"

Not once I'd sold my soul, no. Not without it costing everything.

My spirit shivered as Autumn's face flashed through my mind.

Guilt clawed at my insides. "I came here tonight already on edge, and that's on me. Karl's been messing with Tessa. Threatening her. Not sure I can control it when it comes to her."

Fury clouded Trent's expression. "Did he touch her again?"

"We went to get her stuff. Fucker didn't know I was there, and he got his hands on her, thinking he was gonna take what she didn't want to give."

His jaw clenched while the violence I'd just tamed screamed.

Trent pushed from the desk and knelt in front of me, his voice as dark as my heart. "We fight for the ones we love, Milo. It's who we are. It's in our blood. And we fight to the end."

Except I hadn't fought hard enough for Autumn.

"I won't let that bastard get near her."

"Good, because if you don't do it, then I will."

Grinning, he stood.

"You okay?"

Hardly.

I choked out the scrape of a laugh and the somberness rolled in. "I have to control it, or I'm going to lose my kids forever."

Trent set his hand on my shoulder, and he dipped down, his voice low with emphasis. "You fight for them, too, Milo. With everything you have. Whatever it takes. I know you, man, you've been hurting for a long fuckin' time. It's time for you to find what you've been missing."

And I needed to remember that was my kids.

I stepped into the vapid shadows of the cabin. It was late, the darkness thick, my spirit heavy.

I needed to drag my ass to my room and take a shower.

But no.

I couldn't stop myself from quietly edging across the floor to her door.

Drawn.

Persuaded.

Moved.

Her influence more than I could resist.

She'd left her door open a crack, and I nudged it the rest of the way so I could check on her.

Make sure she was whole and safe.

That she wasn't tossing with the fear of the monster that I wanted to end.

Her breaths were long and deep, the woman lost to sleep, her slight frame silhouetted by the blanket draped over her body.

I eased forward, my heart jackhammering in my chest, no longer sure what the fuck I was supposed to feel.

Not *this*, I was sure of that.

The ache.

The need.

The urge to reach out and caress the curve of her cheek.

Soft, red locks spilled out over her pillow, and all that wild, warm energy was subdued. Locked in her sleep.

Like a fool, I reached out and let just the tip of my finger trace the edge of her beautiful face. This girl who'd made me feel something for the first time since the day my life had gone dim.

A spark of light in the darkness.

She whimpered at my touch, then I froze when my name ghosted over her lips.

"Milo."

That feeling swelled.

Close to overflowing.

Swallowing, I forced it down and walked from her room.

Because I knew better than toying with what I couldn't have.

Chapter Sixteen

Milo

Ten years ago

SHOUTS RAINED FROM THE DANK, DARK SPACE, ECHOING WITH the call of bloodlust against the thick block walls of the seedy basement.

The ceiling was low in the pit. The pipes exposed. Water dripped from the orifices and gathered on the dingy ground in blackened puddles that rippled with the stomping of feet.

Heat overwhelmed the space, fire on his flesh and old, ugly hatred in his soul.

Here, where the shroud was ripped away and the vileness came to play.

Milo stalked the edge of the ring, watching his opponent like prey. A gash on the side of the man's head gaped open, and blood poured from the wound and streaked down his face. One eye was swollen shut, and bruises had begun to welt on his sides and chest.

Milo lifted his shoulder to swipe the blood that gushed from his mouth, the pain nothing but fuel that fed the frenzy that pounded in his brain.

The chants rose, filled his ears, "Finish him! Finish him!"

They'd learned quickly if they wanted to line their pockets with dirty money, they'd do best when they were shouting for him.

"Come and get me, pussy," his opponent taunted as he bounced on his toes and gestured at himself with his blood-stained fists.

"You little pussy. Good for nothin'. Pathetic waste of space. Just like your mother. Should put a bullet in both your heads."

Milo snapped. He flew forward and released the violence that seethed in wait just beneath the surface of his skin. His fist rammed into his enemy's face, knocking him from his feet.

Milo descended in a blaze of fists and fury. Old hatred that he poured into the wrath that he unleashed.

Hit after hit.

Crack. Crack. Crack.

Darkness enclosed, and the basement walls spun and blurred into one with the cement floor that pooled with the man's blood.

Vengeance shouted in his ears.

Louder than the calls that hurtled from the monsters who chanted their greed. "Finish him."

He delivered another blow, and the man went limp. Hands were suddenly all over him when he went for another hit, yanking him back and pulling him up.

In the middle of the ring, his hand was tossed into the air in a victory Milo would never really win.

He stumbled back to his corner and looked at the man he'd beaten to within an inch of his life.

His skin covered in welts and blood and the grime of this disgusting life.

Gore.

Milo shook as he fell back against the corner of the ring, barely able to stand.

A hand clapped him on the shoulder. "You did good. That's ten thousand in your pocket."

He swallowed down the bile before he slipped out of the ring. He shoved off those who sought to talk to him like he was a hero rather than a monster, and he stalked down the darkened, desolate hall to the old locker room that had been used for employees before the industrial building had been abandoned.

Bought for *renovations* by a man who was as dirty as they came.

He went directly to the shower and turned it on as hot as it would go. He didn't bother to peel himself from his trunks before he stepped into the spray. He stood beneath the scalding water with his forehead pressed to the grungy tiles as he searched for a cleansing breath.

For a way out of the desolation.

He pushed his hands to the wall, his back bowing as he writhed, his mind in search of sanity and his soul filled with the abhorrence of who he'd become.

The molecules in the space suddenly shifted. Changed and took new form. Intensified and deepened.

He shifted to look over his shoulder at the girl who peered back at him through the jaundiced light that glowed in the space.

His ugly heart nearly stopped.

Maybe it was the residual aggression.

The adrenaline that instantly spiked in his veins.

It was her…the same girl who'd been there to watch him two times before. Out of place, so fucking gorgeous he thought his brain had short-circuited and tripped.

The girl who'd become an infatuation in his mind.

"You should probably leave," he warned, his voice low.

She stepped forward. "I think it would be better if I stayed."

Chapter Seventeen

Tessa

A LOW ROLL OF THUNDER PULLED ME FROM SLEEP. I'D BEEN riding just below the surface of coherency, anyway, caught in one of those dreamlike states where you were partially aware of reality. Where the pictures in your mind were distorted by the fears and what-ifs and unknowns, twisting them into untold horrors.

I wouldn't deny it.

I was nervous.

I was usually the rush right in and experience life kind of girl, but my spirit warned of what was riding on tomorrow, and it'd manifested itself into every terrible thing that could go wrong.

Mainly the idea of letting Milo down. That he wouldn't find the fullness of this life. That what he was missing might not be restored.

Tossing off the covers, my bare feet hit the floor, and I padded out into the lapping darkness of the main room. Rain pattered against the roof, and lightning lit at the bank of windows that overlooked the back. For a flash, the mountains were alight and the blackened lake alive with the torrent that pummeled from the sky.

Thunder rolled, and my spirit shivered when I heard the distinct rumble of Milo's old pickup truck approaching in the distance.

I glanced at the clock that glowed from the microwave in the kitchen.

3:14 a.m.

A thrill slipped beneath the surface of my skin.

Every time he came home, it was the same reaction.

Excitement.

Another week had passed, living in his home. Each day, I wanted him more. Each day the idea of *him* increased.

It was no secret I'd lived vicariously through my friends.

I'd always played it a joke. Like I was just being a nosy friend who wanted to goad them for the dirty details in their lives.

But the truth was, I'd been afraid I might never experience it for myself.

That I might not ever realize the desire to be touched.

To be pleased and adored and revered.

To understand what it was like to be taken by an all-consuming need.

To understand freedom in ecstasy.

To me, it was a mystery.

A fantasy I'd played through my mind a million times but had never known for myself.

Through them, I wanted to believe it was real.

The kind of connection they shared with their husbands.

I wondered if Milo touched me if I…

My stomach twisted, and I forced myself to stop that dangerous train of thought and turn back to the gorgeous scene of the summer storm bearing down on the mountain.

I had to reel in these feelings that were getting out of control.

Stop myself from believing this hoax could become something real.

I was setting my heart up to get broken.

I knew it.

That didn't keep it from racing when I heard the tires of his truck crunch over the gravel as he came to a stop in front of the cabin. The spray of his headlights lit through the front windows.

A charge of energy sparked in my spirit.

That expectation was only amplified when his engine shut off, and I could all but hear his big boots pounding up the steps to the front porch, though it was dulled by the constant drone of the rain that pounded the roof.

A key slipped into the lock, and crap, my nerves zapped in anticipation.

Excitement and need and a thrill.

A little fear, too.

No question, what I was feeling was reckless.

Fraudulent and a clear contraindication to this bogus relationship that we'd fashioned.

Because it felt all too real when the door slowly creaked open and I felt his presence wash over me from behind.

Bold.

Severe.

Potent.

All that intensity was nothing but a lure because I couldn't do anything but turn to look at him from over my shoulder.

He'd frozen in the doorway when he saw me there. His black hair was wet and dripping down his face to crawl into his beard.

His face so gorgeous it'd become a direct threat to the strength of my knees.

His black T-shirt was drenched at the shoulders, the fabric stretched tight over his wide, wide chest, though his jeans were barely wet, the top of him taking the brunt of the downpour battering the earth.

It was those honey-dipped eyes that did me in.

Tender.

But I swore I saw them flame with greed.

The man was an absolute hazard to my heart.

He might as well have had me on a lead because I was compelled by his movement as he stepped the rest of the way inside and clicked the door shut behind him, and my body turned in anticipation of his approach.

"Tessa, what are you doing up so late?"

I shrugged. "I think the storm must have woken me." I glanced back through the windows. "It's absolutely gorgeous."

He edged in farther, his big boots thudding on the hardwood floors. His steps were measured, as if he recognized he needed to be careful, as if he understood he was treading into dangerous territory.

Where my heart had gone haywire and the dirty ideas in my mind had spun out of control.

Tension thickened the air, and everything felt too full and tight.

"Gorgeous, yeah," he rumbled, but those eyes never strayed from me.

Lightning flashed, illuminating the room in a strike of energy.

His aura glowed within it.

The warmth now a slow-burning fire.

He edged closer.

The man was all dark Viking and sexy manipulations.

Seriously, he made my mind mush.

"How was your night?" I rushed.

"Long. Couldn't wait to get home."

"Right. You have to be exhausted."

"Not really," he rumbled in that low voice.

"Oh," I peeped. Brilliant, I know.

Milo took the last step until he was a towering shadow that eclipsed me, his big body vibrating with this severity that knocked every rational thought from my brain.

"Don't like leaving you here by yourself night after night."

My mouth went dry, and every drop of blood in my body raced to forbidden locations. I felt like I could step forward, disappear into the man, and I might get lost and never find my way back to sanity.

I wouldn't mind staying there forever.

"I can handle myself just fine. I already told you I'm used to being alone."

He angled down, his breath a hot wisp over my cheek.

Honey and the woods and the fall of summer rain.

A needy sound slipped between my lips without my permission.

"I know you can take care of yourself, Tessa, but that doesn't mean I'm not goin' to worry about you."

"Well, that's what good fiancés do." I struggled for light.

"Well, I do plan on treating my girl right." His delicious mouth tweaked into a half smile.

Snap. Crackle. Boom.

My tongue raced over my parched lips.

I searched for space because at this rate, I was seriously going to make a fool of myself.

Climb him like a tree, like I was aching to do.

I took a fumbling step back and hit the long pane of cool glass.

Milo erased that space, too.

Like maybe he couldn't stand the distance.

I gulped as my belly flipped, and that sweet spot between my thighs throbbed.

Was he thinking the same things as me? What it would be like to run his hands over my body? Tear my clothes off like a wild beast? Take me?

With Karl over and done with, every sordid fantasy I'd kept tucked away of Milo had been unleashed and had taken on a very vibrant new life.

Heat burned up the bare space between us, and I could see the way his chest was jutting with each panted breath.

His jaw was clenched in restraint, and his eyebrows slashed downward in severity.

But his lips—they were plump and soft and full and, oh my God, was this mountain man going to kiss me?

His big palm went to the side of my face. The contact sent chills scattering far and wide, and I was most definitely getting lost in this fantasyland that I wanted to make my home.

Stake a claim in it.

Discovered terrain never known before to exist.

Tessa's territory.

It had a really nice ring to it.

A frown dented his brow. Close to pain. "Are you ready for tomorrow?"

Oh.

Right.

That's where this severity was coming from.

He was worried about the visitation with his kids.

I so got it, and I refused the disappointment that wanted to sprout up between the hope.

I met his fierce gaze through the shadows. "I think it's likely that's what really woke me up. I'm pretty nervous, honestly."

His nod was tight. "Me, too."

"Do you think we can pull it off?"

"I do." He stated it without question.

Like it was fact.

And his hand was slipping farther up my jaw, his fingertips just dipping into my hair.

"Is it wrong I'm excited for you to meet them?" His smile was almost shy.

I gulped. "No, because I can't wait to meet them, either. I just hope they like me."

"Don't think it's possible for someone not to like you, Tessa."

"Oh, I've had a few foes in my life. Third graders can be total bullies. Terrifying, if I'm being honest." My voice was a wisp of light.

A deep chuckle rolled from his chest. "That so?"

I nodded frantically.

Gah.

Why was he tucking me closer?

Another slow roll of thunder rumbled the sky, driving the intensity between us. Waves of vapor that was completely intoxicating.

He hesitated for a second before he murmured, "I was afraid to hope before you came here, Little Dove, and now…"

My fingertips found the spot where his heart hammered at his ribs.

Violent yet steady.

"I want to help you find your joy, Milo. I'm not sure I've met anyone who deserves it the way you do."

"You hardly know me, Tessa." A warning tolled in his gravelly voice.

My blunt nails scraped at his chest. "I don't need to know the details to know you, Milo. I don't need any of it to feel who you are."

A flash of guilt speared through his expression before he urged, "And if it comes to gettin' on the stand and testifying to that? Taking an oath that's a lie?"

"Are you trying to run me off again?" I forced a shaky smile.

He pressed my hand flat to his chest, covering it with his in a desperation that made me want to weep. "I want it so badly, but this week, it's become abundantly clear what I might be putting you through."

I huffed like it was nothing. "Pssh. Lying under oath? I've done it a hundred times."

It wouldn't be a lie, though. What I felt for him. Who I believed him to be.

The smallest grin curled his lips. "A hundred times?"

I shrugged a small shrug and peered up at his intimidating beauty, struggling with all the needy bits inside me to keep this thing light. "What can I say? I'm a rule breaker."

He gruffed out a chuckle, his voice so low and smooth.

Raw liquid silk.

I wanted to roll around in it.

"Rule breaker, huh?"

"Yep, of the worst kind."

Because my thoughts about him were slanting criminal.

"Murder?" His eyes widened with the tease.

"You'll never know," I played right back.

Somehow, he'd drifted even closer, and his free hand had found its way to my hip, and crap, the other was lifting my hand that sported the ridiculously gorgeous ring that I only could have imagined in my dreams. It was so perfect for me it kind of made my heart hurt looking at it.

One he'd picked himself, like he knew me, inside and out.

He held it up between us, watching the big diamond shimmer in the flashes of light. For a moment, we both stared at it before his gaze drifted to mine.

"You don't seem like much of a rule breaker to me," he mumbled so low, the words ripe with affection.

My tongue swept over my dried lips, my voice cracking on the truth. "I think I'd break any rule for you, Milo Hendricks."

He pulled me against him then, to the hard, hulking planes of his gorgeous body, and he pressed his face to my neck, his breaths harsh and shallow where he exhaled them just behind my ear, his hold fierce and unrelenting. The man was as close to me as he could be without taking me, but I wondered if it might be just as intimate.

"Thank you, Tessa. Thank you for saving my heart and what's left of this life."

And I knew right then, I'd give him anything he wanted.

Chapter Eighteen

Milo

IN LIFE, WE ALL HAD CHOICES TO MAKE.

Some were cut and dry.

A line that clearly delineated right and wrong.

Others were grayed in uncertainty and ambiguity.

By circumstance and morality.

Some were distorted by greed and selfishness and egocentric behavior, and others in insecurity and doubt.

And then there were the ones that were a composite of so many factors that there was no defining the right answer except for the one you held in your heart.

My heart that was currently lodged in my throat and constricting airflow as I pulled my Tahoe into the parking lot of the city park nestled in the center of Redemption Hills.

Tessa clung to my hand the same way as she'd done the entire ride over, neither of us saying a word, both lost to thoughts of every one of those factors above.

During it, a quiet support had settled over the cab of the SUV.

Wrong or right, we were in this together.

No matter what.

Slowly, I pulled into a spot two spaces down from Paula and Gene's Range Rover.

It still shocked the shit out of me that they would allow themselves to become so lowly that they'd set a meeting place in a public park, but it wasn't like they were going to extend me an invitation to the country club.

I didn't realize how hard my hand was shaking until I removed it from Tessa's, put the SUV in park, and killed the engine.

Silence descended.

Thicker than before.

My attention was out the windshield to where I could barely make out my children in the distance, little more than specks of color climbing the jungle gym.

Paula and Gene were facing them with their backs to us, off to the side the way they always remained, stoic sentries guarding their charges.

I was thankful they loved them so intensely, but I wouldn't lie and pretend I didn't hold an animosity so fierce toward them that I had to keep my spite under lock and key when I was around them. Going apeshit on them wasn't gonna win me any points with the courts.

Besides, I had to remember grief changed people, made them resentful and bitter, desperate to bring punishment on the one who'd brought on their sorrows.

I knew it firsthand.

Old anger flared in my spirit.

The pressure.

The judgment.

The curl of Paula's nose the first time she'd met me like she'd caught a whiff of something bad.

It wasn't as though they ever liked me, anyway.

I'd never be anything more than a piece of trash in their eyes.

"This is it," I mumbled, having no clue what form of hostility we would be met with, but make no mistake, there would be hostility.

"Paula isn't going to be excited to see you," I reiterated for about the tenth time, trying to prepare Tessa for the shitshow that was likely to go down.

"I know, and that's okay." The words were barely wisps from Tessa's mouth.

She peeked over at me.

Ocean eyes swam with a thousand different currents.

A riptide where I was going to drown.

An encouraging smile lit on her sweet mouth. "We have this, Milo Hendricks. We make a great team, remember?"

My guts fisted when I looked at her.

"Yeah, we make a great team." The words were shards, filled with these broken feelings I couldn't get free of my skin.

Hot and sticky.

She rubbed her palms on her jean-covered thighs like she was wiping the feeling away, too, before she popped the latch to her door. "Ready?"

"Yup."

I opened mine, and we climbed out. We rounded to the back, where I lifted the tailgate and pulled out the cooler we'd packed this morning at the house before we'd left.

Tessa grabbed the picnic blanket, a Frisbee, and a football, the giant bundle tucked to her chest. It was piled so high that I could barely see her face from behind it, the girl so goddamn cute as she shuffled anxiously from foot to foot.

"Got it," she asserted with a resolute nod.

We started across the rambling lawn of the park. We passed by a smaller playground up front, a soccer field, and ramadas housing picnic tables and barbecues.

My pulse thudded harder with each step that I took, knowing I was leading Tessa into the eye of a quiet, deathly storm.

I knew when Paula felt our approach, the way her spine went rigid and revulsion crawled over her flesh.

A palpable hatred that gutted me all over again.

It took her a second to gather her strength before she finally turned to look back at me. Her angry, grief-stricken eyes widened in surprise before they narrowed in spite when she saw I wasn't alone.

She whipped the rest of the way around and all but ran toward us, cutting off our path.

Tremors rocked from Tessa as she prepared herself for a fight.

Paula started hissing as she quickly closed in, her voice held from my kids who still hadn't noticed we were there.

"What the hell do you think you're doing?"

Autumn's mother was younger than my own, but her hair had fully grayed, the lines on her face carved by the torment she'd succumbed to for the last four years.

I swallowed down the hurt that wanted to spew from my mouth as hatred because she was good to my kids, and I knew what it felt like to have your heart ripped out.

It was the same pain that made Paula strike at every turn.

I set the cooler on the ground, took the blankets from Tessa, and set them on top of it, trying to keep my shit together, to guard myself from the loathing that flooded from Autumn's mother.

I wound my fingers through Tessa's and tugged her to my side, clearing my throat. "Paula, this is my fiancée, Tessa McDaniels."

I might as well have kicked her in the gut with the way she took it as a physical blow.

Her body swayed, and her hand wrapped around her stomach before she was rebounding and forcing herself upright.

Disgust and pain left her on a condescending laugh. "Your fiancée?"

"Yes."

Tessa fidgeted at my side, though she did her best to hide her nerves. "Hi, it's very nice to—"

"I don't want your whore anywhere near my grandchildren."

I wanted to tear into her, get in her face, but I forced myself to keep control.

Not to let go or give into the demons that howled.

Monday had been a glaring reminder of how easily I could.

I clutched Tessa's hand. The girl a lifeline. "You don't get a say in that, Paula. This is my day."

I'd already confirmed it with my attorney when I'd set an appointment for the upcoming week.

"Not if it puts my grandbabies in harm's way," Paula spat.

Tessa swallowed, hurt and sympathy coming off her in waves, the girl drowning in this turmoil, too.

"I can assure you I'm no threat to them. I'm a teacher at Redemption Hills Christian Academy, and I run the Hope to Hands Foundation. I'm CPR and first aid certified, and I—"

"I don't care what you are." Venom whipped from Paula's tongue, cutting Tessa off.

I should have expected it.

Hell, I had.

Still, there was no stopping the rush of protectiveness that exploded in me. The way I wanted to wrap Tessa up and shield her from Paula's vile slurs.

I pulled Tessa closer. "You can direct your anger at me, Paula, and I'll take it, but Tessa doesn't deserve it, and I won't stand for it."

"You won't stand for it? I don't think you have any say in the matter."

Tessa inhaled a sharp breath. Yeah, I'd warned her, but I doubted much that she could imagine a single person being so cruel.

Gene was suddenly there, touching Paula's arm. "Come on, sweetheart. Now's not the time for this."

She shrugged him off, and hateful tears brimmed in her eyes when she angled toward me. "How dare you think you deserve joy when you've stolen mine. How dare you move on after you did what you did. Just leave us alone."

Her accusation nearly knocked me to my knees.

The truth of them.

Why I couldn't have what my heart kept aching for.

And there I stood, squeezing Tessa's hand, anyway.

"Dad!" Remy's sweet voice suddenly powered through the air from where she'd seen me from the top of the playground that was fashioned to look like a castle.

My chest squeezed tight.

Love erupted.

Overflowed.

"I'm sorry, Paula, but you know that's not going to happen."

I gave Tessa's hand a tug before I released it and leaned down to pick up the cooler and everything on top.

"Come with me," I told her.

I rounded Paula and strode with the whole pile toward the call of my heart.

My kids.

Tessa kept up at my side, her mouth pinched and dread spinning from her spirit.

"I'm so sorry," I muttered under my breath.

"It's okay," she whispered back.

It wasn't. But there she was, refusing to leave me.

Scout came blazing out from a tunnel slide, all bouncing brown hair and bright eyes and these giant lips that were so cute my heart twisted in a fist. My Remy Girl was right at his heels, the child tall for her age, lanky, her spirit reserved and intuitive and the best sight I'd ever seen.

And I was dropping the cooler in that spot and rushing that way, falling to my knees on the grass at the same second my kids were colliding into me.

"Dad! Dad! You got here!" Remy's arms encircled my neck, and my arm went around her waist.

I breathed out the weight sitting in my chest as I hugged her close.

Relief.

Relief.

Scout was all giggles as he threw himself onto my back. "You're a dad-*sammich*. Right in the middle of me and my sister."

My other arm wrapped around him, holding him tight against me, and I wished for a fucking miracle that I would never have to let them go.

Remy swayed me back and forth, her thin arms as strong as steel. "I missed you so much."

"I missed you, too, Rems. So much."

"Then why does it have to be so long for me to see you?" Confused distress filled her voice.

It drove a blade of pain deep into my soul, and I breathed out, just hugging her because how the hell did I answer that?

"I thought about you every second," I finally said.

"Me, too!" Scout piped in from behind. Thank God he hadn't quite figured out the distance the way his sister had.

He didn't remember his mother, our family, the way it had once been, and I was afraid it was the ghost of it that was going to haunt Remy for the rest of her life.

"You did, huh?" I tried to tease and keep the heaviness out because I didn't want to waste a second of the time I had with my kids.

"That's right, Dad. All'uve 'em. Every single one," Scout said in his adorable, slurring voice.

It flooded me with an adoration so intense it physically hurt.

This ache in my soul that only abated in the moments I got to spend with them. I ignored the thought they kept abating when I was with Tessa, too.

I couldn't go there.

Couldn't lose sight.

I relished in holding on to my children for the longest time, my eyes squeezed tight as I savored the connection.

In the midst of it, I could sense the presence hovering off to the side.

Warmth and affection.

The light.

The rising of the sun.

And fuck, it was so wrong, the way I felt when I shifted my attention that way, when I slowly peeled my children off me and tucked Remy to my side and drew Scout around so his back was against my chest.

My chest that felt like it was about to blow.

Tessa stood about ten feet off, a hand pressed to her throat like she was trying to stave off the emotion vying for a way out.

It radiated around her, anyway.

Bright, blinding rays.

Shocks of fiery red hair whipped around her face, kissing her freckled cheeks, her mouth set in a soft, red bow.

But it was those eyes—those sea-blue eyes that were filled to fathomless depths with a devotion I didn't come close to deserving.

I attempted to clear the roughness from my voice, but it scraped when I murmured, "There's someone really special I want you two to meet."

Remy shifted into me when she realized I hadn't come by myself, her cheek pressed to my shoulder, the child hiding behind the thick locks of her brown hair as shyness took her over. She warily peered out at Tessa, who remained floating at the fringes of my broken little family.

I felt the full force of Scout's grin. "Is that who we gotta meet?"

"Yes, it is. Her name is Tessa, and we are going to…"

The lie locked in my throat before it could reach my tongue.

Yeah, Tessa and I had talked about this. How to handle our *relationship*. How it was going to affect my kids.

Even with the precautions we were taking, with the sacrifices Tessa was making, I knew in my gut that this sham wasn't going to come without consequences. It wasn't going to come without disappointment and more confusion and wounds that I fucking hated inflicting.

But I was fighting for something eternal with my kids.

For a home and their peace and their knowledge that they were the meaning of this life.

That they weren't secondary.

That they were worth a hell of a lot more than one goddamn afternoon a week.

"This is Tessa, and she and I are going to get married." I tried to keep the roughness out of the confession, but it came out sounding like a double-edged blade.

A blessing and a curse.

A tremor rolled through Tessa, head to toe, and her mouth tugged at the side while she waited there like she wasn't sure of her place.

"You don't got a wife." Scout giggled like it was absurd.

"Well, since I don't have one, I wanted Tessa to be mine." Fuck, this was rough.

Unsure, Remy trembled in my arms. Both curious and distraught.

"But what about Mom?" she whispered close to my ear.

Agony cut me in two.

Grief.

Guilt.

My arm tightened around Remy's waist, and I shifted so we were facing each other, so I could connect with her golden eyes that were just a shade darker than mine. "Marrying her will not replace your mom, Remy, and I will love her forever, but it's okay for us to love someone else, too, since Mom's not here to be with us."

The heresy abraded my throat, razors cutting through.

Remy warred, unconvinced, peeking back at Tessa who glowed in the backlight of the sun before my daughter was whispering to me like a secret, "She looks like sunshine."

My spirit flailed. "Yeah, she does, doesn't she?"

I lifted my chin, asking Tessa to come closer, and the woman slowly crossed the space before she was getting down onto her knees in front of us, so cautious and careful and with such discretion and mindfulness that I was terrified I fell for her a little bit right then.

"Hi," she whispered, attempting to tuck wayward locks of red hair behind her ears that kept flying into her face. "I'm Tessa. It's so wonderful to meet you both."

Scout got to his hands and knees, hopping toward her like an excited puppy. "Hi, Tessa. Look it what I got!"

He dug a little metal spaceship out of his pants pocket and started flying it through the air in front of Tessa's face while making a bunch of rocket noises.

"I'm gonna be an astronaut when I grow up."

A giggle slipped from Tessa, and her gaze slanted to me for the barest flash, one of those looks that promised we had this.

Could only pray we did.

Because I knew the risks.

It was hazard and peril, but it was also a newfound hope.

All those blurred lines promising the only right choice was the one of our hearts.

Resting her butt on her feet, she turned back to my son. "You are, huh?"

"Yep, I'm gonna go to space."

"To the moon?" she drew out, her eyes wide in awe.

Scout frowned. "No way. People have already been to the moon. That's old news. We gotta go all the way to Mars if we're gonna discover somethin' new."

"Oh, well, then, that's going to be awesome, just like I bet you're pure awesomesauce."

She poked his belly, and he tried to grab for her finger, cracking up, his voice twisted like she was crazy. "Awesomesauce? You mean like apples-sauce? Because my gramma says it's okay to eat the apples-sauce, but I can't get no more cookies, and I am starvin'. Did you even bring lunch because I really hope so?"

He popped up on his knees, bouncing six inches in the air.

Affection pulled tight across my chest, and Tessa was fighting laughter, this softness about her that was soothing the air that burned with chaos.

It was a chaos that for the last four years I hadn't known how to tame.

Stuck in a windstorm that would never cease.

And now...now it felt like there was a chance at peace.

"We sure did. Just how hungry are you?"

"The hungriest. I got the growls." He rubbed his stomach.

God, how desperately I loved this kid.

Affection kissed Tessa's pale cheeks, and she carefully shifted her attention to Remy, who still stood reticent at my side. "Hey, Remy."

"Hi." Remy's voice was quiet.

"It's nice to meet you."

Remy blinked at her. "Do you love my dad?"

Right.

Okay.

I shouldn't have been surprised it would be Remy who put us to the test.

Flustered, Tessa let go of a haggard breath.

She warred, and something flashed through her expression when she glanced at me, something that shouldn't have been there, something that should have been missing when she whispered the lie, "I do. Very much."

I could feel Remy searching her, like the child wished she could dig through her mind, that her trust wasn't quite there, which was no surprise since this world hadn't given her much to believe in.

I cleared my throat, unable to take the tension for a second longer. "We should get set up."

Scout hopped to his feet without care. "Lunchtime!"

I pushed to stand. Remy remained pinned to my side, though she barely made it to my waist. Reaching out a hand, I helped Tessa to her feet.

"Thank you," she murmured, her eyes on me for a beat before they were on Remy, her expression riddled with this empathy that made emotion clot up my throat.

Then she reached out and ruffled her fingers through Scout's hair. "Let's get you fed, Rocketman."

Scout giggled like it was the best thing he'd ever heard, then the two of them went skipping toward where I'd dumped our things.

A playfulness took over Tessa as she said something that made Scout crack up. She grabbed the blanket and started to spread it out under the shade of a tree, and Scout was right there to help her, fumbling to get a grip on one side. He tripped and fell backward onto his butt. Instantly, he popped back up, still holding onto one side of the blanket, the kid likely making the job a whole ton harder.

All while a quiet sadness and confusion emanated from my daughter.

"You good, Remy Girl?" I mumbled, still staring ahead, tucking her closer to me where I had my arm slung around her shoulder.

"It just feels weird that you came here with someone," she whispered like she was ashamed of admitting it.

"Are you okay with that?"

Pain clouded her eyes when she looked up at me. "I don't like you being alone, but I heard Grandma say you don't deserve love and that you don't have any of it to give, either."

My attention snapped to where Paula sat at a picnic table under a ramada.

Anger burned in my guts.

How could she fucking say something like that in front of my kids?

Turning to Remy, I knelt in front of her and brushed the locks of brown hair from her precious face. "Your grandma is still very, very sad, Remy, because she misses your mom so much, and it's really hard for her to see through it. It makes her say things that aren't true."

I took her by the outside of her shoulders. "But no matter what she says, I need you to know that I love you with every part of me. You and Scout? You are my life. You are what is important to me. You are the reason I live."

She blinked, processing, before she murmured, "And Tessa, too?"

Fuck. I looked to the ground for a beat before I returned my gaze to my daughter. "Yeah, Tessa, too, but what I feel for her will never take anything away from what I feel for you and your brother. Do you understand?"

"I think so."

"Okay, good. Now how about we go get some lunch before your brother eats it all?" I forced an easy smile.

Remy gave me one of her half-lopsided grins. "We'd better. Grandma said he's eating her out of house and home."

Yeah, well not for long.

∞

"Go, go, go!" Tessa jumped up and down, rooting on Remy who'd thrown the Frisbee and was currently rounding the bases.

I scooped Scout into my arms, and he and I raced toward the Frisbee that'd rolled out the right side of the baseball field.

Scout was bouncing all over, his laughter filling the air, my little guy kicking my sides like I was a horse. "Hurry, Dad, hurry, Remy is so really fast, and we gotta catch her before she gets all the way to home base."

I dipped down to snag the Frisbee, holding tight to Scout as I tipped him upside down, making him holler and laugh uncontrollably while Tessa was shouting, "You're almost there, Remy! Whoop, whoop! Team Remy-T Wreckers coming in for the win. Yeah, baby!"

Scout's eyes went wide. "Go, Dad! We gotta catch her. Rocket speed!"

I shifted him, tucking his side to mine so he could stretch out his arms like he was flying, and I was supplying the rocket propulsion as we bounded back the opposite direction, a bunch of sounds bubbling out of my mouth as I found a lightness I hadn't felt in a long, long time.

Remy rounded third base.

Tessa jumped up and down on the pitcher's mound, waving her hands in the air and cheering on my kid. "Go, Remy, go!"

Both their faces were red.

Joy radiated all around.

Guessed it was my joy, too.

This feeling in the air that might have been the best thing I'd ever felt.

Scout kept himself rigid, still zooming through the air. "After burners, Dad!"

I increased my speed a fraction.

Remy screamed and laughed as she ran for home, my daughter soaring free when her steps were often laden with reservation.

Her load too heavy.

I made sure that we just missed her as she stomped onto the base.

"Ahh, dang, you're too fast." I feigned the grumbled complaint while my little girl squealed in victory and shouted, "I did it! I did it!"

Tessa ran her way, her arms in the air. "You did it! You are a rockstar, Remington Hendricks!"

They jumped, high-fiving each other with both hands.

"Oh, man," Scout whined. "We got a tie. How do we even know who's the best?"

I pressed my lips to the top of his head. "Means we're all the best, little man."

"That's Rocketman to you," he told me.

A chuckle got free, and Tessa was giggling nonstop, her smile so bright, happiness this glow of warmth that surrounded her.

She poked Scout's belly where I'd shifted him upright. "Pure awesomesauce, I tell you."

He jumped out of my arms and into hers.

She caught him like she was completely accustomed to pint-sized shenanigans. "There's my Rocketman! You're off to Mars!" she sang as she swung him around.

Peals of his laughter rang in the air, and Remy moved to hold my hand, grinning in a way I hadn't seen her do in so long that I'd almost forgotten what it looked like.

God, I wasn't even sure how to navigate through it when I kept getting struck with an urge to capture it.

Hold it and protect it forever.

"Okay, I think that's my favorite game." Remy was almost shy to say it, though it was adrenaline and glee rushing all over her face.

"So fun!" Tessa agreed.

Everyone was panting with the exertion, sweat slicking our skin, and we moved back to where we had the blanket set up in the shade.

Tessa flopped down onto her back on it, Scout still held in her arms. Remy flopped right down beside her.

Tessa rolled her head in Remy's direction so they were staring at each other where they lie on their backs. "Thank you for being on my team."

"Best team ever." Timidity might have filled Remy's voice, but joy shined in her eyes.

They just sat there for a second, smiling at each other, something special moving between them.

Scout climbed off Tessa, and he crawled to the cooler and tossed open the lid. "I spy with my little eye a blue Popsicle."

Like he hadn't spotted it earlier when we were passing out sandwiches and fresh-cut fruit.

He reached for one.

"You're supposed to ask first, little man," I told him.

"Is it okay, Tessa?" He beamed at her. I was pretty sure those full lips would be enough to swindle the last dollar out of a starving man's hand.

I blinked at him. "Excuse me? What am I, chopped liver?"

Scout shrugged. "Tessa's got my back."

Tessa sat up, pressing her fingertips to her mouth like she was trying to keep back her laughter.

"What are you giggling about?" I asked, voice low as I climbed down onto my knees at the edge of the oversized blanket.

"I think I found myself a couple of new besties." Her smile softened, pure affection as she glanced between the two of them.

Remy smiled, too, and fuck, my chest tightened.

I loved to see my little girl happy.

"I'll be your best friend because you brought me a Popsicle," Scout supplied as he grabbed a handful of them and started to pass them out.

"One for Daddy-Doo, one for Remy-Roo, one for Tessa-Too."

My kid, he was a poet.

"Dad, you better kiss her if you're gonna marry her," Scout said so nonchalant as he peeled the wrapper and stuck the blue bullet into his mouth. "Because in a minute, she's gonna have blue lips, and that's gross."

I knew we were going to have to get these displays of affection right, but my nerves decided it was a fine time to short-circuit.

To go zapping and zinging in all those places she kept bringing to life.

Shaking me down and tightening my guts in a flurry of want as I looked at the woman who watched me with such a tenderness that my spirit groaned.

"You've got love, Dad," Remy whispered.

Soft encouragement that cut me to the quick.

My child's belief filling me full after I'd lost it.

Warily, I crawled forward on my knees, already towering over Tessa where she sat on the blanket.

My friend.

My friend.

Curling my hand around the back of her neck, I drew her closer.

Fire flashed.

That feeling rising that I had to keep at bay.

But those blue eyes, they were so intense and deep and filled with this trust that spread like fingers through my senses.

The girl a lure.

Her lips barely parted as we sat there with an inch of space separating us.

Hovering.

Hesitating.

Unsure.

My heart thundered too loud, and I finally drew her the rest of the way in and pressed my lips to hers.

Somewhere between firm and soft.

A second.

Then two.

Breathing her in.

Torment and bliss.

Scout cracked up at our side, and I closed my eyes for a second more, relishing in it, in what I couldn't have, before I forced myself back a fraction to look his way.

"You do got the love bug, Dad. Miss Longmier said it was a horrible disease," he giggled around his Popsicle.

I glanced back at Tessa, who withdrew, timidly licking her lips as she sat back.

My dick stirred.

I wanted to kiss her again.

Guilt cleaved through my spirit at the errant thought, but I didn't have time to fully contemplate it before a voice cleared, bursting the bubble we'd built.

"It's time to go," Paula said, barely controlling the spite in her voice.

"Oh, man, already? I just got my Popsicle," Scout complained.

Sadness rushed from Remy, and in an instant, she had moved and was clinging to me. It was the same way she always did when it was time to say goodbye.

I held her tight, one arm around her waist and my other hand spread over the back of her head while she buried her face in my chest.

I was caught in her pain, in the hatred that burned from Paula, in the sympathy that radiated from Tessa.

"Finish it up quickly." Paula pursed her lips in disdain when she glanced at where I was on my knees hugging Remy.

Scout took it as a challenge, though half of it melted on his face and dripped down onto his shirt.

When he finished, we all reluctantly stood.

Somberness stole the mood as Tessa and I packed our things.

Tessa held onto the blanket while I carried the cooler back across the park.

Scout and Remy walked along at either side of us. Scout prattled on, thankfully unaware of the melancholy that had descended.

Paula and Gene were already waiting by their car. We set everything on the sidewalk, and a sticky disquiet crawled over us as we walked the kids to the parking lot.

Remy took Tessa in a fierce hug.

"I'm really glad I got to meet you today. It was so fun," she whispered, like she needed to keep it a secret.

Tessa gently ran her hand down the back of her head before she eased back so she could meet her eye. "It was one of my most favorite days I've ever had."

An affected smile tweaked Remy's mouth before it dimmed, and she moved to throw herself around me. She burrowed into me as I held her close.

I nearly buckled when I felt her crying.

How many times could my soul shatter before there was nothing left that existed?

I eased her back, tipped up her chin, held it between my thumb and forefinger. "It's okay, Remy Girl. I'll see you next week."

One side of her face tremored as she tried to hold her sorrow back. "Okay."

"I love you."

She nodded, the words whispered directly into my chest when she squeezed me again. "You've got love, Dad, and I love you back so much."

She finally peeled herself away and climbed into the back of the SUV.

I picked up Scout and flung him around a little, making him laugh before I pulled him against my chest, holding him as tight as I could without crushing him. "You be a good boy, Scout. I'll be thinking about you."

"Every single second." He grinned.

"That's right." I pressed a kiss to his temple.

Paula all but ripped him out of my arms, scowling at me as she buckled him into his car seat.

"He's a mess, Milo. I'd appreciate it if you had a little consideration next time."

Right.

Popsicles.

I was a horrible parent.

I didn't bother responding because it didn't matter.

There would be no getting through to her, no changing her mind, and the only way any of this would change would be fighting it out in court.

We stepped back as Paula slammed the door shut, and she rounded and got into the front passenger seat.

Gene backed out.

Tessa eased up to my side.

Energy thrummed.

Quiet.

Intense.

Sorrowful.

She threaded her fingers through mine, and together, we watched them drive away.

I'd done it for close to four years.

Stood there, alone, breaking all over again.

But this time, I did it with Tessa at my side.

This time, I did it with a spark of hope.

Chapter Nineteen

Tessa

I SET MY E-READER ON THE NIGHTSTAND. TONIGHT, I WAS unable to focus on the words that kept blurring together.

Reading romance was my jam.

I loved getting to experience the tension. The angst. The attraction. The mystery.

I loved the triumph over trauma.

I loved getting to fall in love over and over again, a million different times in a million different ways.

I wanted to experience the beauty of it rather than succumb to the numbness I'd felt lying next to a man I would never love, night after night.

One who would never spark a flame or incite a riot of wings in my belly.

But tonight, I couldn't fall into that safe haven. Couldn't settle into the fantasy when I could feel the torment of Milo, who roamed the cabin as if he were lost.

Today had been brutal.

Beautifully brutal.

It had opened my eyes wide to what he was going through. The fight he was up against, and what he was fighting for.

He'd been quiet on the ride home.

Quieter still once we'd gotten here.

He'd been the same way after last week's visit, but I didn't think there was a way to understand the full magnitude of what it meant until I'd witnessed it for myself.

The joy.

The love.

The hurt.

The pain.

The harsh hatred from his ex-mother-in-law that'd had me biting my tongue so hard I'd actually made myself bleed.

But the urge to get in her face and demand she look at the damage she was causing had been close to overwhelming.

How she wasn't only hurting Milo, but her grandchildren, too.

But going all fiery friend on her ass wouldn't help things.

It'd only make it worse.

I doubted there was anything I could say that would make her change her mind.

The second we'd gotten home, Milo had headed directly outside and begun to work on the treehouse.

I hadn't followed him because I'd known he needed space.

Time alone to process.

To mourn.

And I solemnly swore that I'd made a real, valiant attempt at not sneaking peeks.

But I'd worried about him.

Truly.

Not that it'd helped the sticky situation when he had to go and peel the shirt from his body when he'd gotten hot and sweaty.

Hot was the keyword here.

Like, how on all things holy could one man be so spicy?

One glance and I caught fire.

It was like the man had become written code in every fantasy that had ever sprouted in my mind. Had become every hero in every book. Every image of what I ultimately wanted.

But tonight?

It'd been more than just the attraction that burned between us.

It was riddled with the harsh desperation that had surrounded his being while he'd worked on the treehouse.

As if his mind had strayed to faraway places while determination had strengthened his movements. He'd stayed out there until long after the sun had set, and my name had been a bare grunt of goodnight as he'd passed through the house to take a shower an hour ago.

I'd retreated to my room, but now, I could feel him moving around the cabin.

That energy potent and provocative.

My care for him too much.

When I couldn't handle it any longer, I slipped out of bed, keeping my movements quiet as I moved to the door, quieter still as I cracked it open and tiptoed out like some kind of creepy stalker.

I slipped out to the squared archway, and I hung on to the edge of it as I peered out.

My breaths turned shallow.

The only lights on in the cabin glowed from beneath the top cabinets in the kitchen. It was just enough to illuminate the severity of his profile from where he stood at the kitchen sink, though he wasn't doing anything except staring out the window.

He'd showered, his black hair damp and rumpled, and he wore a fresh white tee that hugged the massive width of his shoulders.

Muscles bulged from his back and arms.

Heck, his entire body was this hulking, monstrous thing.

Every inch of him bristled with strength.

The man was pure, masculine poetry.

A shock to my senses.

Bottled mayhem.

Beautiful Beast.

My lips burned with the memory he'd imprinted there this

afternoon when he'd kissed me, and my insides quaked with the way it'd felt to be his for a moment, even when being *his* was nothing but a farce.

And I guessed it was the reason I felt frozen where I stood. Because I didn't know how to hide it any longer. What I really felt for him. I hated that it'd come to feel like some kind of dirty secret.

"What are you doin' over there, Little Dove?"

A buzz slipped down my spine at the sound of his grumbly voice, with the fact that he felt me from across the room.

I stuffed the attraction down because this shouldn't be about my crush. Slipping out from behind my hiding place, I wrung my hands and whispered, "I wanted to make sure you were okay."

He shifted a fraction to look at me.

It sent a ripple of his intensity vibrating through the dense air. I almost stumbled into it, but I kept moving closer.

The way his eyes devoured me from across the space was enough to set me aflame.

In an instant, I was burning up.

"It must be becoming apparent that I'm not in the best frame of mind on Sunday evenings."

I rounded the end of the island and came to stand directly across from him just as he turned to face me. He crossed those massive arms over his chest as he leaned against the countertop.

"That's understandable. Today was..." I trailed off, unsure how to put it into words.

"Rough." There was an apology in his voice, and he picked up the bottle of beer he had sitting open and took a swig of it.

My head shook, my voice quieted. "No. It was wonderful, not that there weren't parts of it that weren't hard. It was just...worth it."

Devotion carved itself deep into his expression. "They're worth everything to me."

Emotion thickened my throat. "They're truly amazing. The sweetest things."

"You did good, Tessa. Really, really good."

I forced lightness into my shaky laugh. "Well, I've been told I'm a great actress. I might have missed my calling."

He surprised me by stepping forward.

That big body filled the space to overflowing, the man stealing the breath from my lungs.

I stumbled backward with the force of it.

Energy flashed as he eased even closer, and I shivered when he angled down so close to my face that I could taste all his yummy deliciousness.

"That wasn't acting, Tessa. That was your kindness. Your gentleness. Your care. The way you made my kids feel like they were the center of your world. There is no faking that."

"No, that part wasn't acting." The confession breezed out in a thin wisp from my lips.

I swore he inhaled the words.

"Remy liked you." He muttered it low, a pain seeded so deep in his being when he spoke of her.

"She misses you." I prayed he could feel my belief as I gazed at his unforgettable face. At the stark, defined angles of his jaw and brow. At the softness of his mouth.

He gave a tight nod. "She remembers livin' with me. What our life used to be like. Felt the trauma of it being ripped apart."

I shouldn't have, but I reached up and gently scratched my nails through his beard.

Everything about Milo Hendricks made me want to crawl right inside.

Hold him.

Maybe let him hold me, too.

Because there was no missing the way our emptiness ached, and maybe those vacancies wouldn't hurt so bad if we let each other fill them.

"I can see that she is also fiercely strong, like her dad. Quiet and insightful. Kind and gentle."

He breathed out a harsh breath. "That's what you think of me?"

"I do."

A rough laugh curled from his throat. "That's me trying to control who I really am."

My head shook. "Don't you see that in your daughter? All of those amazing qualities?"

His brow pinched. "Everything about her is amazing."

My nails kept scraping through the prickly hairs of his beard. "And she is so very much like you."

"Tessa…"

"It's true."

He blinked like he wanted to believe it but didn't know how.

"And Scout…" I murmured with a smile pulling at the edge of my mouth. "He's a perfect little handful, just like you said."

"They're my world. The meaning of this life."

I nodded. "You're a great dad, Milo."

"I'm tryin' to be."

"There's no trying to it. It radiates from you. It's powerful and all-consuming, and I promise you that your kids feel it. I promise they know your love for them. Even from across the miles. Even when they're not here with you. They know."

Torment moved through his expression, and I let my fingertips slide up his face until my palm was on his cheek.

Did he feel the connection? Did he grasp this same feeling that I had for him? The one that kept growing stronger each day?

His hand slipped over mine, and he pressed my palm firm against his face. "And you have given me the chance to erase those miles, Tessa."

A flood of warmth washed across my skin, and my tongue swept out over my lips.

The energy was so thick between us it'd become the oxygen.

Flames crackled, and his eyes flashed.

"They deserve to be with you, Milo. They love you and you love them, and it is clear that you would do absolutely anything to protect and provide for them. This is right, what we're doing."

He could barely nod. "And dealing with Paula?"

"She's horrible, Milo. Her aura, what radiates around her? It's not just broken, it's ugly, and it makes me sick, what she's putting you and the kids through, but I'll take her ugliness on, too."

His gaze flashed with anger. "Don't want to put you through that."

"We're in this together. Remember?"

He warred for a beat before he nodded. "Yeah."

Then something that was close to a grin flitted over his mouth, and somehow, he drew me even closer as he studied me.

"Her aura?" He quirked a brow, somewhere between a tease and true curiosity.

A self-conscious giggle slipped free. "I just…see things about people in ways I'm not sure anyone else does."

"That why you treat people like you've always known them from the moment you meet them?"

Heat flushed my cheeks. "I usually can tell if someone needs a friend. Support. A person there to encourage them."

He hesitated before he asked, "And what is it you see when you're around me?"

My fingertips went back to scratching through his beard, my words soft rasps of affection that I couldn't keep contained. "I see a warm glow that wants to bleed out, but it's shuttered in pain. I see this goodness that got twisted in some kind of guilt that holds you hostage."

A low grunt left his mouth, but he didn't move. He just stood there, swaying with me, the two of us caught in a moment of understanding.

But I thought it might be more than that, the energy that whispered and lured and pulled between us.

Hungry eyes searched me in the shadows, and I could feel the intensity steadily building between us with each second that passed.

"What are you thinking right now?" he finally demanded, words a rugged caress over my face.

And crap, I should lie, keep up with this charade, but the gusty confession left me on a plea. "I was wondering what it would be like if it were real. If this wasn't faked. If you kissed me because you want me, the same way I want you."

Oh, man, I'd really done it then. Pushed him over a line he didn't want crossed. Darkness blazed through his eyes in a way I'd never seen it do before.

Fury and ferocity.

He reeled back by three inches.

It tore my hand from his face and created a chasm of volatility that roiled between us. One that was going to suck me to the bottom of it.

His expression was set in fierce restraint.

His eyes pinched in desperation.

His jaw clenched in disgust.

I went to grab him by the shirt so I could hold on to him. Tell him I was joking, that I didn't mean it.

Convince him I was just being that goofy Tessa who no one took seriously and hope he didn't get that I was begging him not to go.

I started to toss out a thousand lies when he snapped.

His big hand flew out so fast I couldn't process the movement. He had me by the back of the neck and was pulling me forward with so much force my feet nearly slipped out from under me.

Or maybe I was just flying when his mouth crushed against mine.

My entire body lit in a show of fireworks.

Snap. Crackle. Boom.

Oh, yes.

I couldn't even stop the moan that rolled up my throat as a volatile concoction of relief and need and desire went sailing through my system.

My hands drove into his shirt as I struggled to keep up with the shift.

With this perfect fantasy that I'd been dying to experience.

It wasn't gentle.

It was a plundering.

Decimation.

My complete ruining.

His mouth moved over mine in an obliterating push and pull.

A gasp ripped up my throat when his tongue stroked through my lips to dominate the kiss.

It was all kinds of demanding.

Possessive.

I liked it. God, I liked it so much.

My hands roved, needy in their search, palms rushing the hard planes of his chest, up and over his shoulders and diving into his hair.

Bliss.

A torrential downpour of bliss was what I felt.

A grumbly moan rolled off his tongue and spilled into our kiss.

"Tiny Tease, wrecking my mind," he mumbled as his hand skidded down my side, taking greedy handfuls of my flesh as he went.

I yelped when he grabbed me by the bottom and tugged me against the delicious expanse of his hulking body.

Flames roared. An inferno that combusted in my belly.

A full-fledged fire.

I whimpered. Milo moaned.

"Is this what you wanted to know, Little Dove?" he warned at my mouth as he continued the plundering. "Did you want to know what it'd be like if I took you? Owned you?"

"Yes." It was complete surrender.

My feet were suddenly no longer touching the ground, and on instinct, I wrapped my legs around his waist when he hoisted me up.

"You need to feel it, Tessa?" He used his hand that was kneading into my bottom to grind me against his massive erection.

Desire erupted.

A needy throb at the juncture between my thighs.

Holy fuckballs.

Salem was right.

This bad boy would split me in two.

I was so here for it. For all of it. For everything he had to offer.

"I've always wanted you." The admission gushed in a torrent of need. "Show me what it's like, Milo. Please, show me."

A growl rumbled in his chest, and he dove back in. Every stroke of his tongue was possession. Every touch of our hands frantic.

Disorienting.

Perfecting.

So much.

So good.

His kiss consumed, and I was in a frenzy as I struggled to touch him everywhere I could, wanting more, but not sure I could handle all that he was.

But, oh, was I ready to try.

My fingernails raked desperately at his shoulders and rushed down his back, searching for a way to get inside. "Milo. Do you feel this, too? Did you feel it for all those months?"

The question incited him farther, his groan pained.

Close to agonized.

The kiss became punishing as he continued to grind me against his cock.

"Please," I begged. "Please…please touch me."

Lust clouded my sight.

A fever that I'd never experienced before.

Something I didn't know but wanted to discover in Milo.

I gasped when he suddenly plopped me onto the counter, and he fisted a hand in my hair, the man close to rough as he dragged me to the edge.

"You wanna come, Little Dove?"

I couldn't even speak. I was lucky I got out an erratic nod.

He grabbed me by the knee and spread my legs.

Breathless, I gaped, unable to believe that Milo Hendricks was actually wound between my thighs.

A fortress that towered.

So big and burly and positively dripping with sex as he stared at me with this look that told me I'd better be careful what I was asking for.

"Please."

All self-preservation had gone *poof.*

He scraped his callused palm up the inside of my thigh.

Shivers raced, then I was gasping when he jerked the crotch of my sleep shorts to the side and circled a fingertip just at my entrance.

My head spun, and my hands shot to the edge of the counter to keep myself upright while his tongue raked over his bottom lip as he placed his full attention on where he was touching me.

"Look at you, sweet girl, dripping for me."

A blush streaked my flesh, and I wasn't even shy.

The words heaved out with a shattered breath. "Every time I think of you, I get wet, Milo. I can't stop it, the way I wonder what it'd be like to feel you. If you...if you—"

He cut me off by pushing two giant fingers inside me.

"Oh my God," raked up my throat, "Milo, you—"

He silenced the rest when he tightened his fist in my hair and dove back at my mouth.

His kiss was rough as he pumped his fingers at this perfect, mind-bending rhythm while he used the pad of his thumb to circle my clit.

Oh yes, did the man know what he was doing. I didn't have to wonder any longer what he could do with those big, rugged hands.

Pleasure clouded my sight, and I held onto his shoulders while he stroked me into oblivion.

Bliss built so fast I wasn't prepared.

A tsunami that struck from out of nowhere.

A summer storm that hit.

I split apart.

A complete rupturing.

An ecstasy I'd never known plowed through my body, leaving no stone unturned.

I cried out as the orgasm ripped through me.

Nothing else existed but this.

This.

"Milo."

He swallowed that, too, the man holding me like a treasure as I nearly floated off the counter.

In his arms, I shook and bowed, arching toward him in this plea to get closer as little shocks of pleasure continued to scatter through my body.

The O was so yummy, it should have sustained me for a lifetime.

Call me needy, but I wanted more.

One taste was hardly enough.

For the first time, I really, really wanted it because I found the one who I wanted to share it with.

"Take me, Milo. Take all of me."

I wanted to disappear into his beautiful being.

Stay there.

Fill him while he filled me.

But I'd never been so sure than right then that the man was a tornado.

The kind that touched down and destroyed everything in its path as it passed through.

Gone in an instant but the wreckage insurmountable.

Bottled mayhem that had been shaken so fiercely it blew.

Because Milo jerked away while I still tried to cling to him.

Horror cut through every line of his striking face as he stared at me like I was an apparition.

Or maybe the monster who'd shoved a knife into the sanctity of his ghosts.

Because it was all there.

Regret.

Shame.

All up against the lust that hazed over his eyes.

It didn't help that pleasure still rolled through me. Tiny sparks that kept going off while he looked at me like I was the manifestation of his every sin.

Slowly, he backed away, peeling my fingers from his shoulders as he went.

"Milo." His name barely made it from my lips, was barely heard, though I might as well have stabbed him with the way he recoiled when he heard it.

He roughed a shaky, tatted hand through his hair, voice a ragged scratch of desolation. "Have to go."

Without saying anything else, he turned, snatched his keys from the counter, and stormed out the door.

The walls rattled when he slammed it behind him.

A second later, I heard the rumble of his old truck.

Disoriented, I sat up, my limbs trembling uncontrollably, my mind still muddled with desire and my heart spilling out onto the floor.

Trying to get my bearings, I gulped and inhaled, mind scrambling to process what had just happened as his truck roared off into the night.

The man stole the fire when he went.

It left me cold and adrift.

Hurt.

Because what the hell? Kiss me? Touch me? Then just…walk out?

But the worst part was I was stuck there.

Floating hopelessly in his pain.

Lost to the misery of where Milo Hendricks lived.

Chapter Twenty

Milo

Nine years ago

MILO TREMORED WHERE HE SAT AGAINST THE WALL IN the murky shadows of the dingy hall. The shouts and cheers of the depraved echoed from the bowels of the basement.

He thought their greed had grown claws and sank into the concrete, chains that clanked and clanged, shackled to his bitter soul.

Holding him hostage.

He struggled for a breath and brought his blood-stained fists to his eyes.

The violence spent.

Another man beaten close to death.

The stench of the possibility hung fast to the sordid atmosphere.

It was what fed the morbidity. The barbarity and inhumanity that brought men here in droves.

And he prowled through it night after night, like a rabid beast in a cage.

He slammed his head back against the rough blocks like it could knock him out of the vengeful cycle that would never end.

The weight of it lessened a fraction when he felt the shift in the air.

The cool breeze of her presence.

"There you are," Autumn murmured as she neared.

He rolled his head to look at her, his heavy heart lightening at the sight. "Were you looking for me?"

A flirty smile edged the side of her mouth. "I'm always looking for you."

"Is that so?"

"Mm-hmm."

"Come here," he muttered, stretching out a hand as he straightened his legs out in front of him. Autumn didn't hesitate to straddle his lap.

Relief wafted around him like a summer breeze, and he exhaled as he curled his arms around her. "You shouldn't come here anymore."

She pulled back, studying his face in the wisping shadows that haunted this place. "Why not? This is where I found you, isn't it?"

She touched his face, her fingertips running over his lips. He took her hand and pressed it closer, the gentle kiss to her knuckles filled with devotion.

He wanted to take her away from this place.

Protect her from it.

Protect her from *him*.

"Still don't understand that," he muttered as he kept sweeping his lips along her knuckles.

She pulled back, care written in the curve of her brow, her brown eyes sincere. "How I could love you?"

His nod was hard.

She shook her head. "I loved you from the second I saw you."

"I think you just loved the idea of slummin' it with me to get back at your parents." He forced a grin, sick with the idea that it might be true.

Autumn frowned. "You know that's not true. Yeah, I came here that first night because I wanted to piss them off. Among a thousand other places I went that they would never have approved of. But it was here that I found *you*. And you are the reason I returned. The reason I stayed."

His chest stretched tight. "You'd do a hell of a lot better without me."

The lines on her pretty face deepened, and she sat up higher on her knees to hover over him. He tipped his head back so he could meet her stare, and she slipped her hand up his jaw until she was cupping his cheek.

So soft against all his hard.

"You don't have to listen to that voice inside your head anymore. He doesn't matter. You aren't worthless, and you don't have to prove anything to anyone."

She inhaled a desperate breath. "Your father can't hurt you, anymore. Can't hurt your mother. And he can't hurt *me*, either—not unless you let him. Not unless you give him that power and you push me away. We deserve each other, Milo. *You* are what matters. We are what matters."

"Autumn." It was a plea.

A plea for freedom.

A plea to be someone else.

Someone better.

"Let's leave this place, Milo. Let's leave and never come back."

"Need to have a way to support you."

God knew he didn't have anything else going for him.

At his response, her gaze dimmed.

She knew his reasons went so much darker than that.

That he fought for release.

To *prove* he was something. Someone to be feared. Something to be revered.

And now, he fought for Stefan. Other than his mom, he had been the one person who had believed in him. Picked him up and made him someone when he'd been little more than a kid.

Shown him he had value. Gave him a direction to channel the wrath.

He was indebted to him, but that debt had twisted itself into something morbid.

In the end, he'd only fostered what his father had bred in him.

A sickness there was no healing from.

Gore.

Both her hands came to frame his face. "You don't have to fight anymore, Milo. I don't need anything but you."

Thickness clotted his throat, and he reached out and ran his fingertips along the angle of her jaw, forcing out the confession, "I've only loved two people in my entire life...my mother...now you."

Tears blurred her brown eyes as she stared down at him. "Well, now you're going to have to love one more."

Fear curdled in the middle of him, all while hope came sprouting up through the rubble.

He touched her flat belly. "You sure?"

She nodded frantically before she flew forward and wrapped her arms around his neck, hugging him hard as she begged, "Let's leave and start something brand new. No more blood, Milo."

His arms curled around her, and he stood without letting her go. "Okay, baby. Let's go."

He knocked on the door outside Stefan's office in downtown San Francisco.

He kept his legitimate businesses here, the rest he'd brought to Milo's door.

"Come in."

Milo's chest tightened as he stepped inside.

Stefan studied him, his brow pinching at the look on Milo's face.

"Why do I get the feeling I'm not going to like the reason for this visit?"

Dread raced his throat, and he forced out the words. "Because I can't fight any longer."

Stefan scowled. "What do you mean, you can't fight?"

"It's time I moved on and did something honest with my life."

A scoff rolled from Stefan, and he eased forward in his executive chair. "Men like us don't do honest, Milo. Why do you think I picked you up and took you under my wing? Molded and shaped you into the man you are today? Because you are just like me, and you always will be."

"Maybe I don't want to be him anymore."

Eyeing Milo, Stefan rocked back in his chair. "I gave you everything. Laid every opportunity at your feet. You would be nothing without me."

A flare of hatred burst in Milo's spirit.

It'd started out that way. Stefan filling his head with promises, feeding into his wounds and into his pride.

But in the end, Stefan had just wanted to use him.

Use him for power.

For his greed.

For his twisted hungers that Milo hadn't recognized before it'd been too late.

He'd allowed himself to be led astray.

He knew it then.

"Autumn gave me more."

In an instant, Milo knew he shouldn't have admitted it.

Dark amusement played through Stefan's features. "So, this is about the girl."

"I'm leaving this life behind and starting a family."

Stefan grunted. "I am your family."

"Not anymore." Milo started for the door.

Stefan pushed to his feet.

"You owe me, Milo. Everything you have is because of me. Wherever you go, don't forget that. I created you. Made you. Own you. But I'll let you go. Because you need to see for yourself who you are. Because I love you like a son. You'll return when the time is right."

Milo held his scoff.

Stefan was delusional.

He was never coming back.

⁂

Milo clung to Autumn's hand where they stood outside her parents' mansion hidden in the woods.

Its pitched roof was so tall it became a fixture in the heavens, the grounds pristine and manicured.

Autumn's mother stood on the front porch since she refused to invite Milo inside. Disgust poured from her as she glowered at him. "What are you thinking, bringing this trash to my doorstep?"

Trash.

Milo fought the voices that stirred in his mind, and Autumn clung tighter to his hand like she could protect him from the ugliness that wanted to climb from the pit where he'd locked it away.

"Please, don't be like that, Mom. I love him."

Paula scoffed. "That's not love, Autumn. This is juvenile infatuation. I promise you'll come to your senses and get over it soon enough. Now, come inside where you belong."

"It's not infatuation. I love him. So much. We're getting married and having a baby."

Her mother blanched.

Her face stark white.

Horror bowed her back, and her hand darted out to grip onto the railing. "I won't stand for it."

"You don't have a say." Milo couldn't keep the words locked on his tongue, the sound of them close to savagery.

"The hell I don't. She's *my* daughter. *Mine.* And I won't let some lowlife swoop in and destroy her future."

"Mom," Autumn wheezed. "Please don't be this way."

"I'm only protecting you, Autumn. Don't you see your life has spiraled since you met him? You're going to amount to nothing if you stay with him."

Knives pierced his flesh, but he held the fury back.

"If that's what it means to be with him? Then so be it."

Autumn turned and started to drag him down the stairs.

Thank fuck, because Milo didn't think he could stay there for a second longer.

"You're going to regret this, Autumn," her mother shouted. She rushed down the steps behind them. "Don't do this. Please. If you walk away now, you're walking away from everything. You'll have nothing. Your bank account is gone. I'm warning you."

Didn't she know her daughter at all?

What she wanted from life?

Milo turned, his voice haggard and hard. "You don't have to like me, but I love your daughter, and I will protect her, fight for her, and take care of her forever."

Her nose curled and pained disbelief huffed from her mouth. "I doubt you know what that means."

⤲

A tiny giggle rippled from her lips, her smile pure adoration. "I know you better than you think I do, Milo Hendricks."

He could only smile back, propped on an elbow as he gazed down at her where she lay on their bed in the trailer on his land.

"Is that so?" he teased.

"Yup. I see it written all over you. I feel it in these hands." She ran her fingers over the calluses he'd gotten from building their cabin.

Their home.

Where they were going to raise their family.

He'd given his mother the other half of the money he'd saved during his years fighting, and she was having a house built on the property next to them.

Once the cabin was finished, he planned to start his own construction company.

Build their lives up with the strength of his hands.

Because Paula was wrong.

Stefan was wrong.

He would take care of his family, and he didn't need anyone else to do it.

"And I see it every time you look at me." Autumn ran her fingertip down the side of his face. "It's so very plain to see how much you love me."

He ran his hand over her swollen belly. His heart soared, and he touched her face. "More than you'll ever know. I promise you always, baby."

"Always," she whispered back.

Chapter Twenty-One

Milo

MY HAND CLAMPED DOWN TIGHTER ON THE STEERING wheel, my jaw locked in agony as I took the twisting mountain road. Night eclipsed me on all sides and pressed down in a crushing weight from above. The edge of the dense, thick forest that hugged the pavement barely lit in a blur as I passed.

I had no destination in mind. I just had to get the hell away from the regret that was tearing me limb from limb.

Away from the draw I could feel calling me back to where I'd walked out on Tessa like a total prick. No better than the fucker she'd finally gotten free of. Touching her like she was meant for me when I knew better than getting her involved in the dumpster fire that had been my life.

Getting her involved.

I scoffed.

What bullshit.

I'd sucked that girl in so deep I could feel her seeping into the fractures, bleeding into the cracks. Finding her way into the places I had to keep her from, though I'd been the fool who'd invited her in for a front-row seat.

Today, she'd gone and wrecked all my reserve.

I wasn't sure what I'd expected, but she'd gotten up and taken an active role.

She'd spent the day with my children like they'd become the most important thing in her life.

Made them feel alive and whole and cherished.

Safe.

And fuck, I guessed it was me who wasn't feeling so *safe* right then.

Every barrier and wall I'd constructed had been damaged. One more chink in them and they'd crumble at her feet.

My stomach fisted, and my dick pressed at my jeans.

I could still taste her on my lips. Could still smell her on my fingers. Could feel her all the way down in that spot that longed to be filled.

Every cell in my body was knotted in want.

That was bad enough.

But it was my stupid heart that was angling in a direction I couldn't let it go that had nausea curling through my stomach.

How in God's name could I know something was so damned wrong, so at odds with every promise I had made, and crave it like it might be the only thing that could sustain my next breath?

Guilt hurtled through my bloodstream, and I scrubbed a palm over my face like it could wake me from the nightmare.

Keep me from the demons that hunted.

Their howls in my ears screaming of what I'd done.

Thought maybe they'd physically manifested themselves in the glare of the headlights that blinded me from behind.

It'd taken me a minute to notice they'd come closer and closer with each tight turn my old truck had taken up the narrow, winding road.

A road that was normally deserted this time of night.

Squinting, I glanced in the rearview mirror, trying to get a take on who was riding my tail.

All I could make out was a large SUV.

Black.

Indistinct.

I slowed a bit to let the asshole pass.

Instead of going around, they edged even closer than before. Right up on my ass, so close that if I tapped my brakes they'd likely collide with the back of my truck.

A slosh of adrenaline dumped into my veins, and I inhaled around the disorder that began to pound.

Heart beating heavy.

Stoking this dread I felt slither through me as I looked out the side mirrors to gauge what was up.

Had seen enough trouble in my life to know when something was off. When evil had come to collect.

Karma had a way of rearing her ugly head in the moments you'd begun to hope for something different. When you'd been fool enough to hope for something better after you'd already carved out the consequences years before.

Your destruction written in time.

I'd been the fool to go and let hope spark like sunshine in my mind.

Warmth to my life.

I tapped my brakes.

Fucker drifted into the other lane, and he gunned it, coming up to my side before he slammed back on his brakes and whipped back behind me.

"Shit." My heart sped.

Violence whispered in my ear. I tried to stuff it down.

Focus.

Whoever this piece of shit was, he was here for me.

No question about it.

It wasn't too hard to guess who wasn't my biggest fan right about then.

Had known when I'd knocked the bastard out there'd likely be retribution to pay, but I'd gladly pay it a thousand times if it got Tessa safely out of that house.

If it showed her that she had someone there fighting for her, too.

Wanted her to know she wasn't alone, and she didn't have to stay there and take his bullshit anymore.

I just didn't know how far he would push it or the lengths he would go.

No question that the dickhead was slime. Hell, he was the sludge at the bottom of the barrel.

All shiny and pretty on the outside, completely foul on the inside.

I increased my speed, taking the next curve fast, my old truck roaring in the night. The dashed line in the middle of the road blurred into one stripe as the forest swished by on either side.

He accelerated. The glare of his headlights became blinding.

My entire body jolted forward when he knocked into my fender, hard enough for the impact to rattle through the truck, but not enough to send me into a tailspin.

Violence throbbed and pulsed, boiling up from the chasm where I tried to keep it contained. Where it seethed and swelled and festered and became something every bit as disgusting as the dickhead eating up my tail.

My heart thundered as I struggled to keep my mind clear.

He rammed me again. Harder this time. Enough that the back of my truck swerved with the impact.

And there was nothing I could do.

Aggression broke free of the barriers, jumping into my veins like a mask. A cloak of violence that couldn't be contained.

Slamming on my brakes, I skidded off to the side of the road, though there wasn't enough room to get my truck completely off. I braced myself because he was so close I knew there was no chance that he could stop himself.

He crashed into me hard.

Metal screeched and tore, and my truck was forced forward, both of our tires squealing as we came to a shuddering stop.

I didn't hesitate.

Didn't think.

I was out of my truck and striding toward the blacked-out SUV that had careened to a stop sideways about ten feet behind me.

I only paused long enough to dip my hand into the bed of my truck so I could grab the bat I kept bungeed to the side.

I stormed that way, lifting it and smashing it into his windshield.

Asshole was going to learn fast he'd fucked with the wrong person. He didn't have the first clue who he was dealing with.

Because I felt myself slip over the edge.

Control gone.

Tripping me back to the place where there was only violence and brutality.

Where vengeance meant survival.

Where savagery meant you had another day.

Darkness enclosed like a heavy blanket. The glare of the vehicles' headlights that speared at odd directions was the only glow that broke the night, so there was no making anything out, thanks to the broken windshield and the tinted glass.

"Come on, motherfucker." I drew the bat down on his hood. "Let's see what you've got."

Both front doors plus the back driver's side opened, and three men climbed out.

Masked and wielding pipes.

Menace in their stance and bloodlust in their bones.

"Shit," I mumbled under my breath.

Wasn't like I had never been outnumbered before. On the receiving end of a match that hadn't been stacked in my favor.

Maybe I was the fool who'd thought this prick would come alone, that he'd stand up and fight his own battles.

Clearly not the case. Should've anticipated he was a straight-up pussy.

I went for the driver, swinging my bat wide the second he cleared the door. He dodged it, but he went to my right just like I knew he would. I threw a punch that direction, clocking him in the jaw.

He stumbled left and slammed into the opened door of the SUV.

The fucker behind him came at me. He swung his rod.

I jumped back as the metal whizzed through the air, the end of it missing me by an inch.

He kept swinging, forcing me back, while the third came around the front of the SUV to box me in.

Before I could get around to head him off, the guy behind me swung.

His rod cracked across the middle of my back.

Pain splintered down my spine, fracturing out like a web of agony.

A guttural roar ripped up my mouth.

It only amplified the fury.

The need to destroy.

I spun, swinging at the same time, slamming the asshole in the ribs.

A wail tore out of him, and the fucker bent in two.

I whirled back around, going for the second, only the first was back on his feet.

The two of them enclosed on my left and right.

As soon as they got close enough, I swung the bat, hitting the guy on my right in the shoulder.

At the same time, the one on the left got in a brutal hit to my side.

Another, then another.

Agony blasted through my bones.

I let loose.

Throwing fists.

Kicking.

Fighting with all I had.

I nailed the piece of shit on the left and sent him flying back before I spun and slammed two fists into the face of the fucker on the right.

Grunts and a barrage of curses filled the air.

I fought the three of them with all I had.

Blood poured as skin busted open.

Bones cracked.

"Fuck you, you piece of shit," I roared, never backing down.

Because I was fighting for Tessa.

But I was losing hope that I was going to come out on top.

I had plenty of experience, but this?

It was a coordinated attack.

The men trained.

Hired.

Of that, I was sure.

Karl, that sleazy fuck, had taken his offense to the extreme.

The men took the blows, and they returned them as savagely as I gave them.

I doubted much they were anticipating the fight they were gonna get, though.

Surprised at what they stepped into.

They weren't getting out of this unscathed, but I was losing footing.

Strength.

Each blow nearly dropping me to my knees.

A crack landed at the side of my head.

A flash of metal.

A strike inflicted with purpose.

Just hard enough for pain to go splitting through my brain and to drop me to the ground, but not hard enough to do me in.

I gasped for air, trying to get my bearings, to stand up and finish this.

But before I could get to my feet, one of the pricks ran up and kicked me in the gut.

I dropped to the pitted pavement, facedown, groaning in agony.

Two more strikes landed on my upper back.

Blackness clawed at the edges of my sight.

Consciousness faded in and out.

"Tell that asshole he's a pussy for me, would you? Sending three of you," I rasped, delirium setting in. I tried to stand again before I was dropped flat with an elbow to my temple. Then a mouth was at my ear, a low warning that tolled, cutting into the oblivion with a blade of wickedness.

"You didn't think you were going to get off that easy, did you? Did you think he wouldn't come to collect? And he will collect."

Footsteps receded, and tires screeched as the SUV was thrown in reverse before it took off in the opposite direction as we'd come.

While I lay there in the middle of the pavement with harsh, agonized breaths wheezing through my throat.

As a true sort of terror took me hostage and dragged me under.

20

I staggered into the darkness of my cabin, groaning like a bitch and heading straight for the cabinet.

I pulled out a bottle of Jack, opened it, and chugged down three giant gulps, welcoming the fire that raced down my throat and landed in a pool of relief in my stomach.

Glass clattered on the countertop as I fumbled to set it down, and I clung to the neck of it while my head dropped forward.

I had my other hand pressed to my side like it could keep it all from hemorrhaging out.

"Motherfucker," I rumbled, trying to catch my breath.

The pain didn't have a thing on the rage that bristled and blew like a dark storm at the edges of my sight.

Uncertainty tugged me in every direction.

It couldn't be.

It couldn't.

I'd hunted that motherfucker for years.

He was dead.

Dead.

It had to be Karl taking things to the extreme, but it was the man's parting words that kept repeating in my mind.

Torment twisted through my being, and it didn't have a thing to do with the fact that I'd been beaten to shit.

Guilt laying siege.

My intentions skewed.

My reserves depleted.

It didn't help that Tessa had my emotions all fucked up.

I chugged down more whiskey.

Delirium seemed like a mighty fine plan right then.

Every promise I had made screamed in my ear.

Always.

Always.

I stilled when I felt her approach from behind.

I almost laughed.

Of course, she'd come to me right then.

Taunting.

Tempting.

Tiny Tease.

I had no clue how to deal with her.

What to fucking say after the shit that had gone down tonight.

Wariness billowed through the air, and I could physically feel her hurt.

The hurt I'd inflicted.

But this was Tessa we were talking about, and rather than telling me to go fuck myself, there was something riding on the current that was kind.

Genuine.

Radiating all that sweet, sweet light that I didn't deserve to feel.

The girl the sun rising on a darkened day.

God, I didn't know if I wanted to weep and hold onto her with the little strength I had left or tell her to run. To get the fuck out of my house and never look back before it was too late.

Before I completely lost it.

Before she realized who I really was.

"Milo, are you okay?" she whispered through the lapping shadows, and I thought it was just then she realized I wasn't in a good state.

She eased forward another step.

Energy snapped in the air.

She touched my shoulder. "Milo?"

I fumbled around to face her.

She gasped, and both hands flew to her face. "Holy shit! What happened to you? Oh my God! Oh my God!"

She started flapping her hands all over.

Spastic.

Frantic.

"Oh no, Milo."

In a frenzy, she blinked. "I'll call an ambulance. Right. Yes. An ambulance."

She started to dart back for her room.

"Don't you dare."

She whirled around, shrieking at the same time, "You're bleeding!"

She had no idea the blood I'd shed.

"I'm fine."

A frown curled her adorable brow, and she slowed, swallowing, still looking like she might pass out at the sight of me. "Who did this?"

"It's fine," I grumbled.

She opened her fingers enough that she could peek at me through them. "It's not fine. Please tell me Karl didn't do this."

Funny how she didn't want it to be him, and I was praying it was.

That asshole would be so much easier to deal with.

"Don't know. Three guys jumped me."

"Oh, God," she whimpered, and she looked around like she was searching for an answer before her attention returned to me, her voice curdled with disbelief. "Please let me call an ambulance."

I lifted the bottle. "I have everything I need right here."

I tipped it to my mouth, my sights set on draining it.

Oblivion.

It's what I needed.

That or her touch, and that was something I'd be a bastard to take.

I'd already proven that earlier.

I let the bottle fall to my side, dangling it by the neck.

From where she stood halfway across the room, I stared at her silhouette.

At her care.

At this woman who was going to do me in.

It didn't matter that one of my eyes was almost completely swollen shut. That I could hardly make her out. She was the most gorgeous thing I'd ever seen. "Just go, Tessa."

Worry split through her features. "Do you really think I'm going to walk out on you, Milo? Do you really think that's who I am? Because I don't walk out on my friends, not when they need me."

Chapter Twenty-Two

Tessa

HORROR HELD ME CAPTIVE AS I LOOKED AT MILO FROM halfway across the room.

Dread and sickness a spiked ball that I swallowed, ripping up my throat and tearing holes in my stomach.

I felt…shattered.

Shattered at the sight of Milo who'd been shattered, too.

Physically, and in a bad, bad way.

Blood saturated his white T-shirt that was ripped at the side. What wasn't red was soiled with dirt and debris. He had an oozing gash at his temple, the blood dried and sticky where it'd trailed down his cheek and into his beard. His right eye was so swollen it was merely a slit.

My sweet mountain man was a mangled mess.

But I thought it might have been his heart that'd been battered the most. That broken crown mangled where it barely clung to his head.

His spirit was this darkened veil that murmured of secrets and atrocity.

His pain and guilt at touching me.

I wanted to wipe it from his being.

But it was my own guilt that threatened to suffocate. The proof of what I'd dragged him into.

Hatred burned through my being, infiltrating every fiber.

Karl was a monster.

A disgusting pig.

His pathetic ego so vile and inflated that he would stoop to this.

I eased back Milo's direction.

Energy flashed. Strikes of electricity that zapped in the night.

I tried to protect myself against it, against the memories of Milo having me propped on the island that were so vivid I had to grind my teeth to keep from moaning.

His kisses still alive on my tongue.

His touch still trembling through my body.

"Tessa," he warned. I thought the man might be so in tune with me that he'd read every sordid, beautiful thought that had traipsed through my mind.

"Let me take care of you," I murmured as I reached out to pry the bottle from his fingers that he seemed set on emptying.

I set it on the counter, trying to find composure and balance, my tongue swiping my bottom lip as I steadied myself to look back at his marred face.

Pain hit me again.

God, how could Karl be so cruel? So vicious?

I wrapped my shaking hand around his. "Come with me."

"You don't have to—"

"Please." Reservations curled deep in the lines of his face, but he finally nodded and gave, threading his fingers through mine.

Relief pummeled me when he did, that connection coursing through our touch.

I slowly led him into his room.

Everything about it was as masculine as the man. That enormous bed and the chunky, rustic furniture, his pride in the pictures of his children that he had displayed all over.

There were a couple that were of him and his mother, and damn it, that was sweet, too.

Milo was a dichotomy of rough and soft. Menacing and sweet.

I forced myself not to get too wrapped up in it as I continued through to the ensuite bathroom.

I flicked on the light, and we blinked against the intrusion.

"Fuck," he rumbled.

My eyes widened all over again, and my stomach dropped to the floor.

Nausea boiled, my heart aching in a way that I couldn't process.

"I'm thinking *fuck* is about the correct description right about now." The words were splinters of distress.

In the light, it became apparent bruises were welling all over his body.

His skin blackened and abraded, his arms scraped and oozing, his face blemished by the violent attack.

Biting down hard on the side of my cheek, I fought the tears that burned at the back of my eyes. "I'm so sorry. I can't believe he did this to you."

Milo shifted in unease, though he was guarding, an arm wrapped around his ribs protectively.

But it was me who wanted to be doing the protecting.

I wanted to stand for him.

Fight for him.

Hold him.

Love him.

God, I'd gotten in so deep.

"We don't even know if it was him who was responsible, Tessa."

"How couldn't it be? I mean, I asked you to go over there with me, and then you hit him, and then he was so mad when he showed up at my office, even though it was completely that jerk's fault. Of course, it's him," I ranted.

I tried to distract myself by opening the cabinet below his sink and rummaging around for a clean washcloth, the whole time fighting the vicious vibrating in my chest.

"I can't even believe he could do this," I continued through the torment. "I knew Karl was a total asshole. I mean, a giant, huge, gaping asshole, but I never imagined he would stoop this low. I should have known it. God, I should have known he's a monster. This is my fault."

"Either way, I had it coming. Instant karma."

A tear slipped free when I blinked. "Don't say that, Milo. You think you could possibly deserve this?"

For kissing me?

For touching me?

I nearly gagged that he considered it such a sin.

But I'd already known his heart was in tatters. His ace played. He had nothing left for me. I'd been begging for the pain thinking there might be a chance.

My hands were shaking like crazy as I stood and ran the washcloth under warm water.

Milo reached out and stopped my frantic movements. "If it was him? I'd gladly stand between him and you time and again," he rumbled.

My throat nearly closed off, and tears started streaming free. "I can't stand the idea of you getting hurt for me."

"Would die for you, Tessa. Kill for you. Destroy what threatens you. Already told you that."

"You shouldn't have to," I croaked. "We need to go to the police."

Hesitation warred through his being. "Don't think I can risk that right now."

I blew out a frustrated sigh, one he took as my fear.

Ferocity wound into his features, and his hold tightened on my wrist. "I don't know what that bastard is capable of, Tessa, but I won't let him get to you."

"So, what, you're just going to take the beating for me?"

Rage blistered in the air, and his strong jaw snapped shut, the words hissed between his teeth. "There will be no beating when it comes to you, Tessa. He touches you, he dies."

I blinked through the confusion. Through the sudden disorder that whipped through the bathroom. How could he feel so intensely when he looked at me like I was a transgression?

A mistake?

"Let's not get carried away now." I tried to make a joke because come on, he wasn't serious.

"You think I'm playing, Tessa? Know you see me a certain way, but I'm not a good man." His low voice cracked on the warning.

Apprehension unfurled, as cold as ice, skating up from our connection point and spreading through me like a bad dream.

My mind raced to the company he kept.

Trent, Jud, and Logan.

I knew what they were capable of.

Somehow, I'd never associated Milo with that kind of brutality.

I sucked for a breath, tried to smile and pretend the grimness that swallowed the room in foreboding wasn't alive and real. "What do you mean?"

"It means bad things have a way of landing themselves at my door."

"Me?"

He breathed out a pained sound. "No, Little Dove. Not you. But you need to know Karl isn't close to being my only enemy."

The atmosphere thickened, his eyes flaming with something I knew he didn't want to feel.

I tried to swallow around the fullness of it, holding my breath like it could keep this need that glowed within shrouded as I moved forward and carefully reached up to dab the warm washcloth against the cut at his temple.

He winced, though he kept watching me like he was terrified of being close to me and wanted to erase the bare space that thrummed between us at the same time.

I struggled to focus on what I was doing, but my attention kept slanting back to the intensity that burned from his gaze.

"I don't believe that you're bad, Milo Hendricks. I know things, remember?" I tried to inject some lightness into it.

Casualness.

But there wasn't a single thing casual about this moment.

"That's because you don't really know me, Little Dove."

I feel you.

I see you.

I know you just by being in your space.

I peeked at him as I kept gently pressing the cloth to his face. "Would you let me know you? If I asked you to?"

His mouth tipped down at the side. "I let Autumn go there, and it destroyed her."

I hated myself for the flame of jealousy that lapped through my consciousness, and I knew this crush was no longer just a crush.

It'd likely never been.

It'd been distorted by my twisted loyalty to Karl.

And now that my spirit was freed, it gushed toward what it wanted.

I moved to dab at the small cut at the corner of his swollen eye, my intentions wrong, razors that I felt slash through the atmosphere. "You're still in love with her."

He let go of a brittle sound, his response cutting us both in two. "I'm the reason she's dead."

I froze.

His response answered nothing but only bred a million questions.

Torment clotted his words. "Because I was too late. Too reckless. Too fuckin' ignorant to see what was happening."

"I—"

"Fuck," he spat, spinning away.

He set both hands on the countertop, and he bent over, trying to catch his breath, or maybe he was just wishing he could reel the confession back in.

"Milo—"

"Just leave it." His voice was raw.

I blinked, unsure of what to do, and my eyes wandered down his back, over his tattered, shredded shirt and the gnarly wounds that were visible underneath.

"I think you need a doctor, Milo."

"I don't."

"You might have—"

He lifted his battered face to glare at me through the mirror. "I don't, Tessa."

A war tore through me. Finally, I stepped forward. "Then at least let me help you get cleaned up."

He blew out a strained breath as his head slumped between his shoulders, the words coarse as they scraped into the heavy air. "You should go. Forget everything I got you wrangled into."

Mine was a confession. "I don't think that I can. Your kids…"

Agony blazed through his expression. "What if they're better off with Paula and Gene? What if I'm being selfish, trying to get them back? What if I'm only going to end up hurting them in the end?"

"No."

It was a promise.

My oath.

"You're wrong if you think you're not what's right for them. I saw it in all three of you yesterday, Milo. You belong together."

Somberness moaned through the atmosphere.

But something else hit it, too, when he slowly turned around.

Something fierce.

Unrelenting.

Powerful.

He looked down at me, all the intense angles of his face held in restraint, his eyes drenched with the fears and hurt he didn't have an answer to.

"You have to fight for this, Milo. With all your strength. With all your love. With everything you have."

His brow slashed in severity. "And what if letting them go is the best thing I can do to show my love for them?"

I pushed forward, my voice twisted in the hope I had for him. "Is that what your heart tells you? That they'd be better off without you?"

His thick throat bobbed beneath his beard when he swallowed. "No. It's tellin' me to fight. To protect. To give them the life that Autumn and I had dreamed of giving them before we lost her."

"Then that's what you do."

"It might be ugly, Tessa." It rang with a dark warning. "And still, after everything, you want to stand by my side?"

"I've never been surer of anything. I know it might be ugly. You already told me, and I already accepted it. But sometimes, we have to make it through the ugliness to find the beauty on the other side. Now, we need to get you undressed."

I said it like it was no big deal.

Like the thought of getting this man naked had never crossed my mind.

Ragged breaths pumped through my lungs, and my tongue stroked out to wet my dried lips as I slowly knelt in front of him.

He towered over me. A fortress that had been battered but still remained standing.

More ominous than ever.

It felt like some of the secrets he'd tried to keep disguised had been lifted to reveal the darkness that writhed beneath.

Milo exhaled a shaky breath. "And sometimes, the sun rises when you least expect it."

The words were low. Riddled with a dark affection.

My chest stretched so tight I was struggling to breathe as I fumbled through the laces on his boots. I worked to get them loose, then struggled to get the giant things free of Milo's massive feet.

Tension pulled between us. Growing as an acute silence poured into the confined space. I could feel the heat of his gaze.

It only amplified when I finally got his socks off, then slowly climbed to my feet.

The air ripped from my lungs, stolen at the sight of him, at the way he watched me as I stepped forward so I could remove his shirt.

His strong jaw clenched tight, his eyes creased at the corners as if he were frozen in restraint.

My fingers curled around the fabric, and I slowly, carefully began to pull it up.

A grunt left his mouth, and I whimpered when I saw the magnitude of his injuries.

His abdomen was covered in blackened patches where bruises blossomed.

His skin scraped and abraded.

His side was seeping with a deep cut.

What had my chest clutching was the recognition that not all the injuries were new.

Milo was littered in scars.

I guessed I hadn't been close enough to see him those times when he was outside working without a shirt.

They were unmistakable now.

Some jagged and knotted and gnarled.

Others deep, long slashes where it looked like he'd been carved.

"Oh, Milo," I mumbled as my spirit wept.

"I've had worse, Little Dove."

How, and to still be standing?

He took over for me when I'd made it up to his armpits, and he groaned as he lifted his arms to pull it the rest of the way over his head.

Maybe I shouldn't have let them, but my eyes raced, devouring every exposed inch of him.

His shoulders massive and muscled, his arms solid, his chest so freaking wide.

Most of his flesh was covered in ink.

Designs that whispered of beauty against the darkness that reigned underneath.

The scars were woven into the images as if the sum of them had made up his life.

Along his side was one word.

Written on him like a brand.

Gore.

Gulping, I struggled for clarity.

Sanity.

Control.

Something other than this dangerous path I was taking.

Milo had already proven he didn't want to go there with me, but there was no stopping it.

That train had already left the station.

Barreling ahead as my attention raked down to the flat, chiseled planes of his cut abdomen. This area was barren of tattoos and completely ripped.

And holy jeez, that V-cut that dipped below the waist of his jeans was even more defined.

I tried to swallow.

The man was hotter than Hades.

Rugged and hard.

Beautiful Beast.

He never looked away when his fingers went to the buttons of his jeans. He ticked through his fly, then carefully pushed the jeans down, bending just enough that he could shrug them all the way down and off his feet.

Milo straightened.

I nearly fainted.

What was even happening?

Was I dreaming?

Coma by orgasm?

Because the man stood there in nothing but these tight black briefs that came down to the top of his thick, muscled thighs, and he was staring at me like he was daring me to look.

He was hard.

So hard and giant he was nearly bursting out of his underwear, the shape of him forever immortalized in the thin fabric and emblazoned in my mind.

It turned out my fantasies had erred on the side of pathetic when it came to Milo Hendricks.

An offense to all that he was.

No justice at all.

"Not supposed to want you, Tessa." Agony twisted out with the rough words.

Oh, no.

This poor, wonderful man.

But I got the sense he was begging me to run and pleading with me to stay.

Something flared in his gaze.

"Want you to suck me, Tessa."

I was pretty sure my eyes bugged out of my skull.

So blunt.

"You're hurt."

And you don't want me but you kind of do, and I think all of this is a really terrible idea that I want to try out, anyway.

"And I think you might be the only thing in this world that could make me feel good."

"Is that what you want? For me to touch you?" I managed some shaky version of what he'd asked me earlier tonight, when the man had undone me in the span of two minutes, then left me questioning every convoluted emotion I felt.

Half the night I'd spent toiling in bed until I'd finally heard his truck return at close to four this morning.

Now, dawn threatened around us. The quieted, slowed hour that dripped into a new day.

Pregnant with possibility.

Or maybe it was only ripe with reckless ideas.

"I've wanted that sweet mouth wrapped around my cock since the second I saw you. How many times I've imagined you on your knees for me, Little Dove."

I dropped to them like I had no strength left.

Compelled.

Arousal burned across his flesh.

The way his pained breaths had turned jagged with want.

Stepping forward, he brushed the pad of his thumb along my jaw, inciting a frenzy in me so intense it quivered all the way to my bones. Then he was running his thumb over my lips, back and forth, and my nerves were firing all over the place.

"Are you going to let me fuck that mouth?"

"You can have any part of me that you want."

I knew it was true.

Possession flashed through his expression, and my hands shook out of control when I rose higher on my knees and dipped my fingers into the band of his underwear. Those shakes turned into straight up tremors as I carefully drew them down his legs, setting his penis free.

It bobbed up high on his stomach.

My belly twisted, and I was pressing my thighs together as a new-found desire throbbed like a life beat at my center.

He was thick and fat and so freaking long, and the air was getting locked somewhere on the way out of my lungs.

Honestly, I had no clue what to do with that thing.

But I wanted it.

I wanted it deep and everywhere, and I was pretty sure Milo knew it because his hand fisted in my hair, his warning a low desperation when he growled, "You'd be better off if you didn't take to looking at me like that."

"You act like I can stop," I whispered as I reached up and wrapped my hand around the base of him.

My spirit trembled, and my heart raced, a drum, drum, drumming that pummeled my ribs.

His hand twitched in my hair, the man so gorgeous where he towered over me. Every hulking muscle in his body was tense, bristling with strength.

"Don't fall for me, Tessa."

"Don't worry, Milo, it's just fake, remember?"

"Is it? I think you're a liar, Little Dove."

I figured we both were.

I leaned forward and licked him from base to tip, riding up to the fat, swollen head of him.

I gently kissed the tip.

His stomach flexed as he jolted forward. "Tiny Tease."

I ran my tongue over the slit, wondering exactly who I'd become when I found myself relishing the salty taste of the precum that leaked from his dick.

Awed that my freedom was here.

That this was no longer chains or obligation.

It was only the truth that Milo wanted me, and I wanted him, no matter what faulty bargain we'd come to. The terms that it would end.

The only thing that counted in this single moment was *this*. This broken man who needed to be touched. One who thought himself wicked when I was sure he might be the best man I'd ever met.

I curled my lips around his head, applying the smallest amount of pressure, before I flicked my tongue over the little notch at the base.

Milo hissed, and his hand curled tighter in my hair, the muscles in his abdomen flexing in greed. "Are you playing with me?"

The threat of a smile pulled at my lips, and I whispered against his tip, "Never."

I sucked him deep. As far as I could take him, my lips stretched so wide around him that I was having a hard time not using my teeth.

Milo grunted. "Yes, baby, just like that. That mouth...knew it was going to be my ruin."

I tightened my hand at the base, stroking him in time with my mouth because there was no chance I could take all of him.

I rode him back to his head, sucking before I gave him another good lick.

Milo grumbled and shook. "Fuck me, Little Dove."

His hips began to rock, pulsing deeper and deeper with each stroke.

My body glowed with want. With the perfection of giving him what he needed. Of touching this man in a way I'd wanted to touch him for what felt like forever. Like maybe I'd been coming up on this moment for my entire life.

Yeah.

I was so going to get my heart broken.

I knew it, the way emotion gathered and swept and gusted through me in an unrelenting force as I twisted this man up in oblivion.

In ecstasy.

I could feel it in the sheen of bliss that built across his beautiful body.

He moaned as his hips began to snap.

I felt it the second he let go.

When he drove himself into my mouth as deep as I could take him.

Milo came with a roar.

With a thunder that pounded the room as he pulsed and jerked, pouring into my throat.

He held me by the back of the head while I swallowed him down.

I led him through his orgasm before I slowly eased him out of my mouth, and the man had me by the chin, forcing me to meet his gaze.

This battered man who looked like chaos. A perfect disorder. A flawless tragedy.

My Beautiful Beast.

"You are better than I ever could have imagined," he murmured.

Emotion clogged my throat. "I liked it, pleasing you."

His thumb swept over my swollen lips. "Nothing's ever felt so good as you."

The second he said it, I could see the guilt that streaked through his expression.

"I guess it might have been a good distraction." I forced a weak smile.

He blinked, so soft. "That's exactly what you are, Little Dove. A perfect distraction, and I'm afraid I'm gonna lose sight."

"And what if I can help you see?"

Another bout of regret.

Right.

My attention dropped to the floor as my stomach got tangled in his guilt.

His hand returned to my hair, tugging my face back up to meet the ferocity in his. "Last thing I want to do is hurt you."

An awkward, self-deprecating smile pulled at the edge of my mouth. "I think it's likely too late for that. But I'll take whatever time I have with you."

I just threw it out there.

My heart tossed at his feet.

Reservations held his tongue, and when he didn't say anything else, I blew out a sigh and pushed to my feet. Turning away from him, I went to his shower and turned on the showerhead, and I stood there while it warmed.

Steam began to fill the room.

"You need to get in and get those cuts cleaned. I'm going to get you some ibuprofen."

He gave a slight nod, the man completely bare as he eased toward me.

My pulse got all erratic and thready again.

He came up right to my side, and his hand spread over my left cheek while his mouth came to my right temple. "Thank you. For taking care of me."

"I told you before that I wanted to be there for you."

"Because that's what friends do?" There was an edge to it.

God, I felt lost. Teetering on unknown ground.

I swallowed around the rock lodged at the base of my throat. "Yeah, because that's what friends do."

He stepped into the spray and shut the door, and I darted out into the main room.

Trying to catch my breath.

Or my sanity, really.

My self-preservation.

Because really, Tessa McDaniels, what the hell do you think you're doing?

I kept tossing myself at him, begging him to break me.

I inhaled a shaky breath, and I moved into the dimly lit kitchen. I rummaged around in the cabinet where he kept his medicines. I found the bottle of ibuprofen, and I shook out four because I knew he might be tough, but no man was immortal.

I ran a glass under the faucet, then I had to steel myself all over again when I crept back to his room.

He was already shutting off the shower when I got back inside. The shower door clicked open, and he grabbed for the towel that hung on the rack.

He wrapped it around his waist, the man wet when he stepped out.

Droplets dripped from his long, black hair and down into his beard, and he had streams of glittering rivulets running down his marred chest.

Gah, why did he have to be so everything?

"Here you go," I whispered as I eased forward. He tossed all four of them back and chugged the water.

"Are you sure you don't need to go to the ER?" I chanced again.

"Think I got all the medicine I needed."

Right.

Blow jobs saved lives.

"Let me at least bandage the cut on your temple."

"Okay."

I was almost surprised that he agreed, and he sat down on the edge of the bathtub like a good little patient.

I tried to hold my breath as I gathered the bandages and ointment from the medicine cabinet.

I wasn't sure I could handle more of him.

His aura that'd turned haunting yet hummed with want.

A dark, glowing amber that I could almost feel slipping through my veins.

He kept slanting his gaze up at me as I applied the ointment with a Q-Tip, then carefully placed the butterfly bandage on his temple.

So attuned.

So right.

"There."

He gave me a tight nod, then stood.

Warily, I backed away.

He flicked off the bathroom light, and I made a beeline for his bedroom door.

I whimpered when he looped one of his giant arms around my front, yanking me back against his chest. His mouth came to my ear, a low roll of seduction. "Stay with me tonight. I don't want to be alone."

My eyes squeezed tight.

I should hightail my ass right out of there.

Stop this thing that neither of us understood.

My spirit ached.

Because I wanted it.

To be there for him when he needed me.

I nodded, letting this man, who was going to do me in, lead me to his bed.

He lifted the covers. "In you go, Little Dove."

There he was, back to all that softness he wore at the club.

The quiet protector.

The gentle monster.

He moved across the room to his dresser and opened a drawer just as he dropped his towel.

I forced myself to stare at the ceiling as he pulled on a fresh pair of underwear, but I couldn't look away when I felt the tremoring of the ground when he slowly edged back toward the bed.

My breaths turned shallow.

His big body filled the space.

Intimidating and rough and overpowering.

The bed creaked when he crawled onto the mattress.

A tremor rocked me when he tucked my back to his chest, the two of us lying on our sides.

Silence stretched long, both satisfying and insufficient.

"Wish I had my heart to give you, Tessa. Peace. Safety," he finally murmured into the dense air.

I clutched at his big hand he had stretched out over the booming in my chest. "I don't need your heart, Milo."

And I was sure, as I drifted to sleep in his arms, that it was the greatest lie I'd ever told.

Chapter Twenty-Three

Milo

"WHAT IN THE WORLD DO YOU THINK YOU'RE DOING?" A fiery ball of red came streaking out the back door, full of steam and lookin' like the best kind of fantasy.

Stealing my breath and sanity, because clearly, I had lost my goddamn head.

She came bounding down the porch steps, barefoot, hair wild and her stunning face glowing, girl still wearing those sleep shorts and tank she'd had on last night when she'd climbed down onto her knees and blown my mind.

I arched a brow at her from where I was leaned over the worktable measuring a 2x4, and I ran a pencil along the ruler to mark my cut. "Working."

She came to a stop on the other side of the table, a hand propped on her hip, sass flying from her mouth. "Um, yes, I see that, and you got beaten to a pulp last night. Are you insane? You cannot be out here working today."

She flung a hand in the direction of the wood I was measuring.

A grumble of a laugh left me.

She was fucking cute when she was mad. Hell, she was cute all the time.

Asleep in my bed with all that hair around her.

In my arms and making these tiny noises while she was lost to a dream.

On her knees with my cock in her mouth.

You pick.

"I'm fine."

"You're not fine. You should be in a hospital right now."

My head shook, and I focused on getting the line just right, mumbling, "Best way to heal from something like this is just gettin' up and moving. You sit still too long, and your muscles seize up."

On a huff, she crossed her arms over her chest. "You're going to make it worse."

"I'm not."

Ocean eyes caught me up, her demeanor shifting like she was seeing the scars written on me anew.

This girl, nothing but a riptide.

Unexpected.

Everything I hadn't anticipated.

Everything I shouldn't want.

"And I'm guessing you know this from experience?"

Her eyes drifted over my shoulders and chest that were now concealed by a tee. But she'd seen it plain last night, all because I was a fool who couldn't stop from exposing myself.

I'd wanted to take something good for a minute when I'd been sure I was going to succumb to the bad.

"Fighting is in my blood, Little Dove." The admission barely made it into the air as I leaned down to guide the 2x4 through the table saw. The engine whirred and the blade spun, and the sound of the wood grinding in two didn't stand the chance of blocking out the questions that flared from her.

The plank broke apart, and I let go of the button. The sawblade spun slower and slower, quieting to her soft intensity that was rippling between us like shockwaves.

"You're the gentlest man I know, Milo." There was a question behind it.

A scoff got free. "That's bridled anger, Tessa. That's me keeping who I am under lock and key."

"Maybe they're both part of who you are."

I grunted. "You keep trying to see someone you want me to be."

"Maybe I like everything I see."

My gaze snapped up. Damn it, I never should have given in yesterday. Touched her. All but demanded for her to touch me.

Because that energy sparked in the air.

Shocking between the two of us.

Lust and greed and something far more dangerous than either of them.

"Think it best if we don't go there," I warned low.

Her eyes narrowed. "Sorry to break it to you, Milo, but I think we already did."

I heaved out a sigh as I started to organize the pieces of wood I'd cut for the rest of the treehouse ceiling.

My side burned like a bitch, every inch of my body in the clutches of an unrelenting ache, insides spiking with sharp shocks of pain that sheared through me as I pushed through every movement.

I ignored it because I did know from experience.

Moving was the only way I was going to make it through the day.

How many matches had I been in that I'd been beaten to within an inch of my life, then had to jump right back into the ring the next night?

I didn't get there from lying around moaning, that was for damned sure.

She kept watching me, waiting for a response, the weight of her stare ten-thousand pounds on my back.

"We shouldn't have," I finally rumbled.

"I think we're of two differing opinions."

Turning my back on her didn't seem to work because her voice kept coming at me from behind.

"Because the way I see it, I think you really want me, and you're just trying to pretend like you don't. I mean, have you seen me?"

She pushed out one of those teases she usually played, except when I shifted to look at her from over my shoulder, there was nothing remotely comical on her face.

It was just the hope cut in the stark angles of her gorgeous face.

Cheeks flushed and that smattering of freckles striking in the rays of light.

My chest tightened.

A red-headed flame.

The sun rising on a darkened day.

"Never said I didn't want you."

"Then take me." She said it so simply. "Let's see where this goes."

Autumn's face flashed through my mind.

Every oath that I had made.

I promise you always, baby.

Always.

I squeezed my eyes as guilt came stabbing through, as gory as a slasher flick.

I propped my hands on my hips and turned away like it could keep Tessa from seeing the corruption that clawed through my spirit.

I roughed a frustrated hand through my hair.

I felt her move slowly.

Caution and care.

She must have been two feet away from me when she whispered, "Talk to me. I'm right here."

Agony cleaved me in two, and I gulped around the sorrow as I let go of a little bit of myself. "I haven't been with anyone since she died, Tessa. Haven't touched anyone. Kissed anyone. Not until you."

Tessa exhaled a shaky sound, this woman the first who'd made me let part of that go. One who fucked with my mind and made me break the oath I'd made.

My whole life, Autumn…I promise…it belongs to you. Nothing can change that. Not time or circumstance.

Misery burned a hole in me. It terrified me that Tessa might be the only one who could fill it.

Her fingertips slowly drifted down my back.

An embrace.

Support.

A friend who'd come to mean too fucking much. "I'm sorry you lost her."

"You don't have to feel sorry for me."

I could almost feel the pinch of her brow, the gravity of her breath. "Hurting for you and feeling sorry for you are two different things. And I hurt for you."

She hesitated, then whispered, "But everyone deserves to be touched. To be loved."

I turned to face her. "Not me."

But I'd taken her affection and used it up, anyway.

Her lips tipped down at one side, tenderness full in the soft twist of her mouth, red locks of hair flaming around the sharp lines of her face.

"You're wrong, Milo. You deserve happiness. Joy and peace and safety. Pleasure. All the things you've been giving me."

Affection burned through her expression.

So intense, I swore it was scorching my skin.

"I don't deserve any of those things."

Hurt flashed through that unrelenting gaze.

A gaze that could see all the way to the hidden places inside of me.

"Even if you think you don't, I still need you to be safe. What happened last night? I refuse to let you get hurt again because of me."

"I'll be careful," I promised. "Need you to be, too, until we find out what's going on."

Who was responsible for this.

"I don't even know what Karl wants." She bit down on her bottom lip.

If it was him?

I knew exactly what he wanted.

I couldn't help but slide my palm to the side of her face, my thumb tracing over the freckles beneath her eye. "You, Little Dove. He wants you."

Tenderness overtook her features, and she let lightness weave into the heaviness that had saturated our conversation. "Well, he obviously cannot have me, since I'm engaged to you."

"Obviously," I told her, going for a grin that likely cracked.

She angled her head. "How about I call in today and help you with the treehouse? Remy and Scout are going to be ready to play in this thing before you know it."

Air puffed from my nose. "Sounds like you just want to keep an eye on me."

Honestly, I didn't want to let her out of my sight, so it wasn't going to take much for her to talk me into it.

Her eyes widened in feigned offense. "Who, me? You think I'm some kind of schemer?"

"Positively diabolical." A grin tugged at my mouth.

"Well, it fits because if I catch you trying to pick up one of those heavy pieces of wood, I'm going to make you pay for it later."

She winked at me and wiggled her hips.

Tiny Tease.

I grunted. "Don't tempt me, Tessa."

"Um, last night, you gave me my first orgasm that I didn't give myself. I'm pretty sure it isn't me who is doing the tempting."

Surprise bound with the hunger, and I snatched her by the back of the neck. "What did you just say?"

Her eyes rounded in surprise, and I had to stop myself from devouring that mouth all over again.

"Yeah…well…Karl," she stammered. "It wasn't like I was having any of those with him."

"And before?"

Redness filled her face in a way I'd never seen it, embarrassment lighting her up, though she tried to joke, "Oh, I was saving that V-card like it was going to be something special. But we know how that turned out."

I wasn't prepared for the rush of disgust that sped through my veins, clashing with the lust that banged through my body.

Karl was her first?

I wanted to put my fucking fist through a wall.

"You deserve to find someone who loves you, Tessa. With everything they've got. Treat your heart and this body right."

She blinked up at me, the words tremoring when she murmured, "Yeah, Milo, you're right, I do."

Then she twisted herself out of my hold and moved to the pile of wood I'd been making.

I dropped my head.

Shit.

How the fuck was I supposed to be around her now?

With that mouth and those eyes and those hands?

With the knowledge that last night I gave her exactly what she needed?

With this girl who made me wonder what it would be like to give it to her forever.

"This treehouse is pure awesomesauce. Remy and Scout are going to lose it. Plus, I'm pretty sure your neighbors are going to get a complex," Tessa rambled as she swished the paintbrush over the floorboards of the steps. "There's going to be no keeping up with the Joneses after this baby gets finished."

I let go of a playful grunt. "Only neighbor within ten miles is my mother."

"And she's going to be horribly jealous. Green with envy. Like, seriously, it's kinda sad." She grinned, all wide-eyed. "But there's really not much you can do but build this to its intended grandeur. You know what they say, bigger is better."

She winked.

The girl was a goddamned flirt, and there was a distinct chance I liked it too much.

The lightness she exuded. The warmth. She was a life raft when things got too deep.

Like she was doing her all to get rid of the pressure over what we'd fallen into last night, but it wasn't forced, either.

It was easy.

Right.

It was just me and Tessa.

Our friendship.

Our teasing.

This bond that strengthened with each layer of me that she peeled away rather than her running, like I'd expected her to do.

"Is that so?" I asked, letting her innuendo weave in with my response, playing with fire, but since the girl was a ball of it, I didn't know how to stop.

"Mm-hmm. Who wouldn't want their margarita bigger? Or their pizza? Or I don't know, the mountain they're about to climb? It seems like more of a challenge, don't you think? At least the one thing I know for sure is that I like my things super-sized."

Mischief pranced through her expression, though her eyes told a different story, this softness there that was riddled with fierceness and vulnerability.

This was a woman who would just lay herself on the line if it felt right.

If she believed in it.

All while staunchly believing in the end it would turn out all right.

"Thanks for spending the day out here in the heat, slogging along beside me," I told her.

"What can I say? Some things are worth working for. Or working beside."

She shrugged like what she said didn't matter, like she wasn't slowly undoing me with every word that fell from her mouth, with every glance she cast my way.

I stared at her for a beat. Her flaming hair was hidden beneath a ball cap and tucked behind her ears, the rest of it a lush fall down her back.

This morning, she'd dashed inside to change into something appropriate to work in.

I wouldn't have exactly called it that.

She'd strutted out wearing cut-off shorts that showed off her long, long legs, and a tight red tank top.

Shocker.

My favorite color.

The tank hugged that sweet, tempting body, the neckline scooping down to reveal a bit of cleavage.

My mouth had instantly watered, and I'd been wondering why I'd been such an idiot last night that I didn't take the time to get a peek at her tits while I'd had the chance.

Thought she was purposefully trying to drive me out of my mind.

Drive me to desperation.

All that pale flesh flushed from working out in the heat.

Glistening and kissed by the sun.

A bead of sweat rolled down the side of her face.

Fuck me.

"You're hot." It was a low grumble.

"It's like a thousand degrees out here, and you're working a woman to the bone. And you're like…all broken. How are you even standing right now?"

"Not broken, Tessa."

Her expression softened. "No, Milo. You might be battered, but you're not broken."

"Little Dove." It was caution and this adoration that kept climbing to the surface.

She angled her head in thought before she tossed her brush into the near-empty container.

"Come swimming with me." It wasn't even a request.

Bad idea.

"I've got work to do."

"We've been out here for hours, and we're almost finished. I painted the entire deck, steps, and railing. One more day and we can bust this thing out. See how great it is to have friends like me? Seriously, what would you do without me?"

Her grin was coy, so sly, as she started to edge down the lawn in the direction of the lake that was shimmering behind her.

All sweet seduction.

"Only have a few more boards to nail in to get the ceiling finished."

"Come on, Milo," she whined in that playful way. She tossed the hat from her head and began to spin around with her face upturned to the sky, red locks whipping around her. "You have all of this, and you don't stop to enjoy it? Look at this view."

She stumbled out of her spin then directly proceeded to peel that tank over her head to reveal the lacy red bra she wore underneath.

Shit.

What was she doing?

Lust fisted my guts, and then she wound out of her shorts, too, kicking both them and her shoes off before she ran for the lake in nothing but her bra and underwear.

Girl a mile of legs and slender curves and tempting shapes.

Tiny Tease.

Hell, I was right—she was goddamn diabolical.

My stomach growled.

She spun around to walk backward. "Are you coming or what? Tell me you don't want to swim with me. I dare you."

She hopped onto the dock and sprinted down the planks. She didn't hesitate to jump.

She threw her arms into the air as she catapulted off the end.

Freedom rang from her mouth.

A shout of excitement.

Water splashed as she went under, then popped right back up.

She swished the drenched locks of hair out of her face, grinning so huge that it panged right in the middle of my chest.

"Get that cute butt in here, Milo Hendricks. You'd be crazy to miss out on this," she shouted while she bobbed up and down in the water.

"You're the crazy one...that water's fuckin' freezing."

She giggled and started to float on her back. "It's exhilarating. It's all in the perspective, don't you know?"

I'd edged that way, slower and slower as I approached the water.

My stomach twisted.

Images flashed.

"For a giant who can take himself a beating, you're a big baby," she teased.

Fuck it.

I'd been on my canoe a thousand times.

I could get in the water.

I peeled my shirt over my head, ignoring the aching that wanted to remind me of my place.

My pace increased as I hurried to meet her where she bobbed in the water.

Her smile was enormous, blue eyes taking me in like she'd just seen the light of day.

I shucked out of my boots and socks, then fumbled out of my jeans, leaving it all in a pile before I hustled to the end of the dock and jumped in, too.

Cannonball style.

Cold water swallowed me up as the momentum drove me under.

I was right. It was fucking freezing. But Tessa was right, too. It felt amazing.

Like bliss.

A small dose of liberation.

I felt it expand my chest as I floated beneath the surface for a second, in this place that was supposed to be my sanctuary before it had become no better than a burial ground.

Had hated these waters for the longest time, but I was remembering their freedom when I broke the surface.

Tessa giggled. "That was a straight ten. Bonified gold, baby."

A chuckle broke free, and I pushed my fingers through my hair to toss back the wet locks from my face. "You think so, huh?"

"Absolutely. And not even like when I tell Gage it's a ten when he's doing karate. Like for real. The best cannonball I've ever seen. I think you missed your calling."

Tessa tried to hold back her laughter.

I skimmed my palm across the water, sending a small wave of water sailing her way. It splashed her in the face.

She gasped, her eyes going wide, her feigned outrage leaving her spluttering. "What was that for?"

She immediately sent a wave right back. I turned to the side, and it splashed against my cheek. "Come on, take it like a man, Milo."

Her eyes were wide.

"You take it." I splashed her again.

Laughter rang.

Hers and mine.

Two of us treading water in the middle of my lake while we splashed and teased and laughed.

Our legs kicked beneath the surface.

Skin brushing skin.

A ripple effect.

And that feeling was there that I needed to deny.

What I needed to lock down.

Reject.

But my arm was reaching out, and I snatched her by the wrist and drew her to me.

Surprise flittered through her expression before she exhaled a happy sound.

Her body was pressed to mine as my palm found her cheek, and she stared up at me with this awe like I could be the man I'd once attempted to be.

Hesitation warred. What was I doing?

And she was whispering, "It's okay, Milo. While we're in this, why can't we make each other feel good? Be there for each other? In every way?"

That was one second before my mouth was crashing against hers.

My hand tangled in her wet hair, and my tongue dove in on a hunt for hers.

While we're in this.

Liar.

Think we both knew.

We knew that none of this was going to come without consequences. That this was impossible. That my heart didn't belong to me.

Still, I kissed her like I meant it.

Devouring this woman who'd awoken a dead place inside me.

Tessa giggled into my mouth, then she drew away and sent another wave of water splashing into my face.

"Oh, you're gonna pay for that," I warned.

Her smile was soft, those freckles alight. "Let's see it, mountain man."

I dunked her head under water.

Just a tiny, playful shove.

She bobbed up, her mouth flapping for a breath. "Oh, that was a low blow. You're going down, buddy."

She jumped on me, throwing her arms around my neck and trying to drag me under.

The two of us were tangled.

Wrestling.

Teasing and playing. *Free.*

I hadn't had a moment like this in so long.

Maybe in forever.

Because I'd never been with someone quite like Tessa McDaniels.

This wild little thing with the softest spirit.

One who right then was making *mine* sing.

She shoved off me and began treading away, that smile dancing all over her face.

"Where do you think you're going, Little Dove?" Words were abraded, harsh with the need she'd spun up in me.

"Wouldn't you like to know?"

"Tiny Tease."

Redness flushed her face, my favorite fucking color.

"Is that what you think I am, Milo Hendricks?"

"I think you're teasing me with what I can't have. With what I can't keep."

"Who said you couldn't have me, *fiancé?*"

She drew the last word out as she swam around the end of the dock and toward the beach. When she got to the depth where she could stand, she began to clamber out of the water on her feet, more and more of that tight body exposed the higher she got.

Fuck.

She was gorgeous.

A mind-bending beauty that messed me up.

Heart shattering, and that didn't bode so well when mine was already in pieces.

The girl nothing but a goddess, who giggled when she looked at me from over her shoulder. "Come and get me."

Like I said...diabolical.

I followed because she just might have a leash around my neck. My strokes were fast as I swam before I was able to stand. I rose up, coming out of the water.

From where Tessa stood on the bank, she gasped, and the playful energy between us shifted.

Charged.

Loaded.

Dense and teeming with everything I was supposed to be refusing.

"You steal my breath, Milo. Did you know that? Did you know the first time I met you I froze, my lungs locked because I'd never seen a man who affected me like you?"

"Tessa," I warned.

"It's true."

I slowly eased the rest of the way out of the cold water, the warmth of the sun skipping across my wet skin.

Or maybe it was her.

That heat.

The flames.

The burn that scorched me in a passion I'd never felt.

The sun rising on a darkened day.

"Thought I got punched in the gut the second I saw you." The confession was thick as it rolled up my throat. "When you came waltzing into that club with your bright eyes and your big smile. With that sweet confidence. With that sexy body wrapped in a tight red dress. Did you know it then that it was my favorite color?"

"I might have imagined I figured it out that night." Her words were choppy, laden with this need so dense I thought it would suffocate us.

"Never before had I been tempted. Not once. Not until you." The admission curled through the air. "You make me feel something I never thought I'd feel again. In a brand-new way, and I don't know how to fuckin' deal with the truth of that."

Air wheezed from her lungs as I edged up the lawn in her direction, the girl standing there, soaking wet, her pale, freckled flesh sparkling with the droplets that trickled down her body.

Her small tits were perfect beneath the red fabric of her bra, her nipples pebbled and peaked. Her underwear was soaked, and rivulets were rolling down her legs.

The rest of her exposed.

Her belly. Her chest. Her thighs. That thing that kept flaming in her eyes.

My cock hardened to stone, need trembling to my bones.

Her eyes drifted to my dick that was trying to burst out of my underwear.

"Tessa." Her name rolled out on a bolt of lust.

She turned around like she was going to keep up this game.

She started to run, wanting me to chase her.

She squealed as I closed in on her fast, and I snagged her around the waist. The momentum sent us tumbling to the ground. The lawn was soft below us, and Tessa was on her hands and knees.

Giggles rang, and Tessa went to start crawling away like this was all in fun, then froze when I kissed a needy trail down the line of her back, mumbling as I went, "Is this what you want? You want me to chase you?"

She whimpered, and I pressed my nose to her skin, inhaling her delicious scent.

Strawberries and cream. The sweetest, most tempting thing.

"Is that it, Tessa, you want to do me in?"

"No, Milo, I don't want to do you in. I want to make you feel alive, the same way you make me feel."

A desperate moan rolled from her when I barely sank my teeth into the flesh of her round bottom, my fingers burrowing into her waist as I drew her closer to me.

Her perfect ass in the air was nearly more than I could take.

Desire radiated from her being, saturating her flesh.

"What do you need, Little Dove?"

"You. Just you."

My finger slipped beneath the crotch of her underwear, and I drew the wet fabric to the side.

"Shit, baby, look at you."

Her slit was pink and swollen, her silky arousal seeping out at the seam. I traced the tip of my finger through it before I watched myself drive the single digit in.

All the way until I was to the knuckle in her tight cunt.

"Your pussy is so sweet, Little Dove. Knew it was going to be."

"Milo." She rocked back.

Delirium.

That's what I had to be suffering from.

No sense.

No rationale.

Just this girl and this moment and taking her to that heightened place where she wanted to be.

I drew my finger out and drove it back in slow, before I pulled it all the way out so my tongue could take its place. Using my hands, I spread her cheeks wide.

I devoured her.

Her clit.

Her pussy.

Her asshole.

Wanted to make every single one of them mine.

Fuck her. Keep her. Love her.

I squeezed my eyes closed at the barrage of thoughts, focusing on bringing her to the ecstasy that she kept affording me.

She mewled this desperate sound that landed like lust on my brain.

"Milo, please."

I flipped her over onto her back, catching her off guard. She gasped in surprise before her hips were jutting off the ground as her heels dug into the grass.

Begging.

The girl dripping and pleading.

I angled back so I could rip her underwear down her legs, and there was Tessa, all spread out on my lawn, her chest heaving, her belly flat and quivering, her tits barely concealed by the red lace of her bra.

Her hair was stringy from the lake, spread all around her, red tendrils that snaked around her face.

A dark goddess.

A red siren.

My seduction.

My ruin.

So fucking sweet when she looked up with those eyes that pierced me through.

Sharp as a blade.

Deep as a knife.

"Take me."

"Not gonna fuck you, Tessa, but I'm going to make you fly."

I gripped her by the hips and lifted her high, hooking her legs over my shoulders as I dove back in. My tongue drove deep into the well of her body before I changed course so I could suck and lap at her engorged clit.

I plunged two fingers into her pussy.

Deep, deep, deep.

Her nails dug into the soft soil of the grass like it could keep her grounded. "Please."

My cock was so fucking hard, this sweet thing so tempting. My free hand curved around the top of her thigh, and my fingers burrowed into the flesh while the others stroked deep inside her body.

I wound her to the place that had her writhing.

Her head swished back and forth, and her pleasure became something tangible in my hands.

Took only a minute for her to come unglued.

For bliss to break. For this treasure to crack.

Her walls tightened around my fingers when the orgasm blew through her body.

Tessa soared and flew.

Every muscle in her body trembled.

That rapture seeded way down deep.

Air rasped from her lungs, and she was nearly levitating from the ground as her pussy throbbed around my fingers.

I was the fool imagining it was my cock.

What it'd be like to just let go.

Get lost in this girl.

In her sweetness. In her belief. In the faith she kept pulling out from the wreckage like everything broken could once again belong to me.

I couldn't go there.

Couldn't.

I wouldn't make it back.

Instead, I shoved down my underwear to my thighs, and I stroked myself while Tessa watched and writhed and whimpered at the sight.

"Tessa." It was a twisted prayer getting loose of my soul as I dumped all over her belly.

We both struggled for breath, to come back down to reality.

A second later, Tessa flung an arm over her eyes, hiding her face as she let go of a wispy giggle. "Oh my God."

"Are you going to get shy on me now, Little Dove?"

I reached out to tug at her arm so I could look at her, my chest stretching tight at seeing that adorable smile tugging at the edge of her lips.

"Where did you get that magic mouth, Milo Hendricks?"

A chuckle rumbled free because Tessa McDaniels surprised me at every turn.

"Funny, I was thinkin' the same thing about you just last night."

Everything about her went tender, and she reached up and set her palm on my cheek, her thumb soft as she ran it under my eye. "Well, we can't deny it, now, can we? It's a fact. We make a really great team."

Chapter Twenty-Four

Tessa

MY CHEST SQUEEZED IN BOTH SORROW AND JOY WHERE I paused outside Bobby's door. I'd come as soon as I'd finished up work for the day, needing to see his face.

Today, he was in his bed, the head of it propped up so he was upright.

Late-afternoon light spilled in through the window where he sat unseeing, the rays filtering over him in a shimmery spotlight.

The focus on my big brother.

I forced a bright smile onto my face, wearing it to camouflage the pain that seeped through my bloodstream.

Because I missed him.

I missed his voice.

I missed his smiles.

I missed his teasing and his jokes and his devotion.

The way he'd fought like crazy to give me a good life, then lost the potential of his in a single moment.

Dreams stricken.

Stolen away.

I eased forward, keeping my footsteps light.

His left side twitched, and my heart throbbed with the bare hope that he at least was aware of my presence.

"Hey, Bobby," I whispered as I rounded to the side of his bed. I scanned him, searching for signs that he was still being well cared for. That he was healthy and whole, at least in the form of his current condition.

His russet hair was brushed, his clothes were clean, and they continually shifted his position so he wouldn't end up with pressure sores from sitting in one spot for too long.

I was suddenly so thankful for the gift Milo had offered that I felt too unsteady to stand, knowing what it meant for Bobby.

A gift that came without chains or expectations, which was funny, considering I would give him anything.

Pulling a chair to the side of Bobby's bed, I sat down and reached out to carefully take the hand that he held against his chest. I opened his fist, and I touched the round locket as emotion crept up my throat. "Have you been thinking about me, Bobby? I know I've been thinking about you."

I looked up at his face, still so handsome, though it'd thinned a ton since his accident.

He'd once been muscled and fierce.

My hero.

He might be frail now, but he was still my hero. That was never going to change.

"It's a beautiful summer, isn't it?" I kept as much lightness in my tone as I could.

I glanced behind me out the window to the flowering Crape Myrtle just outside.

Turning back, I curled my hand around his and decided to broach the subject that I really wanted to talk to him about. "So, remember that friend I was telling you about? The one I'm staying with?"

I got no response. It didn't matter. I just prayed he understood. "He's pretty amazing."

There was no keeping the affection out.

My heart fluttered just thinking Milo's name.

"He's helping me take care of you while I figure things out, so we at least don't have to worry for a little bit," I rushed. "He's truly so good to me."

I wouldn't torture Bobby with the sordid details about the epic afternoon Milo and I had shared in his backyard two days ago.

It was hands down the sexiest thing that had ever happened to me, and we hadn't even had *sex*.

Afterward, Milo had hovered over me for the longest time, like he was memorizing the moment, the way we'd both felt, before he'd pushed his lips to my ear and whispered, *"Want you so bad, Little Dove. Want you in a way I don't understand."*

There had been so much fear behind his statement, so much reservation, so much guilt.

I wanted to show him that there was still life after trauma.

Love after loss.

"I think I'm falling for him, Bobby." I choked out a soft, disbelieving laugh. "Of course, I'd be the girl to go after the one guy who doesn't think he can love me back. Shocker, right? But there's something about him that makes me feel like I'm tied to him. Like we belong together. Like we can soothe each other's loneliness."

I rubbed my thumb over the back of Bobby's hand. "I miss it, Bobby. Having a family. Is it wrong to imagine I could have one with him? He has these two kids…"

Emotion clogged my voice. "They're amazing, and I think I'm falling for them, too. And they think I'm marrying their dad. Can you believe it? It's all fake, Bobby, but it's the realest thing I've ever felt."

I tightened my hold on his hand. God, I wished he could respond to me. Tell me I was being crazy. Neurotic the way I was. Or maybe give me his blessing. Tell me to chase after what I loved because losing it was what would be the tragedy.

"I get myself into some messes, don't I?" Through bleary eyes, I smiled at my brother. His eyes were distant, but I could feel the steady pound of his heart.

I had to believe he was right there.

"You probably want to kick my butt and tell me to get my life together right now, don't you? But I think I finally am. At least I'm finally understanding what it is I want."

I wanted my brother cared for.

Healed because I'd never stopped believing it was possible. Never stopped praying for that miracle.

God, if he could hug me one more time? What I wouldn't give for that.

Beyond that?

I wanted a connection. The same thing I got to see in my friends.

A devotion and need that went beyond imagination.

I wanted to be cherished.

Adored.

And I wanted the gift of cherishing someone, too. Of them experiencing my love and my faith in them.

I wanted *my person.*

"I love you, Bobby. So much. And I will always, forever be fighting for you." I curled his hand back around the charm, and I pushed to my feet and leaned over him so I could press a kiss to his forehead. "I could never ask for a better brother. Thank you for loving me, too."

I eased away, my affection whispering around my lips. "I'll see you in a few days, okay? And know I'm thinking about you...always."

Chapter Twenty-Five

Milo

TESSA'S HAND TREMBLED IN MINE.

"Holy fuckballs, I'm nervous," she mumbled as she stared out the windshield to the restaurant where we were meeting my attorney.

A rough chuckle scraped out, though I'd be a liar if I said my knees weren't knocking, too.

"You're lucky I'm a fantastic actress, Milo, because shit just got real."

She shifted her head to look at me from over the console.

Red hair swishing around her shoulders, freckles alight.

But it was a tidal wave of worry in those ocean eyes that rushed for the shore.

"Thought you said you'd lied under oath a hundred times?"

I attempted to keep it easy. Like this was no big deal. Like this whole plan wasn't hinged on this moment.

Tessa gulped. "Well, I *lied* about that."

Fuck, she was cute.

"You've got this, Little Dove. You're the one who keeps telling me what we're doing is right." My hand squeezed around hers. "Can't do this without you."

How big of an asshole did that make me?

Felt like I was toying with her.

With her goodness.

With her kindness.

Because I'd given in three times, touched on her beauty, ate it up like I would never stop because finding pleasure beneath her hands was the best thing I'd ever felt.

Standing in her light.

Burned in her blaze.

But I couldn't keep touching her if it only left me riddled with guilt.

Couldn't put that on her. Couldn't let her think for a second she'd become part of my shame.

Because she was everything that mattered. She deserved joy and love.

She deserved it all.

Someone who matched her radiant soul.

Someone who was decent.

Someone who was honest.

Someone who didn't have ghosts following them to bed.

She exhaled a rough breath and smiled at me. "It's an honor I get to do it alongside you."

That feeling lifted and rose while we sat there staring at each other for a beat. I finally cleared my throat. "We should get inside."

"Yup, let's do this."

She pulled her hand from mine and swiped her sweaty palms on her skirt, then she grinned over at me when she said, "Not the only place I'm sweating, in case you wanted to know."

Laughter rumbled. Ease mixing with the anxiety.

"Wait right there," I told her.

"Oh, right, yes, that's what a good fiancé would do." A tease played through her features.

I hopped out of the Tahoe, and I rounded the front and moved to open her door, taking her hand to help her out.

That energy rolled, a thunder in the air, this pure understanding and support radiating from her when she set those eyes on me.

Belief.

Affection.

Something else I needed to shun.

But right then, I threaded my fingers through hers and held on for dear life.

"You've got this, Milo Hendricks. You're one of the best dads I know, and I know soon, your children are going to be home," she whispered just for me as we walked together to the casual restaurant.

Opening the door, I let go of her hand so she could walk in front of me, though my mouth came to her ear as she passed, "Because of you, Little Dove."

She glanced back at me, her smile so sweet. "Because of us, Milo. Because we're a great freaking team."

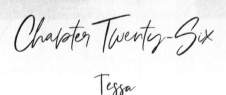

Chapter Twenty-Six

Tessa

I WASN'T LYING. I WAS SWEATING IN VERY UNMENTIONABLE places. Because it was me, I'd mentioned them, anyway.

But bejeebus, I'd never been so nervous in my life. And we were going to have to take this to the stand? Holy mother, I'd probably look like I'd been dunked in the lake.

Milo kept his hand on the small of my back as he led me through the restaurant. Dark brown booths ran along the walls, and a bunch of plain wood tables sat in the middle.

Servers bustled through the space during the dinner rush, and most tables were filled.

Milo guided me toward a small square table in the middle where a woman sat sipping a cup of coffee.

She was probably in her mid-forties, her hair down and curled in loose waves, wearing a pantsuit and soft determination on her face.

"Mr. Hendricks, it's great to see you again," she said as she pushed up from her chair and extended her hand over the table.

Milo shook it as he said, "It's good to see you, too, Ms. Anderson."

He shifted back, nudging me forward. "This is Tessa McDaniels, my fiancée."

Her eyes lit. "Miss McDaniels. It's a pleasure. Please sit."

She gestured to the open chairs, and Milo pulled the one out for me that was directly across from his attorney.

Ever the gentleman.

"Thank you," I mumbled, chanting silently, *Do not screw this up and accidentally blurt out that this is fake.*

We'd be dead in our tracks before we ever made it out of the gates.

Milo leaned down from behind and pressed a kiss to my temple. "Anytime, baby."

My heart pattered.

Fake.

Remember it's fake.

But for the love of God, don't say it out loud.

Nope, this was not messing with my head or anything.

"I appreciate you meeting with us," Milo said in his rumbly voice as he took the chair between us.

Her smile was coy. "Well, it is my job, but I must admit, I've been anxious to hear about this one."

She shifted her attention to me.

I itched on my seat and sent her a little wave.

Milo chuckled and reached for my hand over the table. He squeezed it in a clear show of support.

We had this.

"Tell me about yourself," she prodded.

Well, then, we were going to get right down to business and no one had even offered me a margarita.

I swallowed my nerves and lifted my chin. "Well, let's see…I work as a third-grade teacher at a private Christian academy here in Redemption Hills. I'm also the executive director of Hope to Hands, a nonprofit supporting the community."

Milo's attorney looked much happier to hear it than Paula had.

"I also have an older brother…his name's Bobby." Affection wobbled out. "He lives in a long-term care facility after an accident in which he sustained a severe brain injury. I'm his power of attorney."

She nodded, obviously pleased.

"And you met Milo…?"

"Through our friends where he works."

Her attention shifted back to Milo. "The club? Absolution?"

Milo gave her a tight nod, unease flitting through his being.

She blew out through her nose. "I feel like that is the biggest issue you have going against you, Milo, if I may call you that?"

"Of course," he said, but the words were sticky.

Discomfort rippled through his big body.

I squeezed his hand tighter.

"I would urge you to move beyond your current profession. The court isn't going to like the idea of you working at a club, being away all hours of the night when your family might need you, especially in that type of atmosphere."

I knew it was part of what Paula had used against him before.

"I'll be there at night with the kids." The promise whipped out without consideration.

But I'd told him I would be there.

For him.

For them.

I'd meant it.

"That is a good start, but I think it would be helpful if Milo had higher aspirations."

I didn't love that she was demeaning his job, but I got it.

The idea of a bouncer came with a certain impression, and it typically wasn't the good kind. Paula could easily twist what he did into something sordid.

A war went down in Milo's psyche, a severity firing from him in sparks of pain, like he was stuck and didn't know how to move forward. He seemed to have to pry the words from his mouth. "I plan on starting my own business…a construction company."

What?

That would be awesome.

I had to bite my tongue to keep from squealing and demanding to know all the deets. From telling him how freaking proud of him I was.

A good fiancée would already know these things.

But honestly, it was perfect. So fitting for him. I'd already seen what those big, bare hands were capable of. The rugged beauty they created.

Ms. Anderson smiled, but Milo didn't return it.

Worry for him curdled in my stomach.

"That is wonderful, Milo," she encouraged. She jotted down a few notes. "I think you're in a good position to have your rights restored. Honestly, I'm surprised the judge didn't rule in your favor the last time you contested their custody. It's obviously time that you and your children were reunited."

She continued writing a couple more things down before she lifted her head and pinned her attention on Milo. "When would you like to get started with this process?"

"As soon as possible." It ripped from his mouth on desperation and a shock of hope, his entire body bowing forward in relief.

"Great, I'll file the petition tomorrow."

Expectation and disbelief blistered through him, and I found myself leaning farther over the table toward him, clinging to his hand.

Staring at him with a smile splitting my face.

This was happening.

His attorney hummed. "You two are adorable. Your love is really apparent. I think we have this one in the bag."

The smile I sent her was feigned.

Right.

Totally apparent.

The problem was, it wasn't all that hard to fake it.

"Expect a call from me after I have more information," she told Milo. "In the meantime, show your faces around town more often. I like the look."

She gestured between us, then gathered her things and strode out.

Five minutes and it was done.

I exhaled a ragged breath. "Holy crap, we did it, Milo."

He squeezed my hand back, those honey-dipped eyes swimming with hope. "Told you that you could pull it off."

"I'm a great actress," I mouthed.

His expression deepened, and I knew what he saw because I couldn't hide what I felt. "Yeah," he murmured, his voice laden with appreciation.

I sat back to break the intensity before I got lost in it, and I wagged my brows at him. "It looks like you owe me a big, fancy steak dinner, fiancé."

His brow arched. "Fancy, huh? Not sure that's what I'd call this place."

"Are you kidding me? I'll bet you twenty bucks they have a killer chicken fried *steak*. Now show me the love, Milo Hendricks."

"Love, huh?"

I grinned at him. "Mad, mad love."

I grabbed the plastic menu and started to peruse it before it came to mean something I couldn't let it.

I gasped when Milo clutched my knee from under the table. I lowered the menu, peering at him from over the top. My breaths shallow, and my stupid heart racing.

"Thank you," he rumbled, so low.

I forced down the truth of what I felt. "It's all good, Milo. It's what friends do."

"That's it. I'm not standing here and letting him get away with this crap. I won't be bullied."

We'd come out after dinner to find Milo's windshield smashed in.

I mean, seriously, what a freaking jerk. Ruining our win. This evening that Milo and I had spent like normal people, laughing and joking over dinner.

A really freaking delish chicken fried steak dinner.

I dialed and had the phone pressed to my ear before Milo could stop me.

"Tessa, what are you doing? I don't think—" Milo wheezed just as the bitter voice answered on the opposite end of the line.

"Tessa." Karl's laughter was cynical.

Or sinister.

Was there a difference? I couldn't tell.

"I take it you've realized the error in your ways."

I couldn't even scoff out a witty rebuttal. Because tears stung my eyes as I gritted my teeth and hissed, "That's enough, Karl. I hurt your ego. I get it. You're upset. But what you're doing? This isn't okay."

"What the hell are you rambling about, Tessa? I don't have time for your nonsense."

That time, I did scoff. "You don't have time for this, but you have time to come to my office and threaten me? Time to have Milo chased down and beaten? Time to bash his windshield in? Nice, Karl. I'd call it childish if what you're doing wasn't so dangerous."

He laughed a disbelieving sound. "As much as I'd love to witness your boyfriend get the beating he deserves, I sadly can't take credit. I'm in London right now."

Air huffed from my nose. "Save it, Karl. I know you hired someone to hurt him. This ends now, or I'm going to the police, and yeah, you can toss your connections all over the place, but everything you said is on video at my office. So why don't you save your pride and tell your colleagues and friends I got a horribly bad case of the herps and died. Or maybe I give really terrible head. Or heck, here's an idea, you can just say you and I ended up not working out. Whatever it is, just leave us alone. And to be clear, I'll be paying you back. It will be slow, but I will get every dollar you spent on Bobby back to you."

I had a plan.

Aspirations, too.

It wasn't like I could let Milo take care of Bobby forever.

Milo, who was a shaken bottle of that mayhem beside me.

Pacing one step back and forth while he looked like he was about to rip the phone from my hand.

Or go on a rampage.

I held a finger up at him like the gesture could keep him tamed.

Milo grunted.

"If you think I'd take that kind of risk for you, Tessa, you're delusional." Condescension lined Karl's voice. "I'll wait until you come to your senses. It's only a matter of time before you come crawling back, and I guarantee it will be with you on your hands and knees."

Confusion clouded my head, and the words were thin when I released them. "You tried to force me…"

"You should get over yourself."

I stared blankly.

Get over myself?

Was he serious? After everything he'd done?

I felt lightheaded as a rush of unease flitted through my consciousness. I shifted to look at Milo, who had opened his door.

Milo, who had frozen in shock.

I could physically feel the cold chill that slithered down his spine.

I ended the call without saying anything else because I didn't give two craps about Karl.

There was only one person who I did.

My brow pinched together as I took two careful steps toward Milo, who was clutching a piece of paper in his hand.

I reached over and pried it out, squinting in confusion as I tried to process the significance of what it said.

To think I was betting on you.

Confusion whipped through on a gust of wind.

Dread clutched Milo, and he slowly turned around, searching the parking lot, terror stampeding through his being.

I touched his arm. "What does it mean?"

"It means when demons run, they don't always stay hidden."

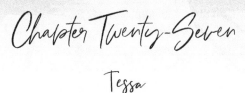

Chapter Twenty-Seven

Tessa

I EASED UP BEHIND MILO WHO STOOD WITH HIS PALMS pressed to the island countertop with his head drooped between his shoulders.

Late afternoon light streamed through the windows, casting his giant frame in shimmery rays that made my stomach clench and my heart fist.

Everything about him was overpowering.

Overwhelming.

Big and intimidating and rough.

Soft and kind and real.

I wished with all of me he could see himself the way I saw him.

That he could understand the way he made me feel.

I slid my hand up his spine, praying I could offer him comfort.

A shiver raced through his body.

He'd been in turmoil since we'd found his windshield bashed in and the note in his truck on Thursday night, the man in this constant war inside his head that I had no idea how to fight.

Because he'd shut down and shut me out, though he watched

over me like he was terrified I was going to disappear, all while looking at me like maybe he wished I'd never existed in the first place.

Like I might be the source of his pain.

"It's almost time. We need to finish getting ready," I murmured.

"Not sure this is a good idea anymore."

A frown curled my brow. "The party, or are you talking about
your kids?"

Tonight, we were supposed to be celebrating.

It was our official *engagement* party. It had been Milo's mom's
idea. Heck, she'd pretty much insisted on it. At the time, Milo had
agreed, but that had been before Thursday.

We'd thought, what better way to profess our love to the rest
of the world than to come together with the people closest to us to
mark it.

Yeah, we were full steam ahead with this little charade, and if we
were putting on a show, we needed to do it right.

But this charade had come to feel too real and complicated and
complex.

The ground no longer solid beneath my feet.

Because when Milo shifted to look at me from over his shoulder,
my heart stalled out.

It was like my spirit needed the extended beat.

A moment to recognize the profound fullness of what I felt.

I was in love with Milo Hendricks.

Completely.

Wholly.

And I was petrified he might not ever see through his past to
love me back.

God, I'd gotten in deep.

Tangled in this man.

So invested I wondered if I'd remain whole when the deceit spit
me out on the other side.

But I also knew, no matter how much this hurt me in the end, it
was worth it.

He was worth it.

His children were worth it.

It didn't mean it didn't hurt like hell.

"All of it." Torment rolled through his gruff words.

"If I know one thing about you, it's that you deserve to have your children in your life…and they deserve to have you in theirs."

"Not if it puts them in danger."

The dread I'd been sporting for two days slashed at my resolve. My voice shallowed out. "How are they in danger, Milo? Tell me what's happening."

Milo scrubbed a tattooed hand over his face, and he looked to his boots when he rumbled, "I—"

We both froze when the front door opened without warning.

Milo shot upright, instantly on edge, even though workers had been coming and going all day to set up.

His mother popped her head through the door, one of her affectionate smiles alight on her face, though she appeared a little frazzled as she wrangled in a large white box.

"Oh, my goodness, I'm finally back, sorry about that. Debbie had to show off the cake before she would let me take it. She claims it's the best she's ever made, which I'm going to have to agree. Of course, she made it extra special for the two most special people in my life."

She grinned as she set it down beside us on the counter. In the same beat, she reached for my hand and squeezed just as she set her hand on Milo's cheek with the other. "Don't be nervous, Milo. This is a good day. I know you're not about all the hubbub and big parties, but this is worth celebrating."

Milo visibly swallowed his reservations, forcing a big smile to his face as he looked at his mom. "I'm good, Mom. Don't worry about me."

"I always worry about you." She ran her thumb under his eye as if he were a little boy who needed the support.

Emotion swam through my chest, and I cleared the roughness away with a forced giggle.

"It's not like it's that big of a party, anyway. Just our closest friends and family."

Mine were one and the same.

Not one blood relative to my name.

Bobby's face flashed through my mind, and my chest felt like it just might cave. What I wouldn't do for him to be here. For him to experience this.

And it wasn't even real, so what in the world was I thinking?

I'd gotten it all convoluted.

What this meant.

I did my best to keep the sorrow out of my voice when I spoke to Cheryl. "And you went and made it extravagant, anyway."

Cheryl's black hair swished around her shoulders, and she angled her head to the side as she tightly gripped my hand.

"Only the best for the people I love." She swiveled her attention to Milo. "Besides, it's Milo who spent years taking care of me. I think it's time I return the favor."

My teeth raked my bottom lip.

So many questions.

Why'd I have to go and fall for a man who was so not an open book when I really liked reading between the pages?

"All right, what else needs to be accomplished?" Cheryl asked as she stepped back, shaking herself out of the intensity of the moment.

The party was taking place out back.

Twinkle lights had been strung in the trees. Round tables were set up beneath them, and they were covered by white tablecloths. Each was decorated with white and pink floral bouquets.

A dance floor was off to the side since Cheryl had asked me my favorite thing to do at a party, and there was an open bar to the left for our guests to enjoy.

It would be a blast if it were real.

If Milo wasn't second-guessing everything.

If this all hadn't turned into a cluster that I had no idea how to sort.

"I think that's it. This guy needs to get changed, and we'll be ready to roll."

I jostled my hip into his.

He grunted a grumbly sound, then he was breathing out in pained relief when I reached out and took his hand and threaded our fingers together.

I glanced up at him.

We have this. We're a great team.

He just had to let me off the bench if we were going to win.

Music played softly from the speakers that had been set up around the yard, and a gentle breeze blew through, rustling the trees and making the twinkle lights dance across the lawn. The lake was calm and glittering behind us, and light laughter trickled through the atmosphere, voices soft and carrying, the mood easy and right if it weren't for the man who was tacked to my side.

All burly and grumpy and intimidating, wearing dress pants and a button-down, the sleeves rolled up his tatted arms.

Need quivered in my belly. I'd never seen the man look so delicious.

He and I had found ourselves in the shadows of the yard, watching as our guests finished eating their dinners.

Cheryl had organized this big buffet that was full of every kind of dish.

The woman was so sweet.

So kind.

So hopeful when I could feel her son losing hope.

Milo's arm twitched where he had it wrapped around my waist, his nerves as jumbled as they'd been earlier, before his mom had walked in.

"We have this," I muttered under my breath again.

"Don't you dare leave my side. Need you, Tessa." It was a bare grunt from his throat.

And I guessed I was having a really hard time differentiating the counterfeit from the factual.

Delineating his feigned affections from the concrete.

Because his fingers dug into my side as if I'd become his anchor when his spirit kept floating adrift.

The man casually nursed a beer while he tried to hide the uncertainty and doubt.

To camouflage the shadow of shame that hovered around him like a merciless reaper.

"I'm not going anywhere, Milo. I don't care what you've done in your past."

He shifted until he was towering over me, the man an obliterating fortress that ripped the breath from my lungs. His hand came to my jaw. "You don't know what you're saying."

"Then tell me."

I didn't even realize we'd gotten lost in our own little bubble until a hand clamped down on my forearm.

My attention whipped that way. Eden pinned on the biggest smile that was completely faked.

"You wouldn't mind if I stole my BFF for a minute, would you, Milo?"

His expression promised he most assuredly did.

"Eh, sure, of course."

"I'll be right back. Promise."

His nod was tight.

Eden began to drag me to a secluded spot on the opposite side of the yard. I couldn't help but look at Milo fading into the distance as we went.

I whipped back around when she rushed under her breath, "What is going on with you two?"

I pinned on a feigned smile, completely innocent. "Who, me and Milo?"

"Um...yes...you and Milo."

"We're getting married, obviously."

"Tessa." Her tone lowered in seriousness as a worried dent formed on her brow.

I blew out a heavy sigh and mumbled, "I have no idea what's going on."

"It looks like something is going on to me."

"Oh, I don't know, does it look like I'm glowing from the two amazing orgasms he gave me?"

"Shut up," she choked as she tugged me closer. "You had cake, and you didn't tell me?"

Laughter ripped from me, still half-disoriented from the impact of it. I still couldn't process it. "God, and it was so good, Eden. Like, decadent, dark, delicious chocolate cake."

I would never get enough.

She giggled. "My bestie finally got herself some good lovin'. Tell me you ate it all."

"I wish. It was only a tiny taste. I'm, like, still *starving*, and I'd really like Milo to stuff me." I angled my head to stress the point.

She cracked up, her laughter ringing over the lawn.

A bunch of faces spun our direction, and I turned my back to them, hoping I remained hidden in the shadows.

My hands shot to my face like I could cover the need that wanted to rush out. "I'm so screwed, Eden."

She pried a hand from my face, and she dipped down to meet my gaze, all the lightness draining from her expression. "Hey, you're not screwed…you're just…in love, aren't you?"

I blew out a sigh and glanced back at the man in the distance. Trent, Jud, and Logan had joined him, and he sipped at a beer, the faint lines of one of his sexy smiles tipping up behind his beard at something one of them said.

Hello, volcanic eruption spewing out the hotties.

But Milo was the only one I could see.

This man who'd changed everything inside me.

Stood up for me.

God, how desperately I wanted to stand beside him.

I slowly turned back to Eden.

"He's my Ace, Eden. The one I never could have anticipated or expected. The one who makes me feel alive with just a glance. And when he touched me…" I trailed off, my mouth going dry at the memories.

"I felt like a treasure for the first time in my life. Like I found the person I belong with. My match. But he doesn't see it the same."

Sympathy deepened her features. "You're blind if you don't see the way he looks at you."

Emotion thickened my throat, this love and this pain knitting together and becoming one. "He might want me, but he won't love me, and I won't settle for anything less. Not ever again."

Affection wisped through her eyes. "No, don't settle, not ever. But don't give up on him, either. I've seen that look before, and that's not lack of love, Tessa. It's fear of feeling it when he thinks he shouldn't."

Possibility blossomed. It only took a second for it to get trampled by the fear.

"He's got these demons…" The word hitched in my throat, and I looked at Eden in this broken hope as I touched that achy spot on my chest. "Secrets. I'm afraid he might be in trouble. He got jumped the other night by a bunch of men."

I warred, wondering how much to share with her, if I'd be breaking Milo's trust by confiding in my bestie.

Worry eclipsed her joy, and she barely nodded as she glanced at the group of men who looked like a pack of yummy, gooey trouble standing beneath the stars that shined down over the party. "And if he is in trouble? What then?"

"Then I face it with him. Help him get his kids back, whatever it costs."

Eden squeezed my hand. "I'm pretty sure it's you *he* could never expect. You who's bringing faith back into his life after he lost it."

"We all need someone to stand by our side."

Eden wrapped her arms around me and hugged me tight. "And he's lucky it's you."

Moisture stung the back of my eyes, and we both let go of these affected giggles when I stepped out of her embrace. Eden always got me.

Understood.

No judgment.

"Come on, everyone is going to be wondering where the bride-to-be ran off to. They'll think you got cold feet."

Hand-in-hand, we started walking back toward the party.

"Is it wrong I wish it were real?" I whispered so only she could hear.

"No, Tessa, there is nothing wrong with wishing for the things we want. The things we need. For believing in the chance of them, even when it feels impossible."

"There you two are. I was beginning to feel left out. Way to leave a nursing mother over here sitting all by herself." Salem sent us a pout, though there was curiosity blazing in her blue eyes, obviously catching the severity of what was riding on our demeanors. She had her sweet baby boy, Grant, pressed to her breast, where she sat at one of the round tables, her hand running over the back of his tiny head as he ate.

Baby Kate was asleep in the mobile crib Eden and Trent had brought.

Juniper lifted her head from where she was sitting next to her mother, coloring.

"You're not by yourself, Mommy, you silly willy. I'm right here, and you've got my *brover* right there."

Juni used her crayon to point at Grant, who grunted as he suckled.

"Hey, what about me?" Gage's eyes were pure offense as he looked up from his coloring sheet to Juni. "I'm right here, too."

He and Juni Bee were tied at the hip, the two so adorable the way they couldn't go anywhere without the other, their lives forever linked.

Eden had gotten the sweet bonus of Gage when she'd married Trent, and his brother, Jud, was lucky as hell to get not just the amazingness that was Salem, but her daughter, too.

"I would never in ever forget you, Gage," Juni told him, so serious.

He seemed to breathe a sigh of relief. "You better not, especially since we're gettin' married."

Neither of them had quite figured out that they were now cousins by marriage and that was not going to happen. But they'd been claiming it for so long, everyone had pretty much given up correcting them on it.

They'd figure it out.

"Maybe we should just have a double wedding," I teased as I moved around the table and pressed a kiss to the top of Gage's head. He angled back so he was beaming up at me.

All adorable dimples and these big brown eyes.

My chest stretched full.

Holy crap, how much I loved these babies. This makeshift family I'd never expected to receive.

"Not old enough yet, Auntie Tessa. Doncha know nothin'?"

A giggle got free, and I swept in to press a kiss to Juni's cheek as I mumbled, "Apparently, Auntie knows absolutely nothing."

"What's nothing?" Aster asked as she came walking over, carrying a pink, bubbly drink with a bunch of maraschino cherries floating in it.

"Tessa knows nothing," Salem supplied.

"Oh, right, yes, I already knew this." Aster grinned as she plopped her adorable pregnant butt onto a chair.

"Oh, I see how it is," I drew out, then my brow was drawing together. "And are you giving me crap when you're sitting over there drinking a Shirley Temple?"

"Would you rather I have a margarita?" She arched a brow as she took a sip. "Besides, I'm pretty sure it's you who deserves all the crap with this… This is quite the party," she drew out. She lifted her glass and waved it around, indicating the mess I'd gotten myself into.

Sighing, I plunked onto the chair next to her and leaned my head on her shoulder. "Pathetic, right?"

She took my hand. "No, honey, you're just doing what you feel is right."

"And you're doing it so well, Jud hasn't even asked a thing about it," Salem added.

"Yeah. It was hard not to let something slip coming over here. This is a lot, Tessa," Aster murmured, her voice close to a warning.

I could feel a thousand silent questions screaming from my friends.

Salem arched an inquisitive brow my direction, her words held in code. "Why are you over there looking so loved up?"

"Ugh," I groaned.

"Because she's gettin' married, Auntie Salem. She's got the love." Gage said it like her question was so ridiculous I was surprised he didn't tack a *duh* to the end of it.

"Hmm," Salem mused.

Guilt came lighting on my cheeks, and I itched in my seat.

"Oh, you little faker," Salem wheezed as she leaned closer to the table. "Tell me now."

The clinking of a knife against a champagne glass and Cheryl announcing she had something to say had me hopping to my feet. "Oh, that's me. Gotta go."

"You're in so much trouble, Tessa McDaniels," Salem called after me.

Oh, I was in trouble all right. She just didn't know how deep it went.

Chapter Twenty-Eight

Milo

"S̶o, Tessa, huh?" Logan elbowed me in the ribs as he sipped at his scotch, the asshole grinning behind it as he razzed me. "Now that is some wild shit that came from out of nowhere."

Night had taken hold of the air, the stars alight and alive where they danced over the party that was supposed to mean something, our friends there to celebrate us, to cover us in their love, when it was nothing but a sham.

Guilt of it had me in a stranglehold, everything catching up. Could feel that what we were doing was about to blow up in our faces. Did we really think we could get away with this without repercussions? Did I really think my past wasn't going to catch up?

My guts twisted as I thought of the note that had been left in my truck. Not that I hadn't been thinking about it twenty-four seven since I'd found it. Since the abyss that was my life had sucked me down in a spiral.

When I realized that it wasn't over.

That I couldn't drag my kids into this.

Couldn't drag Tessa into this.

I didn't deserve a single one of them in my life.

Not with what I'd done.

I might have tried to change, but it didn't *change* anything. The damage was done.

Jud quirked a brow.

"Nowhere? This fucker's been salivating over Tessa since the second she came into the club. You didn't think we missed that shit, did you, brother?" He chuckled as he took a swig of his beer.

Unease stretched across my chest, and I forced myself to return his smile.

Because *that shit* had gotten deep.

Taken a direction it wasn't supposed to go.

"Guess you got me," I mumbled.

"Okay, okay, the whole salivating over our sweet Tessa thing was clear. But this whole wedding bit comes as a surprise," Logan argued.

Trent grunted at his youngest brother. "Says the guy who proposed to Aster three weeks after she came back into his life."

Logan shifted to gaze at Aster, who was laughing where she sat at the table with all their wives.

Tessa had her head leaned against Logan's wife's shoulder, mumbling something that I'd really like to hear.

My dick twitched.

She was all the way across the yard and still the sight of her had lust knotting in my guts.

Logan swiveled back to Trent. "I've loved that woman since I was eighteen. I would say that proposal was about a decade delayed. Not that you didn't get yourself pussy whipped the second Eden came into your club."

Another grunt from Trent. "Not complainin.'"

Jud gazed at his wife, his dark eyes devoted as he watched her nurse their son. "I'd have to say not one of us has a thing to be complaining about."

He put his beer out in the middle of the circle we'd made. Logan and Trent were quick to clink their glasses against it.

Warily, I clinked mine, too.

"To four lucky assholes." Jud chuckled.

"Here, here," Trent agreed.

My spirit rumbled.

Thunder that vibrated through my being. One that warned a storm was coming.

The clinking of glass suddenly pulled me out of the stupor, and my mother was over by the cake that was set up on a round table near the buffet. "I have something I'd like to say."

That had guilt constricting, too.

My mother's joy too potent.

Too profound.

And I'd been the fool who'd insisted we needed to keep her in the dark.

Tessa popped up from her chair, and she whirled around. That gorgeous face lifted in this smile when she caught my eye. It nearly dropped me to my knees.

Like the sight of me made her feel like she was soaring.

She stretched out her hand toward me. She wore another red dress because she had this thing about driving me out of my mind. This one was flowy and swishing around her knees. Tonight, her freckles seemed to glow beneath the twinkle lights strung up over her head.

I gulped.

Sweet fuckin' temptation.

In an instant, my body was a tangle of want.

Problem was that need refused to remain skin deep. It was something that had seeped and infiltrated, penetrating all the way down to the bone, getting way too close to the darkened depths where no one else could go.

Where *her* ghost lingered, and my soul stayed trapped.

Jud patted me on the back. "Looks like your girl is waiting on you."

Right.

My girl.

I slowly edged across the lawn in her direction.

Energy snapped and fired, and fuck, what the hell was I doing?

Because our friends and family were clapping, shouts and cheers going up in the air, and my mother was looking at us like a long-dead dream had come to life.

My head tipped down, then I was breathing out a shattered sigh when Tessa wrapped her hand in mine.

She squeezed and canted me one of those looks that promised, *We have this. We make a really great team.*

But how could that be true when I was dragging her toward destruction?

Tessa led me up to where my mother stood, the girl barely touching me but wrapping me whole.

Mom cleared some of the roughness from her voice, her eyes bleary just from looking at us.

Our guests all settled down.

"I wanted to thank everyone for coming tonight on such short notice…but I think we can all agree that Milo and Tessa's engagement took all of us a bit by surprise, can't we?" my mother teased as she set her gaze upon us.

Her love poured out and flooded the space.

Hell, I felt it coming at us from all sides, laughter rolling across the lawn as our guests called out their agreement.

My heart jackhammered.

"Okay, okay, we can tease these two all we want…" Mom waved a hand like she wanted everyone to understand the seriousness of what she was speaking, and her voice deepened in emphasis. "But there's something I've learned in my life. Love can come on fast or it can come on slow. It doesn't matter. Not one kind is stronger than the other. It's just born differently. And what I can say for sure is I've never felt a love so strong as the one that was born between Milo and Tessa."

My throat thickened, and I struggled to breathe.

Mom turned her full attention on me. "I've prayed for this day to come, for you to find your way to joy again. That you would find a path that would lead to the place where you belong…and that's with Tessa."

She lifted her glass. "To the happiness that you deserve because you, my son, you deserve it more than anyone I've ever known."

Her voice got choppy, soggy with the affection that rippled out.

She shifted her adoring gaze to Tessa.

To the woman who stood beside me vibrating with emotion, too.

It's not real.

It's not real.

It's not fucking real.

I chanted it to myself like I could make it so, but Mom had her hand on her chest like she was trying to keep her heart in place while she whispered, "And I am so thankful it is you. Tessa, you beautiful girl, the morning I showed up unannounced and found you here, I knew there was something so extraordinarily special about you. You are the hope that this family has been missing, and I will be forever grateful for you showing us that it's a possibility. I love you, and I know that's new, too, that it came on just as fast, but it's true. I'm so happy to have you as my daughter."

Tessa gulped, and I felt her spirit flail.

Her own loss stark.

This beautiful woman who'd lost so much.

It was a rare day my mom hadn't stopped by to say hello, and they'd established a bond unlike anything I'd witnessed before. It only made this that much harder.

"I love you, too," Tessa barely was able to murmur.

My mother nodded, and Tessa was moving forward and throwing her arms around her.

Their hug was fierce.

Different from when they'd first met.

Because in it was a promise.

A promise of a new life.

They finally separated, and both were wiping tears from their faces, whispering something under their breath.

And fuck, I nearly fell apart when Mom turned and wrapped her arms around my neck.

I had to bend down, and I was leaning into her as her mouth came to my ear and she murmured, "I see you terrified of finding love again, my son. I see you're scared of losing it. Let this love be strong enough to carry you through it. Let her hold you when you feel like you can't hang on any longer. Cling to each other, build each other up. And most of all, you let your beautiful heart live."

I'm not sure I know how.

She pulled away and lifted her glass, gesturing it around to our guests.

"Now, I think we should officially announce these two as engaged with a special dance, don't you?" My mother's voice lifted at that.

Wariness took me hostage.

The music was turned back up, and everyone was standing, and the air was getting dense, even though a breeze whispered through.

Because these feelings were too heavy.

Too big.

Too much.

And Tessa was turning and grinning up at me.

Sly.

Sweet.

Alight.

The sun rising on the darkened day.

I felt her burning me through.

Scorching when she looped her arms around my neck. I banded one arm around her waist and pulled her flush against my chest.

Relief at her touch belted through my being.

"There you are," she whispered up at my face, and she fluttered her fingertips down my beard, this precious woman who'd offered me everything.

My forehead dropped to hers, and I inhaled her deep into my lungs that kept aching for a way to fully be filled.

Strawberries and cream.

We barely swayed, just stood there together, me breathing her in as that energy burned around us.

Calling me to a place that I couldn't go.

"Are you going to stand there all day or kiss the poor woman?" Logan shouted from the sidelines.

I eased back and found what was written on Tessa's face.

The adoration.

The loyalty.

And that feeling rose up again.

Felt it struggling to pull me over.

Trip me up.

Telling me it would be fine to slide into the safety of a girl who wasn't really mine.

Tessa's lips parted, and there was no tease to it.

It was bare-naked hope.

Mad love, Milo. Mad, mad love, she mouthed.

Fuck.

I couldn't do this. Couldn't.

I pecked the quickest kiss to her mouth before I tore myself away, putting as much distance between us as I could, waving at our friends like everything was just fine.

While Tessa looked at me like I'd just rammed a knife directly through her heart.

Chapter Twenty-Nine

Milo

Five Years Ago

MILO PRESSED A SOFT KISS TO HIS DAUGHTER'S TEMPLE, the little child long asleep within the darkness of the small room. He brushed back the wild locks of her brown hair and stared at her precious face where she rested.

His spirit flailed.

He would do whatever it took to provide for his family.

He would fix this.

Make it right.

"Goodnight, my sweet Remy," he murmured below his breath before he stood and walked out into the cramped living space of the trailer.

Autumn was asleep on their makeshift bed, their son asleep in the playpen they used as a crib.

God, they were beautiful.

A treasure he didn't deserve.

Every molecule in his body clutched.

You're pathetic. Worthless. You'll never amount to anything, just like your mother. I should do the world a favor and put a bullet in both your brains.

Milo eased over to Autumn, ran his fingers through her hair, and swept his lips over her cheek.

She hummed in her sleep, and before he woke her, he pushed to standing and moved to the door. He carefully clicked it open.

He felt the shuffling from behind.

"Where are you going?" Autumn's voice hit him in confusion.

Chaos and perfection.

Warily, he turned to look back at her from over his shoulder, his eyes taking her in where she'd pushed up to sitting.

"I have to run an errand."

She frowned. "Where? It's late."

"I'll be right back."

Worry traipsed through her features, though she forced a trusting smile. "Okay…just hurry and come back to me."

He nodded, then he slipped out into the night.

Twenty minutes later, he was standing in front of Autumn's parents' door.

He struggled and warred, searching himself for strength.

For a way to swallow his pride. To take back his promise.

He gulped around the disgust because what he felt didn't matter. It held no bearing on what he had to do. He reached out and pressed the doorbell.

It seemed like an eternity passed before a light flicked on downstairs.

He could almost feel the animosity burn through the peephole from someone glaring at him from inside, and he sucked in a steeling breath when the metal slid and the latch gave.

Autumn's mother barely cracked open the door, hatred in her eyes as she peered out. "Is my daughter safe?"

"Yes," he wheezed.

She was safe. But she was none of the other things he'd promised she would be.

"What do you want, then?"

Bile lifted in his stomach and coated his tongue. Swallowing it down, he lifted his chin. "A loan."

Her laugh was incredulous. "You're standing here asking me for a loan?"

He could barely make himself nod. "I am."

Paula scoffed and widened the door enough so that she could angle toward him. "Why would I ever give you anything when you stole everything from me?"

Old hatred flared. Vibrated through his being. Boiled hot in his blood.

Paula could have easily been a part of their family. Could have been a part of her grandchildren's lives. She just chose not to. She had all but written Autumn off for loving him.

He refused the spite, the intense urge to lash out.

Fight.

He wasn't that man anymore. He refused to be. Wouldn't give into the depravity.

"I know you hate me, Paula, but I really need help finishing our cabin. I'm trying to give your daughter and grandchildren a good home. But after the investment in the business, I'm coming up short. We have some big jobs in the works. Things will come together, and I'll be able to pay you back quickly."

He prayed sooner rather than later, but he was worried that wasn't going to be the case. He'd invested everything in the construction company. Running a business and profiting from it was a whole ton harder than he'd ever imagined.

But he would make it work.

He just needed more time.

"I just need the money now so I can finish our cabin."

At least he'd already gotten his mother's place finished, and he was more than halfway done with their cabin, but the time and cost investment were greater since it was more than double the size of hers.

Maybe he should have waited until he'd been completely fin-ished with both places to try to start the company, but Autumn had pushed him, telling him it was time, that they needed to make a change and have a steady income coming in before the money he'd saved from fighting ran dry.

He understood.

He wanted that safety net, too.

He wanted to provide.

To do right by his family.

And there he stood like a pathetic beggar, groveling at Paula's feet.

She angled back. "Did you know my daughter called here crying the other day?"

Milo blanched. What? He gritted his teeth to keep himself from demanding to know why. He needn't worry because Paula was dead set on throwing it in his face, anyway.

"It seems she's realized just how miserable life is going to be with you."

His head shook.

"Do you really think she wants to raise two children in a trailer, Milo?"

"Our place is nearly finished."

"But it's not, is it? And you can bet your life I won't be helping you do it, either. I want my daughter home, where she belongs, not depressed and sleeping on your couch. She's worth so much more than the life you're giving her. My grandchildren are worth more. You will never give them what they need. If you love them at all, you'd walk away."

He breathed out the shock and pain, a low, horrified laugh leaving his mouth that he turned toward the ground, trying to gather himself.

His thoughts.

His strength.

To make a rebound on this desperation because he knew what Paula was spewing had nothing to do with the quality of life Autumn and their children had.

It was about him.

Paula wanted him gone.

"Now, get off my property. You will never be welcome here, but my daughter and grandchildren will always be. Autumn will return, just as soon as she comes to her senses and finally sees who you truly are."

"Paula—"

She slammed the door in his face.

Desperation streaked through his spirit, and he started to rush forward, to pound on the door and demand she listen. But it wasn't going to change a damned thing.

She would never see him as anything but scum.

He turned and headed back to his truck, climbed inside, and took off down their long drive.

He was barely able to see through the haze of loathing.

For Paula.

For his father.

For himself.

He struggled to see through the disorder. To find a reason. A way.

His teeth gritted, and the blood sloshed through his veins, and he jerked to a stop on the side of the road.

He picked up his phone, stared at it as the voices whirled through his mind.

The hunger.

The hate.

The thirst for destruction.

Gore.

He squeezed the phone as hard as he squeezed his eyes closed, his throat clotting off.

Before he lost his nerve, he thumbed into the phone and made the call.

He pressed it to his ear, close to panicking as it rang.

But he had no other choice.

No way to be the man he'd promised Autumn he would be.

The dark voice answered on the second ring. "Hello?"

"Stefan." Milo needed only to say his name for Stefan to recognize him.

A beat passed before Stefan blew out in surprise. "You are finally ready to return?"

"I told you I'm finished with that life. I just need one fight."

Hurt curled through Stefan's voice. "So, you only call me when you want something? This is how you treat me after everything I've done for you? What does that say about you, Milo?"

Desperation clawed at him. "I just need one job, Stefan."

Enough to see him through.

"You know it doesn't work like that. You're in or out. And you should know the stakes are much higher than they used to be."

Apprehension billowed through his spirit. He gulped it down. "I'm in."

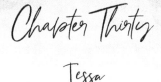

Chapter Thirty

Tessa

"Goodnight," I called to Cheryl from the front porch. She was the last of our guests to leave, staying long after the party had ended since she'd insisted on helping clean up.

"It was the best time. Thank you for letting me share it with you. I'll see you both soon." She blew a kiss in our direction before she climbed into her car. She started the engine, and her headlights sliced through the dense, toxic air.

Suffocating.

Excruciating.

At least that's the way I sensed Milo's presence, where he stood behind me like a dark mirage.

The hope of something beautiful, but when you dipped your fingers into it, it filled your spirit with poison.

It was my own freaking fault that I'd come to imagine a future he would never allow.

His rejection earlier had hurt.

In a big way.

I'd felt—embarrassed, I guessed. Too hopeful in a moment that felt so real. Lost to Cheryl's love and support. The love and support of our friends. Milo could have at least taken one for the *team* and kissed me like he meant it.

But I knew down deep it was all me.

That I'd come to a breaking point.

The realization that I couldn't keep doing this to myself. Putting myself in a position where I kept getting hurt.

Yeah, I was the one who'd encouraged it. Pushed it. I'd wanted him to open up to me so badly that I'd laid myself out like an offering. Hoping he'd feel it in my touch. That he'd understand.

After tonight, I knew it. Felt it. I couldn't pretend any longer.

Cheryl backed out and drove away, and I felt the shift in the atmosphere, the low roll of thunder as he turned and moved back into his house, leaving the door open behind him.

I followed, slow to move back through the door, freezing when I was struck with the low, anguished bellow that ripped from his massive body.

Guttural.

Pained.

It was a sound I was sure I could hear from a thousand miles away.

A hook that embedded itself in my soul from where he stood at the island with his back to me.

Slumped over again, though this time, his posture was riddled with stark, gutting grief.

The kind that couldn't be understood unless you'd experienced it. Been right there to witness it. Felt the desolation of its effect.

"Milo." His name trembled from my throat and struck the room like a plea.

Energy pulsed. Intense and dark and compelling.

It was a pull I knew full well I needed to resist, but I had no idea how to defy the call of his heart, as if our souls were linked in some way.

Because that connection hummed in the air, though tonight, it keened and moaned a quiet lament.

Potent and powerful.

Fierce and broken.

My pulse raced with determination, a furious thrumming that rushed out to meet with the man who thrashed in the wreckage of his past.

Tied to a place where he was alone.

Where demons possessed and monsters roamed.

The problem was, Milo somehow viewed himself as one of those who crawled the underbelly of this sordid hell where he held himself prisoner.

Chained.

Stuck in a moment he couldn't change or take back.

And I wanted to free him of his binds. And if I couldn't, then I needed to free myself of the ones he'd locked around me.

Because I couldn't do this.

Couldn't keep pretending that what I felt was fake.

So, I inched closer to the mayhem that flailed and whirled, a dark, dark storm that battered his soul.

I felt it flooding back. A swell that crashed and beat against the shores of my spirit, as if he were seeking refuge.

"Milo," I said again.

His shoulders tensed before he finally turned around.

My breath hitched.

The sheer size of the man was terrifying, but it was his agonized expression that knocked my knees, the sight of him that reached into my chest and yanked my heart right out of my ribs.

That mountain of a man stood raging.

A hurricane.

Lost to a torment that I didn't know how to erase, but I wanted to find a way to possess for him, anyway.

To whisper it away for a moment.

To promise him I would hold it if he'd let me.

But he had to let me in. I could no longer stand on the sidelines.

He stared at me through a bleary, disordered gaze, the man held captive somewhere in the recesses of his mind, though I could feel those eyes calling out for me somewhere in the misery where he lived.

Like he thought maybe I could be his rescue. A way out. Or like I might be his condemnation.

"Little Dove." It was half a plea, half a warning. "You should go to bed."

I edged forward a step. The air shivered. The energy leapt.

"You keep asking me to walk away from you, Milo. You keep pushing me away. And I can feel it, when you need me." I clutched at my chest.

Unease flitted through his big body. "Keep telling you that you don't want to go there."

I lifted my chin, the words hard and desperate. "I'm strong enough to handle what you need. I think it's you who's not strong enough to handle me."

Shards of pain left him on a moan. "Tessa."

My head shook, and I took another step forward. "I can't do it anymore. Can't handle this push and pull. Can't keep ignoring what this is."

Blinking, he took a step away like he could shield himself from the severity. "Warned you it was going to be messy."

"But neither of us knew it would be like this."

"I already told you—"

"Stop it. Just stop it, Milo. Stop lying to yourself and stop lying to me. This isn't fake, and if you think it is, then you're a fool."

"I warned you not to fall for me," he grated.

"Too late."

His jaw clenched beneath his beard. "I can't give you what you want, Tessa. What you need."

"You're wrong. Everything I need is right here." I pointed at the floor. "Right here with you. And I know you think you've done something in your past that precludes you from being loved, but you're wrong, because I love you."

The confession whipped from my tongue.

So hard it smacked through the oxygen like a sonic boom.

A reverberation that banged against the walls.

"I love all the sweet and protective parts about you, and I love the harsh and fierce ones. I love the hope you have for your children, and I love your broken parts, too. I love you," I whispered that time, begging him to see.

He squeezed his eyes shut, words a scrape of denial. "Tessa...don't."

"I love you, Milo. I love you."

His head shook, and he refused to look at me. Refused to acknowledge what I'd said.

"I'm in love with you, Milo. Wholly and completely."

Pain lanced through his expression. "Please...don't."

"Tell me you don't feel it."

He just stared at me, refusing to say anything.

Rejection curdled in my throat, closing off the hope, and I began to nod as I forced myself to accept it.

"Okay, then."

My words were so low, filled with the pain of the realization that this had to be it. He'd made me promise to tell him if it became too much. I doubted this was what he'd meant, but here we were.

Me at my end, and Milo stuck where we'd started.

"I'll be here for your kids, like I promised. But if you can't admit what you feel for me? Then this..." I gestured between us. "It has to end. I have to protect what's left of my heart."

No more pitching between want and rejection.

No more stolen touches and shameful hands.

Because I wouldn't be a sin.

Wouldn't be something he regretted.

"Goodnight, Milo."

I turned in the direction of my room, fighting the burn of tears. I needed to hold on to them at least until I made it to the safety inside.

He might know how far I'd fallen, but he didn't need to know the pain of landing there.

I'd almost made it to the door when a flurry of footfalls echoed behind me. He looped a massive arm around my waist and yanked me against the hard planes of his body.

His voice was even harder as he rushed the words at my ear, "You think I don't feel this, Tessa? You think I don't know it's real? But I'm terrified of letting you down. Of failing. Of destroying something good."

"I'm not afraid, Milo. You're worth the risk," I rasped through the haze. "What you have to ask yourself is if I am. Am I worth the risk?"

A growl ripped from his chest, and he had me spun and pressed to the wall before my senses could catch up.

Electricity cracked.

A whip in the air.

Amber eyes had turned molten.

Lava.

Scorching a fiery path as they seared me through.

"Am I?" I demanded. He didn't need to tell me he loved me back, but I at least needed this.

A promise that this was more.

That *I* was more.

My shoulders were pinned to the wall, but my back heaved forward, my body making a play to meet with his.

Milo stared at me, his breaths ragged, that severe brow slashing downward in intensity. His lips plush and his jaw hard and his heart hammering.

"You're worth it, Tessa. You're worth everything." He swept me off my feet and into his massive arms. "Every. Fucking. Thing."

I lifted my chin. "Then prove it."

He carried me through the cabin and directly to his room, all hulking power and steely determination.

He tossed me onto his bed, and I bounced against the mattress.

A giggle got free. I didn't know if I wanted to weep or let go of a shout of victory.

Loving Milo Hendricks for the win.

"What are you laughing at, Little Dove?" It almost sounded like a warning as he gazed down at me where he stood towering at the side of the bed.

He was looking at me the way I'd imagined he would do in my dreams.

In this way that made me feel like he was both going to ravage me and keep me.

Ruin me and cherish me.

All bristly fierceness and gentle adoration.

I felt it glow and warm and seep down to my bones.

"That I can't wait until you wreck me."

"You want me to break you, Tessa?"

Every glorious muscle in his giant body flexed.

I writhed on his mattress, my breaths shallow, the words a plea, because for the love of all things holy, I needed him, and I needed him now. "I think you already have."

"Think it's safe to say it's the other way around."

"No, Milo, I don't want to break you. I want to show you everything you deserve."

"And what do you want in return?" His voice turned all sexy and raspy, and God, this man did things to me that shouldn't be possible.

Things I should probably be terrified of because I was completely laying myself bare.

Offering it all. But we were long since passed caution.

I'd tossed it to the wind the day I'd agreed to stay here with him.

"Well, I'm thinking right about now that I want you to touch me."

I sent him a teasing grin, though the need was verified.

A dizzying desire streaked through my body, and I was tingling just looking at him.

A heavy breath escaped him, and his tongue swept over his plush, decadent lips. "Why's it feel so good with you? Why's it feel so right?"

"Maybe because we're right where we belong, right now, in this moment." The words were thin wisps that rushed from my lips. "What if we were meant to be here, Milo? What if the heartbreak and loss we've both suffered warped us into a new shape? What if it bent us so we had no choice but to turn a different direction? A place where it was impossible for us not to meet? What if we were supposed to become something brand new together?"

His fingers tickled along the outside of my calf, just above the strap of my red heel.

An anxious breath sighed from my lips.

"And what if I ruin you, Little Dove?"

My heart ravaged my chest, every beat chaos, my spirit whipping through the room in a bid to meet with his.

"I already told you that you were worth the risk."

A compulsion wound around us.

Enveloping.

Enshrouding.

Or maybe it was cocooning.

Weaving a safe place.

This bond of protection that we could only find in one another.

I eased up to sitting, and I stared up at him as my fingers moved to his belt, my voice a low promise as I worked the buckle free. "I'll stand by you, Milo. I'll stand by this gentle man who's so intimidatingly fierce. A man who will do anything to save his family. A man who is willing to fight. But one who also has the softest spirit. A man who adores his children. A man who looks at me like I might be a treasure."

I pushed to standing.

Energy flashed.

I set my palm over the erratic thunder of his heart.

"And whoever you are in the darkest places in here? Whatever you've done? Whatever you're prepared to do? I'll stand by him, too."

"That guy's not good, baby." He gathered my hand and kissed across my knuckles, his breaths shallow and hard.

I pushed up higher. My fingertips traipsed into his beard. "But I still want that guy to be mine."

"I want to give you the entire fuckin' world, Tessa."

"How about you just give me *you*?"

"Is that what you want, Little Dove? You want this? You want this mess?"

Everything about him darkened and slowed.

Energy crackled.

Pinpricks of light.

Every part of us knew this was it. Milo and I were no longer at a precipice. We'd pushed ourselves to the edge and there was no place to go but over.

Our only choice was to fall into each other's arms.

And I'd gladly, recklessly fall into his.

"Yes. I want it all."

"If I have you, you're mine." The words came as possession as they cut from his mouth.

A claim.

A call.

"I already am," I whispered.

I had no time to even anticipate it before his lips captured mine in a savage kiss, his mouth hot and his tongue demanding.

He fisted a hand in my hair, and he angled my head to the side so he could devour my mouth. His other hand splayed wide, riding down my spine until he was cupping one side of my ass.

He squeezed and kneaded before he tugged me closer, up against the rigid expanse of his gorgeous body.

I yelped a tiny sound that was driven by lust.

By this cloud of desire that filled the room.

Disorienting.

Bewildering.

Empowering.

The roiling heat combusted, his kiss, his touch, the room consumed in flames.

He touched me everywhere, palms impassioned as they glided up my back, running around my sides, pushing up between us until he was palming my breast as he continued to kiss me. Never letting go of my mouth while he worked every inch of me into a frenzy.

A blaze erupted in my insides.

A flashfire that seared across the surface of my skin. Rising up and pouring out from that sacred place that'd cried out to be set free. To find the place where I trusted fully. Where there was no question. No ulterior.

Just pure desire.

My desire for him and his desire for me.

A low, throaty moan reverberated from Milo's chest as he pulled me closer, and he slipped his hand under my dress. He lifted me by the bottom into his arms and ground me against him.

I burned.

Begged.

"Milo, please."

"You think I'm not going to take care of you? You think I don't know what you need or how to give it to you? I'm going to own you. This sweet body that I've been dying to get lost in."

"Do it now." I almost whined it as I rubbed myself all over him, my core throbbing, this desire so intense he was the only breath I could find.

A rough chuckle skated free, dripping from his tongue and sliding into me, his tongue stroking slow as he murmured, "Are you eager, sweetness?"

I clawed at his shoulders. "I need this. I've never felt this way, Milo."

"And now you're mine, and I plan on havin' you feel this way forever," he rumbled.

Oh, holy mother.

I was not going to make it.

Especially when he shifted me in his hold, keeping me writhing against him with one hand while he dragged the zipper of my dress down with the other.

And they said men couldn't multitask.

He somehow peeled me out of my dress without setting me on my feet, leaving me in only my underwear and heels, while I was ripping at the buttons of his shirt.

Our kisses barely broke long enough to tear our clothes from our bodies.

Relief whooshed from my lungs when his chest was finally bare, his shoulders so wide and his pecs so big and hard, and God, was this man beautiful.

I crushed myself to his magnificent body, rubbing my boobs against him because I really needed the friction.

Needed it everywhere.

Had to sate this burn.

"Tiny Tease," he rumbled at my mouth.

"No teasing to it, Milo. This is real. It's real," I rushed back.

Every inch of him tensed, and I thought he was going to withdraw again, but instead, he was laying me out on his bed, his gaze devouring me as he went.

"So fucking gorgeous." It was a grunt of lust. "What I'm going to do to you. The pleasure I'm going to bring you. Again and again."

My hips bucked in an emphatic, *yes, please.*

He never looked away as he toed off his shoes, then he was shrugging the rest of the way out of his pants and underwear, and I was dying all over again at the sight of Milo completely bare.

My eyes raced to take him in.

Tracking every inch.

Hulking, rigid muscle and the sheen of want that coated his tattooed, scarred flesh.

His cock was enormous, thick and fat with the kind of hunger that made my knees weak.

Beautiful Beast.

"I'm going to expect you to make good on that promise, Milo Hendricks." I tried to play it light, but my throat was tight, and these tingly shivers were streaking all over my skin.

He leaned over and began to peel my underwear down my legs, murmuring, "I'll do my best," as he went.

A desperate sound got loose of my mouth.

I couldn't help it.

Milo chuckled, then he took me by the knees and spread me wide.

That time, I gasped, "Milo."

"You've got the sweetest pussy, Little Dove." He dove in for a taste, his tongue pushing deep between my lips.

My hips bucked. "Please. I'm on the pill. Hurry."

His mouth moved higher, leaving a trail of kisses as he climbed onto the bed.

My hip bone, my lower belly, my ribs on my left side. "Eager girl," he murmured across my heated skin.

He rode up until he was winding himself between my thighs before he took the hardened nub of my right breast between his teeth.

Warmth streaked, and my fingers drove into his hair. I held on for my quickly dwindling sanity as he licked me into oblivion.

My eyes nearly rolled back into my head when he pressed his hot cock to my center.

Erratic anticipation rushed through my veins and sent chills skating over every inch of my flesh.

"Milo."

He pulled back, and his fingers softly traced the angle of my jaw. "I have you, Little Dove."

It was a pained oath.

"Then take me."

He gazed down at me.

My hair all around and my heart in his hands.

Did he know?

Did he understand what it meant?

Did he know it was unconditional?

Eternal?

"I love you," I whispered.

And I'd love this man to his dying day if he'd let me.

Honey-dipped eyes dimmed, and his palm slipped to my cheek. "And you own me, Tessa McDaniels."

There was a dose of sadness behind it as he pushed up onto his hands, the man an intimidating refuge where he hovered high.

The bare space between us groaned, and our connection thrummed.

He adjusted himself between my shaking thighs, and he ran just the tip through my center.

"Oh." My arms curled around his neck, and I couldn't do anything but hold on, though my mouth was near his ear, my confession quiet but bold. "I want you so bad, Milo."

So bad I hurt.

"Does that mean you're ready for me? Ready for me to take all this sweetness?"

My stomach flipped in need, and I frantically nodded where our cheeks were pressed together. "I've been ready forever."

"Hold on, baby."

Milo began to nudge his cock inside me.

So slow because *holy crap*.

He spread me.

Inch by torturous inch.

My mouth opened on a moan, on the perfect, blissful, pained pleasure as he worked himself into my body.

I expelled a shattered breath when he finally filled me full, so full I was gasping short, jutting sounds that I couldn't control.

Milo's hand flexed where he held me by the back of the neck.

No doubt, he was struggling to keep it together.

Close to snapping.

To freeing the intensity I could see radiating from him, the clench of his jaw and the flex of his abdomen and the sheen of sweat that glistened on his flesh.

He grunted a hard breath, and his arm came around the top of my head like he could hold every part of me beneath the hedge of his protection.

His body a shield.

His aura was dark and light and thrashing.

Everything.

Everything.

"Can't believe I'm here like this with you, Tessa. Can't believe it's real. You have no idea what I'd do for you. The lengths I would go."

The words were gravel.

The grinding of a threat that wasn't meant for me.

His mind traipsing to the dark places he was terrified for me to see.

"I will follow you there."

He eased back so our lips barely brushed, our breaths rasping together.

Our hearts meshed.

He pressed up onto one elbow and began to move.

Milo took me in a way I'd never been taken before.

Fully.

Wholly.

"Do you have any idea how good it feels being inside you?" It was a grunt from his mouth.

Energy fired and flashed.

A flame that could never go out.

"Your pussy hugging my dick. So goddamn perfect. Could live inside you forever."

Air wheezed up my lungs, and I clung tighter to him as he spread his hand around to my bottom.

"You can have me forever, Milo. Always."

Something flashed through his expression, like his spirit that had been held back by chains suddenly broke.

He pulled out, then filled me with a possessive thrust. "I want it, Tessa. Want to give that to you."

He picked up a reckless rhythm, and I clawed at his back.

He took me hard. Desperate.

The two of us left without caution.

Pure abandon as we got lost in this relief.

In what neither of us believed we'd ever have, but we'd found in each other.

We became this writhing, thrashing, undulating thing.

Liquid.

One.

No separation.

Nothing to keep us apart.

Not even his past that hovered at the fringes of the room, phantoms that waited for the moment they would consume.

I wanted to possess him the way he possessed me, and I lifted to meet his hips with each desperate thrust, fully giving myself to him with every pitch of my body.

"Milo," I rasped.

"It's only the beginning, Tessa. You understand, baby? You're mine now."

Pleasure flickered at the edges of my sight, and it only grew brighter with each jut of his hips.

He angled back onto his knees, changing position.

He rubbed his thumb over my clit.

"So good. So good," I mumbled frantically because oh, my God, it was.

"Told you I was gonna take care of you, Little Dove. You get it easy this once."

I probably shouldn't shout how much I really loved that idea.

He drove deeper, harder, faster.

And it all became so intense.

Blinding.

This bliss that built.

It rushed and gathered.

A swarm of ecstasy.

A buzz of rapture.

Beautiful in a way that infiltrated my chest and seeped into my spirit.

Acute.

Profound.

Exquisite.

I gasped and whimpered and begged in the moments before I split.

One second later, I shattered.

Broke apart in the safety of his arms.

Milo had it all wrong when it came to him and me. There were no gilded cages. No clipping of my wings.

Because he touched me, and I soared.

Flew.

He and I together?

We were free.

I trembled all around him as the orgasm barreled through me.

An obliteration.

A detonation.

Every cell slayed.

Complete, blissed-out rubble.

Milo jerked as he came, every muscle in his rugged, gorgeous body flexing as he grunted my name.

We led each other through.

Rocked and shivered in this glorious aftermath.

We slowed as the sensation ebbed, both of us twitching and shaking.

He shifted us onto our sides so we were facing each other in the lapping night.

Everything had grown so still.

Like the earth had been set to pause to honor this moment.

His gaze moved over my face, taking in my expression, his fingertips tender as he ran them down the angle of my jaw. "You believe in me, Little Dove?"

The pain in his voice brought tears to my eyes.

I nodded against his pillow, and I scratched my nails into his beard. "Yes, Milo, I do."

Chapter Thirty-One

Milo

DARKNESS SWATHED THE ROOM IN SHADOWS.

Ocean eyes gazed at me through them.

A thousand currents.

Unfound depths.

Belief.

Trust.

Love.

My chest tightened as I held her in my arms. Our limbs were tangled, our breaths slowed but jagged as we floated through the type of tranquility I wasn't meant to possess.

"I believe in you," she whispered that time as she dragged her fingers through my beard, riding down until they were playing over the designs on my chest.

Tiny Tease tapping out a love song that was supposed to have no beginning but begged for no end.

Wanted to give it to her.

All of it.

All of me.

Always.

I curled my arm tighter around her, breathing out a sigh as I pressed a kiss to the top of her head. "It's been a long time since someone has."

The softest smile played over her lips that were swollen from my kisses. I couldn't do anything but trace it with my finger.

"I think your mom has always believed in you."

Affection tugged at my insides. "Yeah, guess she has, hasn't she?"

"Mm-hmm, she sees just how incredible you are."

A grin pulled to one side of my mouth, this feeling too light as I held Tessa in the darkness. "Think she might be biased."

"I think she knows exactly what she's talking about." An easy playfulness edged her words.

"Hmm...I'm thinking someone else might be a little biased, too." My fingers threaded through those fiery locks of red.

Tessa all but grinned. "Well, I guess someone did knock me out with his giant cock."

A surprised chuckle raked free as my brows shot toward the ceiling. "Knocked you out, huh?"

She nodded emphatically. "Oh, yeah. TKO. I'm done for. I might not have my faculties about me any longer. There'll be no thinking straight from here on out."

Air puffed from my nose. "I hope you know what you're doing. That all of this isn't about me blowing your mind with my dick."

Tried to keep that light, too, but the words were rough.

"I know exactly what I'm doing."

Her fingers kept exploring, tracing the lines of my tattoos, before she was running her fingertips over the word stamped on my side.

Gore.

It stood out over the rest, right over that deep scar on my side.

"What does this mean?" she whispered, in tune with me and already sure it held significance.

A tremble rocked down my spine, my mouth going dry.

Tessa leaned up a little bit. "You can trust me, Milo. I already told you there is nothing you could have done in your past that would make me stop believing in you. Make me stop loving you."

She touched my jaw as she emphasized it, and my lungs pressed full with her beauty, with that fiery, sweet loyalty that made her extraordinary.

Just like my mother had said.

"Told you fighting is in my blood."

She barely flinched, but I still felt it, felt her spirit prepare to be led in a direction that would likely send her running out my door. "You did."

"First time it happened, I was in middle school. These kids… they were always fuckin' pushing me. Rubbing it in my face that we were poor. That my father was a drunk. Wasn't like I didn't show up at school with black eyes half the time."

"Milo." Sympathy rushed through her expression.

My head shook to cut her off. If she wanted me to get this out, I was just going to have to spill it.

"One of them called my mom a whore, which seriously? My mom's a fuckin' saint. That was it. I lost it. Beat the fuck out of that kid. It felt so damn good."

My teeth ground when I admitted it.

When I gave voice to the violence that seethed underneath.

Barely held.

Barely constrained.

She wanted my darkness? I was going to give it to her. Make her understand. I was sure she still didn't have the first clue what she was getting into.

"Well, I think I want to kick that kid's ass, too." Her voice was choppy with affection, blue eyes racing over me like she was trying to see through the veil, which apparently, she didn't have to look too hard because when it came to her, there was no denying her.

"It got worse as I got older. Fought so much in high school, they finally expelled me. It was after my mom left my father."

I paused, an onslaught of ugly memories impaling me. "My father was this nasty bastard who took his misery out on my mom and me whenever he got the chance. As I got older, I did my best to take the blows for her, but I swear, every fuckin' time he hit me, this monster inside me grew. It got to the point where I think I craved it…him hitting me so I could return it. When I was sixteen, I came home one night to him hitting on my mom. I beat him so bad I don't know how he ever got up again. That was the night my mom finally cracked. Knew we couldn't stay there anymore. She and I took off while he was still bleeding on the floor, and we came here to Redemption Hills."

Regret blistered hot across my flesh. "But it was like once I stopped having to fight him, I needed somewhere else to turn the aggression."

She started to say something, but her questions stalled out, like she knew I wasn't ready to answer them.

Not yet.

"I got involved in some bad stuff, Tessa." Barely was able to force the admission out.

"My grandparents were still alive when we came back here. There was this shitty trailer sitting on this property, and they gave it to us, not that they had much else than the land to their names, either. Mom and I made it the best home that we could, but *it* was still there, Tessa. The *rage*. This feeling that threatened to boil over. We were broke as fuck, so when I was presented the opportunity, I took it."

"The opportunity?" Tessa's voice was thin, held in concern, but without any judgment.

My hand tightened on her hip, and I focused on the way her bare body felt against mine.

The warmth.

The goodness.

The hope.

The sun rising on a darkened day.

Regret churned through my insides. Hate and violence and thirst for retribution seething underneath.

"I'd met this guy. Stefan. I guess he'd seen something in me, and he took me under his wing. He started having me do random odd jobs. Gave me money. Made me feel like I was something more than the piece of shit my father told me I was. Treated me like his family, and that's the way I'd come to think of him. I'd respected him, or really, maybe I'd just wanted to be like him. At the beginning, it was all good. I was already in thick when it started to become clear that he ran this underground shit. Drugs. Prostitution. Gambling. Fighting, which looking back now, I know that's why he'd singled me out. What he'd wanted me for. He'd seen that potential in me."

"Like Fight Club?"

A rough chuckle scraped free. "If you mean a bunch of assholes beating the shit out of each other in a basement, then yeah. But it was different. Money was on the line. It was all bred of greed. It was ugly, Tessa. Dirty."

She gulped. "People got hurt."

"Yeah." The word was thick.

"Like…how bad?"

"Bad."

Her fingers were back to running over that word. "Have you… killed someone?"

I could barely breathe, and I shifted, pushing out the confession toward the ceiling, "I have."

A tremulous sound quivered from her lips, but this girl didn't seem swayed. She just shifted onto her elbow, her brow twisted as her palm slid up to my cheek. "On purpose?"

I blinked through the sordid memories. "Sometimes you're pushed against a wall so hard you have no choice but to fight back."

She nodded like she understood. "You can't blame yourself for that."

My hand came to cover hers, and I met the intensity of her stare. "The only thing I feel guilty about is that I don't regret it."

"We all do what we have to in order to survive. I see it, Milo. It was survival."

I clung to her hand as the hatred ran hot. "Working for Stefan was a trap."

I needed her to understand what was on the line.

"I'd finally gotten out of that life, even though Stefan didn't want to let me go. I didn't hear from him for years, so I'd believed he was dead," I continued. "Most likely chained and floating at the bottom of the ocean somewhere because that was the kind of life he led."

My throat burned as I forced out the dread. "But I'm certain it was him who had me attacked. Had my windshield bashed in."

Terror blanched through her defined features, though she tried to keep it under wraps. "What does he want?"

"I don't know. Money. Revenge. To show me he owned me all along. We'd been close... I viewed him as a father figure at one time. He'd warned me I could never walk away from him...and when I did..."

Grief clamped off the confession, unable to let the words free.

I needed to tell her.

Shit, I needed to tell her.

But I couldn't force it around the sickness that clawed through me, and instead, I was clinging tight to Tessa as I made a promise to her and myself. "I'm going to end it this time. He won't get near you or my kids. Whatever it takes. Do you understand?"

She seemed to hear the threat in my words, and she was trembling when she shifted up higher so she was close to laying on top of me. Her pale skin was bare and sprinkled with that wash of freckles, her face so fuckin' gorgeous as she gazed down at me.

She stole the breath right out of my lungs.

"I understand," she promised.

My hand slipped up her back and over her shoulder so I could tuck her closer.

"This could get ugly," I warned around the lump that sat like a stone in my throat.

She went to fluttering those fingertips over my face, red hair raining around her.

"It's already ugly, Milo, and you're still the most beautiful thing I've ever seen."

My head shook. "I'm afraid there's not a whole lot of beauty here, Tessa."

"You're wrong. You are my beauty." She slipped her fingers through my beard.

Soothing.

Encouraging.

"You are the one who filled up a place inside me that I never thought would be filled. You were there for me when I needed the support after I walked away from Karl. Terrified. But you helped me see through it that I needed to believe in myself. That I deserved more. And you've shown me more, Milo. Even when you were terrified to do it, you showed me what it was like to be cherished, just in the way you looked at me."

Her fingers raked and her voice softened.

"In the way you were there for me. In the way you touched me."

She shifted until she was fully hovering over me, all that red hair around her angel face. "You are your children's beauty. Their hope. Where their hearts belong. And you have become mine, too."

Her tongue stroked across her lips. "And no matter what you've done, Milo, you deserve redemption. Forgiveness. You deserve to be loved."

You've got love, Dad.

Remy's little voice filtered through my mind.

That feeling lifted and swelled.

Wasn't sure I even wanted to fight it any longer. My fingers played through her hair as those blue eyes devoured me.

Pulled me closer.

Sucked me under.

"Never thought I'd see the sun rising again. Thought I'd live in this darkened eternity for the rest of my life," I murmured.

She let go of an affected giggle, though her head tipped to the side in question.

The pad of my thumb ran the contour of her sharp jaw. "You are the light, Tessa. The warmth when every part of me had gone cold."

Affection poured from her features, so sweet that my chest was going tight, and my heart was slugging out of time.

"And you sparked to life something inside me that I've never felt before," she whispered. "I know what I really want for the first time."

"And what is it you want?"

"I want to fight for my happiness. I want to keep building the Hope to Hands foundation and expand it so we can help more people. People like my brother who need long-term care. I want to respect myself for who I am and cherish the parts I'm still working on. I want a family so I can share this love that burns inside me. And I want my person to share it with."

"Your person, huh?" It was gruff.

She smiled, her shoulder coming up to her ear. "Maybe."

"Do I know this guy?" I teased.

"Well, he's big and burly and kind of gruff and crazy hot and good in bed."

"Really?"

"Really," she drew out.

"Well, I think he might have found his person, too." My voice was thick, cracking on the truth. I forced down the traces of guilt that kept trying to erupt.

Redness flushed her cheeks, and she trailed her fingertip down my neck. "We make a really great team, don't we?"

"Yeah, we do." I brushed a lock of hair from her eyes. "Tell me about your brother. About your life before I knew you."

Pained devotion moved through her expression, and her voice went soft.

Held down by old sorrow.

"When my parents died, it was this giant shock. Like how the hell were my parents just gone, you know?" Her brow dented as she blinked.

Hated taking her back to that time, but I needed to understand her, too. Get her the way she got me.

"I was devastated, Milo. Crushed and scared and lost. Everything I knew no longer existed. Our grandparents had already passed, and the only sibling either of my parents had was my dad's brother, and he definitely didn't want anything to do with two teenagers who'd been orphaned."

My thumb traced along the sharp edge of her chin. "I'm so sorry, baby."

Her shoulder barely hitched. "Me, too."

"So, what happened?"

"We basically had two options. Either I live with Bobby and have a social worker come in and check that I was in a safe environment, being cared for, or go into foster care. Bobby was nineteen, free to live his life. But for my brother? There was no consideration. No other choice to make."

She inhaled a shaky breath. "Luckily, Hope to Hands was able to help us at the very beginning, and Eden's father, Gary, was there a lot, making sure we were okay. He'd even offered for both of us to live with him until we got things sorted out. But Bobby? He chose to take care of me. He stepped up and did everything he had to in order to provide for us. He worked so hard, every day, to give us the best life he could."

Air wheezed from her nose, and sadness clouded the blue of her eyes.

"I lived with him until I graduated high school and left for college." She dipped her gaze as she murmured, "You know he paid for that, too?"

My hand ran up her back, encouraging her to continue, promising to hold her burdens, just as she'd done with mine.

"He put his entire life on hold for me, so when he had his accident, there was no way I'd consider a different option, either. I didn't care what it cost." Her head shook as she stared at me, begging me to understand what it'd meant to her.

I threaded my fingers in her hair. "He sounds awesome."

She choked over the affection. "So awesome. I wish you could have known him."

"What happened to him?" I hedged, heart aching at the suffering she'd gone through.

Sorrow wrapped her whole, and for a beat, she glanced away before she returned her attention to me. "Bobby was this super outdoorsy guy. He was always wanting me to go camping with him. Explore the wilderness."

Tears brimmed in her eyes. "He'd gone hiking by himself and fell down a ravine. Someone found him the next morning. They estimated he'd been lying out there for at least fourteen hours. Alone. I just pray he wasn't in pain, that he wasn't afraid, that he didn't blame me for abandoning him."

Agony clotted the words as she released them.

Fuck.

I wished for a way to change it for her.

But I guessed that's what caring about someone did.

It made you want to erase their pain.

Soothe their sorrow.

Even when you had no goddamn control other than to be there for them.

"I'm so fucking sorry, Little Dove."

She sniffled. "I wish I would have somehow gone with him that day. He'd finally given up on even asking me, since I usually had other plans. Every weekend, there was either some party or friends I wanted to hang out with. I always had some dumb excuse not to go. Some reason more important than spending time with him."

Life had a way of showing us what was important when we no longer had the choice, didn't it?

"He'd teased me that I was too much of a girly girl who didn't want to get her hair messed up." Regret tipped one side of her face into a broken smile.

A tender grin took to my mouth, words a soft tease meant to hold her up. "You are kind of a girly girl."

She choked on an affected laugh. "Hey, cute shoes speak to my soul. Don't judge me."

"Never. Kinda partial to those shoes myself, if I'm being honest."

"Have you been fantasizing about me in my heels, Milo Hendricks?" Lightness spun through the sorrow, and she laughed a disbelieving sound as she twisted so she could glance at the heels she still wore.

"Can you blame me?" My voice turned needy.

"Um, no, have you seen me? I'm a total catch."

"Have I seen you? I can't look away, Little Dove."

Tessa smiled this slow smile that warmed and inflamed.

Everything about her right and good.

She bit down on her bottom lip, adoration pouring out, and she climbed up to straddle me.

"Shit, baby."

My hands shot to her waist, the girl completely bare, her small tits perfect and round, her pebbled nipples the same color as her hair.

All that pale skin was on display.

A gorgeous goddess.

My ruin or my salvation.

"I love you," she murmured.

Salvation.

Definitely my salvation.

"You sore, Little Dove?" It came out gruff with desire.

She canted me a sly grin, greed lighting in her eyes. "Not sore enough."

A groan held deep in my throat, and I gripped her by the hair.

"You're about to be."

Chapter Thirty-Two

Milo

I TOSSED HER ONTO HER BACK IN THE MIDDLE OF MY BED while I slid off to stand on the side.

She gasped, panting as she looked up at me.

In an instant, the room took on a new intensity.

The oxygen thickened.

Overflowing with this need that could no longer be contained.

She was exposed, an expanse of that milky skin shining through the dimness that echoed through the room.

Bare except for the red heels she was pressing into my bed as she writhed, hips undulating like a plea.

My dick hardened at the sight.

"On your hands and knees."

My wicked little angel grinned as she complied, swinging around until she was on all fours, her round bottom hoisted in the air.

My mouth watered.

She looked back at me from over her shoulder. "It seems you have a thing for me in this position, Milo Hendricks."

"What can I say, I like that sweet little ass." I gripped two handfuls, making her moan, before I dragged her closer to the edge of the bed.

"Milo," she whimpered. "Please."

One second and she was already begging.

A groan rumbled in my chest as a flood of lust streaked through my veins. My fingers twitched where I held her, my hands nearly encircling her waist.

"You want it, Little Dove?" It was a warning.

"I already told you I could handle all that you are. Turns out, it's quite a lot."

"I'm going to give it to you, sweet girl. Everything that you've been missing."

"Don't tease me," she whimpered when I pressed my cock against the cleft of her ass.

I almost laughed because it was her that did the teasing.

The tempting.

"Make me lose my head," I rumbled as I leaned over her so I could kiss along the delicate slope of her back.

A tremor rolled the length of her spine. "And you've shown me exactly what I want."

I eased back. "Spread your knees."

She exhaled a shaky sound as she did what she was told.

"Good girl."

Tension bound the air.

Sparks of energy.

A shimmery lust that radiated from her skin.

A thrum of our connection.

I grabbed her by the waist and jerked her hips out, tilting her ass upward so I could get a good look at all her sweetness.

Surprise jutted from her mouth, and Tessa's fingers dug into my covers as I positioned her right where I wanted her.

I smoothed a palm over her bottom.

Heat raced, every inch of her aflame.

This ball of fire that was going to do me in.

I slipped my hand between her shaking thighs, brushing my fingertips through her folds that were soaked again.

"Always so wet."

Her head dropped between her shoulders as she wheezed, "Always. Every night when I'm across the house and you're in here, I'm imagining what it'd be like for you to take me."

I drove my fingers into her pussy once before I pulled them out and ran them up to her clit.

I barely pinched the engorged nub, eliciting a squeak of desperation from my girl.

"Oh." She rocked away before she was pushing back for more. "Yes, right there."

A chuckle rumbled out. "Know what you need."

"Then give it."

"So eager."

"Only for you." The words were nothing but a breath.

I pushed my thumb into her pussy and rubbed her clit with the pads of my first two fingers.

In an instant, Tessa's hips started rocking, driving my thumb in and out.

"Look at you, riding my hand." I murmured it like praise because shit, she was the hottest thing. "You've got the sweetest cunt."

She whimpered.

I circled my fingers faster while she increased her speed. She started to rock and push back harder while I held her by the hip with my other hand so I could guide her.

Her skin glistened.

Every inch of her glowed.

This girl, a firestorm that came to life in front of me. My palm on her hip moved to her butt cheek, and I spread her so I could stroke her asshole with my tongue.

"Holy shit, yes, Milo, I'm going to—" She split right then, before she could get the whole thought out, and she came apart in a flash of ecstasy that cracked through the room.

She writhed and rolled and whimpered, and she was groaning when I eased back, her breaths shallow when I lifted her hips higher.

"You want it?" I teased her with the head of my cock at her dripping entrance.

"I think we've established I want it. I want you."

"Going to give it to you hard, Little Dove. Are you okay with that?"

Another spastic nod, and I held her by the front of the hips as I drove into her in one solid thrust.

She clawed and scratched at the bedding, harsh breaths rushing out as her cunt squeezed my cock in a needy fist. "Milo."

"You good?" I gritted through clenched teeth because shit, I'd never felt anything half as perfect as this.

"Good. So good. A thousand times good."

I pulled almost all the way out before I drove back in to the hilt.

Nearly lost my shit at the sight.

My dick buried in her body, her walls hugging me so tight I thought I might pass out.

I used her hips as leverage as I began to take her hard.

Our bodies banging with each jut of my hips.

I loved every needy sound that escaped from her as I pounded into her.

Tessa met every savage thrust.

Red hair wild and whipping around her, her pleas filling the lust-soaked air.

"Please, don't stop. Don't ever stop."

I slid my hand around her waist to her stomach, riding down so I could stroke her while I fucked her hard because whatever my girl wanted, I'd give her.

Friction sparked.

The energy whirled.

I needed her closer.

Needed more.

I jerked her up to her knees and plastered her back to my chest. My free hand came to her jaw, and I twisted her face toward me so I could devour her mouth.

I kissed her like mad as I thrust up into her, the fingers of my free hand strumming over her clit.

Every stroke ruthless.

Merciless.

I slowed my fingers when I could tell she was about to come.

"Please, oh my God, Milo. Don't make me beg. Is that what you want? Me on my knees?" she whispered into the frantic kiss.

I had her picked up and spun around and pinned to the wall before she could comprehend the movement.

Her eyes were wild.

The air combustible.

I pushed back into her tight pussy, the words nothing but a groan as I grated, "No, Tessa, don't you get it yet, baby? It's you who owns me."

In an instant, everything shifted around us.

Slowing.

Growing tight.

Intensifying.

This connection there was no use denying.

Tessa touched my face. Tenderness and care.

Slowly, I pulled out, then eased back in, and, on a long moan, she arched from the wall to meet me.

Our breaths were a tangle.

Our spirits meshed.

Eyes locked.

Everything chained.

I kept thrusting up into her while she rode me, her fingers burrowed into my shoulders as she rocked me into oblivion.

In this position, her clit rubbed over my cock with each pass.

My hand slipped to the curve of her face, and I could feel the emotion rising, cresting, overwhelming.

She nodded against my palm.

Like the two of us just knew.

And my mind flashed to my daughter's words again.

You've got love, Dad.

Maybe it was right then that I understood I didn't have only one chance at it.

It wasn't in the past.

It wasn't secondary.

And the words were rumbling out as Tessa held my gaze.

"I love you, Tessa. Fuck. I love you."

We came like that, orgasms rending through us as every other place inside us was being torn apart.

Wave after wave of bliss.

A perfect, unending pleasure that wrote itself onto our souls.

Damage or not, it was done.

Gasping, my forehead dropped to hers as she clung to me, her breaths so sweet as she panted them at my neck.

When we'd come down, I pulled her from the wall and carried her into my bathroom that was lit by the glow of a light in the closet.

I set her onto the counter, and I knelt down in front of her so I could unfasten the buckles on her heels.

So I could cherish her.

Praise her.

Worship her the way I felt.

I kissed her ankle as I drew one heel off, then did the same to the other.

She lightly fluttered her fingers through my hair.

Love.

I dropped them both to the floor and had her back in my arms. I carried her to the shower, opened the door, and fumbled to turn on the showerhead, and I held her there until it warmed.

When steam began to fill the space, I stepped with her into the spray.

We washed each other.

Carefully.

Tenderly.

A new awareness thrumming in the atmosphere.

No words were needed.

It was just Tessa and me.

Love.

I turned off the faucet and grabbed a towel, and I wrapped it around her before I had her back in my arms.

I took her directly back to my bed and set her in the middle of it. "There you go, right where you belong, fiancée."

She giggled and flushed, but it went deeper than the surface, those eyes on me as I crawled into bed next to her and pulled her into my arms.

Pressing my mouth to her temple, I murmured, "Sleep, Little Dove."

But it was me who fell into it.

This peace that I should have known could never really be mine.

Chapter Thirty-Three

Tessa

I SHUFFLED TO THE DOORWAY AND PAUSED TO PEER OUT AT THE man who lumbered around his kitchen the same way as I'd seen him do so many mornings since I'd started staying with him.

But today…today it was different.

The way the sunlight streamed in through the massive bank of windows.

Or maybe the way the birds seemed to be chirping a little bit louder. Or maybe the coffee brewing in the pot smelled like it might have an extra shot of caffeine in it.

Okay.

Fine.

It was entirely, 1000-percent, hands down due to the way Milo looked at me when he shifted around after he sensed my presence.

Like he was looking at the dawning day.

His gruff demeanor was softened, and his eyes deepened with affection as he perused me like I was his to take.

Heat blossomed in my belly, and I shifted on my feet.

I stood there in one of his enormous shirts that swallowed me whole, so huge it nearly went down to my knees, my hair undoubtedly a flaming red mess, my lips still swollen, and every inch of my body aching in the most glorious of ways.

Could anyone blame me if I wanted to eat cake all freaking day? Hell no.

Because a sly grin pulled to the edge of his mouth, his voice all grumbly and sexy as he murmured, "Mornin', Little Dove."

"Good morning," I peeped, popping up on my toes for a beat before I snapped myself out of it and moved toward the kitchen.

He filled a mug of coffee and already was setting it in my spot before I'd made it there, and he grabbed the creamer and set that in front of me, too.

So sweet.

"Thank you," I said as I slipped onto the stool.

From across the island, he reached out with one of those big hands and tipped up my chin. "Gotta take care of my girl."

Butterflies swarmed.

So thick they might have been a plague.

Alrighty then. It was settled.

Milo Hendricks was most definitely a stone-cold charmer.

"You took care of her pretty nicely last night," I muttered, fighting a blush. I wasn't even shy, but holy mother, the man wasn't *shy*, either.

Those eyes gleamed. "That's just the start."

Everything tingled. "I'm going to hold you to that, Milo Hendricks."

"No need. Already told you that you're mine now."

My belly buzzed, and I pressed my thighs together.

"You'd do well not to go looking at me like that." Did he just growl?

"I'm not sure I can stop."

"You're going to have to keep those needy little hands off me for a minute." His mouth twisted in a delicious smirk. "We need to get packed and get out of here soon."

Hope burned through his expression, and my body that was vibrating shifted and hummed in a new way.

I touched his face. "Are you excited for today?"

He took my hand and threaded our fingers together. "I'm always excited to see them, but…"

He trailed off like he was searching for the right words.

"It feels different today," I pressed.

I could already feel it.

Anticipation alight in the atmosphere.

Wisping through our beings.

Filling these once-vacant walls with hope.

He nodded, his attention downturned to our joined hands, before he lifted his striking face to look at me, his brow slashed in all his intensity. "Yeah, it feels different, Tessa. I'm not walking into it feeling like I'm just going to have to turn around and walk away. It doesn't feel like torment. It feels like I'm on the cusp of something good. A change. A change toward something better."

I squeezed his hand. "That's because better things are on the horizon. We're getting your kids back."

His thick throat bobbed when he swallowed, and he ran his thumb along the outside of my hand, his voice heavy with implication. "Because of you."

"Because of us. Because we're a great team." My tongue swept out to wet my lips. "Have you heard anything else from your attorney?"

"Just that the paperwork is submitted, and all parties have been notified."

That was the only time his expression dimmed.

Paula was not going to be happy.

So be it.

"It's time, Milo."

He rounded the edge of the counter, and his big palm spread across the side of my face before he slipped his fingers all the way into my hair. He tipped my head back. "It's time."

Then he kissed me.

Kissed me tenderly and profoundly, his hand framing the back of my head as he did.

He pulled back as I clutched at his shirt.

"You ready, Little Dove?"

"Yeah, I'm most definitely ready."

Chapter Thirty-Four

Milo

I PULLED INTO THE PARK'S PARKING LOT THE WAY I'D DONE WHAT seemed like a thousand times over the years, and I took the spot two spaces down from Paula and Gene's Range Rover.

But this time, it was entirely different.

I was doing it with Tessa at my side.

No pretenses as to the way we felt.

Reaching over the console, I took her hand and ran my thumb over the ring she wore on her finger.

She shifted her attention my way, that affection flooding out on this promise that we hadn't made aloud, but it was there.

Always.

The two of us.

The truth that this wasn't faked. Hell, it'd probably never really been from the get-go. It'd been fated or some shit, not that I believed in any of that, but I'd also never believed that I could feel this way again, either.

Never thought my heart might soar at the sight of a beautiful girl.

Never thought my spirit would clang against its confines when she touched me.

Never thought anyone could help me heal from the loss.

But there she was, smiling at me in all her soft support.

Red hair wisping around her face, her fucking adorable nose and those tempting lips and those eyes that saw things that could never remain hidden from her.

The thing about Tessa was her beauty was written in her being.

In her sweet, giving spirit and her gorgeous, vivacious soul.

"Funny how I was terrified to introduce you to my kids as my fiancée, worried I was going to cause them more pain in the end, and now today…today, I get to mean it."

"Mean it?"

"Yeah…because it doesn't have to be a lie anymore."

Confusion marred her expression, though the gentlest tease was playing around her mouth, her tone entirely joking. "Are you asking me to marry you, Milo Hendricks?"

"Yes."

I said it simply.

Wholly.

Her sweet brow drew tight when she caught up to the seriousness of what I was implying. "What are you saying, Milo?"

"I'm saying that I want this forever. You and me and my kids. I want to promise you always, Tessa, when I didn't think I had always to give."

She threw herself at me then, kissing me fast and hard before she ripped herself away. Without saying anything, she straightened herself out, clicked open the door to the rental SUV, since mine was in the shop, and began to climb out.

What the hell?

Then she tossed me a grin as she hit the ground. "That was a yes, in case you didn't know it."

A chuckle rolled out because Tessa McDaniels was something.

Something special.

Something amazing.

Something extraordinary.

And she was mine.

I killed the engine and followed her out, rounding to the front to take her hand.

My kids saw us first this time, and they came clambering off a jungle gym and beelining our way.

My chest expanded to bursting.

Tessa's hand squeezed mine, feeling it, too.

Impossible but right.

Scout was all grins as he came barreling up, his messy brown hair bouncing around his face, his smile so wide as he ran with his little arms thrown over his head.

Hitting me with a thud, he threw his arms around my thighs. "Dad! Dad! Dad! You got here with my Tessa!"

Tessa let go of a surprised sound, and she leaned down and curled an arm around him just as Remy came up behind him.

More reserved, the way she was, but different this time, too.

Like she could feel the blaze of hope that shone down from the endless expanse of the blue, blue sky.

Rays streaking through.

Chasing away the shadows.

"Hi, Dad," she said quietly when she wrapped her arms around me, and I was sinking to my knees and taking Tessa with me so we could wrap my children in our love.

I kissed the crown of Remy's head, holding her close, my other arm locked around my son as I breathed out in relief. "I missed you two."

"We missed you both a lot," Scout promised. "Every second, just like I said."

All of us stilled when the darkness descended, and I gritted my teeth to keep from spitting my anger at Paula. To keep from shoving what she was doing in her face. But it was Gene who spoke. "Can we have a word with you, Milo?"

His frame was rigid, and Paula was positively quivering with hate.

A frown took to my brow as I eased back. I gave them a tight nod. "Sure."

Tessa glanced at me in confusion, with her support, with that belief that promised *we had this.*

"Why don't you two take Tessa over to the playground so I can talk with your grandma and grandpa for a minute?" I suggested, though it was firm.

Worry trudged through Remy's spirit, her hesitation full, though she nodded. "Okay."

Tessa pushed to standing, and she stretched out both hands. "Come on, let's see how high you two can climb on the jungle gym."

"I can go all the way to Mars!" Scout shouted, jumping toward the sky as he threw a fist toward it.

Tessa tenderly ran a hand through his hair, love coming off her in waves. "There's my Rocketman."

He giggled and took her hand. Tessa led them across the park to the playground on the right.

I stood there, staring, unable to look away.

A beautiful pain sawing at my chest.

Gene cleared his throat.

I ripped my attention away to where the two of them stood. Gene seemed unsettled, and Paula looked like she was going to fly into a rage at any second where she faced away and hugged herself.

There was no secret she hated even looking at me.

"What's going on?" Caution filled my voice when Gene said nothing.

Paula whirled around. "Like you don't know exactly what's going on," she hissed.

"Oh, you mean the petition." There was no keeping the challenge out of my voice.

She laughed like I was stupid. "Obviously, Milo. The petition. The truth that you're trying to steal my grandbabies away from me…trying to take them from the one home they've known. After everything that you've done."

"I never wanted to keep your grandchildren from you. You just left me with no choice," I gritted.

She scoffed. "No choice? If you had any soul at all, your choice would be to walk away."

Anger pulled at my insides. I ground my teeth to keep from saying something I would regret. Something she could use against me in court.

"Turning my back on them is not a *choice*, Paula. At least it's sure as hell not one that I would ever make. Do you think that's really what Autumn would have wanted? For me to turn my back on our kids?"

"She's not here to tell me that, is she?" It whipped from her mouth like a slur.

Gene pushed a hand out in her direction. "We didn't come here for an argument. We came here for a discussion."

My brows shot up. Not once had they ever wanted to *discuss* anything with me.

Gene rushed a palm over his face like he had to prepare himself for whatever he wanted to say, then he was looking at me with his head angled to the side. "Listen, Milo, we talked to our attorney, and he feels it's best that both parties come to a resolution without this getting messy."

Funny, it'd been messy for years, but they didn't give a shit about that when the odds had been in their favor.

Still, I stood there and listened because a part of me got it.

Their daughter was dead because of me.

I hated myself for it, too.

His throat bobbed when he swallowed. "We don't want to lose them, and it's time we also accepted that you shouldn't, either. We thought maybe they should spend the night with you tonight, and you can bring them back to our place in the morning."

Paula choked.

Clearly, this wasn't her idea.

And I wanted to drop to my knees in joy. In gratitude. In relief.

But I also wouldn't allow them to manipulate the situation or continue to hold the upper hand.

"That doesn't mean I'm just going to drop the petition. They're my children, and you've kept them from me for a long, long time."

His mouth tipped down on the side. "We realize that, but we love them, truly, and it's time we recognize their love for you."

I could barely nod.

He inhaled a shaky breath. "We brought overnight bags for them. They're in the car."

"I'll get the kids and meet you there," I said, before anyone could change their minds. I swiveled on my heel and started in their direction.

Tessa was laughing like crazy at some antics Scout was tossing out, her hair flying all around, her spirit so right, and my Remy Girl was tacked to her side, the same way as she normally was with me.

Like she didn't want to let go.

And for the first time, she wouldn't have to.

My voice was ragged when I called from about twenty yards away, "How about we take this party to our house?"

Tessa whipped around.

Bewildered.

Shocked.

But what was most apparent was her faith.

"We get to go to your house?" Remy was clearly hesitant to hope.

I made it to them, and I ran my hand down the back of my daughter's head just as Scout was attaching himself to my leg.

I wound my arm around Tessa's back. "Yeah, sweetheart, you do."

Chapter Thirty-Five

Milo

I EASED THE SUV DOWN THE WINDING GRAVEL DRIVE TOWARD the cabin tucked deep in the woods, where it waited for us like the sanctuary Autumn and I had dreamed it would be.

Old sorrow whispered through my spirit, her voice and every promise I had made trying to get me in a stranglehold.

I fought it.

Fought the welling of guilt.

Fought the shame that pushed up from my conscience to remind me of what I'd done.

I couldn't go there right then. Not when Scout was chattering from the back seat, over-eager as he tried to push against his booster seat straps so he could see out the window. "Oh, wow, is this almost it? I can't wait, Dad! I've been wondering where you live. I bet it's awesome."

That panged, too.

The truth that neither of my kids really knew that much about me other than the little glimpse they got on Sunday afternoons, but I prayed it was enough.

Prayed they knew the fullness of my devotion.

Prayed Remy could feel it rushing toward her like an embrace as I glanced at her through the mirror.

She sat quietly.

Nervously.

Like she wasn't quite sure of her place.

I couldn't wait to prove to her that her *place* was right here. This was where she belonged.

"Yep, we're almost there," I promised as we rounded the last turn, and Tessa sent me an encouraging smile as she reached over and squeezed my forearm, like she'd heard every worry that had whirled through my mind on the trip over.

Funny how I'd been fighting for this moment for years, and now that it was here, I felt unprepared. All of it coming at me at once and without warning.

But like Tessa had promised, *we had this.*

I came to a stop in front of the cabin, and Scout had himself unbuckled in a second flat and was standing on the seat and holding onto the back of Tessa's headrest so he could peer out the windshield.

"Oh, cool! Are we going camping?"

A low chuckle got free. "This looks like camping to you, huh?"

"It's like the great outdoors, Dad."

Love rumbled through my being, and I shifted so I could touch his chin. "This is our house, Scout."

I made sure to make it clear that it was *ours.*

They might not have been living within the cabin walls, but they inhabited every board, every plank, every swipe of paint.

Most of all, they lived in the foundation.

"I like it," he said, so casual, a hike of his shoulders like it was no big deal, before he scrambled over to toss open his door.

He hopped out.

A tender smile edged Tessa's mouth, and those bottomless eyes lulled and lapped.

Offering comfort.

Tessa recognized this was huge. Hell, I was pretty sure she could physically feel that my insides were absolutely shaking.

She touched my arm again before she hopped from the SUV to

follow Scout, who was already racing for the porch steps and shouting, "I can't even wait to see inside."

Remy didn't move.

She just sat there.

Held hostage by her worry.

I shut off the engine and slowly climbed out, fighting the thickness in my throat, hating with all of me that she might be scared to come here.

I opened her door, and I swore I sensed her little spirit wobble, this sweet, sweet child who felt things so deeply.

She kept staring at her fingers she twisted on her lap.

"Are you okay, Remy Girl?" The words were shards, scraping through the disorder.

She finally peeked over at me. "My stomach hurts a little bit."

"Because you're nervous?"

Warily, she nodded.

"Do you remember it here?" Could barely choke it out.

She wavered and hesitated, chewing her lip before she whispered, "A little. I feel like it looked different."

She remembered the trailer.

Fuck.

Had to grit my teeth to let her continue.

"And I remember Mom sometimes, and her eyes and the way she used to sing to me, but mostly, I remember the sirens."

Grief stalled my heart before it started racing for a way to meet with my daughter's.

To find a way to mend the memories when there was no fucking way to correct them.

"Come here, sweetheart."

She slid from her seat and onto her feet, and I knelt in front of her and pulled her into my arms. I was probably hugging her too tight, but I couldn't let go. I had to support her as she gave voice to the fears she'd likely been hiding all these years.

God, I wished that I'd always been there to hold her through them.

I could only imagine what Paula had told her.

"I'm so sorry that's the main thing you remember about this place because it's an awful, terrible memory," I told her, my voice drawn low in the strain. In the promise. "But I want you to know that you used to love it here, Remy. You loved this land. You used to run and play and fill this place with so much happiness. It was my favorite place in the world because it was ours. I'm not sure if you remember that part, but know that I do, and if you want to ask me about those memories or talk to me about absolutely anything, I am right here."

I pulled back so I could meet those trusting brown eyes. "I'm right here, Remy. But if you want to go back to your grandma and grandpa's, I understand that, too. I support you, whatever you need to make you feel safe."

Panic blazed through her expression, and she threw her arms around my neck, her voice close to frantic. "No, Dad. I'm not scared of being here. I've wanted to come here for a really long time. But I'm scared that maybe I'll want to stay here always, and I won't get to."

My chest clutched with devotion, and I held her close, tight to the thunder that raged. "I promise you, I am doing everything I can to make that happen. Do you understand?"

She nodded against my neck, and I could feel her tears seeping onto my shirt. "I know, Dad. I know you want us here. Because you have love."

My arms tightened, and I squeezed my eyes shut as I relished this moment. "I do, Remy, I have love. I have love because you showed me I deserve it. I have love because of your brother. I have love because of Tessa."

We stayed in that embrace for the longest time before Remy mumbled, "Is it okay if I still miss Mom?"

Agony sliced me in two, and I pulled back so I could take hold of the sides of her shoulders. I squeezed in emphasis. "You're always going to miss your mom, Remy. Always, and that's okay. You should never be ashamed of it or feel like you're doing something wrong. I will always miss her, too. But we also can love the people who come into our lives after, and we don't have to be ashamed of that, either."

A rock lodged itself in my throat.

Fuck.

I needed it to be true.

Needed Autumn to forgive me.

"Do you understand the difference?"

"I think so."

Tears tracked down her face, and I wiped them with my thumb. "Would you do something for me, Remy?"

She gave a furious nod.

"Whenever you start to question it, I want you to talk to me. You and I can remind each other that we have love. That we deserve it. That no one is allowed to take that away from us. Okay?"

She nodded again. "Okay."

Sniffling, I straightened and held out my hand. "Are you ready to go inside?"

Her smile was small and perfect and everything that was this intuitive, amazing child. "Yeah, I'm ready."

We climbed the porch steps and headed in through the door.

We stepped inside to the stampede of footsteps that pounded the floor.

Scout appeared at the head of the hallway that led to their room, so much joy and excitement on his face it nearly dropped me to my knees. "Oh my gosh, you're not even gonna believe it, Remy. We got our own room and our own tree fort and our own lake and everything. I think we really are camping."

Remy peeked up at me like she was telling me she wasn't surprised that they did have their own room.

Maybe my kids really did know me, after all.

Tessa followed behind Scout, fighting laughter that played all over her face as she crossed her arms over her chest and leaned against the edge of the entryway.

"He's already gone through every room to check things out. Rocket power speed, right?"

She ruffled a hand through his hair.

"It's the only speed I got, my Tessa."

Affection soared as high as my kid.

It blistered between me and Tessa.

The connection strong.

Bold.

Unbreakable.

"You want to check it out, Remy, before I go get your things?" I asked.

"Can Tessa show me?"

I looked back at Tessa, my heart hammering at my ribs, wondering how the fuck I got so lucky. "Sure."

"Remy-T Wreckers back together at last," Tessa sang as she stretched out her hand. My daughter took it, giggling as she did.

And I realized then I'd totally forgotten what it felt like to have the ground sit solid beneath my feet.

Scout zoomed out in front of them so he could get to their room first. "Wait 'til you see it, Remy!"

With the emotion close to locking up my throat, I slipped back outside and down the porch steps. I leaned against the side of the SUV, unable to catch my breath through the rush of bliss.

Inhaling deeply, I dug my phone out, dialed the number, and pressed it to my ear. My mom answered on the first ring. "Milo. Aren't you supposed to be at your visitation right now? Did something happen?"

She tried to keep the tremor from her words.

I gulped around the joy. "Yeah, something happened…the kids are here."

"What do you think we should have for dinner?" Tessa asked as she searched through the fridge.

"Pizza!" Scout shouted from behind her.

"Pizza?" She grinned at him from over her shoulder.

"Um, yes, pizza. Doncha know you can't have a party without pizza, and my dad said this is a party."

Tessa slanted me a grin, affection riding on her mouth before she looked back at Scout. "Well, then, pizza it is."

"I like her, Dad," he told me, so nonchalant from where he was on his knees on the living room rug, playing with a bunch of cars that had been sitting on his shelf waiting for him.

"Yeah, Scout, I like her, too."

Tenderness danced around her being, and I couldn't do anything but wrap my arms around her from behind. I hooked my chin over her shoulder and murmured at her cheek, "Thank you, Little Dove."

"Anytime, fiancé." She grinned back at me.

Shit.

I liked the sound of that.

The truth that rang behind it.

I held her for a second and relished in what we'd been given.

Remy almost blushed from where she sat at one of the stools, but her smile was soft and real, and, God, I didn't think I'd ever been happier than right then.

Everyone's attention snapped to the door when it opened, and my mom was suddenly standing there, her breaths shallow and energy frenetic.

Her gaze swept over the room, her throat bobbing as she took it in, like she was working through her disbelief.

Her hand went to her chest as a rush of tears fell down her cheeks. "Oh my God."

I pulled away from Tessa and moved toward her, stretching my hands out for both my kids to take. Remy slipped off the stool, and Scout came bounding over, and I led them toward the door.

"Hi. I remember you. You're my other grandma, right?" Scout's head tilted to the side.

My mother hadn't seen them for two years, and I highly doubted Scout remembered her much at all. His memories were the pictures I constantly showed him and the stories I told. The way I shared her love, brought them the notes and presents she had for them.

Paula made sure to make my mother feel as unwelcomed as possible. Tainted our visits with her venom. Took it to the place where my mother believed she was only making things worse for my children, to the place where she worried she was stealing more joy than giving it, so she'd stopped coming.

It was no wonder my mom dropped to her knees.

"Hi." It was a wheeze from her soul.

Adoration.

Hope.

Remy reached out and took her hand, the child covering my mother in all her goodness. "Hi, Grandma."

My mother squeezed back, and the tears wouldn't stop falling from her eyes. "I can't tell you how happy I am to see you."

Scout grinned and patted her face. "Well, that's really good because I'm happy to see you, too."

It was strange when the walls of your home had echoed with vacancy for so long, and it was suddenly bursting with life.

Overcome with it.

The scent of pizza sauce and basil overwhelmed the air, and giggles and laughter rang through the room.

My mother sat on the floor with Scout on her lap as he read us one of the books she'd left for him on his shelf.

She'd added to them each year, making sure they were age appropriate, the same way as she'd done for Remy.

She wanted them to know she was always thinking of them. That they never strayed far from her thoughts. That her love would forever surpass this tormented time that had stretched too long between us.

No more.

My heart squeezed tight as I tossed a grin down at Remy, who sat with her shoulder pressed to mine. We were on the floor with our backs leaned against the couch.

"The end!" Scout beamed when he finished the book that was mostly pictures but with a few words sprinkled in.

"Wow, that was really incredible, Scout," my mom told him.

"I'm a great reader, you know. You gotta know a lot of stuff if you're going to be an astronaut, so I've been learning a lot and a lot."

"That's right, my little Rocketman," Tessa shouted from where she was finishing the pizza. She'd insisted we all go hang out while she prepared it. Told me to take the time with my kids before she'd pecked a kiss to my lips to seal the command.

"What do you want to be when you grow up, Remy?" my mom asked softly, being sure to include Remy in the conversation.

Remy hiked a knobby shoulder, a bit of shyness weaving into her demeanor. "I don't know…maybe a writer…but my grandma Paula said it would be better if I were realistic."

"Dreamin's for fools," Scout tossed out, his voice raised, and he giggled because he hadn't figured out yet that the bullshit Paula spewed wasn't funny.

Anger curled in my guts, and I had to keep from spitting the words as I took Remy's hand. "You chase your dreams, Remy. Work hard at them, whatever they are. And they'll probably change some as you get older, and that's okay, just as long as you listen to your heart and those dreams make you happy."

My daughter looked up at me with a timid smile on her face. "I'm happy here, Dad."

I gulped around her admission, and I touched her chin. "I'm happy with you here, too."

The silence that wrapped around us was both fierce and free. The intensity ripping between my mother, Tessa, and me a torrent of devotion.

The determination to bring these kids home permanently.

I just prayed I could do it right.

But I had to be the one to ensure it was safe.

Put an end to this bastard's threat.

Guarantee that he could never taint this beauty again.

Chapter Thirty-Six

Tessa

"**R**EADY OR NOT, COME AND FIND ME!"

I covered a giggle because Scout was honestly too cute. The second I'd gotten to twenty, he was the one who'd called out from his hiding place before I could get a chance to warn I would soon be on the hunt.

I was *it*, which I didn't mind a bit, because I could hear their little giggles rolling through the summer night, the temperature still warm enough for us to be out playing long after we'd cleaned up after dinner.

It was close to ten, but we didn't want to waste a second of the evening, so we'd let them stay up late, promising one more game before it was time for bed.

"I'm coming for you," I called, tiptoeing across the lawn and peeking behind some shrubs that I knew full well none of them were hiding behind.

You know, since I could distinctly hear three different hushed voices behind me on the opposite side of the yard.

Right after he'd brought in the children's things, Milo had come out back to put up the removable safety fence that kept the kids away from the lake so they could run free within its boundaries.

So we could keep them safe.

My heart pounded with the truth of it.

Remy and Scout were now a part of me.

Permanently.

Not in the way I'd promised Milo when we'd first struck out on this venture.

But wholly.

Truly.

I searched behind the small storage container at the far side of the house. "Are you in here?" I called.

"No, I'm over here!" Scout's little voice rode on the breeze.

"Shh." I could almost see Remy putting her finger to her lips.

I pressed my own lips together as the smile spread free, and I shifted, turning the other direction, spinning a circle as I called, "Where?"

Scout cracked up. "Right over here, you cuckoo!"

"Scout," Remy whined, and I could feel the intensity of Milo's chuckle, the ferocity of his love and joy as he got to have a brand-new moment with his kids that he'd never been afforded before.

Joy overflowed.

Joy for the man I loved and joy for his children who I loved, too.

Completely.

I'd known it wouldn't be all that hard to fall for his kids, but I guessed what I'd never anticipated was that it could feel quite like this.

"Right over here?" I drew out as I slowly began to ease up the treehouse steps.

To the sanctified little spot Milo had poured himself into.

Blood, sweat, and tears.

Literally.

Because the entire endeavor had hinged on the hope that his children would one day get to play in it.

And here they were.

I pushed open the miniature door to the adorable fort where I knew they were all hiding.

One of the lights Milo had installed illuminated the space, casting a warm glow over the room.

Or maybe it was just the energy that vibrated within.

The love that emanated.

Because I felt it stretch so fiercely across my chest when I found Milo sitting against the corner with both his children resting in his arms, a blanket flung haphazardly over them like it would keep them hidden while Milo's massive legs and boots extended out from underneath.

Not that I couldn't clearly see their shapes pressed into the fabric, anyway.

I tried to hold my giggle, but a bit of it erupted, eliciting one from Scout, too, who squirmed under the blanket.

I tiptoed over.

"Where are you?" I called again, then I took hold of the edge of the blanket and ripped it off. "Ah-ha!"

Scout shot up and threw his arms over his head. "You found me, my Tessa!"

He beamed, and my heart nearly exploded.

"Barely. I thought I was going to have to be looking for you the entire night, you were hidden so well."

"I already told ya that I'm a great hider, didn't I?"

"You weren't even lying," I told him.

My gaze moved to Remy who was tucked into the safety of Milo's hulking arm, her cheek pressed to his chest, a true, genuine, relaxed smile on her sweet face.

My spirit thrashed.

In happiness.

In completeness.

For so long, I'd been alone. Not by myself, but *alone*.

Empty where I'd lost my own faith.

I was always thankful for my friends—so thankful—but I'd been lost somewhere in the void left behind by the loss of my family.

I shifted to look at Milo who gazed up at me, love dripping from his eyes, his sharp brow lax with tenderness, though everything about him was still overpowering.

Overwhelming.

Big and intimidating and rough.

Soft and kind and real.

I wondered if, for the first time, he could see himself the way I saw him.

If he finally understood the way he made me feel.

That *he* was my family, and his children completed that.

Because he shifted Scout so he could stretch out his hand to me. "Get over here where you belong, Little Dove."

"Little Dove?" Scout curled up his nose.

"Yeah, a dove is a messenger of love, Scout. One who lets you know not all hope is lost. That there is something better on its way."

My heart squeezed so intensely I couldn't breathe.

"And that something better is the three of you," Milo rumbled, still looking up at me.

I eased onto my knees and crawled up beside Milo, picking up Scout as I went and draping him across our chests. I reached around him so I could take Remy's little hand.

Because *this?*

It was the *always* I'd forever wanted.

I pressed a kiss to Remy's forehead where I stood beside her tree-house bed.

Scout was already fast asleep in his, completely tuckered out from a full day of playing.

Darkness wisped around the room, though it danced without caution or fear. The tiniest glow from a nightlight illuminated the child's precious face as I looked down at her. She stared up at me with her trusting brown eyes that I had no idea could slay me through.

Her spirit was slowed, her heart light, but her thoughts ran deep. A divot formed on her brow, and she whispered, "My dad told me your mom died, too."

Sorrow crested, both hers and mine.

Gently, I ran my fingers through her hair. "Yeah. She did."

"How old were you?"

"I was fifteen…much older than you."

She barely nodded. "Do you remember her?"

"I do remember her. Not everything, but I remember her smile and what her voice sounded like and the way it felt to hug her. I also remember a lot of the times I got into trouble, which I think I tended to do a lot." My words were quieted, held in our confession, though the last rippled with hushed laughter.

I'd been kind of a handful.

A grin spread over Remy's face. "You used to get in trouble?"

She said it like she couldn't believe it.

I twisted a lock of my hair around my finger and teased, "Redheads are rarely controlled."

She giggled. "Can I dye my hair red?"

I smoothed my palm over the top of her head. "I think you're perfect just the way you are, Remy, but when you get older, if you still want to, I'm sure that would be fine, but you'll have to ask your dad."

"I think it's better if I ask you both."

A current ran through her statement.

A claim.

Love spread through my chest.

A hot spring rushing with warmth.

Gushing up from the depths where I'd had no idea it existed.

"I would like that."

"Me, too," she whispered.

I kissed her forehead again, then brushed my thumb along the angle of her jaw. "You'd better get some sleep."

Nodding, she snuggled down in her covers.

Breathing out, I straightened, then I was sucking for oxygen all over again at the sight of Milo leaning against the doorway, watching us.

Seeing him there pulled at every place inside me.

Heart and soul and body and mind.

He was mine.

Always.

All hulking, burly mountain man with the softest spirit.

Beautiful Beast.

I eased that way, lured by this energy that would never quell.

His big hand went to my waist, and he tugged me toward him and pressed a tender kiss to my lips.

I peered up at him, scratched my fingers through his beard, and murmured, "Today was wonderful."

He curled his arm completely around my waist and tucked me closer. "It was the best day of my life."

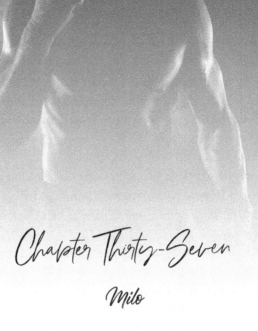

Chapter Thirty-Seven

Milo

I JOLTED UPRIGHT IN BED, MY EYES NARROWED INTO SLITS AS I tried to process what had yanked me from sleep.

An edge cut into my consciousness.

Razor sharp and making my heart gallop in jagged clips.

Night eclipsed the light, the entire room shrouded in it, everything quieted and held. The minutes slowed, bound by something sinister that eddied through the room.

Tessa was twisted into a pretzel beside me, her limbs at odd angles, which I'd come to realize was just the way she slept, her hair strewn all around and her soft breaths filling the air in tiny puffs of peace.

But there was a disorder within it.

A darkness deeper than the night.

Ugly and oppressive.

I steadied my breaths and inclined my ear, listening for anything out of sorts.

It took me a second to realize the noise might have come from one of the kids. To realize they were really here. It'd seemed such an impossibility just yesterday that I doubted my mind had fully accepted the shift.

Only silence echoed back.

An eerie stillness that slithered through the atmosphere in a menacing mist.

Gulping around the spiked rock that filled my throat, I slipped out of bed, keeping my feet light on the hardwood floors as I eased to the bedroom door that we'd left open specifically so we could hear the kids if they needed us.

I peered out.

More of that stagnant tranquility echoed back.

I moved quickly across the space to the hall and down to the children's room, my breaths quiet and shallow as I checked to make sure they were fine.

Both of them were fast asleep, Remy curled up in a ball and Scout tossed out on his back like a starfish.

Relief heaved from my lungs, and I dropped my head between my shoulders so I could get it together.

You're just freaking the fuck out, Milo. Conjuring things because your kids are here.

Blowing out a sigh, I shuffled back out into the main room, on my way back to my girl.

Only I stalled out when I saw the flicker of light through the windows out back.

An icy dread slipped down my spine.

I crept forward and squinted into the darkness. Bare moonlight floated down from the heavens, scarcely enough to cast the earth in shadows, the trees mere silhouettes and the lake a blackened pond.

"Fuck."

I was losing it.

Making shit up.

I started to move when I saw it.

A flash, flash, flash that strobed through the trees.

I was out the door and barreling that way, my feet taking the path down the middle of the lawn in the direction of the lake.

I sprinted across the cool, damp grass.

The only thing I had on was a pair of shorts and a tee.

Barefoot.

Wasn't exactly prepared, but there was no time to hesitate. I wasn't about to give this fucker a chance to get away.

Knew it the second the bastard sensed me. The way he suddenly changed course and darted back into the forest.

Violence erupted from where I held it chained. A straight shot injected into my veins.

He was here.

Here at my home.

Where my children were.

Where Tessa was.

Rage blurred my sight, and I hustled faster, tossing myself right over the top of the fence in one leap. I landed hard on the other side, nearly tripping as I was set off balance, but I righted myself quickly and hurtled into the thick.

The forest rose up on all sides.

It cloaked the faint rays of moonlight. Dimmed them to nearly nothing.

I was surrounded by grisly shadows on each side, spindly branches and fallen trees and the sharp pricks of pinecones and needles beneath my feet.

But I didn't slow.

I ran.

I fucking ran through the forest, an arm coming up to guard my face as branches whipped and lashed at my flesh.

The tangled gnarl of roots below tried to slow my path.

A rock cut into the sole of my foot.

I didn't give.

Didn't slow.

Adrenaline sloshed through my veins, fueling the aggression that seethed.

With all of me, I hunted the light.

Still, it grew farther away with each step.

Fuck.

My heart hammered as I raced through the maze of trees.

The darkness disorienting.

My breaths too shallow.

I suddenly broke out of the forest.

Confused, I looked around, realizing it had landed me halfway down my gravel drive that ran for more than a mile.

The asshole had made a big loop around my property.

Ragged breaths jutted from my lungs as I searched for which direction he'd gone, then I shielded my eyes when headlights suddenly speared through the darkness.

An SUV peeled out from where it'd been hidden just off the drive about a hundred yards in front of me, whipping around and heading in the opposite direction toward the main road.

Gravel spewed as his tires spun, and the fucker gunned it.

I chased him like it might be of use.

Like it wasn't fruitless.

Like I could catch up. Head it off. Stop it before the horrors of my past were the ones catching up to me.

Taillights disappeared around a corner, and I kept lumbering forward before I bent in two, gasping for air that I couldn't find.

A guttural roar ripped from my lungs, rage blustering beneath my skin.

Motherfucker.

He wanted to come here? I was going to *find* him first.

Fear roiled with the desperation.

I knew it. Knew how this would end.

I glared down the road where he'd escaped until everything settled.

The dust.

The scream of his engine as he took off down the main road.

My breaths that I couldn't control.

But it did nothing to settle the chaos.

No peace found in the middle of the mayhem.

Swiping my forearm over the sweat drenching my face, I turned and walked back up the drive, not giving a shit that the soles of my feet were shredded, barely registering I was leaving a trail of blood behind me before I caught sight of Tessa, who was on the front porch freaking out, her arms hugged across her chest as she paced.

She gasped when she saw me in the distance, and she fumbled down the steps and came running my way, wearing shorts and a tank and unlaced tennis shoes she'd clearly stuffed her feet into.

All that red flew around her beneath the pale moonlight, and my chest panged so hard, clutched in this love and this fight.

This girl.

The sun who'd risen on a darkened day.

But how could I ever stand in the light when wickedness still enshrouded?

She threw herself against me with a hard thud, grasping my shoulders when we made contact. "Oh my God, Milo, what happened? I heard the back door burst open, and I went running out there. I couldn't find you. I called and called. I...I wanted to get in the car and come find you, but the kids are still sleeping, and I didn't know what to do."

The words tumbled from her in a deluge of worry.

I curled my arm around her waist and inhaled, struggling to keep my shit together.

To keep from losing it.

She yanked away, ocean eyes searching me in the night.

A frenzied current that battered at the shores of my heart.

"Are you hurt?"

"No," I grunted.

"What happened?" she begged.

"Someone was out in the forest." Could barely force it out around the razors that lined my throat.

Terror ripped through her features. "Are you sure?"

I managed a harsh nod.

"Oh my God..." Her brow pinched in alarm, and she let go of the words like a secret, "Was it him?"

I unwound her from my hold and turned away, unable to face her when my body still vibrated with hostility.

Wrath still firing from my cells.

I looked to the ground. "Likely someone he sent."

Horror wrapped me from behind, her energy throbbing and thrashing and battering against my back.

"I don't understand. What do they want?" she whispered like she was praying for a different outcome.

I whipped back around, the confession tearing out of me on the hatred I would forever hold. "They killed her, Tessa."

Tessa stumbled back like she'd run smack into a wall.

Pale skin blanching a ghostly white. Thought I could see the blood drain from her head and pool in a vat of dread in her belly. "What do you mean?"

My jaw screwed in indignation as my fists curled in malice. "They killed her."

I could feel her heart seize.

My teeth ground as I forced myself to continue. "Because of me."

"No," she whimpered.

My nod was savage.

"Her death was labeled an accident. Paula has always believed it a suicide. I let her believe it."

A barbed cry got loose of her mouth that she covered with shaking hands. "Oh my God, Milo."

"I hunted him...for a full fucking year...I hunted him. Abandoned my kids, gave them over to Paula and Gene without so much as a fight because the only thing I could do was hunt the monster so I could make him pay for what he'd done."

Torment crumpled her face.

Mine and hers.

Did she see it now?

Who I really was?

"I'd taken out a bunch of his men. One after another, trying to get to him."

Tessa choked over my blunt confession.

"Plus, word on the street was he owed a bunch of money to some people more powerful than he was. Guess that was enough to run him out of town and into hiding. He was a fucking ghost. I'd finally given up. Figured someone else had beaten me to the honor of sending that piece of shit to the ground. But I should have known he would come back for me. Should have known he was biding his time until he found the right time to strike."

I stared down at this gorgeous girl who'd stood beside me all this time while I admitted it.

The one I'd warned wouldn't like what she saw if she got too close.

Now that she could see, tremors rocked her.

Violently.

Savagely.

"Milo." It was a whimper.

"And I don't know exactly what his game is, Tessa. But make no mistake, now that he's returned, he won't touch my family again."

Chapter Thirty-Eight

Milo

Five Years Ago

CHANTS LIFTED THROUGH THE GRUNGY BASEMENT, THEIR bloodlust clogging the air with the greed that claimed their tongues.

The cement floor vibrated with the force of it, and from the fringes of his sight, Milo could almost make out the demons that crawled the walls, their talons sunk into the blocks where they stood guard over the depravity.

Dark specters that fed into the wickedness.

Or maybe it was just the remnants of the souls that had been left there.

Where goodness was ground to dust, and the only thing that remained was the corrupt.

Blood spilled from a gash on Milo's right eye, obscuring his vision, but that was just fine because he didn't want to see.

Didn't want to witness the evil that he perpetuated, brought on by his own greed.

He was no fool.

It didn't matter his reasons.

There was no excuse for this.

It was only vileness and impurity.

His opponent clocked him on the opposite side of the head, knocking him from his feet. The man attacked, diving on top of Milo in a bid to finish the job.

Shouts soared. Battered his ears.

"Finish him!"

The man might have thought the position gave him an up, but Milo only grinned. He tossed him to his back before he was the one in control.

Milo's fists pounded into his face.

Gore.

They hauled him back when the man went slack.

Bile filled Milo's mouth as he was dragged away from the limp form laying in a puddle of blood.

His opponent barely clinging to life.

His arm was lifted in the air as he stumbled on his feet, hardly coherent himself.

Beaten to shit.

Dripping blood and broken bones.

"You just earned me five-hundred grand," Stefan murmured in his ear like it was a rumbling of seduction, right as he was pushing twenty-five thousand of it against Milo's chest. "I knew you'd come back to me. This is where you belong. To me, you are my son, and we are going to rule this world."

"What did you do?" Autumn held their wailing infant against her chest, bouncing him frantically like maybe she was searching for comfort, too.

She stared at him through the dim light that burned from a lamp in the small living room. He'd just come crawling home at four in the morning after his first dirty fight in years.

Bashed to hell and riddled with shame and praying to God she was still asleep.

"Told you I'd do whatever I had to."

Her face pinched.

Horror.

Disgust.

Disappointment.

"You promised me you wouldn't go back."

"Yeah, well, things have changed."

Tears tracked down her face, and guilt clawed through his being, steely talons wrapped around his neck.

He never should have done it.

Never should have given into the weakness.

Never should have allowed the voices to control what he knew was right.

But he was afraid it was too late.

"So that's it? This is who you want to be?" Her brown eyes dragged down the wounds that littered his body, his clothes fresh but his soul soured.

"I was always him, Autumn."

Her mouth twisted in pained disbelief. "No, Milo, you are blind if you think this is who you are. You are good. I know you are, and our children deserve that man, and so do I. This is not the man I married, the one I love, and if you can't find him, return him to us, then you can just go."

"Don't fuckin' say that." Grief constricted airflow.

"It's not me *saying* it, Milo. It's you *choosing* it. You're choosing not to have us because I won't let my children be damaged by that life. All for what? Some stupid need to prove to everyone else that you're what...powerful? Or is it just the money?"

Repulsion filled her voice, and Milo flew across the room, pushing in close to where their baby boy howled. As if he felt the turmoil.

Guilt nearly ripped Milo in two. "I'm doing it for you. For them. So you can have a good home. So our children don't grow up in this fucking trailer."

Autumn stepped away, her head shaking as the haggard words fell from her mouth. "Do you think that's what I want? The only thing

I've ever wanted is you. So, you decide, Milo… You decide. That world or us."

❧

"I'm out." Milo tossed the stack of cash he'd won two nights before onto Stefan's desk because if he was cutting ties, he was cutting ties.

He'd come here to San Francisco where he knew he would find him.

The man who'd picked him up and dusted off his knees and fed his violent ego. Sculpted and shaped it, then let it fester over the years until Milo had reached the place where he'd been desperate. Where he had no other choice.

He could see it clearly then, the way Stefan had manipulated his weakness. Used it against him, all while using it for his gain.

Milo could hardly blame him.

It was who he'd been.

But he couldn't be that man if he wanted his family, too.

Like Autumn had told him, he had to choose.

Condescension rolled from Stefan's mouth, and he rocked back in his executive office chair. "You think you can just walk? Just like that?"

"I have no other choice."

He tsked. "I warned you the stakes were higher this time, and you agreed. Do you know what that means, *Gore?*"

Unease shivered through his consciousness. Still, he planted his palms on the gleaming wood and hissed, "It means nothing. Like I told you, I'm done."

Without saying anything else, he turned on his heel and stormed to the door.

Stefan might think he had control over him, but he would prove he was wrong.

He tossed it open, but he didn't make it out before a blade was pressed to his jugular, one of the guards hauling him back into the room and turning him to face the bastard who shook his head.

Milo wanted to rage.

Fight.

But the blade was digging into his neck, and his family's faces were flashing through his mind.

"I wouldn't do that if I were you." He stood, rounding the table as he readjusted his suit jacket. He leaned against the front of his desk and crossed his legs at the ankles. "I have treated you like a son for years, Milo. I took you in. Gave you a chance at a life that you would never have known without me. I loved you enough to let you walk away from me the first time, only because I knew, in time, you would be back. I trusted you when you agreed to the terms. It's now time to stand and be the man I taught you to be."

"And if I don't?"

Stefan cocked his head. "All I can say is I'd suggest you show for your fight this weekend."

He pushed off the desk, grabbing the stack of cash. He slowly strode across the room, his dress shoes clacking on the polished floor.

He angled in, too goddamn close to Milo's face. "See, it's a special night, and I'm going to need you there. I have a lot of money riding on you. You've always been my most prized fighter, Milo, a man I respected, but it's time you respect me after all I've done for you. I won't be made a fool again. After tomorrow's fight, if you do as is expected of you, then you'll be free to go."

Then he shoved the money against Milo's chest and leaned in close to his ear. "Don't disappoint me."

Then he walked out without saying anything else.

Chapter Thirty-Nine

Tessa

MILO SPUN ME AROUND AND PRESSED ME TO THE DOOR of my car. His hands came to frame my face, and his big body covered mine.

A burly blanket of protection.

A giddy sound rippled up my throat, and my lips were dancing all over the place, anticipating one of those kisses I'd come to crave.

The man chaos on my tongue.

Morning light warmed the new day, and he stared down at me as he traced the pad of his thumb along the line of my jaw. It was wild how the man could look at me with such tenderness while I could physically feel the well of violence that steamed beneath the surface.

Every glorious muscle in his body was tense.

Ready to strike.

"You sure you need to go into work today?"

It'd been four days since Milo had found someone lurking on his property.

Since he'd confessed what had happened to Autumn.

To the lengths he'd gone to try to avenge her death.

Ever since, he'd been completely on edge.

Watching out the windows. Pacing the floors at night.

Following me to work.

It was honestly still hard to grasp. That life. What he'd done and what he'd gotten involved in. To fully understand the severity of what he'd warned me about.

Over the past few days, he'd opened up a little more, talking about how he'd been sucked into a life he never should have stepped into. The way he'd tripped into making the same mistakes and it'd cost him his wife.

I'd seen the fear in his eyes. The truth that he believed himself wicked and weak. That he was terrified that he could trip again.

My heart panged as I thought of the way he'd stalled out, unable to speak the full horrors of what had actually happened to Autumn that night.

Or maybe he'd just been trying to protect me, keep me from the sordid details.

He'd expected that I'd run when I found out.

And yeah, I was freaked out. Saddened that he'd done what he'd done, that he'd lived the life that he had.

He was true in saying his past had been dark and ugly.

But I also believed in forgiveness if we'd moved beyond that person. If we'd sought to make a real change.

I knew he had.

I believed in who he was today.

I'd promised him I could handle all that he was, and I'd meant it because the man standing in front of me right then was good and right.

I pressed his palm closer to my cheek as I gazed up at those honey-dipped eyes that roiled with so many things.

Possession.

Protection.

Ferocity.

Desperation.

The culmination of them love.

The kind of love that made my chest feel achy and full and like it still wasn't enough.

He was what I never could have anticipated.

My wild card.

My Ace.

"You know you've asked me that same thing every day this week?" I sent him a sultry smile.

A small grunt rumbled from his chest. The sound trembled through me like a caress. "I've had to since you're so stinkin' stubborn."

"Stubborn? Who, me?" I let the tease wind from my mouth, loving the way his expression darkened as he curled a hand around my hip.

Tingles raced through my body.

I was hooked.

Craving him, and I didn't hesitate to indulge.

Cake.

So much cake.

I'd been glutting myself on it every day.

Morning.

Night.

Noon a bunch of times, too.

It was a yummy, lovely bonus of the fact that Milo would hardly let me out of his sight.

Although I hated the circumstances.

Hated the terror that ridged his brow.

Hated the panic in the tremor of his fingers as they held on to me, like he couldn't stomach the idea of letting me go.

I knew he was worried that his children were with their grandparents and there was nothing he could do about it, all while wondering if they were safer there.

Dread filled my soul because honestly, I didn't know what to anticipate.

Milo had warned me again and again that the man was evil. Sick. Twisted in a way that wasn't right.

Because of it, we were being as careful as we could.

Trying to ease some of his worry, I let my fingertip drag down over his beard until I was fluttering my fingers over his heart, my head tipped to the side as I whispered, "Like you aren't just going to follow me, anyway."

Another grunt.

I was growing addicted to that sound.

"Don't want to let you out of my sight, Tessa. Told you I would do everything and anything to protect you."

"You already are," I promised him.

He slipped his palm around to the back of my neck. "I can't take the risk of something happening to you."

Desperation filled his voice.

"We won't let it." My words were short and heavy with the belief.

Adoration moved through his expression, his voice gruff when he murmured, "Never thought I'd be given a chance like this, Tessa. The chance to love again. The chance to feel what I feel for you."

He picked me up off my feet and kissed me. Kissed me sweetly, though with Milo, it was always underscored with passion. With this need that torched me through.

He had it all wrong.

He was the heat and the fire and the flame.

The one that would forever burn inside me.

He pulled back. "You'd better get that adorable ass in your car so I can follow you to work before I carry you back inside instead."

"Don't tease me."

"Oh, it's not me who's doing the teasin', Little Dove. Think we know that honor belongs to you."

Lightness played across his features.

I hiked up onto my toes and pecked a quick kiss to his sexy mouth. "Fine. I'll see you tonight at the club."

He had to work…and, well, like we'd established, he didn't want me out of his sight. He certainly wasn't going to leave me at the cabin alone until three in the morning.

I wasn't exactly complaining.

"I'll be waiting." He opened my car door for me, standing there like a giant gentleman as he helped me inside.

"Liar…you'll be sitting outside the school, keeping watch, just like a good fiancé would do," I teased.

Need rumbled through him, head to toe.

My spirit shivered with the impact.

With the truth of how desperately I loved him.

"Plan to be the best, Tessa. Best I can be for the rest of my life."

∞

"I cannot believe I let you drag me to the club on a Thursday night." Eden climbed the three stairs that led to the employee side door at Absolution.

"Oh, please, your husband is inside. This is not clubbing, Eden, it's family time. You're welcome."

She tossed me a grin from over her shoulder, and her blonde curls swished around her face. "You're dead set on taking credit for everything related to my family, aren't you?"

I gave her a nonchalant shrug. "I mean, I won't brag about it or anything since humility is kind of my thing, but you know, if the shoe fits and all."

She laughed. "You're ridiculous."

"You know you love me."

Eden grinned, though it was soft. "Mad love."

"It's the only way I'll take it," I told her as I swung open the door.

I was so ready for a good time. Karl had texted me earlier, saying he was back in town and wanted to talk.

Revulsion had crawled through me, and I hadn't even graced him with a response.

Because the only thing that mattered was the man who filled my sight the second we stepped inside.

Talk about mad love.

My stomach bottomed out as Milo came our direction. He looked like a legitimate goliath as he stalked down the hall, wearing all black and ferocity on his face. His shoulders were so wide I thought they might rub against each side of the wall, his head nearly touching the ceiling, his powerful presence erupting from him and pounding through the air with each step he took.

Milo had just texted for an ETA, but since I drove my Corolla like it actually was a Porsche, we'd made it a few minutes early.

He looked annoyed by that fact, all while his gaze was licking over the red dress I'd worn just for him like he was wondering how fast he could get me out of it.

"Told you I'd meet you outside," he grumbled.

"Sorry, we got here, and Oz was out there talking to one of the employees, so we didn't see any harm in it. You know that guy would go GI Joe on that jerk's ass if he dared to show up here, so we were completely fine."

A grunt got free of Milo, the man hesitant to give, though I could see a little of the edge slide from his being.

I slipped my palm up his chest, tipping my head back to take all of him in. Every cell in my body pounded. Lit in recognition.

His arm curved around my waist and yanked me against all that knotted muscle.

Yummy.

"Told you to be careful," he warned low.

"I am," I promised, then I let a flirty grin take to one side of my mouth. "Miss me?"

"If you're not with me, that means I'm missing you, Tessa."

His words were so hard that I gasped a little at the weight of them.

Tingles raced over my flesh.

Giddiness creeping up to take me over.

All mixed up with this heady desire that spun through me like a storm.

Disordered and unruly.

Yup.

Addicted.

And I did not want help.

Eden laughed from the side of us, breaking through the intensity.

"Um, hello, hi, remember me, your BFF?" She lifted her hand in a tiny wave.

I'd given Eden the rundown on the way over.

The fact that Milo and I were now together *together*. That what we had was no longer a sham.

It was real and true.

Along with the rest of the terrifying things that went along with it.

An exaggerated frown puckered my face. "I'm sorry, no, who are you? It seems someone has turned my mind to mush."

"That sounds like a horrible state of affairs." She mocked a gasp as she touched her chest.

"No, it's really not. Believe me, life is much easier this way."

"Where's Salem? She needs to be here so she can see what a goober you really are," Eden said.

I pouted. "I miss her. That damn baby is stealing all my Salem time."

"How dare he." Playfulness danced on her face.

"I know." My head shook with mock sadness.

A chuckle rumbled from Milo. "All right, you two. I should get you to the table."

"Oh, no, Milo, we are dancing tonight."

His brow lifted. "You trying to make my night harder?"

I hiked up on my toes so I could whisper in his ear. "I plan to make it much, much better."

He groaned. "Tiny Tease."

"Only for my beast."

Then I patted his chest and strode around him, snagging Eden's hand as I went so I could strut in front of him.

"You are going to make that poor man lose his mind," Eden whispered so only I could hear.

"It's only fair since that mountain man has stolen my heart."

And I was never getting it back.

I could feel his watchful gaze rushing over me as Eden and I danced. We were on the edge of the dance floor, and I was letting loose because hello, it was me, and I was not the kind of girl who turned down the opportunity for a good time.

Bonus?

I really was going to make Milo lose his mind. The man was positively vibrating with want.

Want for me.

Those eyes continually swept over my body before his jaw would clench in restraint and he'd tear his attention away.

Lights strobed over the crowd that writhed and throbbed in a mass.

Tonight, there was a DJ, the house packed, the vibe different than when a band was playing.

On nights like these, it felt more entrancing.

Hypnotic.

Lust permeating the air and inhibitions crushed.

But my only desire was for Milo, who stalked the side of the dance floor like he was hunting prey.

He was what was mesmerizing.

Magnetic.

He made my thighs throb and my insides quake.

Leann, my favorite cocktail server, came waltzing by, lifting two glasses filled with yummy, sugary, tequila-laden goodness in the air.

"Margarita time!" I squealed over the music. Grabbing Eden's hand, I hauled her off the dance floor to the small round table where Leann was setting our drinks.

"Two margaritas, on the house." She winked and gestured to Trent who stood guard at the edge of the bar, watching over us almost as closely as Milo.

Giggling, Eden took a sip. "Well, I guess I'd better be getting something out of this."

"I'm sure you're getting plenty," Leann told her in her southern accent.

I cracked up. "Oh, she is. I accidentally walked in on that biz one time, and hot damn..."

Trent was packing almost as large as Milo.

Almost.

Eden swatted at me from over the top of the table. "You have no filter."

"There's no filtering that, Eden."

Leann howled. "You're a terrible person, making my mind go there."

"You're welcome." I grinned.

Eden shook her head as Leann walked away and disappeared into the fray. "You are so much, Tessa McDaniels."

"Just the right amount, wouldn't you say?"

"I would have to agree." She clinked my glass.

Emotion rushed me out of nowhere. "Will you be my maid of honor? For real?"

The softest smile edged her mouth, and she reached over the table and squeezed my hand. "Of course, I will be. I am your ride or die, aren't I?"

"Until the end."

There was no erasing the smile from my face. Well, not until I saw Milo pull his phone from his back pocket and freeze. The man just stood there in the middle of the chaos looking at the screen.

Dread slithered down my spine, or maybe I was feeling the wash of his. The ice that seeped from his pores and frosted the air in a cold mist.

"I think I'm going to go check to see how Milo is doing."

"Trent has been eyeing me for some alone time for about the last thirty minutes, anyway."

Light laughter filtered from me, though it trembled with my worry. I forced an easy grin. "Go get yourself some of that cake."

"Don't mind if I do."

She grabbed her margarita and headed to Trent while I worked to gather myself. Praying, praying, praying that it wasn't bad news about our kids.

I nearly toppled over when I realized what I'd thought.

At the claim my heart had made.

Ours.

I meant it to my soul.

And crap, I'd never been in so deep, and there was absolutely no climbing out. But I didn't want to. I wanted to bask in all his glory for my entire life. Wander around in his darkness if it was required, but truthfully, I believed the two of us made each other better.

Held each other's goodness like a treasure.

I'd hold all his bad places, too.

I moved that way just as he was shoving his phone into his back pocket. He felt me coming, and that severity flash-fired across the space when he shifted to find me heading his way.

The world moved on around us while our spirits slowed.

Winding and wrapping and binding.

My hand was extending for him right as he snatched my wrist. He pitched a sigh of relief at the contact.

"Little Dove." His voice was rough.

"What happened?"

"Come with me."

He hauled me through the roiling crowd toward the left side of the expansive building.

Kult was walking toward us.

"Cover for me," Milo told him as he passed.

Kult just nodded, the two of them clearly in sync and used to tossing orders at the other.

I could barely keep up with Milo as he led me down a hall toward the private party rooms, and he tossed open the door to one that wasn't being used.

Inside, it was dark, and he reached over and flipped on a switch that tossed the luxury suite in blue-tinged neon that barely cut through the shadows.

Shivers raced. Both in terror and desire.

"What happened?" I demanded that time when Milo lumbered out into the middle of the room, standing away from me and roughing both hands over the top of his head.

"Got a text."

It wasn't too much of a stretch to guess who it was from.

"What did it say?"

Milo whirled around, fury on his face. "It was an address plus a time and date."

So much hatred rolled out with the response that it nearly swept me from my feet.

"To where?" The question trembled from my mouth.

"A vacant building that's only inhabited by devils and fiends."

A lump obstructed my airflow as awareness hit. "He wants you to fight?"

He swallowed hard, his throat bobbing beneath his beard as he gritted out the words, "It seems so."

"Why?"

"I'm guessing he has a ton of money on me. Or maybe he just wants to prove that he still owns me. That he can push me. Manipulate me. Remind me what he did to Autumn and dare me to defy him again."

"What are you going to do?" The question convulsed through the dense air.

"I'm going to find him and end him before it happens."

"Milo." Fear spun around his name. Fear that he might be hurt. That I might lose him. That he might lose himself if he didn't stop this monster.

Because I could see the darkness there, lurking in the depths of his eyes.

The golden yellow tinged in aggression and violence.

"Warned you that it might get ugly."

"This is more than ugly, Milo. This is—"

My words clipped off when he suddenly stormed my way, erasing the space. Without warning, he lifted me from the ground and crushed me against him.

Energy crashed.

A thunderclap.

A strike of lightning.

He held me against him with one arm while his other hand twisted in my hair. "It's disgusting, Tessa, but men like him are vile, wicked to the bone, and the only thing that can be done to stop them from destroying everything that is good and pure is to wipe their existence from the earth."

Tremors rolled through my body, a rush of alarm.

"You see it now, what I'm capable of?" It was a challenge.

"You're a good man," I mumbled, our lips so close, our breaths panting into the other.

Severity curled through the room.

Flickers of light at the edges of my blurred sight.

"I'm not. But I will be everything I can be. For you. For my kids."

"Then you do what's right. Whatever it takes to protect that."

He dove for my mouth, devouring the words on my tongue.

"Don't deserve you," he rumbled at my lips as he was grabbing a handful of my bottom. A moan got free, mixed with the wisps of words that I breathed back into him. "Everyone deserves forgiveness, Milo. Redemption for what they've done. I think you've paid your penance, suffered enough."

"I could never gain atonement for what I did. And somehow, I got you. You, who's pure fuckin' bliss. How'd I get so fuckin' lucky?"

"I am kinda amazing." I forced some lightness into the madness, but he just swallowed it down with a growl, turned, and carried me to the grand piano on the left side of the room.

The heavy beat of the music filtered through the walls, though it was subdued, and our breaths heaved in a frantic melody.

The keys clanked when he propped me against them, and he took a seat at the bench while he was shoving my dress up my thighs. "Need to taste you, Little Dove."

"Okay, yes, I'm good and fine with that," I whimpered as he ripped my underwear down my legs.

I shucked the little wristlet from my hand, and it clattered against the keys before it dropped to the floor.

A low chuckle reverberated through the desire-drenched room. "Always so eager, aren't you, Tiny Tease?"

He spread me by the knees, exposing me, and my hands were trying to find purchase on the keys, the clanging notes going off as I struggled to find balance.

But with Milo, there was no footing.

No grip.

I was just in a freefall.

Falling forever.

"Such a good girl, dripping for me."

He looked so savagely gorgeous there, sitting between my legs that he held open. He was so wide and rough and rippling with a strength and brutality that attested to the man who he could be.

Grabbing me by the back of one thigh, he pushed one big finger into me to the knuckle.

A gasp jolted from my lungs, and I shifted on the keys.

"Look at your pussy, throbbing and needy." He drove his finger in and out.

Tingles raced, a shimmery pleasure streaking across my flesh, lifting goose bumps along my arms.

"Milo."

"Told you once I had you, that was it. You belong to me now. This sweet, delicious cunt. Is it mine, Little Dove?"

"I'm yours. All of me. Take it and hurry up while you're at it." It rushed from my lips.

"So eager," he rumbled as he was letting go of a dark, delicious chuckle before his tongue was swirling around my clit.

He licked and lapped while he added another finger.

"Oh, crap, yes, Milo."

He flattened his tongue, stroking me just right, his fingers shifting to rub at that spot inside me that had me seeing stars.

He thought I was the sun, but when he was touching me, I was a supernova.

Nothing but a fiery fever that rushed through my body.

And I was whimpering and trying to hold on as he drove me higher, as all the elements came together, earth and water and sun and sky, and I was flying.

Soaring through his darkness.

This man my perfect eclipse.

I pulsed and shook as the pleasure blistered through my being, and Milo was on his feet and yanking open his fly and pulling out his enormous erection.

I didn't even have time to appreciate it before he stuffed me full, then I was totally, completely appreciating it in a different way.

Aftershocks still rolled through my body while fresh sparks of bliss lit up my insides.

"Milo." I clawed at his shoulders like I could keep up with the force of him.

Impossible.

His thrusts were ruthless.

Possessive and deep and hard.

"Milo," I begged again.

"Whatever you need, Little Dove, I'm going to give it to you. All of it. Always."

"Always," I whispered back, and he was yanking me up higher, holding me upright as he drove me up and down his shaft.

Our bodies pulsing and writhing as he slammed into me.

Taking me.

Owning me.

Ruining me.

And I was coming apart in his massive arms.

His.

And he was shouting as he throbbed and poured into me.

And he was mine.

And I believed in him with every part of my being.

My Beautiful Beast.

Sweat drenched our skin and heat covered the air, our breaths harsh and haggard as we clung to each other for the longest time.

Finally, Milo pulled back, though he kept me there, held in his arms, warm eyes flaring with intensity as he murmured, "I love you, Tessa. So fuckin' much. And I hope you know that means I'll do whatever it takes to give you a good life."

"I know, my sweet man. I know."

He squeezed me once before he set me back on my unstable feet, and a giggle was getting free as I searched around for my underwear. "Um, I feel like we sullied that poor piano. I think that was the best action it's seen in years. Probably ever."

Low laughter rolled from him. "Maybe don't tell Eden what went down in here, yeah? Trent might not approve."

"Pssh…keep this from Eden? I'm pretty sure you're written all over me right about now, Milo Hendricks. I'm glowing with the good D. No wiping the evidence away."

He grabbed me by the hip and jerked me against him, his voice rough at my ear. "Exactly the way I want it, to be written all over you. Inside and out."

My tummy tipped.

"Signed and sealed, baby." I did my best to pin on a grin when I was totally serious.

The man had branded my vagina.

Milo's.

I slinked back into my underwear and straightened my hair, and my phone started to ring from my bag.

"That's probably Eden wondering where I got off to, which I'm not quite sure why she'd be concerned since she was off taking a bite of her tasty husband."

Unzipping my bag, I pulled out my phone.

The smile slid off my face, and my heart plummeted to the floor.

"What is it, Little Dove?"

"Bobby's care center."

My hands were shaking out of control as I answered, trying to keep the room from spinning because it was freaking midnight on a Thursday. Maybe he was unsettled, having a bad night, and they thought it was good for him to hear my voice.

That was it.

It had to be.

"Ms. McDaniels?" the woman asked on the other end of the line.

"Yes, this is she."

"This is Pamela at St. John's Meadows. I'm really sorry to call you like this, but we need you to come down."

And I couldn't breathe.

Couldn't see.

Couldn't do anything but drop to my knees.

Chapter Forty

Milo

I SPED DOWN THE DESERTED STREETS OF REDEMPTION HILLS, flying through the intersections and taking the turns hard, agitation driving me faster as I tried to get Tessa to the care facility as quickly as possible.

She was falling apart.

Hell, she was in shock, really.

Shaking in the passenger seat, her knee jittering a million miles a minute and her breaths coming so fast, I was sure she was a second from having a panic attack.

She'd removed her heels, and she looked like she might jump out the door, thinking she could run faster than I could drive.

I reached over the console to try to give her some comfort, knowing words meant little, but still needing her to know she wasn't alone. "Try to take a deep breath, baby. I'm right here."

She wrapped both her trembling hands around my wrist. "I can't, Milo. I can't breathe. What if…"

She trailed off on an agonized wheeze, unable to bear to say it or think it or contemplate it.

"I know, Tessa. I know, baby."

I focused on getting her there, clinging to her hand while I blazed down the streets.

When she'd fallen to the floor, I'd taken her cell and tried to get more information, but the woman had said she couldn't tell me anything over the phone.

I'd had Tessa in my arms and out the door in a flash, shooting a text to Trent to let him know what had happened.

My phone had buzzed back a couple times, Trent telling me to do whatever needed to be done.

The one that had come in from Eden had been completely frantic, and I'd promised that I'd send her details as soon as I had them.

Right then, I just had to get my girl there. Stand by her. Support her. Whatever she needed.

I made a sharp left into the parking lot, tires squealing as I floored it again and came to a jarring stop in one of the spaces at the front, the lot mostly vacant this time of night.

Tessa hardly waited for the SUV to come to a stop before she went flying out the door, her bare feet slapping against the cement.

I was right behind her, holding open the door so she could run inside. Except she didn't stop at the reception desk. She took a turn and went streaking down a hallway.

A woman was behind us, shouting at her, "Ms. McDaniels!"

Tessa didn't listen.

She just ran.

Ran with this misery radiating from her spirit.

Her soul crying out.

Her desperation so intense I could barely move in the wake of it.

I rushed to keep up as she made another turn and increased her speed.

A bunch of people were gathered outside a room, their faces grim, and Tessa was crying out before she even made it all the way there. "No! Please, no, Bobby."

She tried to blaze past the group, but someone grabbed her, holding her back. "Ms. McDaniels, let's talk before you go in there."

She flailed and kicked her feet and fought to get inside. "No, let me go. I need to see him. Let me see him!"

I didn't know whether she broke free or if he released her, but Tessa darted into the room.

I ran in behind her.

She started screaming. Screaming in agony. In this gut-wrenching grief.

She tossed herself on top of her brother who wasn't breathing, holding onto his lifeless frame. "Bobby, no, oh my God, no."

I moved to go to her.

Hold her up when she was falling apart.

But when I got a good look at him, I might as well have gotten impaled with a blade.

It was a face I would never forget.

I stumbled back into the wall, unable to keep standing as horror took over every cell in my body.

Agonized wails kept coming from Tessa as misery sheared through my spirit.

Blurring my sight and sending nausea curling my guts.

Vomit pooled in my mouth.

I stumbled out into the hall, and my hands were shaking so bad it was a wonder I could lift my phone to my ear when I made the call.

"Eden, need you to come here," I grated as soon as she answered.

"I'm already in the parking lot. Trent brought me."

"Good, Tessa needs you."

Because I couldn't stay.

I should have known…should have known…

No matter how hard I might try to change it. Be someone different. My past would be there to overcome. To overthrow.

Because there was no redemption for men like me.

Chapter Forty-One

Tessa

I GUESSED I WAS NO STRANGER TO GRIEF. TO THE WAY everything felt excruciatingly heavy.

Suffocating.

Oppressive.

Your breaths so strained it was a labor to draw them into your aching lungs.

All while you were just…hollow.

Carved out.

Gutted.

Nothing inside.

Maybe I knew the feeling, but I was sure I'd never felt it so distinctly as right then.

Chained, yet floating away.

Wandering through the desolation with no direction.

No sight.

Staring blankly through the large plate glass window that overlooked Eden's lush backyard. Her lawn was manicured, and the hedges trimmed, and she had at least a gazillion pots overflowing with flowers on the patio and filling the planters that lined the fence.

An oasis cradled by the forest beyond.

Beautiful.

But I wasn't sure anything would ever feel truly beautiful again.

Eden set a cup of coffee in front of me, where I sat at the breakfast nook under the window. Easing back, she wrapped her arms around me from behind, hugging me so tight that my aching chest squeezed.

"I am so sorry, Tessa. God, I'm so sorry."

"I can't believe this happened." Forcing the words through the disorder felt impossible, the thought too thin, too vague.

But I couldn't…I couldn't believe it.

Bobby was gone.

Gone.

Without reason or warning. The small parts of him that had still remained ripped away.

And in the middle of it, Milo had walked.

Left me.

Without reason or warning, either.

Tears ran hot down my face, but I didn't have the strength to wipe them, the mess dripping off my chin onto the pajama shirt Eden had given me when she and Trent had brought me back here at close to four o'clock this morning.

Hours had been spent with Bobby before the coroner had come. When they'd taken him away, the only thing I could do was wander the parking lot, refusing to get in the car with Trent and Eden.

I'd been lost.

Dazed.

Numb.

Then a rush of anger had hit me so hard I'd buckled in two, and I'd demanded Trent and Eden drive me to Milo's place so I could find out how he could just leave me.

I'd needed him. Needed him to be there with me during one of the most painful times of my life.

Agony carved through my spirit.

He promised me.

Promised.

I didn't understand.

Didn't understand how the man who was supposed to be *my person* had abandoned me, too.

I choked over a sob, and Eden squeezed me tighter. "It's okay…let it out. Let it out, Tessa."

I clutched at her hands where they were locked around me.

"I don't understand. How could Bobby just…die? He was fine. I saw him two days ago, and he was fine." My voice croaked with the confusion as another sob erupted.

"I know. I don't understand, either. But they'll get answers for you. I promise."

My nod was erratic. "I'm so sad, Eden."

She just kept holding me, my friend who had always been there for me, the one who'd never let me down, the one who loved my crazy and supported my neurosis and never judged me for being myself.

"I'm so sad, too," she murmured with her cheek pressed to mine.

"And Milo. How could he be such a selfish, horrible jerk? I thought he was the one, Eden. My Ace. The one who would always be there. Stand by me and hold me up. Isn't that what love is supposed to be about?"

I could feel her bewilderment, her uncertainty, and she peeled herself away and pulled a chair close so she was facing me. "I am not making excuses for him, Tessa, because I'm really pissed, too. That was a giant dick move, but there was something going on with him last night. I heard it in his voice when he sent out the SOS call to me, and he could barely stand when he came stumbling out of the building. Trent tried to talk to him, but he shrugged him off, got in his car, and took off."

"But why?"

He was supposed to be there for me.

Through thick and thin.

Through everything.

Even when it was hard or it hurt.

"I don't know, sweetheart."

She handed me a tissue that I wadded up and pressed to my nose. "I think I need to lie down."

Eden squeezed my hand. "You do whatever you need. I'll be right here."

"Thank you."

"I'm your ride or die, remember?"

I nodded through the tears.

"The best one I could ask for."

She hugged me fiercely before I stood and fumbled my way back upstairs to the room that she'd always told me was mine if I ever needed it. If I needed a safe place to stay.

I'd never wanted to be a burden, not when she had two children, a family, but I'd honestly had nowhere else to turn last night. Nowhere else to go.

I'd truly, completely lost it all.

I sank down onto the side of the bed.

Lost.

Disoriented.

Tortured.

My gaze landed where I'd set the little round locket on the nightstand last night. The one Bobby had forever kept clutched in his hand. I reached for it, pressed it to my lips, and whispered, "I'm so sorry, Bobby. I'm so sorry I let you down. How didn't I know you were sick? That something was wrong? God."

Tears blurred my sight, and I ran the back of my hand frantically over my face like it could clear the haze, and I opened the locket to the four little pictures of our family inside.

My brother who'd tried to keep me close when he'd been so far away.

"Why did you have to go?"

My mouth kept tweaking at the side as I stared at the images.

The memories so good, but when they were gone, the pain was so great.

A frown curled my brow when I realized each of the pictures was indented.

Squinting, I tried to make them out, realizing they were numbers inscribed on the back.

My hands started shaking when I carefully peeled one from its setting, confusion clouding my senses as I turned it over and saw the individual number written on it.

I repeated it with the other three pictures. Each had a different number.

My stomach swooped in awareness.

The safe.

The safe I'd found in his closet. I'd never been able to open it, so I'd put it in the storage locker with the rest of his things without ever knowing what was inside.

Oh my gosh, I might be able to get into it.

It was weird to suddenly blaze with hope in the middle of this relentless grief, but it was there, the excitement of finding another piece of Bobby.

Frantic, I rushed to change into a pair of jeans and a tee that I'd left here after a drunken night.

I shoved my feet into the same heels I'd had on last night, swiping the tears from my face as I pressed the pictures back into the locket and put it into my pocket.

I scrambled downstairs, my breaths rapid as I raced into the kitchen where Eden was feeding Baby Kate in her highchair. "I need to borrow your car."

Surprise twisted her face. There was no chance she didn't notice the change in my demeanor.

This hysteria that streaked through my veins.

I didn't know why. I just knew I had to get there. To see what was inside.

What if Bobby had left me a message, something important, something that he would want me to know?

"Are you sure? Give me one second, and I can drive you."

"No, I'll be right back. I just need to go grab something."

"Tessa." Worry filled my name.

I forced a bright smile, which probably made me look like a lunatic since my hair was a disaster and my face was stained with tears. "I'm good. I promise. I'll be right back. Besides, you told me whatever I need, remember?"

Her eyes narrowed. "Someone knows how to twist my arm, doesn't she?"

I choked over the affection as I snagged her keys from the counter. "It's only because you love me."

Everything about her softened. "Mad, mad love."

Baby Kate squealed and giggled, a balm to those vacant places that felt so raw and abraded.

I blew them both a kiss. "Mad, mad love."

Then I turned and ran into their garage, punched the button to lift it, and I was flying down the road in Eden's Mercedes.

Taking deep breaths to steady myself.

Completely entrenched in this mission.

I punched in the code to open the security gate of the storage facility. It swung open, and I took the fourth turn into the aisle where Bobby's locker was located. I parked in front of it, jumped out, and immediately started spinning the padlock combo. When it gave, I unhooked it and rolled open the metal door.

Dust billowed out, curling and dancing through the rays of sunlight from the absolute stillness that echoed from inside.

I choked over the pain that stabbed me in the stomach.

He was gone.

He was gone.

I brushed away the fresh round of tears and moved directly for the little safe that was on top of his old dresser. I pulled out the locket and removed the pictures again, turning them upside down.

It took me only a second of shuffling them around to realize it was my birthdate.

0921.

I punched in the code, and the safe buzzed before the latch gave, and I rushed to open it.

Disappointment hit me hard when I found it was empty.

Except...it wasn't.

There was a pocket on the right side, and I dug into it to find one of those tiny manila envelopes. I tore it open and dumped its contents into my palm.

It was one of those old, tiny flash drives.

A disorder blustered through my being.

This sense coming on that made bile lift in my throat.

The truth that something was…off.

Wrong.

My brother hadn't been sick.

He was fine.

I swiped my hand over my face, trying to process, to stop my mind from racing toward assumptions.

To keep from diving into paranoia.

I gathered up the pictures and stuffed everything into my pocket, quick to close the locker door and jump back into Eden's car. I started it and raced back to her place.

"Do you have an old laptop around here?" I called as I tossed open the garage door and jogged back into her kitchen where she was giving Gage a snack.

"In Dad's office. He's got a billion," Gage told me from around a mouthful of apple and cheese.

"Thanks, buddy."

"You know I got your back, Auntie Tessa."

Eden frowned, her worry thick. "What's going on?"

"I just found something of Bobby's I want to take a look at."

Except, I didn't.

I absolutely didn't.

Because on the zip drive was video after video of Bobby in a ring.

Dreary darkness all around. Eclipsing goodness and everything that was right.

My brother fighting.

Being beaten to a bloody pulp.

Him doing it in return.

And the last…the last demolished my shattered heart.

Because Milo was standing over his beaten body, where Bobby lay in a pool of blood, his leg bent at an odd angle. Voices curled through the air, demanding that he end him.

Right before the video cut out.

Chapter Forty-Two

Milo

Five Years Ago

SHOUTS THUNDERED THROUGH THE SORDID AIR, VILENESS riding on the thinned vapors of oxygen that smothered all morality.

Loathing seeped down to his core, infiltrating every molecule.

The disgust at what he'd succumbed to, the revulsion for what he'd done.

Pain throbbed at his right side from what he was sure was a cracked rib, and blood dripped from his ear and down his chin as he stalked around the edge of the ring, weighing his opponent who'd turned out to be far more difficult to beat than he'd anticipated.

No doubt that was why he'd been forced into this corruption, the stakes higher than they'd ever been.

Ten million he'd heard rumbling through hushed voices, the anticipation of it curling through the basement on dark ribbons of greed.

And if he didn't win?

He refused to even consider it.

The man they called Immortal stalked forward, tossing out a blow that landed Milo on the jaw.

Violence screamed, the thirst for it racing through his veins, clouding out reason and sight.

Milo attacked.

Throwing blow after blow, knocking the man back farther and farther across the ring with each hit.

Blood splattered, and Milo could feel the crunching of bone. Immortal fell back against the ropes, and someone shoved him off, and the man lumbered three steps forward.

It gave Milo the perfect opportunity to knock him in the temple.

His fist cracked.

The man slumped forward.

Facedown.

TKO.

Greedy shouts erupted, chanting through the air. "End him. End him!"

Milo turned in a circle, mind jumbled with the disorder, with the aggression that thrived and the disgust that made him want to turn and run.

Nothing making sense.

They kept chanting.

Chanting and chanting.

It was different from before.

Something sinister filling the air.

Nausea spun through his stomach as dread clawed across his flesh.

Vipers that sank their teeth into his soul.

The ref was still standing there, not calling the fight.

He stumbled back to the ropes, realization bottling his conscience into a fist of terror.

Stefan leaned in from behind him, his wicked voice hissing in his ear, "You heard them…end him. I promise you, he's not *immortal*."

Milo spun to look at him.

The twisted fuck cracked a grin.

Disbelief shook Milo's head. "What are you saying, Stefan?"

"I warned you that the stakes were greater than before, Milo. End him. Because it's him or it's you."

Chapter Forty-Three

Tessa

"**I** REALLY THINK YOU SHOULD WAIT, TESSA. TRENT'S ON HIS way home right now." Eden's panicked voice covered me as she chased me back into her garage, begging me to listen to reason.

But there was no reason right then.

There was only agony and pain and the deepest, most brutal kind of wounds.

Had he done it? Had Milo hurt Bobby? Is that why he freaked out and left?

Horror cemented in my throat.

He'd...killed people before.

He'd admitted it.

Tossed it out. Proof that he shouldn't be trusted.

And I'd ignored it like it was rational.

I gulped around the torment. Around his truth he'd confided in me. The confession I'd promised him I would hold.

My head spun through the anarchy that tugged my thoughts in every direction.

Everything I'd thought I'd known at odds with everything I'd discovered.

But Bobby'd had an accident.

He was hiking, and he'd fallen.

Hadn't he?

"Oh my God." A convulsion of pain wrenched through my body, and my arm went to my stomach like I could keep the sickness from overtaking me.

Like I could protect myself from experiencing it.

From feeling it.

Because I couldn't handle it if this was true.

I managed to make it to Eden's car and ripped open the door. She tried to stop me.

"I have to go, Eden. Please. I need to know."

"Wait for Trent," she begged.

My head shook, and I choked over the truth. "I can't."

"Tessa." She looked behind her, torn between me and her children, who were inside.

I felt terrible for putting her in this position, but my soul wouldn't let me wait.

I smiled at my best friend through the soggy blur of my eyes and my heart and my soul, and I whispered, "Mad love."

In surrender, she moved back, giving me the space I was asking for. Tears streaked down her face. "Please be careful."

"I'll be fine."

One day, I would be, but that was not going to be today.

I backed out, my pulse so loud I could hear it chugging in my ears as I drove to the little cabin tucked in the woods.

A cabin I'd believed a sanctuary. The place I'd thought was going to be my home. But Milo had destroyed that, hadn't he? Robbed me of the one person I'd had left?

Bobby.

Grief nearly buckled me, but I forced myself to focus through the disorder, to be careful because I wasn't going to be one of those selfish jerks who only cared about themselves and put everyone around them in danger.

I struggled to keep my breathing even, to keep my cool, to remember I was just coming for answers.

I did my best to convince myself those answers weren't going to annihilate the last part of me, but I knew I was only lying to myself as I turned onto the windy, two-lane road that led in the direction of Milo's house.

The man who'd warned me he would ruin me.

I'd refused to listen.

I choked over my stupidity, the belief I'd given so freely.

But my heart…my heart had assured me he was good.

I wanted him to be.

I needed him to be.

I needed him to wrap me in his arms and promise me it was all a misunderstanding.

I finally made it to the turn off to his property, and I turned onto the narrow, gravel road. The tremoring only got worse as I approached, my speed increasing, the chaos whipping through my brain, thoughts dragging me in a thousand different directions.

When I got to the end of his drive, I rammed on the brakes, the tires skidding on the gravel as I came to a halt.

At the sight of his cabin, panic laced with this love and desperation overtook me.

He had to tell me it was a mistake.

That I was wrong.

That those videos had lied.

I threw it into park, tossed open the door, and raced up the porch steps.

Even though both his truck and the rental SUV were sitting out front, I already knew he wasn't there.

I could feel the emptiness echo back.

His aura gone.

His hope dimmed.

I tried the knob. When it was locked, I yanked at it in desperation before I started pounding on the wood since I didn't have my keys.

I'd lost mine somewhere along the way last night. Fitting, since I'd lost the last pieces of my life then, too.

And I needed them back.

I needed this heart whole.

I couldn't handle it.

Couldn't.

"Milo!" I yelled it through the agony, his name a petition.

A prayer.

"Milo!"

I was begging for it not to be true.

"Milo, please!" I cried through the grief.

Tears flooded, and I choked over the sobs that wouldn't stop coming.

A sea of them.

Wave after wave.

Rising higher.

Sucking in a breath, I raked the backs of my hands frantically over my eyes to try to clear the disorder.

Cheryl.

It clicked in an instant where he would go. She was within walking distance. He had to have gone there.

With purpose, I ran for Eden's small SUV.

I had to get to him.

I had to know.

I was halfway there when I was ripped from my feet unaware.

No warning.

No way to fight or prepare for the arm that wrapped around my waist from behind and snatched me from the ground.

A scream tore up my throat, though it was muffled by a hand that slapped across my mouth. A second later, a knife was pressed against my neck.

Oh my God. Please no.

Panic skidded through my being.

Fear clouding my sight and terror shaking me to the bone.

Another man stepped out from the trees, dressed in a suit, completely out of place.

Ice slicked down my spine at the cold vacancy in his eyes.

He eased forward, so slowly.

Dread and disgust twisted my stomach in a fist.

It was him.

The man Milo kept warning me about.

I didn't need any introductions to know it to my soul.

With a sneer, he reached out and dug his index finger into my cheek, and he dragged it down slowly, as if his whole purpose was cutting me in two.

Revulsion clawed through my senses.

"I guess I should thank you for leading me to Robert."

Robert?

My heart crashed to the ground.

He was talking about Bobby.

Bobby.

Oh God.

Tears rushed down my face, and he continued like he was enjoying ripping out my tattered soul. "You know, I'd believed Immortal dead for all these years. And when we learned of Milo finding a new girlfriend, I decided I should have one of my guys check into you. Imagine my surprise when I was told Robert was still alive. At least we were able to finally take care of that situation permanently."

"No!" It was muffled against the brute's hand who held me hostage against his body.

"He's lucky it was painless this time...so much less than he deserved for his betrayal."

Rage and heartbreak cleaved through my soul, and I kicked and thrashed against the man, no chance of breaking free of his arms. But I wasn't about to go down without a fight.

"No!" I shouted again. He held his palm so tightly over my mouth I thought I would suffocate.

Still, I fought.

Fought and wailed.

Every one of my cries was muffled and pained.

The monster in front of me cocked his head. "You see, I'm just not the type of man who can look the other way when people don't honor their commitments to me. I'd taken both Milo and Robert in. Nurtured them. Gave them a chance. Treated them like sons. They're the ones who turned their backs on me. Ruined what I'd built. I think it's only fair that I'm repaid my generosity, don't you?"

Chapter Forty-Four

Milo

I STARED VACANTLY AT THE PLACID BLUE WATERS WHILE MY insides boiled and raved, my guts a snarl of shock and foreboding. The mess of it was tossed with the heartbreak that severed me through.

Had known all along I couldn't give. That I couldn't fall. That I didn't deserve the light that was Tessa McDaniels because I was just going to stamp it out.

Smother her beauty with the depravity.

I just never could have imagined the tragedy it was going to be.

That our lives could collide quite like this.

I roughed my hands through my hair, fighting the panic as I paced the edge of the lake farthest from my house, unable to sit still within the vacancy of its walls, the hollowness screaming too loud.

Bobby.

Fuck.

I choked out the disbelief that was coated in pain.

All these years, I'd thought *Immortal* was dead.

Guilt slashed through me like a blade, a sharp pain driven directly into my soul.

I deserved this, didn't I?

Should have known it was going to catch up to me.

The only thing I could do now was stop Stefan before the bastard destroyed anyone else.

Gulping down the chaos that spun through the summer air, I let determination slip into my consciousness.

Let the vengeance take over.

I couldn't sit still and wait for something else to happen.

It was time this debt was paid.

I turned and began to weave my way back around the lake. The trail wound around the perimeter, sometimes dipping into the forest in the areas where the beach was rocky. My footsteps were quick as I made my way around, resolution lining my bones, the prayer on my tongue that I could see this through.

My chest tightened as I broke through the line of trees, and the back of my cabin came into view. The treehouse stood proud while my shame oozed from the walls and spread out over the atmosphere in a murky gloom.

Like the rays of sunlight couldn't quite break through.

I hustled through the gate, crossed the lawn, and bounded up the porch steps.

I yanked open the door and strode inside so I could grab my keys and continue the hunt I'd started last night.

Though this time, I wouldn't stop until I found him.

I was at close to a jog when I stalled out, because in my periphery, I noticed a car outside through the front windows. My eyes narrowed as I moved that way and saw it sitting with the driver's door wide open.

It took me a second to recognize it was Eden's.

My spirit clutched.

Tessa was here.

And fuck, how could I face her? How would she ever look at me the same? But I unlocked the front door and burst out there, anyway.

Only I slowed when I felt the stillness that bound the air, the only movement the limbs of the trees waving in the breeze.

"Tessa?"

My gaze scanned the area.

"Tessa?" I shouted that time.

Silence echoed back.

My heart climbed to my throat as a sticky dread prickled across my flesh.

"Tessa!" Shouted it again as I jumped down the steps and hit the ground running.

I searched the car. It was empty.

I ran up the drive a few hundred yards, searched the line of trees, shouting her name.

Anxiety clutched me as I darted around back.

I prayed I'd just missed her. That she was looking for me, too.

And I was calling and calling her name.

My girl who'd changed everything.

The one who'd lit that dead spot that now screamed inside me.

Silence echoed back.

Relentless.

Overbearing.

Crushing.

Panic seized me, and I went running back inside through the back door, flying to the kitchen counter where I'd plugged in my phone after I'd come crawling back here after dawn.

I'd spent the night searching.

Hunting.

Scouring every place I thought the fucker might be and coming up empty.

A ghost again.

No trace.

But I knew he was here.

Lurking.

Hiding.

Lying in wait.

I yanked my cell from the cord.

Horror wheezed out of me when I saw the text.

It was a picture of my girl, bound and tied in the same vile pit where I'd lost myself years before.

Where I'd become a man I didn't want to be.

It'd been completely empty last night, the way it'd been for years when I'd searched for Stefan.

And now, he was there, the sick fucker using Tessa as bait.

And the only thing it said below it was, *Don't be late.*

"You sure you want to do this?" The last thing I wanted to do was put the Lawson brothers in danger.

They'd had enough of it to last a lifetime. I didn't want to bring it on their families or cause them risk.

But I also couldn't *risk* Tessa.

Couldn't put her through the very thing I'd been terrified of bringing to her door.

What my spirit had warned me against—dragging her into my sordid world, tainting her beauty, stamping out the light—while the rest of me couldn't resist the persuasion that was Tessa McDaniels.

I should have resisted.

Shouldn't have given.

She wouldn't be in this position if I had.

Now there was nothing I wouldn't do to free her. To give her a chance at the life that she should have been living all along.

Whatever it took.

My children's faces flashed through my mind, and every molecule in my body contracted.

Fear that I was letting them down, too.

But I had to stand for this woman who'd stood for me even when she shouldn't have.

The deviant had gotten away before, and I couldn't take the chance of it happening again.

When I'd sent the text saying I needed help, it'd taken all of twenty minutes for all three Lawson brothers to show at my door.

Ready to stand for what was right.

Tessa.

"You think we'd let you go this alone?" Trent asked as he stuffed a gun into a holster hidden under his shirt.

"Tessa is family, man," Jud said. "Same as you. Means we're in this together."

Logan straightened out his suit jacket. "Besides, who else are they going to let in there but me? Obviously, I'm the only one around here with this cool sophistication. Best looking one of the bunch, am I right? You're going to need me."

Dude winked, as cocky as they came, and he gestured to himself before he tucked a thick stack of cash into the inside pocket of his jacket.

"These guys are foul. To the core. Nothing good about them," I warned.

Trent's grin was menacing when he clapped me on the shoulder. "Wouldn't be the first time we dealt with these types of assholes, now, would it?"

"No."

Jud smacked his hands together. "Then let's roll."

∽

Darkness reigned, the night thick and deep, the air stifled and stagnant.

Aggression coiled my muscles into one seething knot, and my chest was jutting in these spastic snaps as I forced the oxygen in and out of my lungs. Every part of me vibrated as I stood at the door to the dungeon beneath the blacked-out building.

You would think it was completely uninhabited except for the vileness that seeped out from the cracks.

The evil that oozed out on noxious tendrils.

The dirty *VIPs* gained access on the backside, and you got to it by following a hidden trail that started up on the next street. There was a second door about twenty feet down where Stefan's men came and went.

For years, it'd remained abandoned, and now I could feel the full force of the corruption rising from within.

The atrocity that had found its way back to my doorstep.

The first time I'd come here, I should have known to run far away, but I'd been drawn to it.

Thirsty for the deviance I could still feel curling from the pit below and slithering through the cracks.

Nausea twisted my guts, and sweat slicked my skin, nerves skidding and skipping, firing with violence and possession.

Tonight, it ended.

My attention swiveled both directions, and I caught sight of Trent slipping around the right side of the building at the same time Jud went to the left. When they were out of view, I inhaled a steadying breath and rapped my knuckles against the metal door.

Some meaty fucker peered out at me through the grate, and there was a rustling on the other side a moment before the door creaked open.

Instantly, I was flanked by two guards as they dragged me inside.

One pushed my chest against the wall and patted me down to ensure I wasn't armed.

The other stood guard with a rifle strapped over his shoulder.

"He's clean."

Anxiety rattled through me.

This whole thing was fucked. So dangerous. One misstep, and we were done.

But there was no other option.

Tessa was inside, and I wasn't coming out of there without her.

So, I acted like I was playing by their rules when one shoved me forward, gesturing for me to head down the grungy hall lit by a line of single bulbs that hung from the low ceiling.

In the distance, I could hear the rumble of debauchery. Could sense the wickedness that crawled the walls and haunted this place.

My heart pounded out of time, frantic and hard, while I struggled to keep my shit together. To keep from busting free and racing to find Tessa.

But I had to stick to the plan. Pray I knew Stefan well enough to know exactly what he intended inside.

They kept shoving at me as we took the stairwell down to the basement, and I was tossed into the old locker room.

My fucking head spun, the memories coming at me from all sides.

Every goddamn mistake I had made.

Every misstep.

The greed and the violence and the perversion of who I'd once been.

"Be ready in ten."

With clenched teeth, I gave a tight nod and moved to the sink, where I splashed cold water on my face.

I had no clue what I was walking into, but I at least knew it would be the fight of my life.

Because this fight?

It was for Tessa.

For Autumn.

For Bobby.

For my kids.

I peeled off my shirt and shoes, and I looked at myself in the mirror.

I let the old rage come.

Unlocked the fury.

Gore.

A shiver crawled across my flesh when I felt the presence cover me from behind. Rage brimmed from the depths. The thirst for vengeance. Retribution. The need to destroy him for what he'd stolen from me.

Slowly, I shifted to look at Stefan, who leaned against the wall so casually.

As if the last night I'd seen him face-to-face he hadn't taken the beauty I was supposed to protect and destroyed it as if it were nothing.

Bile ran my throat while savagery hacked through my senses.

Stefan's stare traced me with a sick pleasure. "I see you still possess it."

My teeth gnashed, and it took everything inside me not to rush across the space and snap his neck.

A twisted smile curled on his mouth, like he'd seen the vision play out and he took a sordid satisfaction in it. He tsked. "So angry."

"You killed my wife." It left me like fragments of broken glass.

He shrugged a nonchalant shoulder. "I warned you to do what you were told. It's you who failed to follow instructions. You knew what was at stake."

"I never agreed to anything."

A scoff ripped from his mouth. "Oh, but you did, Milo. The day you came crawling back to me…just like I knew you would. I warned you the stakes were higher, and you said you would do whatever it took. I gave you another chance because of my love for you, and then you turned around and showed me the greatest disloyalty. Do you know how that made me feel?"

Loathing clawed through my body, every muscle bound, curled with the urge to end him where he stood.

But he had Tessa, and I couldn't be so reckless.

He smiled then, pure condescension. "And then rather than learning from your mistake, you hunted my men. You killed them. *Your brothers.* We were all supposed to be a family, and you betrayed me."

His head cocked to the side. "But I trust that won't happen again? One more chance, Milo. One more chance for you to prove your loyalty. The chance to keep the promise you made me when you were sixteen. The one where you promised you'd always be loyal to me, the same day I accepted you into my family. Don't make me regret that decision because then I'll have to make you regret it, too. First, the girl, then your children, then you. Do you understand?"

Terror curdled in my guts, my chest stretching so tight I thought it would rip apart to expose the torment gushing out from underneath.

"I do," I told him, lifting my chin.

I understood this was it.

There could be no blunders or mistakes.

I had to end it.

"Good. I'll see you in the ring."

He rapped his knuckles on the wall like he was signing a deal.

Agony ripped my throat when he disappeared out the door, and

I spun around, holding onto the edges of the sink as I bent over, trying to catch my breath.

To hold on to sanity.

Because I could feel it slipping away.

Logic.

Rationale.

The violence rising up to asphyxiate everything else.

Taking in a steeling breath, I forced myself upright and stepped out of the locker room.

Greed hummed through the desolation, and I could hear the chants of anticipation in the distance.

Bloodlust.

It rippled and roiled, a darkness that pulsed through the cavern.

Striding down the hall, I called on every ounce of strength that I possessed, knowing this was it.

My attention moved around the space to catalogue everything as I stepped out into the vapid light that cast a dingy, hazy glow through the basement.

Shadows played at the walls, darkness hovering in the corners, the pit nearly throbbing with the wickedness that toiled at the fringes.

The ring was in the middle of the immense room, exactly where it had always been. There was no elevation to it, just the bare concrete stained with blood beneath.

It was standing room only for the *patrons* who seemed to boil and froth around it, the mass of them held back by a chain-link fence about three feet tall that encircled the entire thing.

It gave about four feet of space between them and the ring.

These men who stood in expensive suits, accepting tumblers of amber liquid from the near-naked women who slithered through the crowd, amping the greed that only served to increase Stefan's profits.

My stomach twisted.

An aisle was carved down the middle by the same fencing, hugged by the same bastards who vied to get a closer look.

It could have reminded me of the crowd at Absolution except for the fact it was void of any decency. Void of any goodness.

It had been the reason I'd walked that club's floors for years. Hunting out the degenerates and protecting the innocent.

Like I could make up for what happened here, within these walls.

But I should have known there would be no escaping it. No absolution for who I was.

There was no forgiveness for men like me, and the only thing I could do now was make this one thing right.

Off to my left, near the wall, was an exposed metal stairway that led to a pathway that hung from the ceiling above. Wrapped completely in the same chain-link as the fencing below, it was a walkway where Stefan's men guarded over the mayhem.

At its end was a large cage, hanging high above the ring where Stefan sat on his throne like some kind of twisted king who watched over the perverted.

The reigning demon.

He was standing then, his hand pressed to the chain-link, his eyes glinting as he met my glare from where I stood just outside the end of the hall.

A challenge.

A warning.

One of his guards poked the barrel of his gun into my back. "It's time," he said.

Vengeance thundered in my chest, as loud as the shouts that suddenly erupted when I stepped into the tumult.

My eyes scanned, taking it in—I counted at least four guards that were stationed at each corner of the basement, and the three above who walked the elevated path.

More would be outside.

It seemed Stefan had upped his game since the last time I'd been here.

Nerves scattered when I caught sight of Logan with his chest pressed to the fence on the opposite side, standing there with an arrogant smirk on his face like he was just another of the fiends, though I felt the weight of his passing glance.

Blood thundering through my veins, I strode up the aisle, trying to ignore the shouts, the inhumanity, the greed that banged and ricocheted from their vile mouths.

Another round of roars went up when my opponent was pushed out from the hall on the far side of the basement, the man cutting a path up the opposite side where we both came to stare across at each other from our side of the ropes.

He looked to be close to seven feet tall and was pure muscle.

His eyes wild and untamed.

Bouncing on his toes and ready for the fight.

But the only thing that mattered was Tessa.

My guts fisted in rage, and I could barely keep it together when the crowd suddenly split apart, and Tessa was led by a fuckin' leash through them, her hands tied behind her back, paraded in front of these monsters like she was meat.

At the sight of her, a furor of lust ripped through the throng, her pain their pleasure, and I fought the welling of vomit that pooled in my mouth.

They had her all dressed up like she was a prize, wearing a shimmery white dress, though she was barefoot, her fiery red locks matted to her gorgeous face. There was a stream of blood running down her right cheek that had dried from a gash on her temple.

Fury flashed.

Overwhelming.

They hauled her up to the side of the ring, and I nearly buckled when she found me standing there.

The way those fathomless eyes wept.

Churned with grief and fear and a plea.

It took everything in me not to go barreling that way.

Not to say fuck the plan and get my girl in my arms and off to safety.

The guard who hauled her along forced her into the ring. Tears streamed down her face as she stumbled forward, and she turned in a traumatized circle, her eyes wide with grief and fear.

My fingers twitched.

Needing to go to her.

To stop this madness.

Take her away from the place she never should have been exposed to.

This torture that should not be her own.

Wickedness pierced me like a brand, and I looked up to find Stefan staring down at me.

He wasn't parading her for these sick fuckers.

He was parading her for me.

A warning.

A threat that I was prisoner to his twisted game.

The guard yanked at Tessa with the leash, and she jolted forward, her gaze coming to me for a beat of desperation, and I prayed she saw that I'd meant what I told her.

That I would fight for her.

Die for her.

That I hated that I'd dragged her into my mess, but I would do whatever it took to get her out of it.

She was led back down the opposite aisle, chants riding up through the darkened atmosphere as she was forced up the steps and across the walkway to the cage where Stefan waited.

The whole time, my heart hemorrhaged in my chest.

Bleeding out.

While the aggression rose to take its place.

Taking over.

Stefan pulled Tessa in front of him, his arm around her waist and his mouth at her jaw while he glared down at me.

Violence streaked across my flesh, and every muscle in my body flexed, my being rigid and rolling with aggression.

Anticipation rushed through the murky haze as I moved to the ropes and slipped into the ring.

My opponent climbed in on the opposite side.

Bets had already been cast, and there was no question left about what they were betting on.

Death.

And Stefan was sure, this time, I would see it through.

The bastard wielding Tessa like a tool, the threat of what would happen if I didn't concede inscribed in the memories of my wife.

He cracked an ominous grin as he played with a lock of Tessa's hair, baiting me, loving the way the rage burned across my flesh.

He wanted me on my knees.

My teeth ground, and I inhaled a violent breath and focused. Getting distracted wasn't going to win me any points.

The ref gestured for both of us to meet in the middle. He lifted our hands in the air, holding us by our wrists.

My opponent sneered. "I hope you're ready to die tonight."

No question, this wasn't the first time he'd stood in a ring such as this.

He took pleasure in it.

But it wasn't either of us who were dying tonight.

The ref dropped our wrists and jumped back to indicate the start of the fight.

I conjured all the focus and strength I had as the fucker came at me, setting free the rage I'd tried to tame for years, letting it boil over into the aggression.

I punched him so hard that he was out cold.

Dropped like a brick to the floor.

Because we only had one chance, and there was no messing around.

Shouts erupted, "End him! End him!"

It curled around me in a cloud of iniquity.

Only it shifted to confusion when I ran across the ring, heading in Logan's direction.

I tossed myself over the ropes, flying by Logan and snagging the knife he'd hidden at the bottom of his shoe as I went, running for the stairs.

At the same time, I could hear the shouts and screams tear through the vileness as shots began to ring out.

Without having to look, I knew it was Jud and Trent taking out the guards who stood at each corner of the basement.

I didn't slow to verify, no seconds to waste.

I started to race up the stairs, the metal clanging under my feet as I took them two at a time. Shots pinged through the air, missing me each time.

That was the thing about this set up—what I'd been counting on—the cages might have protected Stefan and his men, but it also put them at a disadvantage since they couldn't get in a good shot.

Uncertainty rocketed through the grunge, chaos erupting below.

A toil of bodies crushing into each other as more shots rang out.

I made it to the top just as a guard was reaching the end of the pathway. Before he could whip around the corner and get a shot, I reached around and took hold of the barrel of his gun, wrenching it out of his hands. I shifted around and used the butt of it to slam into his face.

He somersaulted down the stairs behind me, and I had his gun lifted, firing at the next guard who came running my way.

His body rocked back with the blow before he fell facedown, and I stepped over the top of him on the way to my girl.

I could feel the pandemonium that ensued as shots kept ringing out.

Trent and Jud and Logan in a battle below. Undoubtedly, an army of men had descended on the scene as soon as things had gone awry.

My insides ripped and screamed, praying they were good, that my seedy life wouldn't cost more than it already had.

I couldn't fathom it.

Couldn't.

But I didn't pause to give myself time to contemplate.

Because Tessa…Tessa was relying on me, and I wouldn't stop.

A shot rang out as I enclosed on the cage. A guard had edged around just enough that he could pop off a shot.

I felt the heat as it grazed my left shoulder, pain burning through, but I ignored it. I lifted the gun, steady, waiting.

The second he edged around again, I took the chance and fired.

He dropped in a pile at my feet.

Below, people raced everywhere, trampling each other, pussies who were all too keen to watch someone else get beaten to death running for the doors at the thought that they might get caught in the crosshairs.

I rounded the end of the pathway and went into the side of the cage.

Stefan had hold of Tessa, whirling her around to face me as he pulled her back to his chest. He pressed a blade to her throat.

"You've made a grave mistake," Stefan hissed.

Energy zapped from Tessa.

Tumultuous.

Terrified.

Did she see it now? Who I was?

"You're right, Stefan. I made a grave mistake falling in with you. One I rectify tonight."

Sweat gathered at the monster's temples, though he was sneering, taunting me where he stood. "One step closer, and she dies. You know I don't make idle threats."

Except he knew if he hurt her, then he was done. Literally backed into a corner.

"That wouldn't be a good idea, now, would it? So, drop the fucking knife, and you and I can deal with this ourselves," I warned instead, voice low and shuddering with hate.

That would be a fight to the death I would take.

"I saved you, Milo. Picked up a pathetic kid and made him a man. Gave you everything. And you repay me how?"

"You killed my wife." Venom poured from my mouth.

"You and I both know she was the reason you strayed. She needed to go. You were the fool who didn't understand it for what it was. The gift I was giving you. She got in our way."

Tessa whimpered, her sorrow stark, her grief gutting, while my knees weakened at his depravity.

I forced myself to keep speaking, goading him, distracting him. "You think you ever had my loyalty? Do you think you were something special to me? I used you…just like you used me. So why don't the two of us fight it out like men? Let the girl go."

Tessa's eyes were so wide. Wide and terrified.

Spite flew from his mouth. "You should know better than that, Milo."

He angled around her left side, and for a split second, his leg came into view.

Before I could doubt it, I took the shot.

Stefan cried out in rage and pain when blood began to pour from the wound in his thigh.

It was the chance Tessa needed. The chance to rip herself from his hold.

She whipped around and kicked him in the gut.

The momentum sent her falling to her butt.

A cry ripped from her throat.

Fear and terror and relief.

I dove for her, cutting the bindings from around her wrists and shouting, "Run, Little Dove. Run."

She was freed and on her feet, and I was lifting the gun again to take aim at Stefan.

"You die tonight," I seethed, years of hatred pouring out with the statement.

Only another shot rang out.

Pain splintered from my own leg. I tripped to the side, unable to stop the fall. I hit the ground hard.

Stefan was on me in a flash, a small handgun lifted and ready to fire. "I should have come sooner and ended you long ago. What I should have done was left you floating with your wife that night. I should have seen who you really were. Should never have believed in you."

And it was a blur of red and white from the right, and I was shouting, "No, Tessa!" a second before she slammed into him.

A gunshot went off.

A wail of torment lacerated through the air as she dropped to the ground.

Stefan stood and swung around with the gun aimed her direction.

His back to me.

I fired three times.

Making sure this demon would never draw air again.

He slumped to the ground, falling on top of Tessa.

I scrambled to my feet, tossing him off so I could get to her.

She was lying in a pool of blood.

Misery sheared through my spirit. Years of hate culminating to one single point.

"Little Dove. No, baby, no." It groaned from that vacant space that only this girl could fill.

Wept from my soul as I gingerly scooped her into my arms.

My arms that wouldn't stop shaking as I stared down at her where her head lolled on my arm.

"You can't leave, Tessa. You can't. You have to shine. This world needs you."

Ignoring the pain wracking through my body, I ran back with her down the elevated pathway, banging down the stairs and into the havoc that still ensued below.

The shots had ceased, and it was now a confused chaos that banged through the mass. Shouts that the cops were on their way, causing the vile fucks to scatter.

Trent, Jud, and Logan suddenly busted through the crowd. "We have to get out of here," Trent ordered.

"She's hurt." The words cracked, my chest feeling like it was going to cave, Tessa breathing but bleeding out.

"Fuck." Dread splintered through Jud's expression, and I knew it was bad, what they were seeing.

"We have to get her out of here," Logan urged.

"This way." I ran with her down the long, dank hall.

A hall where I'd made a million promises to Autumn.

Promises I didn't keep.

And I might hate myself for it forever.

But I was making one more.

"You're going to be fine. I promise, Little Dove, you're going to be fine."

Chapter Forty-Five

Milo

I PACED THE WAITING ROOM.

Paced and paced, my hands constantly roughing through my hair, the agitation rolling off me so intense I thought I might start pinging off the walls.

But I couldn't sit.

Couldn't rest.

Couldn't do anything but pray that Tessa was fine.

That she'd pull through.

There was no other option.

The world couldn't keep spinning without the sun.

Everyone else had gathered there, too.

Eden, Salem, and Aster.

Trent, Jud, and Logan.

Eden's father, Gary.

The kids were with Salem's grandmother, and the three women had burst through the door about ten minutes after Tessa had been rushed into surgery.

A black, heavy cloud covered the group.

Dread and worry.

Eden was bent over, offering up prayers, Aster rocked in a hard, plastic chair, and Salem was pacing, the same as me.

It took everything for me not to go charging through the door that read *Emergency Surgery*, but how the fuck did I even have the right?

I was the one who'd done this.

The one responsible for it.

And I knew tonight she'd finally *seen* the man I'd warned her about.

She hadn't listened, and now she was fucking here.

Eden had forced me to get my own wounds checked out. One had been sutured, the other only needed to be cleaned and bandaged, not that I cared about my condition.

I'd already given a statement that Tessa and I had been mugged. Had no fuckin' clue if it was going to fly, but at least the cops who'd been here had seemed satisfied with the story, though they would be back to get Tessa's statement once she was able.

And she had to be *able*.

I paced some more, my fingers laced together and propped on top of my head like it could keep the anxiety at bay.

Keep the torment from flooding out.

Keep myself from completely losing it in the middle of a waiting room.

"She's going to be fine." Eden's soft voice hit me from behind.

I shifted to look at her, and her face twisted up in pain when she looked at me. My hands dropped to my sides. "She has to be."

She touched my forearm, then we all froze when a doctor finally came out the door.

"Tessa McDaniels' family?"

Everyone in that room stood up.

"The surgery went well. She's stable and in recovery."

That was all it took for me to bow in half, slammed by relief. If there was only one promise I could keep, it had to be this one. Because Tessa deserved to live a beautiful life. Deserved love and joy and the freedom from this mess. She deserved everything.

∞

Machines quietly beeped in her room, monitoring her heart rate, her breaths slowed and measured while I sat in the chair next to her.

Just watching her sleep.

Just looking at her.

Basking in her warmth.

Memorizing every inch of her gorgeous face.

Red hair spread out on her pillow, freckles kissing her cheeks and those rosebud lips soft in her sleep.

Not like her picture wasn't going to be emblazoned on my brain for all of eternity.

This gorgeous girl who'd changed everything.

But she was battered, too, the bash on her temple now a scab, scratches all over her pale skin, the wound on her side hidden, though I would never forget it was there.

What I'd caused.

I'd warned her I'd ruin her, and I fucking hated that I was right.

Guilt constricted, then my heart rate spiked when she began to stir.

On impulse, I reached out and took her hand, needing the connection, when those ocean eyes blinked open to me.

Confused for a minute before they squeezed in a shock of painful memories. Thought I could see each of them play out through her expression, like she was coming to the acceptance of the horrors that had come to pass.

"Milo." My name was thick on her dried tongue, and I rushed to grab the cup of water that sat on the table and brought the straw to her lips.

"There you go," I murmured as she sucked, probably a little too fast because she began to cough. "Careful. Slow," I encouraged, taking it away for a beat before I returned it to her mouth, every part of me wanting to take care of her but knowing I didn't have the right.

When she stopped drinking, I set it aside, staring at the spot where I'd placed it for too long. A bluster of discomfort dampening the air.

All this shit that had come between us that I wanted to erase.

But I didn't know how.

Didn't know how when it went so deep.

Finally, I forced myself to look back at her. "How are you feeling?"

Her mouth tweaked at the side, and she lifted her hand with the IV in her wrist. "I'm guessing a little too good for what happened. I'm thinking they're giving me the good stuff."

A rough scrape of a sound left my mouth. "I think they probably are."

Her expression dimmed. "Was it bad?"

"You were lucky." It ground from between my teeth. How close it'd been.

Warily, she glanced around like she was terrified of the answer. "Is he…"

"Gone."

She nodded, both in relief and fear.

The rage I'd been holding on to pulsed in my veins, and I leaned forward, gripping her hand in both of mine. "Did he…did he hurt you while he had you?"

Her throat bobbed when she swallowed. "No. I mean, I tried to fight them when they took me, and someone bashed me on the head to shut me up. Other than that, no."

At least that was a consolation. Had been terrified of what I hadn't known. Of what she'd gone through during that day he'd held her prisoner.

"I'm so sorry," I forced out, barely managing the words.

Distrust and confusion and something that looked like a plea flashed through her gaze, and she withdrew her hand from mine.

My heart crashed against my ribs.

Because she was looking at me the way I'd known she always would when she finally saw who I was.

With fear.

Like the monster I'd warned her I was.

She looked away for a beat before she returned her fierce gaze to me, those blue eyes flashing with intensity. "Was it you who hurt Bobby? Was it you, Milo? Tell me it wasn't you," she begged.

Grief cut through the atmosphere.

It hadn't been confirmed yet, but I knew, and I was sure Tessa knew, too, that Stefan had gotten to him.

It was clear that my involvement with Tessa had led him back to her brother.

"There are some things you need to know, Tessa."

She blinked at me when I sat there, not sure how to confess it.

"Just tell me, Milo, tell me what happened to Bobby. I need to know."

I gathered her hand again, that nasty habit that I couldn't shake, and I forced myself to begin.

Chapter Forty-Six

Milo

Five Years Ago

MILO STARED AT THE MAN WHO LAY FACEDOWN AS THE shouts of the corrupt reverberated against the block walls. "End him. End him!"

That voice echoed in his ear. *Because this time? It's him or it's you.* Everything spun.

The room. His mind. The hatred that burned through his veins.

But this hatred was no longer for himself. And he would no longer give voice to the violence that he thought never could be sated.

It was for a man who'd preyed on his pain, one who'd twisted it into something disgusting, one who'd made him betray his wife.

The one who'd crawled down from his wicked throne to witness the brutality firsthand.

One who was asking him to do the unthinkable.

Fine, then the unthinkable, it was.

Before anyone could prepare themselves, Milo spun and flung himself over the ropes. He rushed for the two assholes standing guard at Stefan's side.

He was behind the first before the man could even shout, his neck snapped, flat on the ground.

The second came at him with a knife.

He threw a kick to his wrist, and the knife clattered to the floor. The guard dove for it, but Milo got to it first, grabbing it and spinning around and slashing it across his throat.

Blood gushed.

Gore.

He turned to look for Stefan, who'd disappeared in the moments it'd taken Milo to end his guards.

Deviants scattered through the basement, roaches that fled while Milo stalked back through the mass of them, striking down any bastard who came his way.

He wanted only one.

Only Stefan was gone, running like the pussy Milo had always known he was. His power was born of manipulation and money and the twisted fucks who knelt at his feet.

Except all those men were now dead.

Milo swiped the blood splattered on his face with the back of his hand, and he moved back to the ring.

He hoisted up the man who was still out, tossed him over his shoulder, and jogged with him down the hall. He only diverted long enough to grab his bag that held his keys, then he hurried up the stairs.

Adrenaline pumped through his veins, a thrashing, driving force. It was the only thing that gave him the strength to carry him out.

At the top, Milo busted out the door. Darkness was thick, shadows rushing on all sides, and Milo jogged into the cover of the trees where he laid the man on the ground.

The man they called Immortal stirred and moaned.

He cracked open an eye, fear rustling through him before he slumped back when he found Milo looking at him.

"You didn't need to save me… I'm already a dead man."

Milo blew out a ragged sigh. "Yeah, well, not on my watch. Why'd he set you up?"

Immortal stared at the underside of the trees. "Because this shit

392 | A.L. JACKSON

isn't right, and someone needs to stop him. Clearly, he found out that's
what I was trying to do."

Milo glanced down at him, his heart still jackhammering in his
chest, trying to gather his thoughts, to process what he'd done and
where it was going to lead.

Immortal sat up. "I need to go...have a contact who was recording.
I need to get this evidence to a safe place before it's too late."

Fear curled through the adrenaline, Milo coming to the full realization of what his snap decision meant. The *choice* he'd made.

"Go. I need to get to my family."

The man looked at Milo, something passing through his eyes.
"Thank you."

Milo shook his head as a thousand regrets flooded his spirit. "I
shouldn't have been in that ring to begin with."

"Yeah, neither should have I. But maybe it's the way we walk away
from it that counts."

Milo gave a tight nod before he pushed to standing, and he helped
the man to his feet. They parted in opposite directions, and Milo began
to run, fumbling through the trees to where he'd left his truck parked
in a backlot on the next street.

Barefoot.

No shirt.

Body covered in blood and sweat.

He rushed for his truck where it sat on the far side of the lot. He
clicked the locks as he ran, and he rushed around the front to the driver's side. He whipped open the door only to freeze when a knife was
suddenly at his throat.

A dark vapor hovering over him from behind.

"You failed. Your betrayal won't go unnoticed."

Pain sheared through his body when the blade was impaled at
his side.

He dropped to his knees, hand pressing at the wound that poured
with blood.

But it wasn't deep.

It was a warning.

Stefan's voice was at his ear. "Now, you must be punished, but only because I love you. I hope it will at least bring you to your senses."

Then Milo was clocked on the temple, sending him into darkness.

Rocks flew up from his back tires as he barreled down the dirt road. Sweat streamed from his temple and pooled on his shirt. His clothes covered in the gore from hours before.

His side was still gaping, oozing, but not deep enough to keep him down.

His hands gripped the steering wheel like it might keep him chained to sanity as he struggled to see through the blur of fear.

Rushing ahead to meet it.

To cut it off.

To stop it.

He shoved the gas pedal to the floorboards, the tail of his truck fishtailing as he whipped around the curves.

It was little relief when the building finally came into sight, his headlights illuminating the trailer. The tires skidded as he rammed on the brakes and threw the truck into park.

He didn't shut it off.

He jumped out and busted through the front door.

"Autumn! Autumn!"

Only the vacancy echoed back.

A sickly awareness that sank into his flesh.

Dread.

Desperation.

He flew into Remy's room, terror ripping through him. His daughter was on the ground in the corner, rocking with her hands over her ears, her brother asleep in the playpen beside her.

Relief slammed him so hard he nearly bowed. He raced for her, knelt in front of her, clutched her to his chest. "Do not move from this spot."

He ran back out, and he burst through the back door and into the night.

His footsteps pounded.

The water glittered like black ice.

She was there, floating facedown, twenty feet off the bank.

"No, Autumn, no!"

Milo plunged into the freezing cold.

It swallowed him whole.

An abyss.

A chasm.

Darkness. Darkness.

He pulled her out on the shore, breathed into her mouth, pumped at her chest.

He dialed 911, begged for someone to come.

It took forever for the sirens to come wailing through the night.

But it was too late.

Too late.

She was gone.

Gone.

And that was the moment his life went dim.

Chapter Forty-Seven

Tessa

SORROW WRENCHED THROUGH MY SOUL AS I SAT AND LISTENED to Milo confess what happened that day.

Because I could see that to him, that's what it was—a confession.

Confession for his sins.

For his guilt.

For the shame he carried like tumbled stones.

Stones he was pinned beneath.

Rubble he couldn't free himself from.

All while I struggled to catch up to who Bobby had been. Tried to reorganize everything I'd known and believed of my brother.

Fuzziness blurred my mind, the disorder amplified by the cocktail of painkillers I could feel slithering through my veins.

But it didn't distort this.

The pain that radiated through our connection.

His hands clinging to mine like he would never have to let go, all while I saw the grief that saturated every inch of him.

"Do you know what happened to him afterward?"

Remorse shook his head. "The cops took me in that night. Questioned me. The second they released me once they realized I wasn't there, I started to hunt. Hunted his men. Took them out, one by one. One of them was spitting that he'd taken care of Immortal just like he was going to take care of me. I thought he was dead."

Air huffed from my nose. "Immortal. I can't believe that was my brother. But he wasn't, was he?"

Milo's head shook. "None of us are."

"But you gave him the chance to walk out of that basement. Gave him extra time. Time to leave the message so someone would know."

Although I was sure his time had been cut off too soon, that he'd fully intended to get that charm into someone else's hands.

Maybe into mine.

I just hadn't seen it for what it was.

"You tried to save him, Milo. You stood up for what was right. That's what matters."

Milo's throat bobbed beneath his beard, a breath of refusal leaving his mouth. "I fucked it up from the beginning. Made mistake after mistake."

"My brother made his own."

Milo's nod was clipped. "And it cost him everything. Just like mine did me. My wife died because of me, Tessa. Don't you understand? I did it. I was the one who was responsible. I was the one who made the choice that cost everything."

I couldn't bring myself to point out that he'd spared my brother while doing it, or at least had given him more time. Not when Autumn's life had been the cost. I wouldn't be so selfish to tell him I was grateful when it'd been the greatest sacrifice, nor would I ask him not to regret it.

But I could ask him to see what still remained on the other side of it.

"But you haven't lost everything, Milo. Look at what you have. What remains. You saved me." I squeezed his hand as tightly as I could.

"I almost got you killed, Tessa." The words were coarse. Riddled with self-hate.

"No."

"You know that I did. I warned that I would ruin you, just like I did Autumn. I knew I would, and I was the selfish bastard who wanted to keep you, anyway."

"Because I'm yours."

His head shook. "No."

"Yes."

Slowly, he pushed to his feet.

Tall and towering.

Fierce and soft.

Rough and gentle.

Everything.

But I'd never seen his broken halo as clearly as right then.

What he'd been through.

The reason he'd held himself back. The reason he thought he couldn't love.

The reason fear clouded his aura in a dark, dingy black.

Dread clamored through my senses. A cold, icy slick of foreboding.

He leaned over and pressed his lips to my forehead. "You are a treasure, Little Dove. You are the light. And I won't dim that…not any longer."

He started to straighten, and I grappled for his shirt, curling my fingers in the fabric, pleading, "Please, don't do this. Don't walk away from me."

"I'm doing you a favor."

"You're wrong."

And if it was a favor, I didn't want it.

He uncurled my fingers from his shirt, and he squeezed them once, heartbreak written all over his face as he carefully set them back on my chest, holding them tight there for an elongated beat. "Shine bright, Little Dove."

Then he turned on his heel and strode for the door, so big and massive and everything that my soul ached for.

Craved.

My match.

My Beautiful Beast.

"Don't you dare leave me, Milo. You promised. You promised!"

I shouted it at his retreating form, panic tremoring through my voice.

He stopped at the door with his hand on the latch, his head bowed between his shoulders.

"We're a team," I whispered when he finally shifted to look at me from over his shoulder.

Amber eyes bled with remorse. "Not anymore."

I stared at the laptop screen, watching the clips again and again.

Maybe I was torturing myself, but somehow, it was cathartic.

Knowing Bobby this way. The side of him that I'd never met. The one he'd kept hidden.

No wonder, because I would have kicked his ass myself.

God, what had he been thinking?

It made it more painful to know he'd done it for me.

Gotten involved in these underground fights because it was easy money.

He'd used it to support me.

As a way to pay for my college and my dorm and to ensure that I didn't start off life with a huge debt.

I'd gladly welcome that debt because the alternative was too steep a price to pay.

I should have known there was no way he could have afforded everything he was paying for.

Working *two jobs*.

I'd been young and naïve and blind to what was going on.

It wasn't like it even occurred to me to be suspicious. Bobby had been my hero, and I never could have imagined he'd get involved in something that slanted sinister.

But I imagined, through everything I'd learned, that Stefan had gotten his hooks into Bobby the same way as he'd done Milo.

Twisted the reality.

Manipulated the intentions.

Laid out a plan that had seemed like a no-brainer but had only been a trap.

It turned out the flash drive held my big brother's secrets. We still didn't know who'd helped him record the fights, but Bobby had been compiling video after video of the illegal fights, plus documenting a ton of different illegal activities that were also taking place.

I wasn't sure if he planned to use it as blackmail or if he was taking it to the authorities.

Either way, it had ultimately cost him his life.

Anger pulsed through me at the memory. At everything that had been lost and stolen.

At the wounds that were now permanently embedded in me.

I wouldn't lie and say I'd come out of that day and night unscathed.

It had truly been horrifying.

Terrifying.

But Milo had come.

Well, Trent, Jud, and Logan had come, too, the idiots.

But I guessed I should have known this family didn't turn their backs on those they loved, and maybe it'd taken until then for me to realize I was a part of it.

A true part of them.

That I wasn't an outsider. The crazy friend who showed for drinks and a good time but was forgotten in the day to day.

Grief had a way of skewing it, didn't it? Of making you believe you were unworthy.

Less.

Lost and without a home when it was sitting right in front of you, waiting for you to claim it.

I just wished Milo had figured that out for himself.

Could see he was worthy to be loved, no matter what he'd done.

I'd believed in him. Believed him when he'd promised forever.

Believed he'd fight for me, which he had, and the sad part was he would have gladly died that night to set me free, but he didn't have the courage to stand for me in the light.

His shame too profound. Those demons catching up to him and bending his mind to their will.

The subdued tapping at the door jolted me out of my thoughts, and I pressed pause on the screen.

From where I was sitting propped against the headboard in the guest bedroom, I shifted around to find Eden leaning against the doorjamb.

"How are you feeling?" she asked.

"Like I got shot…oh, and like someone ripped my heart out, too," I tried my best to tease. It only caused a fresh pang of pain.

Sympathy coasted through her soft smile. "I'm sure that's exactly what it feels like."

My nod was erratic, emotion rising up quickly to erase any lightness.

"It feels like it's missing, Eden." I whispered the admission.

It'd been two weeks since Milo had walked out of my hospital room, and each day had compounded the vacancy that throbbed inside.

I fiddled with the locket I now wore around my neck.

Bobby had made it out alive that night all those years ago, only because Milo had chosen my brother, his *humanity*, over the depravity of the call.

Over his own well-being.

It cost him so much.

His wife.

His children for all those years.

Bobby had been wearing the locket on a large chain the day he'd been found, and I could only assume he'd stashed the flash drive and then had written the code on the pictures.

He'd likely been beaten and tossed over the ravine, making it look like an accident.

Left to die.

Except he hadn't.

Grief clamped down on my chest, so heavy and intense I didn't know how to see through it.

It was funny how I'd tried so hard to interact with Bobby, tried so hard to reach him in the recesses of his mind, praying so hard that he could hear and feel me and know I was there. So, I'd pressed the locket to his hand and asked him if he could remember the memories imprinted on those pictures, whispered a story about how he'd been wearing it that day.

He'd curled his hand around it, and I'd thought…thought he was giving me a message.

It was weird to find out he had been trying to give me a message, but an entirely different one.

I'd had no idea.

None until he was gone.

I sucked in a shattered breath, still unable to fully grasp it.

His funeral had been four days ago—three days after I'd been released from the hospital.

I'd been surrounded by my friends.

Wrapped in their support.

And I had to remind myself again and again that I wasn't *alone*.

That I wasn't abandoned.

That they loved me and would support me through anything.

They were my family.

Karl'd had the nerve to show there, giving me feigned sympathies, like he'd ever actually cared about Bobby. It was strange that I didn't even really notice or acknowledge him when he'd once felt like such an obstacle.

He'd become no more than a blip. I hadn't even given him a response, just turned my back on that part of my life.

But it'd been Milo who'd lurked in the distance, a giant silhouette on the boundary of my pain, cut off and alone and bleeding his.

His apology.

His remorse.

But he'd turned and left me there as I'd been swamped in my sorrow, and I thought that had probably wounded me more than anything.

Him turning his back.

On me.

On us.

A tear slipped free, and I swatted at it, whispering, "It all hurts so bad, Eden."

Climbing onto the bed, she laid down beside me and threaded our fingers together. "Love is the most painful of all emotions. The most beautiful and most wonderful and the most painful."

Through the blur of moisture clouding my eyes, I nodded. "Which was why Milo didn't want to fall for me. He thought he would hurt me, but the only thing that hurts is that he turned his back on me. We were supposed to be a team."

The last of the words came out ragged.

All the hopes and the dreams.

His children.

Our love.

I stared at the stupid ring I still couldn't bring myself to remove from my finger.

It glittered and danced in the spray of sunlight.

"I miss him so much."

Eden ran her thumb over the back of my hand. "Because you're missing the piece of yourself you gave to him."

Tears kept streaming. "I don't even want it back, Eden. I'm glad I got to experience it. What it felt like to find my Ace."

"He was worth it. The risk."

"Yeah, and well, the sex was pretty great, too." I sent her a soggy grin.

Soft laughter rolled from Eden. "At least you know what it's like now."

Yeah, I knew what it was like.

I knew what it was like to be cherished.

Adored.

Worshipped.

"He loves me, you know," I murmured. "He just doesn't know how to separate that feeling from his fear."

Eden hummed. "Fear is powerful, but love is stronger. Don't forget that."

Both our phones pinged at the same time, and I picked mine up to find a new message in the Fantastic Foursome thread.

Salem had sent a link with the caption: **Just so everyone can keep up with the local news.**

She capped it with a winky face.

I clicked on it and scanned through the news article that detailed the violent demise of one of the most wanted crime figures in California. Authorities had been searching for him for years.

Apparently, that man had been killed in an internal gunfight that had broken out between him and his men, leaving seven dead.

I'd honestly been terrified when the police officer had come in to question me about the *mugging*. Praying everyone's involvement in this fiasco wouldn't be discovered. Thank God they seemed to have bought it.

"This is all so crazy. I still can't believe it happened. That I was involved in it," I muttered. I glanced over at Eden. "I'm really thankful for everything. That Trent and the guys stepped up for us. I don't know what would have happened if they hadn't been there."

"Trent and his brothers do what needs to be done to take care of their family. And you and Milo are a part of that."

My chest squeezed, both in thankfulness and misery. "I hope you know what that means to me."

"Of course, I do. You're my soul sister, remember?" Her smile was only half a tease, riddled with the true affection she had for me.

"My ride or die," I muttered with the slightest grin.

She gathered up my hand as she turned to face me. "I know you're in pain right now, but you were right to take the chance. Even if he can't feel it or accept it, you know it was real, and I hope you treasure that forever."

My nod was shaky.

"Promise me you'll never, ever stop fighting for that," she continued. "For what you need and what you want, and promise me, you won't be scared of taking the chance again when it comes to you. Because I know it will, and you deserve every ounce of joy in this world, Tessa McDaniels."

I sniffled through a laugh. "I am pretty great, aren't I?"

Eden smiled. "Yeah, you're pretty great."

Chapter Forty-Eight

Milo

I STILLED WHEN THERE WAS A LIGHT TAPPING AT THE DOOR, right before it creaked open and my mother called, "Knock, knock."

From where I was loading the dishwasher, I glanced back to find her peeking inside.

Morning light flooded in around her, and she sent me a tender, wary smile.

Affection throbbed within the void.

"Hey, Mom," I told her, turning back to place the last cup inside.

Quirking a brow, she stepped in and shut the door behind her. "Dishes again, I see."

"Don't you know they're never done?" I made a vain attempt at keeping it light, to keep the misery out of my voice, but I was pretty sure I failed with the way her face pinched in worry.

She slowly approached, her black hair swishing around her shoulders as she angled her head to study me from across the room. "How are you doing?"

A grunt got free. "Same as yesterday."

There hadn't been a day that'd passed since everything went down that she hadn't come to check on me.

I appreciated it, but I wasn't sure what she thought was going to change.

I couldn't stop myself from cringing when she took a seat at the spot I'd come to think of as Tessa's. Couldn't erase that girl from my mind. Couldn't stop wondering how she was. If she was okay.

Knowing full well I was the one who was responsible if she wasn't.

"Coffee?" I pulled the carafe from the stand and waved it at my mom.

"Sure."

I made her a cup, set it in front of her, and tried to ignore the way everything ached.

She took a sip, then set the cup on the counter and exhaled heavily as she sat back in the stool, her expression tightening in emphasis. "It's been two weeks, Milo."

An incredulous huff left me.

Did she think I wasn't counting?

That every fucking day didn't drag by like razors sliding slow across my skin?

Facing away from her, I pressed my hands to the counter, breathing around the pain. "Time doesn't change anything, Mom."

"Well, I was hoping in that amount of time, my stubborn son might come to his senses and go after the person he's supposed to spend his life with."

Guilt constricted because that person should have been Autumn.

She should have been the one I was grieving.

Missing.

How the fuck could I even look in the mirror when that person had become Tessa?

"It wasn't even real, Mom." I let it drop like a bomb because I couldn't take this anymore. Her pushing me in a direction I never should have gone in the first place.

Confusion pulsed through the thickened air, and I could physically feel the weight of my mother's frown from behind me. "What wasn't real?"

I forced myself to look at her. "Me and Tessa. The whole thing was a sham. Faked."

Disbelief streaked through her expression. "What in the world are you talking about?"

I swallowed around the shards that raked my throat, and I confessed the bullshit that Tessa got sucked into. What had dragged her into the depravity that was my life.

"She offered to pretend to be my fiancée to help me get the kids back. It was all a show for the judge."

Horror smacked through Mom's features, her eyes, the same color as mine, desperate to see inside of me. "What? What are you saying?"

My nod was tight, the words thicker because the second I tossed them out I knew it was a bald-faced lie. "We were just two friends trying to help each other out. We were never real, so you can drop it."

It was the way we should have kept it.

But I was the fool who'd gone after something I knew full well I couldn't have.

Knew I didn't deserve.

"You lied to me about the whole thing?" The question trembled from my mother in a bough of disbelief. Aghast and pained. "The engagement? The party I threw for you? Your friends and family?"

Shame blew out on a heavy sigh. "We thought it was best to keep as few people in the know as possible."

"I don't believe you." Her head shook, and I forced myself to keep going, driving the nail as deep as it would go because I couldn't stand for my mother to keep watching me with the hope she kept subdued at the back of her gaze.

"And you know what that agreement did? It almost cost Tessa her life. I got her involved in my mess, and she almost paid the greatest price for it."

Disgust lined my words.

"She got hurt because of me. Her brother is now dead because of me. Because she was exposed to who I am. Because I brought that trouble to her door. Had she never come here, she would have been just fine. So, I think it's best if I let her live out her life, don't you?" My tone went haggard and harsh, barely able to get my lungs to cooperate.

I felt like I was suffocating.

Drowning.

Lost in this darkness I would never find my way out of.

I was clinging to the edge of the counter and trying to remain standing when I felt my mom slip from the stool and onto her feet.

Slowly, she approached me, her energy warm and fierce.

She angled around, getting in my face, forcing me to meet her gaze. "Do I think it's best for you to let her go? No, Milo, I don't. Because maybe you two started out under some guise of a fake relationship, which I'm really disappointed in, but I know here…" She tapped her chest. "I know in here that it was real. There is no faking what you two shared."

She inhaled a rattled breath. "The love you shared? The way she looked at you and you looked at her? It was real, Milo. I know it."

She reached out and brushed her fingertips to the frantic pounding of my heart. "Just like you know it here."

I choked over the implication.

The howl of the demons in my ear refuting everything my mother had said.

Because men like me didn't deserve love. I was selfish for ever going after it.

I shifted so I could fully meet my mother's eye.

"I failed Autumn, Mom. I failed her in the absolute worst way, and I almost did the same to Tessa. I knew this whole thing was doomed from the beginning, and I should never have hoped that it could become something more."

Mom's brow pinched. "But did it? Did it become something more?"

"It became everything." The truth wheezed out of me.

Unstoppable.

She nodded slowly and shifted so she was leaned back against the counter facing me. "Then, what's your plan?"

I returned my attention to the countertop, my head slowly shaking. "I start my business and prove I can be worthy of raising my kids. I fight for them with all I have, then I live for what I've been given."

Contemplation had her biting her bottom lip before her gaze

narrowed as she started to speak, her voice drawn low. "Do you think it doesn't haunt me, Milo? What you went through as a child?"

"Mom—" Didn't think I could handle the direction she was going. She put out a hand to stop me.

"Do you think I didn't blame myself?" Pain quivered at the edge of her mouth. "Yes, it was your father who was ultimately to blame. The one who was a monster. The one who inflicted the pain. But I also made a ton of horrible choices along the way. *Choices* I wish I could go back and change. *Choices* I will regret for the rest of my life."

Agony skewered through the air.

"Mom…it wasn't your fault."

"Please let me finish because you need to hear this, Milo, and you need to *listen*."

Throat closing off, I gave her a tight nod.

"Could you imagine, Milo, if I would have turned my back on you when you were a teenager? If I would have decided for you that I had made choices that had hurt you and you were better off without me?"

"No." The word scored through the air.

My hands curled into fists.

No.

Her voice dimmed in sadness, with prudence, with care. "Or maybe I could let those choices ruin my life now. Maybe I could run away and hide and think you're better off without me because you have to know the shame that I feel for the mistakes I have made will always be there. Or I can *choose* to live. Choose to move forward and learn from my mistakes. Choose to cherish *all* that I've been given."

"Tessa was never really one of those things."

"Wasn't she?" She angled closer in my direction. "And you can either let your mistakes dictate your life now and continue to make them, Milo, live in regret and shame, or you can let what you've learned lead you to where you're supposed to be."

She pushed from the counter, though she paused and touched my arm, her words issued into the room. "It's your choice, and I pray that you make the right one."

Chapter Forty-Nine

Tessa

"A untie Tessa, are you even a teacher?" Juni Bee scrunched her nose up at me from where she was on her knees, eating a bagel at Eden's round table in the kitchen. She'd come running through the gate and up to the back door first thing this morning, asking her Aunt Eden what was for breakfast.

"You gotta know that a Mantis shrimp has the fastest punch of any animal. It's faster than a bullet." Her dark eyes widened at that.

"Are you kidding me?" I feigned disbelief. Well, okay, it was disbelief. I'd never even heard of it.

"She's not even kidding a little, Auntie. It's just knowledge," Gage supplied around a mouthful of fresh strawberries. "They're fast fighters. They get a one, two, three, kapow on their prey." He tossed a fist through the air. "They're done for. That's how they hunt, you know. I read in a book about the best predators and then I told Juni because I tell her everything."

He shrugged, and my heart squeezed.

So freaking cute.

All giggles and adorableness where they shared their breakfast.

Attached at the hip.

410 | A.L. JACKSON

I pushed to standing, moved around the table, and pressed a kiss to Gage's head as I rambled, "I totally didn't know. It seems my niece and nephew sure have the smarts, don't they?"

I moved on to do the same to Juni.

I ignored the pang I felt when Scout's face flashed through my mind. My little Rocketman who was going to study all the things so he could go to Mars. My smile was soft as I imagined him here, how he'd fit right in with Juni and Gage.

A piece of this beautiful family.

But there were times in your life when you had to accept that things didn't always work out the way they should have.

That sometimes we were robbed of the joy and love we deserved.

Whether we kept it from ourselves out of fear or we lost it out of no fault of our own.

Eden hummed from where she pulled Baby Kate from her high-chair to wash her face that was smeared with baby food. She walked with her over to the kitchen sink. "I'm going to have to be careful what books I buy for Gage. Before we know it, he's going to know more than the rest of us."

"You know I gotta get all the A's, Mommy." Eden started to say something, but he held up a hand. "I know, I know, even if I don't get an A, it's okay as long as I do my best. I got it. I even told Juni so she knows."

"We gotta have the grace," Juni piped in. "My Motorcycle Dad said he sure is happy for it, too, because he's not even close to perfect, not one little bit. You can ask my mom."

A giggle ripped from me as emotion crested from Eden, and we shared a look, her smile so soft as she looked at the sight of the kids in her kitchen.

At this incredible family.

I'd made the decision not to let my own grief stand in my way any longer.

It was there.

Of course, it was.

It would always be.

I would forever miss my parents. My Bobby.

The man who was supposed to be my everything.

But I guessed I finally, truly felt a part of this close-knit group.

Saw their love for what it was.

Auntie Tessa wasn't just a flippant nickname.

It was who I was to them.

Baby Kate screeched while Eden ran a washcloth over her face. "That's right, we work hard, we have grace, and we show love the best that we can."

"Ah, I see someone else who is smart." I winked at her, and she laughed a little just as the doorbell rang.

"Here, can you take her a second so I can get that?" She passed Baby Kate off to me without waiting for a response.

"Always, and of course. I love my Baby Kate, don't I, sweet girl?" I lifted her high, and she curled into this adorable baby ball, giggling and throwing her little arms as I brought her down and blew a raspberry on her cheek.

She squealed then got a fistful of my hair.

"You better watch it, Auntie, she's dangerous. I got a bald spot. Dad said I'm gonna be lucky if it even grows back."

I chuckled. "I don't think you have to worry too much, buddy."

"Oh, I'm worried, all right."

Affection wound me tight as I brought Kate to my chest, bouncing her around, grinning when Eden came back around the corner, carrying a box wrapped in thick, brown paper and twined with matching ribbon.

A card was tucked under it.

"Oh, a prezzie," I sang, drawing it out, wondering what Trent had gotten her this time.

The man was kinda obsessed, but I wasn't about to complain that he was spoiling my bestie. She *deserved* it.

Her expression was somber. "Not for me."

A frown curled my brow when she held it out for me to take, and we awkwardly traded, Eden taking Baby Kate while she passed me the box.

I didn't know if it was anxiety or hope or anger that lit inside me.

But it was bright and kinda blinding, and I was having a really hard time keeping from hyperventilating.

Because I saw the handwriting on the card that simply read *Tessa.*

Handwriting I now knew as well as my own.

Milo's.

I just stood there, staring at it.

"Well, are you gonna open it, or what?" Juniper asked, pulling me out of my stupor.

Was I?

Did I even want to know what was inside?

I glanced at Eden.

She angled her head. "Open it."

I sank down onto a chair, and with shaky hands, I pulled the envelope from under the ribbon, close to frantic as I freed the flap.

I pulled out a flat card plus a folded piece of paper that fell onto my lap.

My heart was in my throat as I stared at the hand-painted image.

As I stared at a lake that was so familiar, the same as was painted on Remy and Scout's walls.

Though in this one, the sun stood prominent, front and center.

I tried to gulp around the emotion as I set it aside and picked up the letter, carefully unfolding it, both terrified and desperate to see what he'd said.

My eyes traced that same bold handwriting that had been on the envelope.

Tessa,

I've been a man who's hid behind my mistakes for a long, long time, and it's time that ended. Maybe I'm a coward for trying to reach you this way, but what I've got to say is really important, and I find myself at a loss for words when I'm looking at you. Unable to form a full, rational thought because you steal my breath and every thought in my mind, so I thought it would be best to get it out this way.

See, you stole my heart, too.

You stole it when I thought I didn't have it to give. When it wasn't whole. When it was in pieces.

You stole it anyway, because I think from the moment I saw you, it belonged to you.

And when you loved me back? I thought maybe I could get a second chance. That there might be redemption for a man like me, even though that dark spot inside me warned that I was being a fool. That I had no right. That my heart wasn't mine to give, and I'd committed too many crimes to deserve all that you are.

I thought I saw the culmination of it that night when I stepped into that basement to the horrible reality that you had gotten caught up in my past.

In my mistakes.

In my sins.

In my tragedy.

This world nearly lost you that night, and that wasn't a fate I could tolerate.

The demons warned that loving you was a heresy. That I needed to walk before I ruined you more.

*The thing was, there was no **not** loving you, Little Dove.*

No possible way to stop what I feel for you.

Something bigger than I'd ever felt. More beautiful than I'd been given.

And I could hide from it forever, but it wouldn't change the fact, and someone really important to me told me this one singular truth.

"You've got love, Dad."

Remy kept reminding me of it, and it's finally time I accepted what it means.

And I can either give it, share it and cultivate it, or let it die.

Dying for someone I love has always felt easy to me. Something I could give to show my devotion.

But it's the living for it that I've always had the problem with.

But I have the choice to live chained to my past, or to learn from it and move on.

And I'd like to move on from it with you, if you'll give me that chance.

I know I made a lot of promises to you. Promises I didn't keep.

But that ends today.

Now and forever.

Because you are my always. I promise you.

I'm ready to stand in the light. To hold it in the darkness. To love you through thick and thin. Through this fight for my children. Through each day's end.

I told you they are the meaning of this life.

And that's what you came to be, too.

My meaning.

My hope.

The joy I never thought I'd experience again.

You are the sun in my sky, Tessa McDaniels.

I love you.

Hopelessly.

Endlessly.

Always.

Milo

Tears blurred my sight, and I choked over a sob when I got to the end. "Oh God."

Eden touched my shoulder. "What did he say?"

"That he wants me to give him another chance."

"And what do you think?"

What did I think?

I thought I was terrified.

Angry.

Hurt.

And that I would love him to my dying day.

I swiped at the tears. "I don't know. He hurt me so bad."

Eden urged me to look at her. "I know it's hard to give a second chance. But I also know it's really difficult to *ask* for a second chance, too. To step out on a limb and ask for forgiveness. You have to decide if it's worth it. If *he's* worth it. If what you feel is worth it. You told me that you won't settle for second best…so don't. But if he's it? Your Ace?"

"Would you open the present already? I gotta know what's in it," Juni demanded.

Right.

The present.

I swiped at the tears on my face, setting the letter aside as I tore into the paper.

Inside was a lidded box.

I opened it.

Then I gasped, my eyes wild as I looked between Eden and Juniper. "He got me the Manolos. He got me the Manolos."

Realization stormed through me.

He remembered me.

He knew me.

He loved me.

Eden giggled. "Shoes?"

I reached out and squeezed her hand, nodding frantically before I rushed to wipe the tears from my eyes. "I'll tell you later, but I think I need to go over there and at least talk to him."

I sniffled and stuffed my feet into my wedges, holding the box that he'd sent against my chest. I grabbed my purse that had my keys from the island. "I'll be back."

"Give him grace, Auntie!" Juni shouted.

I choked out a laugh. "I'll try, Juni Bee."

Eden smiled. "Good luck."

Rushing to the front door, I whipped it open, then I froze when I saw the man leaning against the side of his old truck.

So big and burly and right.

Fierce and soft and intimidating.

My heart raced.

My Beautiful Beast.

I choked over another cry as I stumbled across their porch and to the steps, though I was laughing through the middle of it, then I was running down the walkway and straight into his arms.

I knew we had more to talk about, but it could wait.

Getting to him couldn't.

He picked me up and spun me around, holding me so tight, the box smashed between us. He pressed his face into my neck, his voice doing that rumbly thing I loved when he murmured, "I missed you."

It was so simple.

So true.

Our connection hummed.

Then he started to ramble, "I'm so sorry. I'm so fuckin' sorry."

"There's plenty of time for apologizing later. Just love me and do it right and do it forever."

He eased back a fraction. Those honey-dipped eyes swam with affection.

Devotion and love.

Different from before.

"Okay," he whispered.

Okay.

Then he kissed me. Kissed me tenderly for the barest second before his mouth devoured mine with possession.

Heat burned and joy blazed. "Hurry up and take me home."

"Eager," he mumbled at my mouth, never setting me down or breaking the kiss while he opened the passenger door then plopped me onto the seat.

He eased back, his sexy mouth twitching all over the place.

"Just for you. And it's been two weeks and two days. You owe me like…" I started to tick off my fingers before I wiggled all the fingers on my hands in his face. "Fifty orgasms."

His brow quirked. "Fifty?"

"At least."

"Eager *and* greedy," Milo said. He pecked a kiss to my lips before he stepped away and shut the door. He jogged around the front and hopped into the driver's seat. The old engine rumbled to life. He shifted it into gear and started up the round drive, sending me a flirty grin as he took to the road. "It looks like I have my work cut out for me."

"It's a hard job, but someone has to do it. But since you're such a strong, burly mountain of a man, I thought you might be up for the challenge."

A smirk tugged at his sexy mouth. "I think I just might be."

"That's just the beginning, buddy. These shoes are a good start." I waved the box at him. "But be prepared to grovel. So much groveling."

It was only partially a tease. I knew we had a ton of stuff to work on.

"Baby, I'll be on my knees at your feet for the rest of your life."

I dug my phone from my purse and typed out a quick message to Eden, who'd obviously already known Milo was out there waiting for me.

> Me: I just had the strangest craving for cake. I might be awhile. I don't know…like forever.

> Eden: I hope it's delicious.

I gazed over at the man.

At the same second, he shifted to look at me.

Intense eyes stared back.

Amber dipped in warm honey.

My stomach took a swooping dive.

A freefall as that energy crackled and glowed.

So delicious.

So perfect.

So right.

Mine.

He reached out with one of those big hands and squeezed my thigh, his words nothing but a gruff caress. "Mad love, Tessa. Mad, mad love."

Energy thrummed and danced.

And that was exactly what it was.

Mad, mad love.

Chapter Fifty

Milo

Four Months Later

THE AIR VIBRATED WITH ANXIETY, AND I SAT THERE WITH my knee bouncing a million miles a minute, sweat slicking down the back of my neck.

It was probably drenching my button-up, but there was no stopping my nerves from spinning out of control.

Held in this excitement and hope and terror.

Tessa curled her hand tighter around mine where we had our hands twined together on her lap. Her heel was bouncing on the floor, her nerves getting the best of her, too.

"We have this, Milo. Don't ever forget, we're a great team," she whispered so quietly that only I could hear.

I glanced at my fiancée.

My life.

My reason.

This family our meaning.

"We are."

Over the last four months, Tessa and I had started to build our new lives together. We learned each other. Loved each other. Touched and healed those lonely, vacant places we'd each kept locked inside, trusted each other to hold them forever.

She'd encouraged me to finally take that step and start my business—Hendricks Construction.

Sealing our dedication, we'd promised to fight for my kids.

Our kids.

Which was why we were here today.

I didn't look at Paula and Gene.

This wasn't about them.

"All rise."

Apprehension blistered through our beings, riding on the connection, the force of it obliterated by the belief we shared.

Even if we didn't go home with our kids today, we were certain one day we would.

We would never stop fighting.

Would never stop loving.

We stood as the judge retook her seat at the bench. She gestured for everyone to sit.

Tessa and I eased down together, our hands held so tight I was pretty sure it was constricting blood flow.

The judge sat back in the chair and removed her glasses. "These cases are always difficult because when it comes down to it, it's a fight over the love of a child, or children in this case. I can't say that's a bad thing, that these children are loved so fiercely that both parties will fight for what they believe is in their best interest, but it also causes unwarranted stress and pressure on the children."

A knot formed in my gut, and Tessa somehow managed to squeeze my hand tighter.

"It's a stress and pressure that in this case has gone on for too many years. From everything presented to the court prior to this hearing, there is absolutely no evidence to indicate that Mr. Hendricks is unfit to care for his children. It's the court's decision to reinstate full custody of Remington and Scout Hendricks to their biological father, Milo Hendricks."

She hit the gavel on the block and stood.

I flew to my feet right as Tessa threw herself into my arms.

Relief.

Relief.

I held her close, just…breathing.

Fully and wholly for the first time in so many years.

"We did it," she murmured.

"We did it," I whispered back.

Warmth spread through my being.

Bold.

Blinding.

Searing perfection.

And I finally knew what it was like to stand in the sun.

Chapter Fifty-One

Tessa

I WONDERED IF WE ALL KNEW HOW SURREAL THIS MOMENT WAS when Milo pulled to a stop in front of the cabin.

Because the four of us just sat there for a moment. In silence. In recognition. In joy and happiness and some nerves, too, because this was brand-new for all of us.

We were permanently bringing Remy and Scout home.

I glanced over at Milo, who had turned to look at me.

He was so…everything.

Big and intimidating and rough.

Soft and kind and real.

My Beautiful Beast.

He slanted me a tender smile, and my insides lit up.

My man was as yummy as could be, and it looked like we were going to have to curb a little of our *cake* time.

That was just fine, and I knew Milo well enough to know we'd get creative.

A smirk lit on his delicious mouth like he knew exactly what I was thinking, then he shifted the Tahoe into park and shut off the engine.

"We're home."

That deep voice rang with loyalty.

We were home.

Scout was unbuckled in a flash and poked his head up between us. "Is Gramma coming over? She better. I think she's going to want to listen to me read this book."

He pulled it from his backpack, all kinds of hopeful.

Devotion spread across Milo's face. "Yeah, she's going to be here later for dinner."

"I can't even wait to see her. She's going to be really excited about how much I've learned to read since the last time I saw her," he said as he jumped out the door.

Remy unbuckled and shifted forward, and she leaned up, too.

Her demeanor was so different from her brother's.

Each so unique.

"I'm really glad we're here."

Milo shifted in his seat. "I'm really glad you're here, too, Remy Girl. It's the best day of my life."

"Well, I am pretty great." Remy giggled when she said it, testing out the tease.

Milo sent me a faked scowl. "It seems she's been hanging around someone else I know a little too much."

"Get used to it, buddy." I patted him on the shoulder in mock sympathy. "Because Remy-T Wreckers are together at last. Permanently."

I shifted so I could reach out my hand and offer Remy my pinkie.

She hooked hers in mine, her face turning red as we shook, but joy shined in her eyes.

My chest expanded to overflowing.

God, I loved her.

Loved Scout.

Loved Milo, who watched us with this gentleness that sent my insides fluttering.

Nope, I was never going to get enough of the man.

Maybe we'd had some hard times getting to this place—where he could trust himself to love me, but he'd taken the chance.

Made the choice.

And he'd chosen to love me.

Fully and completely and without reservation.

"We'd better get inside before your brother tears down the house," Milo finally said.

"You are not prepared for what you're in for." Remy shook her head, completely serious.

Milo reached out and took my hand. "I'm in for it all."

"You asked for it," she mumbled as she slipped out from the back seat.

Milo...he just smiled.

Smiled this wistful, hopeful, awed smile.

"Thank you for believing in me, Little Dove. For seeing something in me that I couldn't see in myself."

I leaned over and scratched my fingernails through his beard.

Energy thrummed.

A hum of satisfaction, loyalty, and need.

"I'm so glad it got to be me."

He pressed his forehead to mine and murmured in his rumbly way, "It's always you. How could I live without the sun?"

"I love you," I whispered at his lips.

"Mad, mad love."

He kissed me quick, then he angled back as he sent me a grin. "How about we go inside with our kids?"

A rush of anticipation blazed.

"I approve of this plan."

We both climbed out, and he took my hand at the front of the SUV.

We'd done it for months, visiting the kids at the park since Paula had put the kibosh on visitations at Milo's house, going back on the promise that Gene had wanted to come to some sort of agreement.

Milo's goal had never been to keep the kids from their grandparents.

Remy and Scout would be spending Friday nights there, at least for the time being, until their activities got crazy and their schedules changed.

But Milo refused the bitterness that could linger and *chose* grace.

He chose love.

He chose to live for what was right.

And today?

We walked toward his kids who were arguing in the doorway, fighting over who got to sit by their grandma when she came, realizing this was it.

They were home.

I grinned over at Milo.

He grinned back at me, and he murmured, "We have this, baby."

We stepped into the house and into our future, and I shut the door behind us as I whispered, "Yeah, we do."

Epilogue

Milo

I T WAS A GORGEOUS SPRING DAY WHEN I STOOD AT THE END OF the dock, the breeze light and almost cool, but the sky was clear and warmed by the rays that slanted down from the heavens.

The lake glittered behind me, and our friends and family were gathered just on the shore where three rows of chairs with an aisle down the middle had been set up for the very intimate, small wedding, filled with our friends and family.

Bouquets overflowed with white flowers, and a string quartet was in the distance under a tree. The music they played was subdued and mellow, melting the atmosphere into peace.

The minister stood to my right, and Trent, Jud, Logan, and Kult were wrapped along the edge of the dock since it was too narrow for them to stand in a row beside me.

My mom met my eye from the front row. Love poured from her expression. I wondered if she understood the impact of her support and encouragement.

Because I'd had a choice to make that day—to let the negative shape me, conform me to its will, or look to the goodness I'd been given.

And I was looking to the goodness.

A smile played at the edge of my mouth as Tessa's bridesmaids began to appear at the edge of the house. There was a white plank walkway that ran from the side and down to the dock so they could walk in their heels because Tessa had made it clear just how important those heels were going to be.

I'd only laughed and gotten my ass out back so I could build it for her.

Salem and Aster made their way down, then Eden, who was her maid of honor, each of them sending these reassuring smiles as they passed, each so beautiful, inside and out.

Jud had been right.

Not one of us had a thing to complain about.

We were lucky bastards.

Gage and Juniper came next, hands swinging between them where they held onto each other as they skipped along, taking their spots, no chance that the two of them wouldn't stand in the wedding.

Every one of these kids was a piece of Tessa's family.

It was something she and I had both come to realize through all of this. Sometimes grief and guilt could overshadow the love others held for you. When you cut yourself off, isolated yourself in the sorrow, you could so easily feel like an outsider.

Unattached.

Hovering in the periphery of what everyone else had when they wanted you to be a part of it.

We got it now.

That these people? They were family. What it really meant.

Adoration billowed through my spirit when the music shifted, and my son came blazing down the walkway at warp speed.

Rocketman could not be slowed.

His brown hair bounced around his face, and his big lips were twisted in excitement.

My chest panged.

Because this joy was so full, it was close to painful, but that was the type of pain I would cherish every day. I would no longer fear it or worry that I would destroy it.

Because I would stand for what was right. Live for it. Fight for it.

He skidded across the dock, holding tight to the box that held our rings, the kid giggling like mad as he came to stand at my side just to the front of me. I set my hand on his shoulder.

Our ring bearer.

Just like Tessa had imagined.

And everything clutched when Remy came next, a bit timid, the way she always was, but glowing her insight and warmth. She was all dressed up, looking too old, her hair done up in flowers for the day.

She didn't toss petals, instead, she set out bunches of peonies as she went, something she and Tessa had decided together appeared much more grown up.

It was awesome, watching the two of them plan this thing together.

A team.

That's what we were.

The four of us.

And the love, it just kept rushing out, expanding and growing and almost becoming too much.

Because the music shifted again, and there was my girl, standing at the side of the cabin.

The sun.

Red hair and pale, freckled skin, and this white dress that made her look like a fucking angel.

Knew at least I had to be in heaven.

She looped her arm through Gary's, who stood at her side like she was his own.

He began to lead her down the walkway. Tessa was smiling, a thousand emotions rushing through her expression, the girl never taking her eyes off me as she approached.

She was so fucking beautiful I thought my heart was going to explode.

"You sure got lucky, Dad," Scout giggled as he looked at Tessa coming our way.

He'd heard me say it a thousand times, but man, did I feel the truth of it right then.

And I would never take for granted what I'd been given.

She came down the aisle, then stepped onto the dock.

That energy whispered on the breeze.

Warmth and light.

Her mouth tugged in all directions as she walked the rest of the way to me, her dress form fitted, diving between her breasts and cut up to the thigh.

A foot away from me, she shifted to the side and kicked up a single crystal Manolo.

The rough scrape of a laugh made it up my throat.

"I guess I have to marry you since you got me the Manolos, Milo Hendricks," she whispered the tease.

I took her hand, threaded our fingers together, and tugged her toward me. "You can have anything you want, Little Dove. Just as long as you promise me always."

"Always," she murmured.

Love poured from her.

For me.

For our children.

For this family.

I touched her face. "I guess we do make a really great team."

She touched my chest. "The very best."

About the Author

A.L. Jackson is the *New York Times* & *USA Today* Bestselling author of contemporary romance. She writes emotional, sexy, heart-filled stories about boys who usually like to be a little bit bad.

Her bestselling series include THE REGRET SERIES, CLOSER TO YOU, BLEEDING STARS, FIGHT FOR ME, CONFESSIONS OF THE HEART, and FALLING STARS.

If she's not writing, you can find her hanging out by the pool with her family, sipping cocktails with her friends, or of course with her nose buried in a book.

Be sure not to miss new releases and sales from A.L. Jackson - Sign up to receive her newsletter http://smarturl.it/NewsFromALJackson or text "aljackson" to 33222 to receive short but sweet updates on all the important news.

Connect with A.L. Jackson online:

FB Page https://geni.us/ALJacksonFB
A.L. Jackson Bookclub https://geni.us/ALJacksonBookClub
Angels https://geni.us/AmysAngels
Amazon https://geni.us/ALJacksonAmzn
Book Bub https://geni.us/ALJacksonBookbub

Text "aljackson" to 33222 to receive short but sweet
updates on all the important news.